Dear Reader,

Welcome to another month of Harlequin Duets, the series designed to double your reading pleasure!

This new and exciting series is written by authors you love, and published in a great new format. Have you ever finished reading a romance and wished you had another one you could start right away? Well, we have the answer for you. Each and every month there will be two Harlequin Duets books on sale, and each book will contain two complete, brand-new novels. (You'll always have your backup read with you!)

Harlequin Duets features the best of romantic comedy. In *The Cowboy Next Door* by Laurie Paige, the heroine is determined to resist any and all sexy cowboys, until she meets her next-door neighbor. And if you think that's too close for comfort, try *Meant for You* by Patricia Knoll. Here, the hero and heroine, two complete opposites, end up sharing the same house!

Ruth Jean Dale spins a delightful tale of mayhem created by a little girl when she "appropriates" a very special penny in *One in a Million*. Then Kimberly Raye takes readers to the wild, wild West in *Love, Texas Style,* when a New York lawyer goes looking for her own real-life cowboy hero...but doesn't get *quite* what she was expecting.

Enjoy all our stories this month from Harlequin Duets!

Sincerely,

*Malle Vallik*

Malle Vallik
Senior Editor

P.S. We'd love to hear what you think about Harlequin Duets! Drop us a line at:

Harlequin Duets
Harlequin Books
225 Duncan Mill Road
Don Mills, Ontario
M3B 3K9 Canada

## "You big ape. Get your hands off me—"

Suddenly, Cybil realized Mason didn't have his hands on her, except for holding her wrists. "Want your kiss now or later?" he asked, grinning.

"That'll be the day." Cybil jabbed him in the stomach with her elbow.

He tensed his muscles. "Yes, I have to admit I'm looking forward to it." He set her on her horse. "But the best will be—"

She rode off without hearing the best part. He followed, more slowly.

He didn't know whether it was an insight or a wish, but he knew with a certainty that defied logic that there would come a day when she would want him to touch her, to kiss her.

Then there would be no stopping for either of them....

# Meant for You

## *Caitlin couldn't believe she'd won a car.*

She'd never won anything in her life. She had to tell someone or burst with the news.

Before she could give it further thought, she dashed across the hall. She knocked, then did a fancy little two-step while she waited for Jed to answer.

When the door opened, she whirled around excitedly to see him standing in the entrance, briskly drying his hair with a small white towel.

Caitlin's eyes traveled rapidly downward, spied his hands loosely clasping the ends of the towel, framing his chest, sharply defining the muscles. Then her gaze dropped lower...

Completely against her will, her tongue darted out to wet her lips, and her gaze shot back to his face, which was taking on a puzzled look. She hitched in a breath. "You'll never guess...you'll never..." Her words stumbled over themselves, withered up in her desert-dry mouth.

"Do you see something you like?" he asked.

Did she ever! But she'd made that mistake once before....

HARLEQUIN DUETS

ISBN 0-373-44069-3

THE COWBOY NEXT DOOR
Copyright © 1999 by Olivia M. Hall

MEANT FOR YOU
Copyright © 1999 by Patricia Knoll

**Printed in U.S.A.**

# LAURIE PAIGE

# The Cowboy Next Door

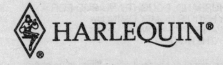

## HARLEQUIN®

TORONTO • NEW YORK • LONDON
AMSTERDAM • PARIS • SYDNEY • HAMBURG
STOCKHOLM • ATHENS • TOKYO • MILAN • MADRID
PRAGUE • WARSAW • BUDAPEST • AUCKLAND

Dear Reader,

My hubby always warns friends and relatives that anything they say in my presence may—and probably will—turn up in one of my books. A case in point: I was at lunch with three friends when one of them brought up the subject of a neighbor who took his wife to dinner at a posh restaurant and told her he wanted a divorce. We discussed how we would have handled the situation. We naturally went over all breakups in recent history—family, friends, movie stars, etc.

That weekend, my husband and I drove over to Eagle Valley in Nevada. Noticing a For Sale sign on the fence post at the entrance to a ranch and a posted Keep Out sign on the other side, I immediately went into my what if mode, as in...what if a man and woman lived on adjoining ranches and what if both had been burned in past relationships, and what if they met and the sparks flew, which would naturally confuse them and make them angry and yet they couldn't stay away, and what if another complication cropped up...well, the rest is history, as one might say. This is how Cybil and Mason's story came to be....

*Laurie Paige*

**Books by Laurie Paige**

## SILHOUETTE YOURS TRULY
CHRISTMAS KISSES FOR A DOLLAR
ONLY ONE GROOM ALLOWED

## SILHOUETTE SPECIAL EDITION
1139—HUSBAND: BOUGHT AND PAID FOR
1178—A HERO'S HOMECOMING
1193—WARRIOR'S WOMAN
1201—FATHER-TO-BE

Don't miss any of our special offers. Write to us at the following address for information on our newest releases.

Harlequin Reader Service
U.S.: 3010 Walden Ave., P.O. Box 1325, Buffalo, NY 14269
Canadian: P.O. Box 609, Fort Erie, Ont. L2A 5X3

To Claudia,
who sacrificed Mother's Day,
the Fourth of July and everything in between
to help a friend.

# 1

MASON FARADAY scowled at the telephone. The last time he'd had a call this early in the day, the caller had been his neighbor and fellow rancher, Cybil Mathews. He sure didn't feel like talking to her at the moment.

Cybil was one of those women whose attitude set a man's teeth on edge. She made it clear she thought all men were, at best, not too bright, at worst, snakes in the grass and not to be trusted. Huh, he could tell her a thing or two about the female of the species.

The only problem was, every time he saw her he wanted to wrestle her to the ground and have his way with her.

Feeling as grumpy as an overworked mule, he waited for the answering machine to switch on so he could screen the call. In the meantime, he opened a desk drawer and filed the court decree he'd received yesterday from his lawyer.

The divorce was final, the marriage irrevocably finished, buried in the past along with other mistakes he'd made. With this one, though, he'd lost more than a few years of his life. He'd saved a nice nest egg during his twenty years as one of the most active stuntmen in Hollywood. For five years of marriage—if one counted the eighteen months they'd been separated—his ex-wife had wanted half his lifetime savings.

Fortunately, the judge hadn't totally agreed with Lorah and her attorney, but his ex had come out of the deal with their house and a big chunk of cash to support her expensive life-style. All in all, he could honestly admit he was relieved that it was over....

The voice of his neighbor penetrated his musing and brought his attention to the problem at hand.

"...and if your boys don't come and get the damn thing within the hour, I can assure you he'll be hamburger before another hour passes."

He clenched his jaw at her tougher-than-buffalo-hide tone and snatched up the telephone. "Well, if it isn't my favorite sweetheart," he drawled at her, making his voice slow and bedroom husky.

"Oh, my favorite poster boy—the one representing all the men who are waiting for a brain transplant," she crooned right back. "Your bull is visiting my cows again."

"Sorry, babe." He could almost hear the anger sizzle from her end of the phone line as he used the endearment, deliberately making the term sound intimate. "He hasn't caught on to the immaculate-conception principle of breeding cows yet. He likes nature's way."

"He'd better learn quick," she warned, a thread of sardonic amusement running through the words. "I might have to perform surgery on him to stop his interest in my cows. Hey, I could transfer his thinking parts to you and save you a heap of money in neurosurgery bills."

"Very funny," he snapped, losing his cool.

Unfortunately, he *had* been thinking with something besides his brain when he'd married Lorah. At thirty-five, he'd been old enough not to fall for soulful, adoring glances and a come-on manner. His ex had been twenty-eight and twice his age in cunning. She'd taken him for a pretty spin.

"When may I expect you?" his neighbor inquired as if she'd invited him to dinner.

"In thirty minutes, honey, and if that bull has one hair of his carcass missing, you'll be sorry."

"Not as sorry as he'll be if you aren't here by seven. Ta-ta, lover." She hung up.

*Lover.* Ha. She wished.

Mason slammed down the phone and pushed his forty-year-old bones out of the leather office chair that had belonged to his uncle Moses since Mason could remember. He groaned under his breath. It had been a few years since he'd worked as physically hard as he had the past six months.

When Moses had called and invited him to become a partner in the ranch, he'd decided what the hell. It was a chance to start over, far from L.A. and the fast lane. He'd been more than ready for a different life.

A ranch was hard work, but it had advantages over other jobs. A man could see it, could crush the dirt in his fist and feel its solid worth, could smell it, hell, taste it if he wanted to, and know it was his.

The land could be a hard mistress, but at least a man would always know it was there, waiting faithfully for him. If he ever found a woman like that...

He snorted at the flight of fancy, wondered briefly

where the hell it had come from and walked out on the porch of the wood-frame ranch house.

The building was almost ninety years old. Built in the post-and-lintel method of yesteryear, the ranch house and barn would last another hundred years if given regular care.

A place for a family to grow up.

The unwelcome thought tore at him. There would be no children for him. Not ever. He was glad now. That would have been another complication in the divorce. He briefly wondered if his ex would have let him keep the kids if they'd had any. Thank God the problem hadn't come up.

Money had been her goal. She'd wanted him to go into some highly speculative land-development deals that were more than a little shady. No way. She'd also wanted him to get her parts in the movies he'd worked in. He'd figured a person should audition and show some talent.

Taking a calming breath, he pushed the past aside and surveyed the valley spreading east and north of the ranch. The Heavenly Valley ski resort, Nevada side, was visible to the northwest, long frostings of snow still nestled among its peaks. Farther north, Carson City, then Reno, sprawled over the desert country.

They were only three days into September, but this was high desert—around five thousand feet. While the days were warm, the nights often dropped into the forty-degree range.

As a kid, he'd loved to spend summers with his uncle. Naturally, as he grew into a teenager, his time here had lessened until he'd finally stopped coming by his sixteenth year. He'd had a job and was saving to buy his first car. He hadn't had time for childish things....

So here he was, a forty-year-old bachelor living every boy's dream. It was just that he'd also forgotten that ranchers had to get up with the chickens, or in this case, an amorous bull.

Uncle Moses had taken to sleeping in since his arrival a few months ago. Mason figured the old man, now in his eighties, was tired and relieved to have someone take over.

He hitched the trailer to the pickup, told one of the cowboys where he was going and headed out. The drive took thirty minutes on the roundabout trip via the county road.

There was a back road connecting the two ranches. His hardheaded neighbor had padlocked the gate and refused to give him a key.

A smile tugged at his lips at the entrance to her ranch. The name of the place, the End-of-the-Road Ranch, was burned into the massive overhead log. On one of the supporting posts, he read the other sign: No Men Allowed. It listed a number to call for permission to enter.

In addition to a cow-and-calf operation, the owner ran a sort of dude ranch for women who were in the process of getting a divorce. She probably advised them on how to take their husbands for the most money.

With a devil-may-care snort, he pushed the gas pedal down and, trailing a cloud of dust along the gravel road, roared up in front of the house that was nearly identical to his own. He waited until the dust settled.

His neighbor came out on the porch. Her face was startlingly beautiful, a perfect oval like those of the blessed saints depicted in old paintings. Too bad her smile was that of a python gazing at a sleeping hog.

She lifted a hand to shade her eyes from the morning sun. The breeze blew her dark, curly hair against her forehead. For a second, he imagined what it would look like spread over a pillow, all in a tangle as she moved her head from side to side in restless passion—

He cursed silently as he tried to banish the image. She wasn't one of those thin, high-fashion women he'd grown used to in Hollywood. There was meat on her bones, something for a man to hold, an easy armful to nestle into....

Heat rolled over him as she gazed directly at him as if dissecting his every thought. Her eyes were light blue, or maybe gray. She carried herself proud. A hint of admiration curled through him until he remembered what a pain she was.

He waited another minute until he was sure his stupid libido was under control, then slid out of the truck.

"Where is Fletch?" he asked, wanting to get back to his own land.

She stepped off the porch and ambled toward him. "Fletch?"

"My bull. My *prize* bull," he added to let her know what she was dealing with. "Grand champion."

He'd bought the animal a few days ago. The bull

hadn't figured out which cows on the range belonged to him.

"I think Don Juan would be more appropriate. What's the problem—you got no cows over on the Faraday place?"

"We have cows," he muttered grimly, vowing not to indulge in a verbal clash and trying not to notice her cleavage, visible just enough to tease a man through the open collar of her shirt. He grabbed a working rope from the bed of the truck. "Where is he?"

A ranch hand came out of the house. She stopped at the side of her boss, her stance protective, her eyes watchful.

Even he, used to beautiful women by the busload, pursed his lips in a silent whistle of stark admiration the few times he'd seen her.

The cowgirl, six feet tall in stocking feet, was a blond, blue-eyed Scandinavian. She was large-boned but slender and whipcord tough from all the ranch work. In her early twenties, he guessed. The youngster could have been a model for any magazine cover. Movie roles would have been offered just by introducing her to a few people.

The two women formed a solid wall against his intrusion, viewing him with definite suspicion of the male half of the population in their collective gazes. He briefly felt sorry for any man who had tangled with either of them and wondered if the poor fools were still whole in spirit…and in body. He smiled sardonically at the thought.

The rancher was close to his age. She wasn't as tall

as her girl, maybe five-eight or -nine, but he had to hand it to her—she had a figure right out of a man's dreams.

To his disgust, his body sprang to life in the nether regions. Not again, he admonished. He'd fallen for a sexy female once, and look where it had gotten him. Nowhere, to be exact. He wouldn't go down that road again.

"He's in the back pasture. I can take you there. Move your truck down to the loading dock," she said, and without another word, headed down the rocky road, her henchman—uh, henchwoman—at her side.

He climbed into the truck and followed the duo of Valkyries to the paddock behind the barn. After backing into position, he joined his hostess by the fence. The blonde had disappeared.

"We'll have to ride. Rains washed out the road. I haven't had time to grade it," she said.

"All right."

The cowgirl came out of the barn with two horses. Cybil motioned him to a big, raw-boned gelding. She chose the mare. Mason was willing to bet there wasn't a stallion on the place. Or any other kind of stud as far as he could tell. He'd heard they had used artificial insemination on their entire herd of cows the previous year.

"I'm surprised you don't have men check their male parts at the gate," he commented after he was up on the gelding. He knew, before the words were out, he should have kept his mouth shut.

She cast him one of her amused, superior glances. "Life would be easier that way. Since that isn't possible, we just don't let them on the place very often. It makes my guests feel better. Safer," she added.

"Any particular reason for the aversion to the male half of the population?"

"Yeah. I was married to one."

"Remind me to tell you about my ex-wife sometime."

"I hope she got a big settlement."

His hand jerked on the reins, and the gelding pranced a bit. He pushed the tension from his body. "She did okay."

"Good."

Her obvious satisfaction had him gritting his teeth. That was the trouble with women. Without knowing his side, without asking if he'd been treated fairly, the smart-mouthed rancher took his ex-wife's side. "So how much did you take your ex for?" he asked.

The mare sidestepped. Cybil patted her on the neck to calm the animal. He smiled, knowing his question had gotten to her. She flicked a razor glance his way. For a second, he witnessed a tumult of emotion in the depths of her eyes, then she matched his smile.

"Half," she said softly.

Mason nodded in pity for the sucker. "The courts give half a man's retirement to the woman now, no matter that he's put in years of labor for it."

She angled around to face him. "My husband and I had our own mail-order business that we'd started together. He tried to move funds from it into a secret stash. I caught on when long-term accounts showed a discrepancy between what was ordered and what was paid. I checked his computer files, found a PIN num-

ber at a new bank and moved the money back to the
business account. A bit of sleuthing disclosed he had
a little nest on the side, so to speak. I opted out.''

Mason grimaced at her lightly told tale. He might
have known she was the injured party. She was obviously one of those women who, once she had a man
in her clutches, would hold on for dear life. He wondered, just for a second, how it would feel to be
wanted like that, to have a mate who would be loyal
for life....

''So why did your wife leave you?''

''Who said she did?'' he drawled, feeling disori-
ented as his thoughts strayed in odd and provoking
directions, leaving him vaguely dissatisfied and definitely grouchy.

Cybil shrugged.

''I wouldn't go into some shady deals that promised
to make us as rich as Bill Gates.''

''Ah, she had a taste for high living, did she? What
about you? You were a big-shot Hollywood stuntman.
Didn't you like the high life?''

''No.'' As old-fashioned as it sounded, he'd wanted
kids and a family and a home. And a loving wife to
round out the picture of the all-American family. He
should have known better than to look in Hollywood
for the latter.

His neighbor gave him a skeptical glance.

''Outsiders only hear about the problems of the
stars. No one cares about the rest of the people in the
industry, those who lead ordinary lives,'' he added,
feeling defensive over his long-lost dreams.

She opened a stock gate and let him through before closing it. "Being a stuntman was ordinary?"

He watched the way she moved as she guided the mare along a washed-out road leading over the ridge that separated the two ranches along here. She was a natural in the saddle and seemed at ease on the ranch, which appeared well cared for. Her hired hand had been protective and loyal. So, okay, she was a good rancher and boss.

He answered her question. "It was fun."

"So why'd you quit?"

"I turned forty."

Her laughter surprised him. "So did I."

"When?"

"A month ago."

"I beat you by six months."

"It isn't the end of the world."

The empty years loomed before him, reminders of all the things he'd wanted and all those he would never have. "Yeah, life begins at forty."

She gave him an odd glance, then clicked her mare into a faster pace. The gelding followed with no urging. Beneath Cybil's shirt, the full, bouncy breasts jiggled with each step. His mouth went dry.

They went through another gate. "There he is."

Fletch was chomping on some alfalfa and looking bovinely happy. The wayward bull snorted when he spotted Mason and edged away.

"You mangy critter," Mason muttered, and considered hauling him straight to the slaughterhouse, but the animal was worth a fortune in stud fees alone.

He circled behind the small herd grazing in a spring-fed pasture and angled in to cut Fletch out of the cattle. Glancing over at Cybil, watching from the sidelines, he realized she was leaving the task up to him. Okay, he could handle one recalcitrant bull.

Once the gelding was sure which animal Mason was after, the horse turned his attention to separating the bull from the herd and anticipating his every move.

Mason relaxed. This would be a snap.

Twenty minutes later, he pushed his hat off his forehead and glared at the beast. Fletch had a mind of his own, which at present was focused on a certain cow in the herd. The bull refused to be parted from her.

Mason glanced at his neighbor. She smiled brightly at him. He felt his jaw muscles tense. "How about a hand?"

She applauded.

"Very funny. Head him off that way, and I'll come around from this side."

Fletch glanced from one to the other, then lit out for the stands of pines and cedars growing on the hills that formed the west side of the pasture. The cow gave a bellow and followed him. The rest of the herd gave chase.

Mason cursed, not bothering to keep his words under his breath this time.

"If we find the break, maybe we can drive him to your side of the fence, then you can do the repairs while I drive the cows back this way," she suggested when he shut up.

"I didn't bring any wire. I thought you would have him at the paddock."

"One of the ranch guests was nearly gored by an

enraged bull last year. I decided then not to tackle any male who outweighed me several times over.''

"I guess that means you're not afraid to take me on since I'm probably only one and half times your size,'' he drawled.

"You wish,'' she scoffed. "I'm particular about who I tangle with…and you're not even in the running.''

He felt the sizzle start in his midsection and burn right up to his brain. He could have chewed horseshoes and spit out nails, as Uncle Moses often said.

"I haven't put any effort into it yet,'' he told her, keeping the words light, but with an undertone of daredevil menace. "If I did, you'd be putty in my hands.''

Pure outrage poured into her eyes before she blinked it away then settled back in the saddle with a laugh. "You do say the funniest things.''

The tingle spread up his arm; the sizzle spread out from his middle. They met somewhere in his chest and formed one certainty. She was a challenge he couldn't refuse.

"Enjoy yourself, darling,'' he invited, his voice as smooth as hot fudge. "You'll be begging for it before the first frost. Now, about Fletch. Let's ride after him. If I can get a rope on him, he'll come peacefully.''

She blinked at the change in subject, then her eyes sparkled with provocative amusement as she recovered and bowed politely from the waist. "After you.''

He led the way up the slope and into the trees. It didn't take long to find the bull and his girlfriend in a clearing a bit farther up.

Mason readied the rope he'd brought with him,

edged closer to the pair and gave Fletch a swat on the rear to get him moving.

The bull crow-hopped around, kicked up his heels a bit, then settled to munching on the grass. Cybil watched with an air of detachment, again from the side.

Cursing at being forced to put on a show for the woman, who acted as if she were at a play or something, Mason slapped the rope against his thigh.

"Move out," he said, trying to sound as if he were the one in charge, rather than the contrary bull.

Fletch tossed his head, angling his chin first to one side, then the other, then bellowed a couple of times.

"You show-off," Mason said, falling into the spirit of the impromptu contest.

He sent the rope upward into a spin, let the rope go, praying it would hit its mark. It did. He'd lassoed the bull around the neck. After circling a tree, he brought the gelding to a halt. Fletch was pulled up short and neatly set on his backside.

"Okay, let's head home," Mason told the bull. He circled back around the tree, gave a tug on the rope and the bull followed, as docile as a lamb.

Mason caught Cybil's look of surprise, then her smile of appreciation as she watched him bring the bull under control. She clapped with genuine feeling this time.

Mason took off his Stetson and gave a sweeping bow, letting a surge of triumph seep into his grin as he met the reluctant admiration in her eyes.

Yeah, they were blue. No, gray. Maybe blue gray.

A sizzle of something hot and raw coursed through

his blood, shocking him again with his body's reactions. This was a complication he definitely didn't need. He'd come to the ranch to get away from women and all the torments they made for a man.

"Next time he visits, he'll come home a steer," his neighbor stated.

"If he comes home without all his parts intact, you'll eat whatever is missing," he promised, his smile as sardonic as hers.

"Ketchup on the side, please."

Damn smart-mouthed woman. Always had to have the last word. However, jousting with her was kind of fun. He liked getting under her skin the way she did his. Sort of. It galled him no end that he couldn't figure out his reactions to her. Neither could he predict them. Nor control them.

He followed her down the slope and across the pasture to the ranch house. A strange sense of excitement bubbled in his blood. He recognized it. After successfully completing the most difficult stunts, he'd wanted to rush home and share the triumph with his wife, then make mad love with her to celebrate.

Yeah, that had lasted six months before she'd made it clear she didn't want to be bothered.

He faced reality now. There was nothing between his mouthy neighbor and him. Well, okay, a bit of heat, but that didn't mean a thing. He had no time for a woman and all the troubles that half of the species stirred up. He had a ranch to run.

First he'd get Fletch home, then he'd have breakfast and maybe, just maybe, he'd stumble upon some of the peace and quiet he'd moved here to find.

CYBIL WATCHED her neighbor drive off with his amorous bull. It had been a fun couple of hours. Even now, her blood coursed through her body at a faster speed.

"Now, there's a man who was made for jeans and boots," Enya, the ranch hand, commented. "Hmm, those tight buns and long legs. He's the same height as I am, though. I like a man to be a couple of inches taller."

"Outside of a pro basketball team, where are you going to find this dream man?" Maria, the cook/housekeeper, asked.

Cybil smiled and headed for the office, leaving them to their discussion. She had to admit to a strum along the nerves herself each time she'd seen the nephew who had bought into Moses Faraday's ranch. He was good-looking in a brooding sort of way. His dark hair was worn short, but tended to feather over his forehead in attractive disarray. His eyes were dark, too, but there was fire in those depths.

Yeah, he struck sparks off her. But along with the flames of passion he ignited—which she hated to admit—he also provoked other feelings just as strong. His arrogant ways made her ache to take him down a peg or two, especially in light of his male swaggering. Beg for it, indeed.

In spite of her exasperation with his typically masculine attitude, she wondered about his marriage and felt a tug of sympathy for broken dreams and vows.

She, too, had learned a lesson the hard way. Married right out of college, she'd moved to Reno with her new husband, filled with expectations of a perfect life. Her marriage had lasted twelve years. They had sold the ranch-catalog business and split the money.

Restless and lonely, with a sizable bank account, she had bought this ranch at a tax auction listed in a notice in the newspaper. It was a return to her roots.

She'd grown up on a big spread in Wyoming, but her parents had sold it when she left for college and had retired to Florida, where her older sister lived. She'd loved the freedom and security of the land around her as a youth, so she'd taken over this place, determined to save it and build a satisfying life for herself at the same time.

A few weeks later, a friend had visited, also seeking solace while her marriage was ending. Thus the refuge for women in the throes of divorce had been born.

For a second, Cybil recalled the awful vulnerability of trust being broken. She would never be that naive again. And the one thing she *didn't* need was the complication of a handsome, virile rancher next door, who made her think of things she wanted to forget—like a strong embrace to lean into, the solid warmth and hardness of well-toned male muscle, the nights of shared passion and laughter....

She fled from her thoughts and returned to the kitchen for a cup of fresh coffee.

"You didn't finish your breakfast," Maria scolded. "I set your plate in the oven."

"Thanks." Cybil retrieved her plate of eggs and bacon and took a seat at the kitchen table. It was nice to be looked after a little bit.

Maria, at fifty-five, was a widow. She had been hired for the summer and would stay through the fall roundup. Her quiet, grandmotherly ways induced their clients to confide in her. She was more sought after than the divorce lawyer in the city who regularly sent referrals to the ranch or the psychologist in the nearby small town who helped the women face and overcome their grief.

"This is delicious," Cybil said, attacking the plate of eggs that were mixed with hot salsa, then scrambled. "The ranch lucked out when you visited your daughter in Reno and saw my ad."

"It was lucky for me. Now I am close to my daughter and grandchildren without being underfoot. I will look for an apartment before the end of the month and maybe another job, although none will be as perfect as this."

"Glad you've liked it. It's been a pleasure for me, too," Cybil said with a wry grin. She disliked cooking anything that took over fifteen minutes, and dust on the furniture didn't bother her at all. The truth was she loved being outdoors. She had found her heart's home here in the valley. Her place was modest by Western standards, but just right for her.

She'd known the ranch itself wouldn't generate heaps of money. According to reports she'd read, farming or ranching earned a three percent return…if one was lucky.

The refuge for divorcées helped with the cash flow, not as much as it could, but she was doing okay. Not all clients had paid for their keep. Some of them couldn't and wanted to work for room and board. She didn't turn anyone away.

Yeah, a softie, that was her.

An image of a roguishly handsome face appeared to her, a smile kicking up the corners of his mouth. She frowned in irritation. She wouldn't be soft toward *him.* Mason Faraday held no attraction for her, not in any meaningful way.

"What are your plans for this afternoon?" Maria asked. She slipped two pies into the oven.

"We're going to round up the cattle that got out last week and move them closer to the home pastures while we repair the fence line."

Maria snorted. "You'd do better to go with just you and Enya. Those other three women couldn't punch their way out of a piñata, much less through a herd of cows."

"They are pretty inept, aren't they?" Cybil laughed and gathered her dishes. She put them in the dishwasher, glanced regretfully at the coffeepot, then grabbed her hat by the door. "Pack us a lunch, will you? It'll be dark before we make it back for supper."

She left Maria grumbling about Cybil working too hard, but it wasn't work to her. She loved every minute of it. She and the cowgirl saddled five horses and, with lunches and canteens, they started out in high spirits.

For one of the three divorcées now staying at the ranch, the merriment lasted about an hour. "This is work," Tippy remarked after following Cybil's orders for driving a stubborn cow and her two calves out of a willow thicket and into the small herd they were collecting.

Tippy was one of those women who insisted on being in the middle of the action, but who was always unhappy, no matter what she was doing.

"How far are we from the house?" she asked, looking down the trail.

"An hour's ride, due east. You can head back if you like. Just follow the fence to the first gate. You'll be able to see the house from there." She stood up in the stirrups and called to the other women, asking if they wanted to go to the house.

They didn't.

"I'll stay," Tippy said with surprising determination.

Cybil paused and let her gaze drift over the lofty peaks of the mountains, then roam the fertile valley. During the summer, the cattle were allowed to graze on the flanks of the mountains in the national forest, thanks to a grazing permit that had come with the ranch. In the late fall, they were moved to the valley pastures. The calves were sold off, and the process started over again in the spring.

The ranch house provided a solid and sturdy retreat, a place to come home to after a day working in the cool, clean air. It would be an ideal place for a family.

She felt an ache in the vicinity of her heart. She'd never had children. The doctors hadn't found anything terribly wrong, but she'd never conceived. After her husband had been tested and found okay, he had pointed out often that there was nothing wrong with him. He'd been right. Last year, he and his new wife had had a child.

So the fault had been hers.

After the failure of the marriage, she'd realized it was a good thing there were no children. However, when she saw pictures of Maria's two grandbabies, she was aware of a tiny ache someplace deep inside.

Well, a person couldn't have everything. She'd been lucky to get the ranch for a price she could afford. Her life was happy for the most part. If it weren't for her new neighbor, it would be perfect.

What the heck had made her think of him! She frowned at her thoughts and started back to work.

By three, they had a sizable herd rounded up and ready to move down from the hills and into the valley. Fifty head, she estimated, mentally counting in groups of ten.

"Ladies, let's go home," she called. "Head 'em up. Move 'em out."

Her guests loved cowboy talk, so she used phrases from movies she'd seen. It made them feel part of the old West. In good humor at getting the job at hand nearly finished, she took the lead and noted which cows followed. An old Hereford with two calves edged out a brindle for the lead, her two ladies-in-waiting falling in beside her. The brindle spearheaded her group off to one side but slightly behind the Hereford.

It amused her how similar to people the cows could be, with their jostling for place in the hierarchy of the herd.

She led the way down the fence line and over the ridge where the Faraday place joined her property. She watched Enya take up a position at the back of the herd, two guests dogging her steps, while Tippy rode a lead position on the far side of the herd.

Cybil watched the other women for a few seconds, then shrugged and angled east with the fence line, her eyes on the barbed wire. She hadn't found the place where the bull had gotten through this time, or the other two times he'd come to visit.

Just as the Hereford topped a small ridge, a scream erupted from an outcropping of rock, partially concealed by a cedar thicket to the right of the herd. The cows bellowed and took off at a dead run.

A mountain lion broke from the cedar thicket, loped in front of Cybil and jumped the fence in one lithe bound.

Another scream alerted her to other problems. Cybil saw Tippy's horse running with the stampeding cows, her reins dangling on the ground.

She cursed aloud and kicked the gelding into a run. She would have to cut across the front of the herd to catch the runaway horse. She hadn't been worried about the cows since there was no place for them to go but the lower pastures. With no main roads to cross, they would be okay even if they broke through a fence or two.

But if Tippy's horse went down, the pretty divorcée could be seriously injured by pounding hoofs, assuming she didn't break her neck in the fall.

Shouting, Cybil leaned over the gelding and charged straight across the herd's path. The cows swerved as one to the side, circled, then headed for the fence. They went through the barbed wire separating the two ranches and disappeared into the trees on the Faraday place.

Tippy clung to her mount, but Cybil could see air between her and the saddle. The woman was off balance and leaning to the side. Urging the gelding even faster, she bore down on the panicked rider and horse.

After what seemed like forever, she drew alongside the pair and grabbed the trailing reins. She eased back on the gelding and brought the animals to a halt.

The mare dropped her head between splayed legs and blew gustily as she got her wind back. Tremors ran over her hide in ripples.

Tippy slid from the saddle. "That horse nearly killed me. You shouldn't keep dangerous animals like that for people to ride."

"It wasn't the mare's fault. The lion startled her, but you were the one who let her go out of control. Why weren't the reins tied together?"

"I didn't like them that way," Tippy stated defiantly.

Cybil thought of leaving her there and letting her walk to the ranch, but they were still nearly an hour's ride from the house. "You're the one who wanted to come along. Now get on the mare or get up behind me, one or the other, but do it quick. I don't have all night."

Tippy shot her a furious glance. She gestured toward the mare. "I'll ride."

Cybil tied the reins. She handed them to Tippy when the other woman was mounted. "Okay, let's go."

The others rode up. "What about the herd?" Enya asked, her worried gaze on the trees.

"We'll get them tomorrow," Cybil told her. With any luck, she would get the cows off the Faraday place and the fence repaired without her neighbor finding out about the mishap.

THE PHONE WAS ringing when Cybil walked into the ranch house ninety minutes later. Maria answered. "Yes, she just this second walked in."

"I'll take it in my office," Cybil said, knowing who it was without asking.

"How many head you figure are on my land?" Mason Faraday demanded as soon as she picked up the receiver.

*Hello and I love you, too.* Briefly, she wondered if they would ever have a conversation that didn't border on all-out war. "Fifty."

"When do you plan on getting them out and the fence repaired?"

"Enya and I will be there bright and early in the morning. It'll take two days to round 'em up again, another day for the fence."

"Not good enough," he snapped. "I've got two hundred head moving that way now. Are yours branded?"

"No."

"That's what Moses said. I thought he must have gotten his facts wrong."

"I see no reason to brand when I'm not mingling cattle on open range. It's cruel and unnecessary. Besides, I use ear tags that have our brand on the back."

"What about when cows go through fences?" he asked. "What about when they lose their tags?"

"What about yours? Aren't they branded?"

"No. They're part of a new herd I bought. Now I'll have to bed them down and hold them while waiting for you."

He heaved a disgusted breath, and she could imagine his frowning like the devil in frustration.

"Sorry to inconvenience you," she said stiffly, half meaning it. Usually ranchers cooperated, but he got her hackles up each time they spoke. He always sounded as if he thought she didn't have any sense at all. Furthermore, he seemed to regard her refuge for women as a laugh.

"See that you don't dawdle on the job," he ordered. "I have a lot of work to do before the season ends."

"Oh, sorry, I thought you sat around reading romances and eating chocolates all day the way I do. That's what I love about ranching. It's so laid-back and easy."

He hung up.

She did the same, then eased her boots off and rubbed her ankle, which had a bruise encircling the bone. She removed the band on her hair and massaged her scalp. The muscles at the back of her neck were tight. Her head hurt.

Tippy had been nothing but aggravation since she'd arrived at the ranch. She'd ignored instructions and warnings. She'd acted as if she knew all about horses, then she'd panicked and dropped the reins.

Ah, well, a few more days and Tippy would move on. Now, if she could only figure out a way to get rid of her tough-minded neighbor...something on the order of a high cliff and an icy stream below. The thought entertained her through a hot shower and well into supper.

"Rain is predicted in the mountains tomorrow. We need to cut that alfalfa field in case it gets over this way," Enya told her during the meal.

"It won't," Cybil said. "Nothing makes it over the peaks at this time of the year. We have other work—"

Enya gave her a sly glance. "Yeah, maybe we'll see our neighbor while we're on his land. He has a new hand, I understand. Six and a half feet," she added with a dreamy haze over her blissful blue eyes. "Dibs if I see him first," she told the other women.

"Not on your life," Tippy countered with a grin.

Maria rolled her eyes at their friendly quarrel over a cowboy neither had seen. Then she looked at Cybil for a long minute.

"What?" Cybil finally said.

"That Mason Faraday is a good-looking hunk. If I were fifteen years younger, I'd go for him."

"I tried to get him to dance with me the other night. He wouldn't budge from the bar stool," Tippy informed them. "Said he came in for a beer and some peace and quiet and that it had been his experience he got neither when women were around."

"Sounds like he had a bad experience," Maria said, immediately sympathetic.

Cybil snorted. She'd like to give him a bad experience—something along the lines of getting knocked end over teakettle by his prize bull.

"Haven't we all?" Tippy said sharply. For an instant, her eyes reflected unhappiness and all the emotions that accompanied the breakup of a marriage.

Cybil could identify with the feeling. Mason Faraday was a born heartbreaker. She could see it in the self-confident set of his rugged shoulders, in the embers that slumbered in the depths of his eyes, in the husky undertone that crept into his voice when they spoke.

Her breath caught in her throat. She wouldn't fall for sweet words or a devil-may-care smile....

Tippy's laughter was hollow. "But I'll not sit around mooning over a man. My motto is, Don't Get Mad, Get Even."

"Did your husband do you wrong?" Enya asked.

Cybil knew the cowgirl thought it had probably been the other way around in Tippy's marriage and she'd been the one stepping out on her husband.

"With every woman on his sales route," she said with a brittle smile. "Fortunately, he has been top salesman for his company for the past five years. His bonuses have been very nice. I'm thinking of taking a cruise with part of my settlement and buying a condo in Tahoe with the rest. Plus alimony, of course."

"Of course," Enya echoed, not quite approving.

"Walk a mile in my shoes," Tippy invited, reverting to her usual acerbic form, "then you'll see how it is."

"I know," one of the other clients spoke up. "My husband was seeing my best friend."

Enya nodded sympathetically when the woman fell silent. "So you lost both your husband and your friend."

"You will find someone better and wiser than that one," Maria said gently.

"I suppose your marriage was the one perfect union," Tippy suggested archly.

Maria's smile was nostalgic. "We had our ups and downs, but overall it was worth every minute."

"What happened to you?" Tippy asked the guest who had arrived that week.

"My husband came home from a fishing trip, took me out to dinner and told me he wanted to be free. He had never had a chance to find himself, he said. He's in Florida now, working on a shrimp boat. He gave up his home and family for that." She looked perplexed.

"He chose a restaurant so you wouldn't cause a scene. I'd have thrown a bitchy, hysterical fit," Tippy declared.

"Me, too," Cybil said, drawing surprised glances. "That would teach him a lesson."

She hadn't thrown a fit. She simply waited for her husband to come home, then she'd asked him, very civilized, what he was trying to pull. She'd been very cool about the situation, but it had hurt.

"Well, I wished him well and left," the woman admitted. "I couldn't stand a scene."

"In my youth, we used to talk about different kinds of marriages," Maria said. Seeing she had their attention, she continued, "For instance, there would be a prechildren period where you could part very simply, but if you decided to have kids, then you had to stay together until they were out of high school. After that, you could renegotiate the agreement. But no fair getting pregnant to keep someone."

"It's easy to see why that didn't work," Tippy scoffed. "It required people to be honorable."

Cybil grimaced at the sardonic tone. She thought the divorcée had been hurt worse than she let on. For a moment, she recalled her own sense of betrayal upon finding that hidden account, then the apartment. She had lived through a long lonely period of grief before coming to terms with it.

While men acted as if they were the ones trapped by marriage, she knew it was women who gave the most. She would never again follow her heart into that snare.

CYBIL AND ENYA rode out at dawn the next morning. They quickly covered the distance to the broken fence. There, they left a roll of barbed wire, then rode onto the Faraday place to find the cows. Fanning out, each headed in a different direction to scout out the herd.

"Watch out for the cat," Cybil reminded the younger woman. Each of them carried a gun. She didn't expect any trouble, but it paid to be careful.

For the next three hours, she drove cattle from the flanks of the mountains and into a clearing close to the break in the fence. By noon, she'd finished two ridges and the valley between them.

She took a long drink from a canteen, then dampened her handkerchief and wiped her face. The temperature was in the low seventies, but it felt hotter. While the nights were cool, the days were unseasonably warm.

Clouds gathered over the Lake Tahoe basin, a sign of possible thunderstorms. That would bring down the temperature. It might even hail. She'd like to get the cattle back on her land and the fence repaired before the weather broke.

A loud retort cracked, then echoed all around her.

Every nerve in her body jumped. She glanced in all directions but couldn't tell where it came from. She rode up on the nearest ridge. Two more shots rang out.

She followed the sounds. Her cowhand had either found the big cat or needed help. Worry ate at her while she rode at a fast clip along an old trail. She disliked being on Faraday land, and the shots could only mean trouble.

In a large sloping pasture filled with cattle, she found Enya. The girl was lying on a blanket, a damp handkerchief on her head. Mason and a cowboy hovered over her, serious expressions on their faces.

"What happened?" Cybil asked while dismounting. She tied her horse to a bush and strode over to the group.

"I fell—"

"Her horse bolted—"

"There's a mountain lion—"

The three fell silent.

Mason continued with the news. "There's a big male cat passing through this area."

"We ran into him yesterday," Cybil told him.

His eyes narrowed. "Did you call?"

"Sorry, I forgot." She felt bad about that. Out here, neighbors kept each other informed of possible problems.

"Moses sometimes forgets to pass along information, too. If you do call, I'd appreciate it if you'd talk to me."

Cybil didn't comment on being lumped in the same boat with Mason's uncle, who was in his mideighties, hard of hearing and absentminded. "Right." She leaned over the blanket. "Are you okay?"

"I hit my head."

"She'll have a goose egg on her forehead, but I

don't see any signs of a concussion,'' the cowboy informed her.

Cybil looked him over. He stood half a head taller than his boss. His wiry physique looked as tough as a rawhide whip. His nose had been broken, but his face was pleasantly composed. His teeth were white and even when he spoke.

"I'm glad you found her. Thank you so much for the first aid," Cybil said.

"He was wonderful," Enya declared, giving him the full effects of her dazzling blue eyes.

The cowboy's ears turned pink while his breathing grew shallow. "It was nothing."

Cybil gave him full marks for modesty and for not being too obviously bowled over by Enya's smile.

"Ohhh..." the cowgirl moaned softly.

Cybil hid a smile as the cowboy readjusted the handkerchief on the small bruise. If melting glances were any sign, the young couple seemed bound for a flaming romance.

She noted the cynical glint in her neighbor's eye when he looked her way. He, too, was aware of the situation. And obviously didn't like it. She shrugged slightly at his accusing glance, which seemed to suggest it was her fault the young people were attracted to each other.

He was certainly a curmudgeon about it all, she decided peevishly, momentarily forgetting her own skepticism about male-female bonding and taking umbrage at his attitude.

"Tony, you can take the pickup and drive..." He glanced from the girl to her.

"Enya," Cybil said, supplying the name.

"You can drive Enya home."

"She may need help changing clothes or something," Tony said, the flush spreading to his cheeks.

"Maria will be at the house," Cybil assured him. She watched as Tony helped the girl to her feet and guided her to the truck as if she might crack into pieces at a stiff wind.

"I'll be okay," Enya called back to them, sounding more sturdy by the second.

Cybil nodded. She checked the time. She figured she could get the small herd moved and a temporary fix on the fence before dark. "Well, I'll be off. Thanks for taking care of Enya."

"Tony did it. He's the one who found her. He was tracking the cat while I watched the cattle."

"After being disturbed two days in a row, the lion will probably head for deep cover."

"That's what Tony thought, too." Mason shook out the blanket, folded it, then laid it on a boulder. "Some of your cattle are mixed in with mine. Since you have a mongrel herd, we should have no trouble sorting them out."

She didn't take offense at his description. His cattle were pure prime Western beef. She bought a mixture of breeds at auction, going for lean and hardy cows who didn't require a lot of care. With only one helper, she had too much to do to pamper a registered herd. Her market was the choice-rated beef for a grocery chain.

"I can't get them today. I have another bunch over the ridge and back a ways."

"I'll help you move them."

"Thanks, but I can handle it." Cybil grabbed the reins on Enya's mare.

"No problem," he said coolly. "The sooner you're off my land, the sooner I can get the fence repaired."

She reined in the instant irritation—nobody got to her faster than this rancher with his sharp tongue and heart-thumping smile—and swung up on the gelding. "I have the wire and staples with me. It'll be done before nightfall."

He whistled. A horse neighed in answer. In a moment, a big chestnut gelding galloped out of the trees. The horse stopped by Mason, who tightened the saddle girth, then mounted. "Ready," he said.

Cybil swung her horse around and headed toward her ranch at a trot, Enya's mare trailing along after her. Mason and his chestnut joined the line.

After a bit, he pulled up beside her and remarked, "You didn't argue about my coming along. I figured you would."

"I generally let people choose their own course."

"Even if you see a big pit in the road?"

"Even then. If someone wants my advice, I'll give it. Otherwise, I don't."

"Uncle Moses said you weren't the usual run of female. I'm beginning to believe him."

Her glance conveyed her skepticism. He surprised her by smiling. She studied him for a minute, disgruntled at how handsome he was. He was a man to make a woman's heart ping.

And break, she added as a reminder.

"Why didn't you become a movie star?" she asked. It was something the women had speculated on after seeing a write-up about him in the paper.

"I liked doing stunts, but actors have to say a lot of damn-fool things with a straight face. It wasn't my thing."

They arrived at the clearing where she'd left her cattle. Mason circled around to the far side, and together they herded them through the gap in the fence. Leaving them in the rough pasture to graze, she and Mason dismounted and checked the broken strands of wire.

While he secured the post that had been knocked out of the ground, she cut a length of barbed wire from the roll. Without conversation, he pulled one broken end toward her and held it while she twisted the wires together. He did the same with each of the five strands until the stock fence was in place once more.

Cybil experienced the satisfaction she always felt when she finished a job.

"I'm on the wrong side of the fence," he said. "I should have left the chestnut on the other side. You got the key to the gate?"

She shook her head. "We can go to my place. I'll give you and your horse a ride home."

"Or you could give me the key so I could cut across the back road."

She hesitated at handing over the key.

"I'll give it back," he assured her, his voice dropping to gritty tones of anger. "I won't even make a copy."

"Good. I don't like anyone having access to my land."

He snorted. "Or any other part of you, I'll wager."

She ignored that.

"I'm not anyone. I'm your neighbor," he reminded

her as they stirred the cattle to a fast walk and drove them to the main pasture where her herd rested in the sun.

Maria came out on the porch while Cybil directed Mason to unsaddle his horse and leave it in the paddock. She did the same and stored her tack in the barn.

"You're just in time. I was about to put everything away," she called out. "I'll set another place." She returned to the kitchen.

Cybil faced the inevitable. "You had lunch?"

"No."

"You're welcome to join me."

She was fully aware of his eyes boring into her back as she led the way inside. He knew she'd had no intention of inviting him to lunch. They washed up in the mudroom.

Cybil felt a light touch along her forearm. She glanced at Mason, next to her at the double sink. A springy mat of dark hairs curled over his tanned arm. Where it had brushed hers, her skin seemed to fill with a strange, restless heat and give it off in pulsating waves. She moved over a bit.

In the kitchen, she took a plate and filled it with pork loin, baked apples, mashed potatoes and green beans from the pots and pans on the stove. Then, instead of going to the dining room, she sat at the kitchen table.

Maria fussed over helping Mason. As if he couldn't dip out food for himself. He joined Cybil at the table.

"How's Enya?" she asked Maria.

"She's fine. She ate a good lunch, then laid down with an ice pack for a nap. The young man who brought her home was very nice. He ate with us, too."

"Good."

"My sweet heaven," Mason said after three bites, "this is the best food I've had in years."

"Who does the cooking at your place?" Maria asked.

He grinned. "Uncle Moses."

While eating the late meal, Cybil fought with her conscience and lost. "I'll go back, get my cattle out of your herd and move them by the back road."

Tippy walked into the kitchen. "Need any help?"

Cybil shook her head.

"I'm bored staying around the house." She eyed Mason like a bear spying a particularly lush berry patch.

"I thought it was your help yesterday that caused the problem," Mason said. "One of my men said you were leading the stampede when he heard the racket and rode up the ridge to see what was going on." He flashed a smile at the sultry divorcée.

Cybil felt her heart seize up. He'd never smiled at her like that. Not that she wanted him to.

Tippy pursed her lips into a pout. "I nearly got eaten by a mountain lion."

Mason scoffed at that idea. "Nah, he prefers deer to cows or humans."

The divorcée joined them at the table and flirted brazenly with Mason while he ate seconds of everything. Maria cleaned up the kitchen and beamed over his compliments on her cooking. She insisted on serving him a big wedge of pie with ice cream for dessert.

The two women fawned over him as if he were visiting royalty. That was the trouble with the male half of the population. They were spoiled rotten, especially when they were handsome and virile and... and...

Cybil stood. "I'm going to saddle up a fresh mount. Tippy can drive you back to your place. You can use my trailer for the chestnut."

"I'll go with you," he said.

She shrugged and headed for the barn. He joined her before she rode out.

"Here, this is an extra key to the gate. We'll bring the cattle back through it." She kept her tone strictly business and refused to look at him.

"You're a funny female," he commented.

"Ha-ha," she replied, not letting herself think about why she felt angry, aggrieved and relieved around him, all at the same time.

# 3

MASON SAID a succinct expletive, which no one could hear for the cattle milling about and bellowing at being disturbed. He shook his head as he watched his newest ranch hand being bowled over by the cowgirl, who had decided she felt well enough to return to the job that afternoon.

He cut a mama and her calf from his cattle and guided them over to the growing pool of mixed breeds belonging to his neighbor. "Try to keep these with the others," he suggested in a wry voice to Tony.

Cybil gave him an amused glance as she brought over two more cows and left them under the cowboy's care.

Mason rode across the rolling pasture with her. He caught her light scent on the breeze and inhaled deeply. His thoughts ran riot along with his libido. They passed Enya herding another cow their way.

"Every time that girl turns her baby blues his way, Tony forgets what he's doing," he complained.

"Yeah, I noticed."

"You find it funny, huh?"

"Well, men are such fools..."

He sucked in a breath and stopped the rising irritation in its tracks before responding. "Nah, we just want what you women flaunt. It's natural, you know. Or maybe you don't." He eyed her as if trying to decide how much she knew about the man-woman thing.

A soft flush slid up her neck and into her cheeks. Ha. Got to her with that one. He settled back in the saddle with a grin of satisfaction, aware that he took entirely too much delight in sparring with this woman. In the back of his mind, he had a feeling this would lead to complications he didn't need in his life.

"Ah, but a thinking person can control his or her natural impulses. That's why science and technology have triumphed over ignorance and superstition. Perhaps you'd better have a talk with your ranch hand."

Mason set his jaw. He could show her a thing or two about nature versus science that would singe that smug look off her face. Before he got through, she would be panting like a derby winner after the big race.

The visions that brought on were dangerous, so he reined to the left when she went to the right. For the rest of the afternoon, they worked on separating her mixed-breeds from his purebred beef. The job was done before dark.

"Tony, Moses will be out to relieve you before long. He'll bring the pickup. You'll have to bed down in it until we're sure the cat has moved on."

Tony nodded. His Adam's apple jostled up and down when Enya rode past. She circled the animals for the trek back to the other ranch, her blond hair, held in a rubber band, swinging down her back. A small bruise curved over her high cheekbone, and another smudged her forehead.

Mason's gaze flicked over to the girl's boss. Her hair was gathered up and stuck under her hat so that her neck was bare. He studied the delicate slope as she bent over the saddle horn to check a galled place on a cow's back.

He'd always had a weakness for a woman's nape. It seemed an intimate place to him, that sweet spot where fine tendrils of hair curled along milky white skin. He liked to kiss a woman there, to sniff the tantalizing scent of perfume, to brush his lips over the soft curls and think of how soft and sweet she was all over.

Cybil, with her pale skin and nicely rounded curves, would be a delicious handful of woman. If she'd ever let a man get close enough to touch her.

The tingle of sexual hunger vibrated along his nerves. As he saw her high, perky breasts shift when she eased back in the saddle, his libido surged to new life. It was maddening the way his body insisted upon reacting to hers. A man his age ought to be able to control his impulses better.

Recalling her admonition about impulses, he bit down on the irritation. Damn, but she was like a rough place in a boot. She just kept rubbing and rubbing on a man....

He cut that thought off as images of other ways of rubbing came to him, ways that were pleasant rather than annoying. Get over it, he advised himself. The lady wasn't interested.

However, she had a different expression in her blue

gray eyes as she watched the youngsters circle each other like two dogs who'd just met and weren't sure how friendly the other was. He would almost swear there was a flicker of tenderness as she observed the couple, who, if he guessed right, would soon be lovers.

So in addition to being a good rancher and boss, the harridan had a grain of humanity and a kind eye for the youngsters. He watched while she and her cowgirl exchanged remarks, then laughed in the way women did when they were sharing secrets.

A hot stroke of need flashed through his system, but it wasn't the pretty blonde with the big blue eyes that drew his attention. It was her acid-tongued boss with the great body that put his teeth and other parts on edge.

"Hell," he said.

His horse plunged to the side and stopped one of his cows from joining Cybil's bunch. From the corner of his eye, he saw the rump end of his bull heading into the trees. He cursed again.

Cybil had also spotted the bull. She took off after him. Mason barked an order for Tony and Enya to keep the cattle in order and headed after Cybil. He heard her yell a swearword or two as she gave chase.

Passing through a narrow place between two trees, he saw why she was aggravated. Her cow was with his bull. They were making tracks for the hinterland. A wry sense of amusement hit him. His bull was chasing after her cow, and he was hot on the trail behind her. There was a certain irony in the situation that he couldn't fail to notice.

"You stupid heifer," she yelled. "Get back here or you'll be hamburger tomorrow, you hear?"

He rode up beside her when she stopped. The cow and bull disappeared into the trees several yards up the trail. They would never track them in the heavy brush.

"You ever notice you do that a lot?"

"What?"

"Threaten people, cattle or anything that doesn't do exactly what you want it to."

She flashed him a heated glance, then wheeled away. "When you find them, I'd appreciate it if you would send her through the gate to our place. I'll check for her tomorrow."

He rubbed his chin thoughtfully. "I'm beginning to wonder if you're using my stud to service your cows."

"Hardly. I rent a bull each summer. My cattle are all bred for this year, thanks."

"Except for that heifer old Fletch is following."

"Yeah, like men, he can't let one flower go untouched."

Mason smiled as she gave him a superior perusal. He reached in his pocket. "Yep, I got two cents," he said. He looked her in the eye. "I said for two cents or less I'd find out something about you."

"What?"

"If you're for real." With that, he reached over and plucked her off the saddle and set her in front of him.

"What are you doing? Are you crazy? Let me go. Right now!" She planted both hands against his chest and pushed.

He caught her hands and held them behind her. "Sorry, I don't take orders very well."

She arched away from him, her eyes—they were mostly gray, he decided—spitting at him like a mad feline. He felt the firm pressure of her breasts against his chest.

"You big ape. Get your hands off me—"

He grinned as she evidently realized he didn't have his hands on her, except for holding her wrists. "Want your kiss now or later?"

"That'll be the day." She jabbed him in the stomach with her elbow.

He tensed his muscles. "Yeah, I have to admit I'm looking forward to it." He set her on her horse. "But the best will be—"

She rode off without hearing about the best part. He followed, more slowly this time. He had a burning sensation in his chest and a hardening one in his groin.

He didn't know whether it was an insight or a wish, but he knew with a certainty that defied logic that there would come a day when she would want him to touch her...just as he wanted her now. Then there would be no stopping for either of them. "I look forward to it," he said softly to her straight back as they returned to the others.

CYBIL FINISHED taking care of the paperwork that went with a working ranch, then yawned. Things had been quiet all week, maybe even a bit dull.

Her neighbor had returned her cow. The key to the gate had been dangling from a string around the cow's neck. He'd also included a note to the effect that he was waiving the usual stud fee for his champion heavy Western bull in the interest of neighborliness.

Very funny—ha, ha.

A smile pushed its way onto her face in spite of her irritation at his flagrantly masculine ego. She was sure he was as stubborn as his bull once he was set on a course.

Heat flushed through her as it had each time she'd remembered his holding her close.

Arrogant brute, part of her scoffed. But another part recalled the strength of his arms around her, the alluring scent of a man who'd worked hard all day and the snug way they'd fitted together.

She sighed. Okay, so she was attracted. Oddly, so was he. It made for an interesting situation, one that was more than a little maddening. Why her? Why him? Why, period? Because there was no rationality to the man-woman thing.

The empty house echoed her snort of disdain. Enya, Maria and the guests had gone into town for a movie. Maria had left a potpie for dinner. It was nice to have the solitude and let her thoughts roam where they would. Cybil went outside to feed the livestock.

Chickens clucked along with her, pecking at grains of corn that dropped from the silage she used to fatten her cattle for the winter months. The barn cat rubbed her legs, then trailed behind, his green eyes flashing in the last rays of the sunset as the chickens kept their distance.

Since the cat had been raised with the ranch critters, he considered them property, not dinner, and tried to mark them with his scent. The chickens didn't go for it.

Finished with the chores, Cybil leaned on the paddock gate and scratched the gelding's ears, enjoying the whuffling sounds the animal made as he angled his head from side to side to get the most from the grooming.

A bellow made Cybil jump. She spun around in time to see Fletch come barreling over the near hill at a rumbling trot, his gaze on the pasture where she'd put the young heifer he'd fallen so hard for. The heifer hung her head over the fence and answered the lowing love call.

After the first start, Cybil, laughing at the thought of Mason's chagrin, opened the gate to an empty paddock and stood aside while Fletch charged at it. He dashed through with only a roll of his eyes for her.

"Gotcha, big guy," she told him after snapping the gate closed. "You'll have to commune with her over the fence."

Sticking her hands into her jacket pockets, she considered her next move. An idea came to her.

No, it would be juvenile...

But funny...

No, she shouldn't....

However, it would serve her neighbor right....

The argument with her better side lasted all of thirty seconds. She went into the house to call a neighbor who also raised heavy Western beef.

Forty minutes later, she pulled up in front of the Faraday ranch house, the trailer hitched to the pickup truck. She blew the horn, then hopped out and rushed to the trailer. Mason was on the porch, pulling on a lined denim jacket, by the time she got the gate lowered to make a ramp.

She backed the prime beef out and led him around to the front of the truck, stopping Mason in his tracks before he came closer. "I brought ole Fletch home."

Her neighbor gave her one of his gimlet-eyed stares, suspicion in every line of his lean body. "That was mighty nice of you."

She grinned as innocently as she could. "Just trying to be neighborly. I believe I've cured him of his roaming ways, too." Now she tried for a sincere expression. It was hard because of the laughter that bubbled in her.

He cocked his head slightly as he considered this latest information. She saw when he made the connection. His eyes widened, then narrowed. His mouth dropped open for a second in a silent gasp, then clamped into a thin line.

Yep, she'd gotten to him this time. She bit her lip to keep from chortling.

"Here." She held out the lead rope.

Instead of accepting it, he bent down and peered under the animal. His eyes snapped back to her.

She smiled brightly while his neck turned an interesting shade of desert-flats red. He opened his mouth, but nothing came out. His chest swelled. The red washed up over his cheekbones.

This was going better than she'd anticipated. After the cad had manhandled her, he deserved everything she could dish out. As his complexion shifted toward magenta, Cybil realized for the first time just how delightful revenge could be.

Mason couldn't think of one word to utter. He hadn't been this shocked since a friend in second grade had confided to him that parents had sex.

His neighbor smiled at him. His prize bull—now reduced to a prime steer—stood docilely beside her, his gaze off in the distance as if he had no interest in the proceedings.

Or anything else.

"My prize bull," he finally muttered, hearing the disbelief in his voice. He shook his head like a boxer reeling from a hard left jab.

"Steer," she cheerfully corrected.

"This is a joke, right?" No rancher in his or her right mind would neuter a prize bull. He peered at the animal again. Definitely a steer. "This had better be a joke." If it wasn't, he was at a total loss about what to do.

She gave him one of her superior-female smirks.

"This isn't a joke," he concluded. It had to be, but he couldn't figure it out. The dazzling shine in her eyes intimated she was pulling his leg. The adrenaline sizzled in his body, a storm of energy that demanded release. Okay, two could play at this game. He could give, as well as get.

"Maybe you don't know what the males of various species are for," he suggested with as menacing a smile as he could muster. "Maybe you need to be shown." He stepped forward.

A flash of surprise rippled over her expression. She backed away. He tracked her mercilessly.

She tried her intimidating glare. He returned it. Each time she stepped back, he stepped forward, making his stride a bit longer than hers so that the gap was closing.

When she hit the truck, she glanced from side to side, then tried to stare him down again.

"It won't work, angel-face. There's no escape." He dropped the register of his voice until it was a nice thuggish rasp. A smidgen of worry appeared in her eyes, which looked the color of polished silver in the twilight shadows. He suppressed a grin.

When she dropped the lead rope and moved as if to dart away to safety, he slapped his hands flat against the pickup on either side of her. The steer moved off to a patch of withered grass and started munching.

"I suppose I'll have to take the cost of Fletch out in trade to make up for the loss. Then there's the matter of his stud fees. That's a yearly income, you realize?" he inquired softly.

She faced him squarely. The self-satisfied little smile that mocked so thoroughly danced defiantly at the corners of her mouth as she recovered her composure. He forgot his revenge and wondered how she would taste when he silenced that smart mouth with a kiss.

But perhaps he should give her a choice.

"You want a kiss or a hiding?" he asked. Looking at her mouth, he thought it was definitely a rhetorical question.

Her eyebrows rose in disbelief. "A hiding? As in a spanking?" she asked, then laughed in derision. "You'd better not try it."

"One or the other," he said. He leaned in closer. "Which do you want?"

"You wouldn't dare." She stuck her chin out.

"A kiss or a hiding?"

The world stopped whatever it was doing and waited. The silence grew. Looking into her indignant gaze, he couldn't decide which he wanted her to choose. Not that he would listen when she did; her mouth was that much of a temptation.

Her lips were fuller on the bottom. They were shiny but pale, as if she used gloss rather than lipstick. There was a flicker of excitement in her eyes and in the slight hitch to her breathing when he bent until their lips nearly touched.

"Choose," he demanded, the word almost inaudible as his voice thickened with the hot flow of his blood.

"You just try, cowboy," she said, warning him of painful consequences whatever he did.

"I won't be sorry, either way."

"You will."

"Never." He could feel the heat of her mouth and body, so close they stood. His reaction was swift and predictable. He felt the way he often had after completing a nearly impossible stunt—overflowing with energy, passion a pounding need that demanded companionship and release....

The odd thing was he knew no other woman would do, only this one. Without further thought, he leaned into her, letting her feel the hunger, letting it grow with each brush of his body against hers—

"What happened?" Uncle Moses shouted, coming out of the barn and around the trailer. "Did Fletch get out again? That blasted bull! We ought to castrate him.''

Mason jerked, a curse of unfulfilled lust coming to his lips. He gazed into Cybil's eyes for a long second, one part of him recognizing the excitement of challenge and desire in her that matched his. He moved back. ''It's already been taken care of,'' he told his uncle. ''Our neighbor did the kind deed.''

The old man walked up and flicked each of them an uncertain glance. ''What're you talking about?''

''Fletch.'' Mason pointed to the steer.

''If that's Fletch, who does that bull in the trailer belong to? He sure looks like that champion you're so all-fired proud of.''

Mason looked at the steer, then Cybil. He saw by her expression that he'd been taken for a hayride down a country lane just as he'd thought. He grabbed her wrist.

To his surprise, she didn't fight when he took off for the back of the trailer. Sure enough, there was a bull who looked exactly like Fletch in there. He zeroed in on her mouth as she tried to control a smile.

''A hiding,'' he decided, resorting to his role as the villain once more.

''Hey, can't you take a joke?''

''Ha-ha.'' He looked around for a good spot.

''You can't give a neighbor a hiding,'' Moses told him, watching the action with unabashed curiosity.

''Okay, what about I hold her and you whale the tar out of her?'' he suggested to his uncle. ''She made me think she'd done Fletch bodily harm.''

Uncle Moses caught on. He slapped his knee and

gave a wheezy laugh that sounded like a moose on its last gasp. "She got you on that one, eh, boy?" he said between guffaws.

Cybil tugged at her arm. Mason let her go. She backed off a few steps, her grin firmly in place.

"When the bull showed up again, I remembered that Sam Whitby raised heavy Westerns, too. I borrowed the steer from him," she explained to Moses.

The old man loved it. "Had you going, didn't she?" He winked at Cybil and bellowed some more.

Mason, unable to hide a wry grin, pulled his hat down securely and backed Fletch off the ramp. He loaded the steer and raised the ramp, then locked it into place.

"You need any help getting this one home?" he asked.

She shook her head and headed for the pickup. Her jacket cupped in below her hips. He watched the way her legs sliced the air. She walked with a sure-footed gait and the confidence of a woman who knew her own mind.

Fletch touched his cold nose to Mason's hand, recalling him to the present. He led the animal to the barn and locked him in a stall for the night. "You're going to get me into a heap of trouble, old son."

The bull snorted softly in agreement.

Mason recalled the pressure of Cybil's breasts against his chest. He had to admit she also had the most delectable mouth he'd ever encountered. Another split second before Moses appeared and they would have been locked in an embrace. She had wanted it as much as he did. Damn. What was wrong with them?

Uncle Moses had been right about her being a woman of surprising facets. She certainly had a sense of humor, warped though it might be. He chuckled aloud in the empty barn. Yeah, she'd had him going...in more ways than one.

It came to him that he might already be in a heap of trouble where his sexy neighbor was concerned.

# 4

"OKAY, HERE ARE the rules. If you ride in with me, you ride home with me. Like Cinderella, we leave at midnight. We stay together at one table. Anyone who tries breaking the rules gets a quick lift back to the ranch. Clear?"

"What is this, kindergarten?" Tippy demanded.

"Something like that," Cybil said. She narrowed her eyes and stared so hard that Tippy gave up trying to hold it after a couple of seconds and backed off.

"Do we have to ask to go to the bathroom, too?" she inquired with an acid smile.

"Yes." Cybil looked each woman in the eye. "If I lose sight of anyone for more than ten minutes, I call in the local sheriff and report you missing. Then we look until we find you."

The other two women looked slightly dazed at this. Tippy looked merely bored. She knew the rules. She also knew they were enforced.

Cybil took the time to explain her reasoning. "You're vulnerable at this stage of your lives. I don't want any of you to do anything foolish or to get hurt."

On the other hand, she knew they needed to get out for some fun and maybe a little ego stroking. Male attention wasn't all bad.

Besides, she liked to dance.

"If a guy calls and asks for a date," she went on in kinder tones, "you have a chance to think about it. You have also presumably met him before. It's too dangerous to go off with some guy you meet in a bar. If you want to see him again, that's your business. Have him call. The ranch number is in the book. If you don't want to go by those rules, you are free to drive in on your own. Fair?"

The women nodded, understanding in their eyes. Even Tippy agreed, albeit with a pout.

After Enya and the three guests were in the ranch wagon, Cybil said goodbye to Maria, then drove to the small town that served the ranching and residential community in the south end of the valley.

The parking lot at the restaurant was over half-full. No surprise there. The food was good, and the locals liked to eat out. She locked the station wagon, then paused to study the heavens while the others went ahead.

The night sky was clear and brilliant with stars. A luminous ring outlined the moon, which silhouetted the peaks to the west of them. An insistent longing vibrated through her. The night was meant for sharing....

She shook her head slightly and trailed into the square log structure to join the others. They were already seated at a large round table that could accommodate eight or ten in a pinch. Noting the number of cowboys, both real and urban, at the bar, Cybil figured there would be more chairs squeezed in before an hour was up.

She was right. Tony and another hand from the Faraday place hurried over before the women had a chance to order drinks. The guys immediately offered to treat them.

"We run a tab and split it even-steven when we leave. You may join us if you wish," Cybil told them.

They did. Two more chairs were pulled up. Tony introduced Jack. Cybil introduced the women. She ordered a pitcher of beer and one of margaritas. The three-man band hired for Saturday night blasted into their first number. Tony asked Enya to dance.

"You dance?" Tippy asked Jack. When he nodded, she grabbed his hand. "Then let's go."

Cybil pushed her chair back and stood. "I'm here for action, too. Let's show them what we can do, shall we?" she said to the two middle-aged divorcées.

Their smiles were rather strained as they sat there staring at the dancers. However, Cybil knew once the fellows saw the women dancing with each other, they would come over and join them. It always worked....

"Good idea," a male voice said behind her.

She whirled around in surprise, her heart thumping all out of proportion to the event. "I didn't see you when I came in." She realized at that moment that she'd looked for him. It was a disturbing thought.

"I was in the restaurant talking to the mayor."

He took her hand and led her to the dance floor. They joined the gyrating bodies to the beat of "Proud Mary."

She wondered if she should refuse. The question was settled when he started moving to the beat. His grin was a challenge she couldn't refuse, and the magic was already getting to her.

Starting out barely moving in time to the music, she let her feet pick out the rhythm. Half closing her eyes, she felt the beat travel the length of her body, moving stealthily from limb to limb until all of her was caught up in the magic.

It was her one weakness.

Her partner was good. He spun and turned her with skill. She flowed effortlessly, like the wind over a quiet sea. The magic strummed in her, a thousand vibrations of delight. She could go on forever.

When the tune ended, Mason held on to her hand. "You like to dance," he said.

"It's okay."

His perusal was intense. She saw puzzlement and something oddly gentle in it. "You feel it to the bone."

The simple statement said he understood more about her than she wanted him to know. She would have to be on guard with this man.

The next number—another fast one—started. "Don't freeze up," he admonished. With a tug, he pulled her to him and executed a fancy dip, a turn, a spin, another dip and turn, then let her spin away before reeling her back to arm's length. He moved his hands to her waist.

The magic latched on and wouldn't let go. She forgot to be wary, to hold herself back. She let the music consume her. When the combo struck the last note, then segued into a slow, dreamy number, she didn't demur when Mason tucked her under his chin and held her close.

She closed her eyes and listened to the lead singer croon words of deep longing that reached to the depths of her. The odd yearning returned.

Once she'd wanted the moon. Now she wanted so much more. She just didn't know what it was or what primitive source the music touched in her soul. Only that it was there, and sometimes it hurt.

Against her breasts, she felt the quick rise and fall of his chest slow with the music. She could feel his heartbeat. And her own. It, too, slowed, quickened, then slowed again as the lights from a crystal ball sent rainbows of color over the darkened room.

A sigh worked its way out of her.

His arms tightened, holding her fast against his strong, lithe frame. When the melody ended, she stepped back from him, her mind hazy with fleeting impressions she didn't care to analyze. He let her go.

"You're with me tonight," he said.

Reality impinged on the magic. She recovered her poise and subdued her senses. "Hardly."

"I'll punch anyone who tries to break in."

"I'll punch you back."

He cocked a dark eyebrow at her. "Why do you always have to be perverse?"

"It's my sunny nature. Dance with one of the other women. They're lonely and need some reassurance."

"Of what?"

"Their allure, their womanhood, their place in the mad scheme of things." She tossed him a challenging smile over her shoulder.

He snorted, but he asked one of the women to dance with him, then the other. On the third number, he claimed her again for the Texas two-step. Cybil noticed Jack had taken one of the other women to the floor. Tippy was with a man Cybil didn't know. Tony and Enya were at the bar looking at the snacks menu.

"Fried mozzarella," she called to them as Mason danced her by. Enya nodded and waved.

"Wow, fried cheese, margaritas and dancing. I never realized the paragon next door had so many vices."

She twirled, letting her arms swing in an arc. Her partner rocked back on his heels.

"Watch out for that elbow," he cautioned. "I might have to haul you in for assault and battery."

"You and whose army?" She tossed her head, liking the feel of her hair swishing along her back with each movement.

"Hey, haven't you heard? I'm a deputy sheriff now. The judge swore me and two others in yesterday."

She leaned against his arm when he drew her close. "I didn't know the county was that desperate."

"The sheriff said you were one, too."

"Yeah. We're called on duty for the big football rivalry between our high school and one in Carson City. The citizens get in a snit if their team loses."

"We don't get to chase rustlers or bank robbers?"

"Not in the last fifty years or so."

He managed an expression of disappointment, but his eyes glinted in the reflected lights of the votive candles at each table as they swirled around the floor.

When they returned to the table, Tippy's new partner and his friend had joined them. With Jack and Tony and Mason, the numbers were now even. Introductions were made, fresh drinks arrived and snacks were served. Cybil felt her efforts as a hostess had been a success.

She dipped a stick of fried cheese into *picante* sauce and munched contentedly.

Mason caught her hand and guided the next bite to his mouth. "Good," he murmured.

She dipped it again and handed it to him, then selected another for herself. "I'm particular about the person I eat after." Sharing food with him seemed too intimate, as if they were lovers or something.

A frisson trickled along her nerves, mocking her caution. The truth was she wanted to dance, to laugh, to forget caution and complications. For just one night. One night of bliss...

No, don't even think it.

His dark eyes roamed over her face, then her Western-cut shirt. "Your eyes are blue tonight. The other day, I would have sworn they were gray."

"It's the shirt," Enya informed him. "The deep blue brings out the blue in her eyes."

"You gals ever wear a skirt?" he asked, raking down her jeans. Enya was similarly dressed in jeans and shirt.

"Do you?" Cybil countered before Enya could answer the sexist question.

A volley of laughter went around the table. Mason grinned amiably. "Only on special occasions."

"Me, too. Weddings and funerals." Cybil let the

tangy coolness of the margarita slide down her throat while she held his amused perusal.

At fifteen minutes before midnight, she told her group it would soon be time to go. Groans of disappointment greeted the announcement.

"It's early," Mason murmured in her ear.

She found it odd to be the center of a man's attention. Mason had made it clear that he was there for her and no other reason. It had been a long time since a man had been so persistent. It was flattering...and disturbing.

Passion bubbled inside her, keeping time to the beat of her heart. She knew it wasn't because of the margaritas. It was the man beside her.

Don't be foolish, she warned, suppressing the urge to give in to the subtle clamor in her body. It had been a long time since she'd been close to another human.

"You can go home with me," Tippy's friend said.

"She goes to the ranch," Cybil stated.

"I meant I'll be glad to drive her," the man—Bill, Bob, Billy Bob, whoever—explained.

When Tippy didn't say anything but simply watched Cybil, a heated gleam in her eye, Cybil sighed and felt the magic drain from her. She hated trouble.

"Thanks, but she goes with us."

"Why don't we let her speak for herself?" the urban cowboy said, his tone threatening.

"Sorry, but that's the ranch rules."

"Says who?"

Tippy's eyes were alcohol glazed. She smiled as her friend's tone became belligerent. Cybil had a feeling she'd been set up. Beside her, she felt Mason shift. He draped an arm over the back of her chair, and she felt his warmth along her shoulders although he didn't touch her.

She looked at the guy. "Me. I'm the boss."

"She your boss?" he asked Tippy.

"She thinks she is, but actually I'm a paying guest. I don't have to take orders from her."

"Sorry, but you agreed to abide by the rules before you came," Cybil told Tippy, worried about the other woman's state of mind. "You come with us—you go home with us." Her open-handed gesture said a rule was a rule.

"Not this time—"

"You heard the lady," Mason interrupted. "Drop it."

Billy Bob stood. "You gonna make me?"

"Hey," the bartender called out. "You want trouble, you go outside and look for it."

"It's time to leave," Cybil reminded her gang. She stood and grabbed her jacket.

Enya and the other two women did likewise. Cybil leveled one of her steely-eyed stares at Tippy, who surprised her by quietly rising and slipping on her coat. Enya led the way out. Cybil brought up the rear.

Mason followed, then Billy Bob. Tony and the other men also trailed after them. Everyone in the bar watched them with interest. Fortunately, the side parking lot wasn't visible from the front windows.

Cybil unlocked the doors and motioned for the women to get in. She wanted to leave.

"You're coming with me," Billy Bob said, grabbing hold of Tippy's arm. "You said you would."

"Oh, let go. You can't even stand up to a woman." Tippy looked him over. "In fact, you can hardly stand up, period."

"I can stand up. I can—"

"I think you'd better move aside," Mason said.

The cowboy took an unexpected swing at Mason, who neatly sidestepped the blow, a grin on his handsome face. Cybil heard the other women gasp as she watched a fist come flying toward her. She realized she should duck. She tried, but the action came too late.

The fist hit her beside the right eye. She actually saw stars, or at least little spirals of light, dance in her vision just before her legs turned to cooked pasta.

"Got you," a deep voice said.

She tried to speak, but no words came out. She could hear herself breathing in shallow drafts. She held on to Mason's shoulders.

"Enya, take the keys and get the women to your place. I'll take Cybil to the clinic up in Carson City. Tony, can you and Jack get Billy home? He doesn't need to be driving."

"Sure," Tony said. He and Jack held the other cowboy between them.

"I'll get you an ice pack," Mason told Cybil.

"I've never hit a woman," the cowboy said in a shaken tone. "Ma'am, I'm really sorry."

Things were sorted out, and Cybil found herself in a pickup beside Mason. She held a napkin wrapped around crushed ice against her aching eye.

"I'm okay. I don't need to go to the clinic." She blinked her eyes several times. "I never realized how much a punch hurts, though. It rattled my brain."

"I can identify with that."

"You've been there, done that," she said, and giggled. "I can't believe I did that."

He flashed her an amused glance and adjusted the heat vents so warm air flowed over her. She was shivering slightly.

"What can't you believe?" he asked.

"That I giggled. I haven't done that since I was five years old."

"You took quite a blow. I'm sorry about that."

"Do you feel guilty because you ducked and I didn't?"

He mulled it over. "I guess I do. I expected him to pull the punch, but he was too far gone. When I realized he was going to nail you, it was too late to intervene."

"Yeah." She sighed and closed her eyes.

"Lean on me."

"Okay."

He wrapped an arm around her. She snuggled against him and let her hand fall to his lap. His thigh contracted. She flattened her palm against him.

"It's been a long time since I've felt muscle this hard," she murmured.

"Ranching toughens a person up. You have strong muscles, too. But you're soft in the nicest places."

She liked the laughter in his voice. She liked the way his arm felt, all warm and snug across her shoulders. The quickening in her chest sent a warning. She ignored it. The inside of the truck was cozy and intimate. Thoughts deeply buried rose to the surface.

"I've wanted to make love with you for the longest time," she confessed.

A muscle jumped under her hand.

"Don't say things like that while I'm driving," he told her. "I would stop, but I'm too old for parking on the side of the road."

"If we did, it wouldn't mean anything. Would it?" she prodded when he didn't answer.

"I don't know," he finally answered. "Is this alcohol talking? No," he answered his own question. "You only had two margaritas the entire evening. I counted."

She slid her hand up his lean torso and under the denim jacket he wore. His heat penetrated her palm. She undid a couple of buttons on his shirt and slipped her hand inside. He wore a T-shirt. She huffed in frustration.

He laughed, a deep, husky note of amusement that strummed along her senses, sending them vibrating.

"Wait," he said. "We'll be home soon."

He pulled into the driveway at his ranch and killed the engine. The silence surrounded them.

Mason felt his heart jump into a faster beat. His felt as if it would leap from his chest at any moment. He wondered briefly what they were doing...and knew he didn't care.

He'd spent the past two years worrying about things, sorting through his life and his broken marriage, trying to piece things together. Tonight was his. He wasn't going to stop unless she ordered it.

Her lips touched his cheek, then moved toward his mouth. He turned his head to meet the kiss.

Fireworks exploded in his head. Yeah, this was what he'd been wanting, too. A shudder ran over him. He felt the answering tremor in her. Whatever was between them was strong and urgent. However, he felt honor bound to call her attention to the fact that they hadn't exactly been buddies in the months he'd been in the area.

"Listen, angel-face, you know where this is heading, don't you?"

She made little "Mm-hmm" sounds in her throat and rubbed against him, as sensuous as a cat. His blood went from hot to boiling. Three hours of dancing and holding her had whet his appetite for the full taste of her particular sweetness.

"The ice has melted," she murmured.

It took a second for the remark to sink in. "Let's go get you an ice bag."

He led her inside the silent ranch house. In the kitchen, he seated her on a stool and removed a gel pack from the freezer.

"Let's see how bad it is," he said, bending down to examine her eye. "Yeah, it's gonna be a beauty."

"My eye?"

"Your shiner. What would you have done if you hadn't had other men around—taken that punk on by yourself?"

"Enya would have helped. We've faced down a smitten cowboy before."

"I'll bet." He lingered instead of moving away, then unable to resist, he kissed her.

When she leaned back, he let his body flow over hers until they were touching in a line from their lips to their stomachs. She opened her legs, and he stepped inside the tight embrace of her thighs.

"You're killing me," he whispered. He felt her urgent heat, the need that swelled between them. "We're consenting adults," he reasoned.

"Yes."

"I don't have anything, any protection." He wasn't going to confess it had been nearly two years since he'd touched a woman. He'd been faithful to his marriage as long as it lasted. As corny as that sounded.

"I can't have children."

He heard the regret. He kissed the side of her neck and tasted the saltiness of perspiration. The faint scent of her cologne filled his nostrils. He brushed the hair off her neck and kissed the sweet curve of her nape.

"Neither can I."

The question hovered in the air between them— would they continue or call it quits?

He lifted his head, cupped her face between his hands and looked into her eyes. "I had a checkup recently. I'm healthy."

She moved those incredible breasts against him. "Me, too."

There was something innocent in the way she said it. He realized she didn't catch the implications. However, he did. His wife hadn't lived up to her vows. He'd had a very thorough physical before he'd moved to the ranch.

"Will you stay?" he asked. His voice sounded far away to his own ears.

The moment stretched to five seconds…ten.…

"Yes." Cybil put her hand in his. Her thinking was sharply focused and very clear. She wanted to stay with him. For tonight? For always? No, not that.

He slipped an arm around her. Together they walked up the dim stairway to his room.

"Where's Moses?" she asked, remembering the old man who had been a helpful neighbor when she was first getting started in her ranching career.

"He sleeps downstairs. Luckily, he's hard of hearing or he'd probably be out in the hall in his Skivvies wanting to know what the heck was going on."

She grinned at a picture of the old man, his false teeth out, his skinny shanks barely holding up his boxer underwear, while he demanded to know what they were doing.

Did she know?

"Yes," she murmured.

"Yes?" His smile questioned her.

"I know what I'm doing."

"Good." He stopped inside the bedroom, closed and locked the door, then snapped on the switch. A lamp came on beside a large four-poster bed of golden pine. There was a matching chest of drawers and an armoire, a square table and one easy chair.

"My father was born in this bed," Mason told her. "My grandmother refused to go to the hospital."

"I don't blame her. Home feels more…natural." She sat on the edge of the bed and grinned at him.

"What?"

"I was thinking of our conversation on nature versus science."

"I wasn't going to bring that up." He yanked off his boots, then helped her.

"You're a true gentleman." She ran her fingers through his hair, which felt springy and soft, like a spaniel's fur. "I like touching you. I know it sounds odd, but I thought about it the first time we met."

He removed her shirt, then his, and tossed them on the chair. His expression intent, he cupped her breasts and took their weight gently into his hands.

"This is something I've wanted to do since first meeting you."

"I've always thought I was too large—"

"No," he interrupted huskily. "You're perfect as you are." He unclipped her bra and laid it aside. "Perfect."

Under his almost reverent attention, she felt perfect, but honesty compelled her to correct his extravagant compliment. "Perhaps Rubenesque would be the more appropriate term." She rather liked the idea of being one of the voluptuous pink nudes the painter was famous for.

He bent and kissed her mouth, then her breasts, before easing her down on the mattress. "Perfect," he repeated. His smile was lazy and sexy. "I like a woman I can squeeze a bit without feeling as if she'll snap into pieces. You're a nice armful, honey."

This time the endearment wasn't edged with mockery. She relaxed, leaving him to set the pace while little whorls of anticipation sent spirals of electricity rioting throughout her body. She couldn't ever remember feeling this way, not once in her whole life.

He kissed and caressed each inch of her as he undressed them one garment at a time. She heard herself sigh several times or catch her breath when he found one especially sensitive spot. Each time, he paused and examined that place more closely before moving on.

"Let's get rid of this," he suggested, grabbing a handful of bedspread. "Hold on."

He picked her up with one hand under her bottom, then swept the covers out of the way. He pressed her to the pillow, eased in beside her and covered them with the sheet.

Her nipples were puckered into tight buds. When he rubbed his chest against them, her breath caught at the sensation that produced.

"We'll soon be warm," he promised, his voice low and husky in her ear.

She turned toward him and caressed his body with her hands and his thigh with hers. She reveled in the total feel of his body against hers. Six months. Why had they waited so long? "That feels incredible," she told him.

"To me, too."

He gazed into her eyes, and for a moment, she recalled when she'd been young and in love for the first time—the breathlessness, the wonder of it—and puzzled on why she felt that way now.

"I'd forgotten the magic," she whispered, aching for that young person and her dreams.

"Yes."

There was understanding in the look he gave her. Pleased, she gave herself over to exploring all there was to discover about him.

His chest and legs were thickly covered in springy

fur that acted as a sort of dry lubrication as she writhed and moved against him. He raked his fingers into her hair and held her face still as he roamed her forehead, eyes, nose and cheeks, leaving kisses along the way. When he came to her mouth, she was eager to participate.

She opened to him and nipped at his tongue when he came searching. She felt laughter rumble in his chest before he bit at her lower lip, then, taking her off guard, slipped his tongue between her teeth and claimed all her mouth.

When he coaxed her into following his lead and carrying their game to his territory, she did so willingly. They thrust and parried, neither seeking a victory over the other. In this game, both would come out on the winning side. That seemed right.

She felt his hands take up a restless journey from her neck to her breasts to her hips and back. His fingers were long and well shaped. The nails were kept short, clean and smooth. She liked that about him.

On his tenth or so trip, he didn't return, but stayed to caress her thighs, down to her knees and back, then down and up along the inner edge. She held her breath as he moved slightly, then she felt a hard warmth slip between her legs. She clamped her thighs together, trapping him there.

He moved against her in subtle little thrusts that mimicked the action of his tongue against hers. Moisture collected where their touch was the most intimate. She was ready for him.

With a low groan, he rolled so she was on her back and balanced his long lean body over hers, his weight on his elbows. His thrusts became more demanding, but he didn't enter her. His every movement increased her hunger.

"Come to me," she invited, her hands on his hips.

"Not yet." His smile flashed white in the soft light. "Ladies first. I can't guarantee my control."

"Then you would have to try again until you got it right," she said tartly.

He laughed. "You expect a lot from a man."

"Only his best." She pushed against his chest until he rose up, then she guided him inside.

He took the journey leisurely, his eyes, like hers, riveted on the point of contact. When the trip was made, he let out a harsh breath.

She wriggled a bit to make some minor adjustments in the close fit of their bodies. He was large, and she was no longer used to a male presence. A puzzled frown appeared on his face.

"Has this been a while for you?"

"About five years," she admitted with a wry grin.

"Not since…" He let the question trail into silence as if he thought it might be too personal. Given the situation between them at the moment, his reticence was appealing.

"My husband, yes." She met his surprised gaze. "I've been much too busy to bed-hop."

"Yeah, I know what you mean." He paused, then said, "Cybil?"

"Yes?"

"My divorce was recently finalized although my wife and I have been separated well over a year. I was raised that a vow was a person's word."

She was touched by the confession. She'd already figured out it had been a long time for him, too. The tremor that had gone through him when she guided him inside her had spoken of his fight for control.

"No more talk," she requested. "Move in me."

"Not yet. Let me…"

He touched her most sensitive spot, causing her to gasp as the magic sparkled through her blood. She imagined she was floating in a warm sea of champagne, that it bubbled inside her, making her dizzy with desire. Her very blood seemed to froth and roil as it carried heat to every part of her. She pushed the sheet from their entwined bodies.

"Yeah, I'm hot, too," he murmured, pressing his face to the side of her neck.

Their skin became slick. He urged her to move against him and let her take her fill of his body. She closed her eyes tightly as the pressure built like a shaken bottle of champagne. She would explode any minute.…

She ran her hands urgently over him. Clasping his hips, she pulled him to her…faster…harder.…

Moans escaped her, little bubbles of passion spewing forth as the need rose higher. He held back when she demanded more from him.

"Not yet, sweetheart," he whispered. "Not…just… yet."

He stroked until she panted and moaned. The pressure built and built. She caught her bottom lip between her teeth and held her breath…and held it.…

"Now," she cried, clutching at his shoulders as the world exploded inside her.

He moved swiftly and deeply now, grabbing her up again and taking her with him as he rode the crest to the fullest. He thrust once into her and held it....

She experienced the pulsating effect of his body deep within her and that of her own stunning release. She planted a row of kisses along his shoulder and tasted the salt from his sweat. When the tension ebbed from him and she heard him exhale deeply, she let her arms fall limply to the bed.

He kissed the side of her face and neck, tasted her with his tongue and brushed the tendrils of hair from her temple with fingers that shook slightly. When he eased to the left of her, she turned, too, and nestled against him, reluctant to separate, content as she hadn't been in...she couldn't remember when.

"That was, you realize, the best ever," he murmured, laughter flowing into his voice, surprising her.

"On a scale of one to ten, it was definitely...a ten," she agreed. "See if you can find the gel pack over your way. My eye is throbbing."

"Yeah, here it is." He placed the pack on the pillow so she could rest her injury on it.

"I have to go soon."

He laid an arm over her waist. "Spend the night."

She hesitated, shocked by her reluctance to say no. "I really can't."

"Okay." He yawned. "Another hour, then."

She didn't refuse. The hour passed, then another as they resumed their sensual romp, a little slower this time, each more comfortable with the other.

He had her home by four. He combed his fingers into her hair and kissed her for several minutes at the door before letting her go inside. "When will I see you again?"

"I... This wasn't the beginning of an affair," she told him, reality blowing the magic aside. She wanted to hold on to it, but all good things...

"A long-term relationship?" he inquired, kissing the back of her neck as she opened the door.

"I don't think so." She spoke lightly.

He tugged her around to face him. "I think it is."

She shook her head.

His expression was disbelieving. "You wanna bet?"

There was only one way to handle a forceful male. She looked him straight in the eye. "I'm not saying it won't happen again, but we're not involved. Not now, not later, no matter what happens between us in the future."

"So this is a kiss-off, huh?"

She wasn't sure how far he could be pushed, but she wanted things in the open. "I'm not a source of convenient sex. Maybe you should find a mistress close by if that's what you have in mind."

He smiled suddenly, and an alarm went off inside. "Nah. You're right. We'll just let nature take its course." He moved to the end of the porch. "By the way, did you notice the frost on the grass tonight?"

Laughing, he tipped a hand to his hat and dashed back to his truck. Cybil went inside, puzzled by his last question. Then she remembered. Mason had told her they would be lovers before the first frost.

She shook her head at the ridiculous situation. She should have learned by now not to take a handsome man at face value. Besides, a one-night stand didn't mean anything.

The house was silent when she went in. No one had waited up. It occurred to her that her friends hadn't worried. Because she was in Mason's capable hands?

## 5

MASON WOKE AT NINE. It was the latest he'd slept in six months. It was also the best sleep he'd had in years.

He dressed quickly, as eager to be up and about as when he'd been a kid visiting the ranch. Uncle Moses was in the kitchen when he went downstairs.

"Pancakes in the oven," the old man said. "Warm up my coffee, will you?"

"Sure." Mason filled his uncle's coffee mug, then poured a mug for himself. The pancakes and sausage were a tad dried out from being in the oven so long, but he ate them with relish.

"Hungry this morning, huh?"

He glanced over at Moses before putting the dishes in the dishwasher, which had been one of the first things he'd installed after arriving. His uncle did the cooking and expected him to do the cleaning.

"Uh, yeah," he answered. Something told him there was more to that question than the obvious. He wondered if Moses had heard him and Cybil—

"Busy night?"

Mason recalled the unexpected bounty of the night. His body was pleasantly stiff in the lower back and buttocks. It had been a while since he'd performed certain exercises. "You might say that."

He returned to the table and picked up a section of the Sunday paper. He noticed his uncle wasn't reading. Instead, the older man watched him over the tops of the half-frame reading glasses he wore.

"Something on your mind?" he finally asked.

Moses shook his head. He looked as innocent as an aging cherub. "She's a fine woman," he said on a note of approval. "Knows what's what."

"Who?" Mason asked cautiously, not sure what the old man had on his mind.

"Cybil Mathews."

Mason hastily swallowed a gulp of hot coffee. "What about her?"

"You two are going to get married, aren't you?"

"What makes you think that?" Mason gave the other man a gimlet-eyed stare to put off any more questions about him and Cybil.

"Well, she came home with you last night—"

"How the heck did you know that?" Mason didn't like what he considered his business being open knowledge. Still, he should have known he couldn't keep it from Moses. The old man somehow knew every damn thing that happened on the ranch without ever leaving the house.

"I was in the hall when you came in. I was going to join you in the kitchen, but you two seemed sort of preoccupied." His smiled widened.

Mason groaned under his breath. "Some clown tried to start a fight. She got in the way of a fist. I gave her an ice pack to put on her eye."

"And kissed her to make it better," Moses concluded. "Then you took her upstairs to your room to show her the Oscar you won for special effects?"

Mason felt the heat rise to his ears as his relative grinned from ear to ear.

"Cybil will make a fine wife," Moses added.

"Huh. She'd take a man's hide off with that tongue of hers if he didn't do what she said."

"Maybe. Maybe not."

"You know her well?" Mason asked facetiously.

"We've been neighbors for five years. She's smart, and a hard worker, too. She'll stand by her man."

"You've been listening to too many country-western songs," Mason advised, but he couldn't help smiling.

Him and Cybil in holy wedlock?

That would be the day. He could imagine what she would say to that idea. None of it would be good.

"A man could do worse." Uncle Moses laid aside the paper. "We need an heir for the ranch."

Again Mason had to swallow fast or risk choking. He shook his head. "It won't come from me, Uncle. Lorah and I tried during the early years. She never got pregnant."

"Maybe it was her."

"No. She went to the doctor. It was me."

"Did you go see the doctor?"

Mason sighed. The old man wouldn't be satisfied until he had the whole story. "I took in a sperm sample. The report came back negative."

Moses frowned, obviously disappointed. "Was it a low number or something?"

Mason didn't remember the exact words. The doctor's office had called Lorah and told her the news. It had been a blow to know he'd never have kids. "Something like that."

"Maybe they could collect enough to artificially inseminate your wife...."

"I don't think so." Mason reined in his impatience with an effort. Uncle Moses was an old man. He wanted grandkids, or the nearest kin to that he could get, to inherit the ranch and keep it going. His own wife had died in childbirth fifty years ago. He'd never married again.

Recalling Cybil's confession that she, too, was sterile, Mason grimaced wryly. They were two of a kind. It wasn't exactly funny, but there was a certain ironic humor in the situation.

Memories of last night—rather, the wee hours of the morning—flooded his mind. She'd been the most responsive lover he'd ever had. Her body had been perfect. Every man's ideal—voluptuous, soft in all the right places, yet firm and well-toned overall.

Heat gathered low in his body. He'd like to go over and spend a leisurely day with her. But not with that passel of women around. "I'm going to ride fences today."

"What about church?"

Moses was a deacon and rather strict about observing the Sabbath. The cowboys had the day off unless there was an emergency. Mason felt a restless need to get outside for a few hours. He had things on his mind.

"I think I'll skip it," he said.

"Yeah, sometimes a man needs to be alone and think about where he's going."

Mason was surprised at the older man's insight. Meeting his uncle's gaze, he saw affection, as well as a certain mischievous twinkle in the depths.

He read the paper, then saddled up and rode the fence line between Cybil's ranch and his. He pulled out shrubs obscuring the strands. That was how he found the low place where the bull got through.

After repairing the broken strands, he cut a cedar sapling and stuck it in the middle of the low point and attached the barbed wire to it. That should take care of Fletch's amorous activities on the other ranch.

Sitting on the front porch later that afternoon, he wondered what Cybil was doing and if she was thinking of him....

"I'LL STRING HIM up by his scrawny neck," Cybil said to Maria. The two women were sitting in the living room. She was speaking of Moses Faraday.

Enya had taken one of the guests to the ice-cream store in town where they were to meet Tony and Jack. Tippy and the other woman had gone to a movie.

"I'm sure he didn't mean anything," Maria said.

Cybil narrowed her eyes and gazed suspiciously out the window in the direction of the Faraday place. "Telling everyone at church that Mason and I are engaged. As if I'd marry that...that..."

"Right," Maria said soothingly.

"Well, I wouldn't."

"Of course not."

"Do you think Mason put him up to it?"

"Mmm," Maria said noncommittally.

"Why would he? I mean, what would he get out it?"

"Not a thing."

"That's right. There would be no point...unless he wanted to humiliate me."

"Mason doesn't strike me as a man who needs to belittle another in order to feed his ego."

Cybil stared hard at the other woman. "I just can't figure this out."

"Why don't you go over and see him?"

"What for?"

"You could ask him about the, uh, situation," Maria suggested delicately.

She jumped to her feet. "Good idea. I'll make him retract it. That's what I'll do."

In five minutes, she'd changed clothes and was ready to go. She took off in the pickup too fast. The back tires threw gravel, then spun uselessly. The back end skidded to the side. Cybil cut the wheel toward the skid and managed to pull out of it without mishap. Taking a calming breath, she drove to the other ranch at speeds too fast to be considered safe.

He was sitting on the porch when she arrived. It was almost as if he expected her. Anger boiled in her.

Surprise darted across his tanned face when he saw who was in the truck. She hesitated. Maybe he didn't know about the disaster. Perhaps he'd had nothing to do with his uncle's announcement on the steps of the church with half the congregation within hearing distance.

He reached the pickup before she'd hardly stopped

and wrenched open the door. "Well, hello," he said in a husky voice that scraped across her raw nerves.

"Don't you take that tone with me. It won't work this morning." She jumped down and faced him, hands on her hips, ready to have this out. "You louse."

"Now, now, sweetheart," he drawled. "If you're going to sweet-talk me that way, we should go to my bedroom first."

"Where's your uncle?"

"He can't join us. He's in town playing checkers with one of his cronies."

Other than that first moment of surprise, he seemed to be pretty relaxed about the entire situation, except for a certain wariness in his eyes as he watched her. She began to suspect he was in cahoots with the old man.

"Did you put him up to it?"

"Up to what?"

She drew a deep breath through her nostrils. "Telling everyone we were engaged."

"What?" The amused watchfulness disappeared. In its place was a fury to match her own. He groaned, then said, "I'll strangle the old buzzard."

"I'll help you," she told him. "What gave him the idea...that is, how did he find out...?" She couldn't quite put into words what had happened last night.

Mason looked a bit sheepish. "He heard us. He got up to go to the bathroom or something and heard us in the kitchen, then on the stairs. He jumped to conclusions."

"Great. So what are you going to do about the rumor flying around the whole valley?"

He gazed at her with narrowed eyes. "Rumor?"

"About our engagement," she said impatiently.

"Didn't you tell Moses it wasn't true?"

"Of course I did. Do you think he listened? He's as hardheaded and single-minded as you."

"Damn." He rubbed his chin, a frown on his face.

Cybil couldn't believe she'd been in his arms less than twelve hours ago, delirious with the passion he stirred in her. A shiver raced over her at the thought and with it, vivid. Technicolor memories of the hours in his arms. He had been the most wonderful lover she'd ever known…like being eighteen again, only without all the clumsiness and uncertainties. The night had been a dream come true—

She shoved the images aside. There were other matters to worry her just now.

"Come on, it's cool out here. Let's go inside and figure out what to do."

She followed him into the house. It was warm, as he'd promised. He left her in the living room while he went to fetch coffee for them. She glanced around, noting the worn furniture. It was furnished for comfort, not style.

*His bed had been extremely comfortable.* She got a firm grip on her libido and studied the room.

After looking at a collection of ranch and family pictures on the wall, she chose an easy chair next to the sofa and perched on the edge.

Mason returned. He handed her a mug and took a

seat on the sofa. "Now tell me exactly what happened."

"Your uncle congratulated me on the engagement right in front of the minister and the whole church this morning. I'm sure the entire county has heard by now."

"What did he say when you told him it wasn't true?"

The blush rose straight to her hairline. "He said since I had spent the night with you he had assumed we'd be getting married, then he mumbled something about the young people of today not taking life seriously enough."

She was gratified to see Mason grit his teeth in disgust. At least he was taking this seriously.

"Didn't your denial take care of the problem?"

Cybil shook her head. "When I stopped at the grocery in town, several people came up and congratulated me. They just smiled as if they knew differently when I tried to explain about last night."

He looked startled. "What did you tell them?"

"That you gave me first aid for my black eye."

"That is a nice shiner you have there."

Her eye was a mixture of purple, navy blue and magenta. "Thanks. Your uncle is still telling people we're engaged. What should we do?"

"You mean after I boil his hide in oil?" Mason set the mug down with a thunk. "Let me think..."

Cybil observed Mason as he sat in deep concentration, his gaze focused internally while he stared at her.

He was a handsome man. Well, maybe not handsome, exactly. His nose had probably been broken at least once. But she liked the clean, strong lines of his face and the crinkles around his eyes…as if once he'd smiled a lot.

So had she. Once, when she'd been blindly trusting. The familiar twinge of anger and humiliation raked her over the coals of the past. Looking back, she realized that was what bothered her now—that she'd been so totally taken in.

Whom was a woman supposed to trust if not her husband?

The reason she was at Mason's ranch surfaced. She had other problems. Why was she thinking so much about the past and times when she'd been younger, happier and foolishly trusting?

"Well?" she said.

"I'm thinking."

"Are you coming up with anything?"

A slow grin spread over his sensuous mouth. "Yeah." His look was so direct she couldn't miss the meaning.

Heat burst inside her, an inferno of spontaneous combustion that scorched her from the inside out. She gave him a level stare as a warning. "Don't."

"Don't remember last night? Don't think about how you feel in my arms? Don't recall how you responded? You'd better get on with the lobotomy, angel-face, if you want to wipe out my memories."

He moved closer and laid his fingers alongside her throat. She became aware of the wayward pounding of her pulse at the same time he did.

"I'm not expecting anyone all afternoon," he said.

Her heart crowded into her throat. She had to open her mouth to breathe.

He muttered an exclamation, caught her up in his arms and stood in one smooth motion.

"No," she said, trying to buy time and regain her senses before things got out of hand. "We have to think. We have to talk and...and..."

She gazed into his eyes.

He held her look until his lips touched hers, then he closed his eyes. Cybil held out a few more seconds, then she closed her eyes and let him deepen the kiss.

"Last night wasn't enough," he murmured. He carried her up the steps and into his room. After placing her on the bed, he walked over and locked the door.

She wondered why she wasn't protesting. "I didn't come here for this." But, she admitted, she wanted it.

"I know."

"We have problems—"

"We'll sort them out." He sat down and pulled her into his arms. "I'll tell Moses to back off."

"Good." She spoke firmly, as if they were reasonable adults who had come to an understanding. "I should go."

He kissed her on the corner of her mouth.

"If you would argue, it would be easier to leave," she complained. She laid her hands on his shoulders, neither holding nor pushing him away.

He chuckled and brushed her hair aside and kissed the back of her neck.

Tingles rushed down her spine. She felt young and inexperienced, caught in the throes of first love again.

The magic shimmered in the air all around them. She had only to reach out to touch it.

"Tippy treats sex as if she were trying a new restaurant to check out its menu," she said.

He dropped her hair and let her face him. "I've never been that casual. Neither have you."

"That's what worries me. Why are we doing this now?"

"Don't beat it to death," he advised.

He caressed her breasts. They sprang to attention. She arched to meet his touch as he undid her shirt. He bent to kiss the flesh above her bra.

The magic, as golden as the sunlight outside the window, invaded her. "My boyfriend died in a skiing accident during our first year at college." She shook her head. "I don't know why I said that."

He lifted his head and looked into her eyes. "I'm sorry."

She nodded. "It doesn't hurt anymore."

"It always hurts. Somewhere deep inside where dreams are born." He lay back on the mattress. "My first love eloped with the son of an actor. He was a typical Hollywood brat. He died of an overdose about a year later."

Cybil lay beside him and laid her hand across his waist. He did the same. They stayed that way for several minutes. It was comforting...almost as if they were friends. He yawned. She did, too.

Then she fell asleep.

MASON WOKE and remained still as he sorted out the situation. A warm body lay against him. Cybil.

He eased up on an elbow and gazed at her. Her face was softer in sleep. The two little frown lines over the bridge of her nose were relaxed. He hoped her dreams were good.

A smile started in him and grew. He wondered if she woke smiling or grouchy. There was one way to find out.

He leaned close and dropped the lightest of kisses on her mouth. Like the rest of her, her mouth was generous and made for loving. Her tall frame fit his perfectly.

Unable to pull away after one taste, he kissed her again. Her mouth moved under his. Heat burst like a tiny nova in his abdomen, radiating passion all over him.

"Once more, angel-face," he murmured. "Let's make it good." He took her mouth in a complete kiss, exploring the textures with his tongue and lips, teasing and taunting until she responded.

He knew the moment she woke and became fully aware of what was happening. Instead of struggling or telling him to get off her, she turned toward him, her arm sliding across his shoulder, her hand cupping the back of his head.

From there, things got hot.

He made it as good for her as he knew how, giving her the benefit of every skill, every nuance he had learned about the female body. She took it all with a sweet greediness that pleased him more than anything any woman had ever done for him.

When she at last relaxed beneath him, panting and sweating from their passion, he smiled and let his own hunger take charge. It was the same as the previous night, a wild explosion that satisfied beyond anything he'd ever known. A slight worry impinged on his contentment, but not for long. Why worry about something that was as good as it could get between a man and a woman?

"What time is it?" she asked aeons later.

He rolled his head to glance at the clock. He groaned and muttered a curse. "Uncle Moses usually gets home about now...."

The words died away as the sound of an engine droned down the road. In another second, the noise of the tires on the gravel reached them, then all was quiet.

"He's home," Mason said.

"My truck—"

"Is plainly visible out front. We had better get dressed and face the music."

Cybil lunged from the bed. Hopping on one foot, she yanked her underwear and jeans up one leg, then the other. She fastened her shirt in record speed.

"This is your sock," he said, and flipped one toward her. He pulled on his boots, then jerked his arms through the sleeves of his shirt before going to the dresser. "You'd better do something about your hair."

She raked the comb he handed her through the tangles, wincing as she hit particularly snarly ones.

"Let me," he said impatiently.

He took the comb away from her. Starting at the end, he worked up her hair until it was as smooth as he could make the curly strands.

"You have beautiful hair. Don't ever cut it."

She snorted and pulled on her boots. "That's easy

to say when you're not the one taking care of it. It's long only because I forget to make appointments for a haircut.''

"Good."

She heard boots in the hallway below, then the bellow coming from Mason's uncle. She checked to make sure she hadn't forgotten anything. No, all was fine; her clothes were on. Nothing was lying on the floor—

"I said, anybody home?" he yelled.

She and Mason exchanged a rueful glance, then headed for the stairs. Moses was standing at the bottom of the steps, gazing up expectantly when they appeared.

"I thought that was your truck," he said.

"I came over to tell Mason about our engagement," she explained. "I thought he would like to know."

Moses smiled in delight, his thin face creasing into more lines than a topography chart of the mountains. "So it is true. I knew it right along. A man doesn't bring a woman into his home unless he's serious. So when is the wedding?"

Seeing Mason's half exasperated, half embarrassed expression, Cybil began to enjoy the prospect of him being on the hot seat. She smiled demurely. "Ask your nephew."

Mason glared at her, then his uncle. "There isn't going to be a wedding. Quit telling people there is."

Moses shook his head sadly. "This isn't like you, boy."

Cybil grinned at hearing Mason addressed as "boy."

"In my day," his uncle continued, "a man married the woman he was humping. If she was a decent sort. Which Cybil is." He gave Mason a stern frown.

"Thank you," she murmured.

"Will you shut up?" Mason snapped. "Uncle—"

"Don't try and tell me you were showing her your awards for the stunts you did in the movies. I didn't fall off the hay wagon this morning. I'm disappointed in you, boy. Just look at the position you've put Cybil in."

"*I've* put her in," Mason said in a low growl. "*You're* the one who's telling everyone in the valley that we spent the night together."

"Well, you did," his uncle asserted.

"No, we didn't."

Uncle Moses grabbed his chest in shock. "Are you telling me that was some other female you had up in your room last night?"

"Of course not—"

"So it was Cybil," the older man declared, a satisfied gleam in his eye.

Mason's jaw was so tight he could hardly get his teeth apart to speak. "Yes. No. That's really none of—"

"I guess next you'll be saying you didn't have Cybil up there in your room when I drove up. Huh. I yelled three times before I got an answer from either of you." Moses narrowed his eyes and gave his nephew and Cybil a crafty perusal. "I guess if I went up to your room and looked, the bed would be made and not tumbled about like a bunch of fighting cats just climbed out of it."

Cybil headed for the door as Mason's face turned ruddy. He was going to explode any minute. She didn't want to stay for the fallout. "I'll see you around."

"Cybil, wait up. I have to talk to you," Mason barked out behind her. "I'll deal with you later," he said to his uncle, who winked as soon as Mason turned back around to her.

She flashed him a flirty smile.

Mason took her arm and guided her outside, not stopping until they were beside her truck. He rested a hand on the fender at either side of her as if she were a captive bent on escape.

"You seem to find this funny now, but you were madder than a wet prairie hen when you arrived," he groused.

"I enjoy seeing a person get his just desserts. I think your uncle won that round."

"He's tough. I'll give him that."

"I like him."

Mason glared down at her. "You would. You and he have the same warped sense of humor." He took a breath. "Look, I think I've figured this out."

"Oh, goody."

He ignored her sarcasm. "We can pretend to be engaged for a while—a month or so—then we'll break up."

"Why?"

"Why what?"

"Why would we break up?"

"Mmm, we can say we're incompatible—" He stopped when she burst out laughing. "Yeah, everyone would think we were incompatible in the bedroom.'' His face softened. ''And that's the one place where we seem to agree with each other.''

She thought of the hour just past. He was an incredible lover. She had never been so pleasured....

He snapped his fingers in front of her face. ''Earth to Cybil, I'm trying to talk to you.''

''Okay, I'm with you.''

For a long minute, he merely looked at her. ''I wish,'' he said on a husky note. He curled a strand of her hair around one finger. ''Anyway, we can break it off later. We'll say both of us decided against marriage.''

''We'll be just good friends,'' she suggested, wrinkling her nose at him in a playful smile.

''Yeah.'' He frowned as if uncertain of that.

''No way.''

''What does that mean?''

''I'm not going to be engaged to anyone. I wouldn't marry again if the groom came wrapped in gold and with a million-dollar bonus.''

''I'm not proposing marriage. For your information, I wouldn't have another woman if she looked like a movie star, cooked like a French chef and had the disposition of a saint, which you certainly don't.''

''Fine. We understand each other. Just straighten out the rumor. I don't care what you say as long as you leave me out of it.''

''Look, I didn't start this mess....''

''He's your uncle.''

''Don't remind me. Shutting him up won't be easy.''

''Try a muzzle,'' she suggested.

Cybil ducked under his arm, climbed into the truck and drove off while he glared at her, his hands thrust into the back pockets of his jeans. It wasn't until she glanced into the rearview mirror that she realized he'd never gotten his shirt buttoned. And his hair was mussed. Mason looked just like a man who had hastily donned his clothing after a tussle between the sheets.

Maria was in when she arrived at the house. ''You got your shirt buttoned wrong,'' she said.

Cybil glanced down. Her shirt hung at a lopsided angle, one button off from straight.

# 6

THE BILLS WERE paid in full. Cybil turned off the computer and propped her chin on her hands. She stared out the windows at the land she loved.

Tippy was shoving suitcases into her car. Her divorce was final, and she was eager to be off. Cybil wondered if she was going to visit the cowboy she'd met at the dance. They had been a constant twosome of late.

One of the other women had obtained her divorce and moved on to make a new life for herself. The other had returned home to attempt a reconciliation after talking to her husband by phone. Cybil wished them all well. She would hate to have to start over again at forty. It had been hard enough at thirty-four.

For some reason, a picture of her maddening neighbor came to mind. Well, she certainly wouldn't be starting over with *him*. She'd tried love twice. Once had been wonderful, like sailing through the stars; the second time—she no longer knew what she'd felt for her husband. There had been the excitement of getting out of college, getting married and moving to Reno, his hometown, and starting their own business. Their lives had been busy.

That was the past. Now she would like to come up

with a way to improve cash flow for the ranch. Depending solely on the price of beef, her guests and the income from stock-market investments left little room for error.

She heard Maria enter the back door. They had the place to themselves. Enya was heading for Reno and the university. The ranch was much too quiet.

She went into the kitchen and poured a cup of coffee. "You want to go to the dance tonight? You haven't been away from here except to visit your daughter and her family for a whole month."

Maria shook her head. "I'm not much for dancing. You go and enjoy yourself. I'm going to read." Maria put away the fresh eggs she'd gathered from the few chickens they kept on the ranch.

Cybil had learned that taking care of living things was one of the best therapies for angry, grieving divorcées, which was why she kept the chickens and brought orphan calves in to be nursed by her guests. It reminded them of life and renewal. It gave them hope.

"I'll finish my book today, too. It's just gotten to the part where the heroine learns her father lied and the information she used to blackmail the hero wasn't true."

Surprisingly, her clients read the romance books she bought and discussed the problems of the main characters as if they were old friends. She thought the heroines' problems sometimes helped them to work through their own troubles.

"I'm reading the one where the hero is a cop and caught the heroine's son shoplifting. Now, there's a great start for a relationship,'' Maria commented with a wry grin.

Cybil stretched and yawned. ''I'm going to take the bills out to the mailbox. Then I'll ride the fences for the rest of the afternoon.''

Maria nodded. ''How about a casserole for supper? I can do one with cheese, potatoes, lima beans and carrots.''

''Sure.''

Cybil gathered up the envelopes with the monthly bills and walked out into the bright September sunlight. The wind had picked up and was blowing strong. A tumbleweed darted past her and collected with others along the fence.

Little rain and lots of wind—that was a fact of life in the desert. But she loved the area and didn't want to leave.

After setting the flag on the mailbox, she saddled her favorite mare and rode up to the ridge to check the fence line between her property and the Faraday place. At the top of the rise, she stopped her mount.

For a moment, her mind strayed to her neighbor. Her pulse kicked up as usual when thoughts of him intruded. She'd been having trouble falling asleep lately. Instead, she roamed the house, unable to settle to any one thing such as reading or watching the late shows on TV.

She had never thought about longing for a man's touch, for the sound of his voice…that it could be a physical thing, like hunger or thirst.

Or that she would wake with the feel of his kiss on

her lips, so real she could have sworn he'd been in her bedroom.

She shook her head slightly to dislodge the images that rushed through her brain like a runaway movie projector. Bringing her attention back to the land, she looked past the ranch next door and gazed toward the east. Sunlight reflected off the steady stream of cars that poured through the valley, mostly going to and from Reno. The area was changing from ranching to developments as more and more ranchers sold out and left. Golf courses were going in faster than her hens could lay eggs.

Shaking off creeping nostalgia, she clicked her tongue, and the mare moved off along the fence. She found where Mason had discovered a low spot with a couple of broken strands and had repaired it, putting in a tall cedar sapling to block the dip under the wire.

Knowing that was probably where the bull got through, she rode on because she liked the solitude. At the boundary of her land, she counted five new houses going in, each with five to eight acres of land around it, on the near hills. The owners would probably have a kid or two, a horse or two and a dog or two. Maybe some cats.

She realized she was being cynical.

Everyone had a dream of the good life. Once hers had been tied to marriage and children; now it was wrapped up in the ranch and the sense of freedom and security it gave her.

She was doing okay, but if she could improve the cash flow, especially with Enya in college, life would be perfect. Climbing the ridge on the way back to the house and seeing the cars on the highway, she got an idea.

Lots of people liked to ride horses and pretend to be a cowboy. She could open the ranch up as a family resort and let people camp out. Yes, that was it!

A small campground in the woods where the creek ran in the spring would be ideal. She could rent horses out by the half day. Retired cow ponies could be bought cheaply and saved from the glue factory. They were already trained and used to people, so that should work.

By the time she entered the house, she was excited about the project. She explained it to Maria.

Maria nodded enthusiastically. "We could serve dinner. With picnic tables under the trees in the side yard, we could put on barbecues. For a reasonable fee."

Cybil mulled over the suggestion. "That would be a lot of cooking. Would we do it every day?"

"I wouldn't mind. Hey, we could do the cookouts on the weekend only, say Friday, Saturday and Sunday."

"Most people go home on Sunday."

"Thursday, Friday and Saturday, then."

"Okay, that sounds good." Cybil grinned at the other woman, delighted that they saw the same vision, then came back down to earth. "We would need another person, to keep things cleaned up and help with the cooking. The campground would be seasonal. It might be hard to find someone for just the summer months. And if you have another job, you wouldn't be available, either."

Maria patted her hand. "We'll work it out. Whatever is meant to be, will be."

"With a nudge or two from me, I hope."

"There's a car," Maria said, glancing out the window. "Uh-oh, I think I'll go to my room and read some more." She disappeared up the stairs.

Curious, Cybil spun in her chair. Her stomach took a dip, then bobbed back into place. Somewhere inside her, an ember sparked and flames started....

Mason climbed out of his truck and slammed the door. He stomped up the sidewalk and onto the porch. For one insane moment, she considered not answering the door.

He knocked.

She gripped the chair arms, as undecided as a schoolgirl about facing him. It wasn't the fact that they had shared an hour or two of bliss that bothered her, or even that her body reacted to each thought of him with an internal clamor of need. No, it was more... something elusive...but insistent...a yearning that got her all mixed up inside.

"Cybil, I know you're in there."

"No, you don't."

"I see your truck."

"I'm gone in the ranch wagon." She started laughing at the ridiculous exchange.

He took that as an invitation and came in. "I saw your girl at the gas station. She said she was heading for college." He hooked his thumbs in his belt. "I take it you would rather not see me?"

"That's right." Her eyes drank in everything about him: the sweep of raven dark hair across his forehead, the smooth fit of his shirt over his muscular chest, the way his jeans clung to his hips and thighs, his hands, his mouth—

"Is anyone else here?" he asked suddenly.

A wicked gleam appeared in his eyes. She frowned to quell any bright ideas he had. "Yes, Maria is upstairs."

"Oh, well," he murmured philosophically.

"What do you want?" She realized that wasn't the right question as the gleam reappeared. She tried again, but in a sterner tone. "What are you doing here?"

"You want to go out for dinner?"

"No."

"Now, now, don't leap all over me in gratitude at the offer. It wrinkles my shirt." His smile was caustic this time. "I think we need to talk some more."

"Why?" She was curious, but also wary. She knew better than to take a man at face value, and Mason was looking very sincere and earnest now. Just looking at him gave her an ache inside.

"We have a problem. Uncle Moses hasn't retracted the rumor. In fact, he ignores me when I try to talk to him. I caught him telling some of his cronies that you and I had had a little spat, but it was nothing. He expects the date for the wedding to be set shortly and told them to watch the paper for an announcement."

"That explains it."

"What?"

"The congratulations I get every time I'm in town, the knowing grins when I explain it was all a misunderstanding."

"Yeah. Come on, let's get a steak. I'm hungry for something besides Moses's burned pot roast. That's all he knows how to cook."

"No, Maria would be left here alone." Another idea occurred to her. "She's looking for a job. She's an excellent cook and housekeeper. Can you use her? Maybe we can share if you can't use her full-time." She calculated expenses. She could afford part-time help all year.

"You aren't going to keep her?" He was incredulous.

"She was hired for the season. That's almost over."

"I'll take her. Full-time."

"Good. I'll tell her—"

"Later. Let's go eat."

She pointed out the facts to him. "If we're seen together, that will set the notion in people's minds that we really are a twosome."

He shrugged. "I've thought about the problem. If we pretended to a long engagement, that would stop others from setting us up with their single relatives and friends."

"Women rarely have that problem," she informed him.

"Yeah?"

"Yeah."

For a minute, she thought of boxing his ears. Men had no concept of what it was like being a forty- or fifty-year-old divorced or widowed female. Most friends didn't know what to do with such a person, and there weren't enough good men to go around. She decided his ego was big enough without her adding to it and kept her mouth shut.

When he sniffed appreciatively, she relented and invited him to dinner.

He accepted, took a seat, stretched his long frame out with a sigh and pulled his hat low on his forehead as if he were going to take a nap. "We branded over two hundred head of cattle this week. One cow nearly put the brand on me."

Cybil grinned. "On your rump, dare I hope?"

"You, woman, are a hard case." He pushed the hat up. His gaze held hers. "I wonder what it would take to break you."

"Don't even try," she warned, her tone more serious than she intended. She'd been down the garden path with one man. She wouldn't take another pratfall.

Maria came downstairs. Mason spoke to her, then turned to Cybil. "Okay if I ask her now?"

Cybil nodded.

He followed Maria into the kitchen. Cybil stayed in her seat and gave them a few minutes alone to sort out their arrangements. She would miss Maria....

Hearing the other woman's laughter, she joined them. "So, are you going to work for this guy? He's probably a slave driver—"

"Nah," he protested. "I'm a marshmallow when it comes to pretty women, especially ones who can cook."

Cybil smiled in approval as Maria beamed and set about putting the evening meal on the table. That was one problem taken care of. And maybe she could lure

Maria back next summer in time for the campground experiment.

"Enya told me you took her in three years ago and gave her a home. You also made her finish high school, and now she's off to college," Mason said after they were seated at the kitchen table.

Cybil nodded. "I still find it hard to believe her mother kicked her out when she was sixteen. She didn't like the competition of another female who was younger and prettier around."

"Did you know them?" he asked, his eyes narrowed on her as if weighing her reasons.

"A friend who was a social worker mentioned the situation. A junkyard owner found Enya living in an abandoned car. I needed some help, so we worked out a deal. She would live here and finish high school, and I would gain a ranch hand until she was ready to strike out on her own."

A sigh worked its way out of her. The girl had a job in the college library and an apartment at the university. She would come home only on weekends or holidays. Cybil thought of the girl as a younger sibling she had raised.

Now Enya, like Maria, was all set for the future. She would miss both of them. "She wants to be a teacher," Cybil finished.

"She wants to be like you," Maria said.

Cybil snorted, aware of Mason's unwavering gaze while she spoke. "She'll do better than I ever did."

"I think she would have to go a long way to match you," he said, sounding thoughtful rather than mocking.

She thought of her past. She hadn't done so well. At forty, she was as unsure and troubled as she'd been at eighteen and first falling in love.

Not that she was in love with anybody, she sternly reminded herself. She'd been down that road twice. Each time had ended in tragedy. Two old sayings came to mind.

"Three strikes and you're out."

"The third time's the charm."

She wondered which would apply in her case. Not that it would matter. She no longer believed in love.

MASON REMOVED HIS hat and shoved his hair off his forehead. He wiped his face on his sleeve. Sweat and dust darkened the material. He watched the cattle trucks disappear around the bend in the road. The last of the cattle were on their way to market.

He heaved a satisfied breath and headed for a hot shower with a slight limp. A steer had stepped on his foot during the loading. The only thing worse than dealing with a herd of cattle was dealing with a stubborn woman.

That brought a picture of his neighbor to mind. His body reacted immediately, as if he were as eager and randy as a teenager. Which he wasn't, damn it.

After cleaning up, he and Uncle Moses headed for town and the quarterly dinner of the local beef growers association. He wondered if Cybil would be there.

A hum started in his blood and wouldn't quit. He hadn't seen her in nearly a month. September and October were swamped with work as they culled cattle, then checked the heavy Western beef before calling the buyer to arrange for the shipment. A restaurant chain gave the ranch a contract for all the prime beef he and Moses could supply.

They were also urging him to provide exotics—deer and ostriches and other so-called wild game, all of which were ranch raised and not wild at all.

At the restaurant, he stopped to talk to a couple of other ranchers while Moses made his way to the private room where the meeting was held. When he joined the old man, he found him seated across the table from Cybil.

"Look who's here," Moses announced as if he brought a message straight from on high. "Our neighbor."

Mason hesitated an instant, then took the seat to her left. "Cybil," he said, acknowledging her.

"Hello, Mason."

He noticed Moses and a couple of his cronies were watching him and Cybil with avid interest. Heat crept up the back of his neck. Interfering old roosters. He figured they were the ones keeping the engagement rumor alive.

"How's it going with Maria?" she asked.

"She was a godsend this past week during loading."

"I saw the cattle trucks coming in and out."

"Aren't you selling any stock this year?"

"Fifty head at the auction next week, the rest to the grocery buyer the day after that."

He nodded. "Your hair looks nice. Different." He'd noticed she'd twisted it into one of those knots that women could do and pinned it on top of her head.

Visions of pulling the pins out one by one came to him.

"Thanks."

It was the most stilted conversation he'd had with a female since his first formal dance in ninth grade. When she went over to refill her coffee at the side table, his lungs nearly stopped working.

She was wearing a dress.

The skirt swished sassily a couple of inches above her knees. Her legs were long and shapely, perfect to wrap around a man, as he well knew.

Moses nudged him.

"What?"

"Move your arm," his uncle said.

The waiter set a salad plate in front of him. Mason realized he'd been staring at Cybil. No wonder. She looked better than any movie queen he'd ever known. She returned and took her seat. The light reflected off the velvety material stretched over her bosom.

She sprinkled vinegar and oil over her salad and picked up a fork. He thought of the sweetness of her mouth, the ticklish spot under her ear and the tender flesh at the back of her neck. His mouth went dry.

"You alone on your place now?" Moses asked her.

"Yes. It seems so strange not to have to yell at anyone about loud music or boots in the middle of the floor. I've been catching up on my reading, especially the farm and ranch magazines."

A man Mason recognized from the county planning office stopped by. "I saw your application for a camping permit," he said to Cybil after greetings and introductions had been made. "You opening a dude ranch?"

She smiled up at him. "Not exactly. I thought I'd put in some camping spots along the creek next summer—"

"Not on your life," Mason stated. When three sets of eyes turned on him with varying expressions, he continued, "Campers and hikers will pollute the creek, which feeds a stock pond on my place. They also increase the fire hazard during the summer."

Cybil frowned at him. "There won't be that many. I'm thinking maybe ten spots at the most."

Her friend cleared his throat. "There'll be a planning-board hearing next week."

"When?" Mason demanded.

"Call the office Monday for the schedule." He looked at Cybil. "See you then."

She nodded, then looked at Mason warily.

"I'm opposed to strangers traipsing all over the place," he told her, taking a patient tone. She evidently hadn't thought out all the problems and complications of her idea. "They leave trash behind."

"I'll see that they keep to my land."

"They have to drive by our place to get there. I can see us having to stop work and stage a search-and-rescue effort for lost hikers."

"I'll buy a coonhound for tracking." She gave him a sardonic smile.

She was a stubborn woman, and he was tempted to tell her so. "What about range fires? What will you do about those?" At her worried glance, he was stabbed with something akin to remorse for hassling her. "Look, if you're lonesome, you can visit us at our place. Or I'll come over and play you a game of checkers once in a while."

He liked the scenario of visiting her on a regular basis. Since their brief trysts, he'd had trouble sleeping at night. She was often in his dreams and rarely far from his thoughts when he was awake. It was a strange experience for him, and one he wasn't sure how to handle.

Her smile became droll. "It isn't companionship I need. It's cash flow. I'd like more money coming in."

"If you need to sell, I'll buy you out," he offered. He knew at once that was the wrong thing to say. Her smile disappeared faster than a rain shower in July.

"I'm not interested in selling, only increasing the cash operations if possible."

"Find some other way. We don't need a bunch of tourists running wild over the place."

"Thank you so much for that gem of wisdom. I'll take it into consideration."

For the rest of the evening, she didn't speak to him unless forced to answer a question. Her gaze flitted past him as if he were invisible. He was as restless as cattle in a thunderstorm during the meeting and the speech by a state representative on land use in the national-forest areas. Since he had no leases on public land, he didn't find the subject interesting and was glad when the speech and the question-and-answer period were over.

Cybil and her plans were a different story. Naturally, he was concerned with the ranch next door. Before he could pursue the topic, a neighbor approached them.

"When are you two going to set the date?" the rancher asked. "My wife wants to plan a shower."

"We've split up," Cybil responded before Mason could.

"It's just a lovers' spat," Moses inserted. "You should kiss and make up. And get on with the wedding. You aren't getting any younger."

The two older men laughed heartily. Cybil, he saw, joined in as if she thought the situation hilarious.

"I don't think it would work out," she explained, her face so pure and earnest she looked like a saint come to life. "He's too stubborn to deal with."

"Don't give up on him," Moses cautioned. "Granted, he is hardheaded, but you're a smart woman. You can handle him if you put your mind to it."

Mason was surprised at the plea in his uncle's eyes. He realized the old man had actually set his heart on their marriage…and the children he foolishly hoped would come from it. Mason groaned internally. He hated to hurt one of his favorite relatives.

"No, thanks," she said. "I haven't the time."

Or the inclination, Mason thought, disgruntled that she seemed unaffected by their time together last month while he was harder than a hickory stick and ready to pounce at the slightest come-on from her.

"Peace and quiet," he muttered. "Ha. A man doesn't stand a chance for either when women are around."

"Go to Tibet. Become a monk," she advised.

Uncle Moses and his checker-playing friend cackled like a whole flock of chickens laying eggs.

Mason leaned close to her. "But then, I might never get to make love with you again, and that would be a tragedy."

Her lashes fluttered downward, hiding her beautiful eyes, but he'd seen the confusion in their depths at his words. He realized he felt as confused as she did about their relationship and wondered, just for a second, if there was something here that both of them were missing....

Nah, he was imagining things.

# 7

CYBIL WALKED OUT of the planning office angrier than she'd ever been in her life. Mason had effectively put a stop to her idea of having a campground on her ranch. Not that the planning commission had issued a flat refusal. Instead, she had to revise her idea to include fire protection within county guidelines and show how it would work...thanks to Mason's suggestions.

"Hey, wait up," he called behind her.

She turned on the second step down and glared at him. He smiled. The sun sparkled off his white teeth and clean-cut features. He seemed to glow with health and vitality. She felt tired, perhaps a tad discouraged.

And lonely?

With Enya and Maria gone and no new clients scheduled until January, she was entirely alone on her 180 acres. At times, she had thought of calling Mason—no, *Maria,* that's who she meant, she quickly corrected, appalled at the slip.

"You can drill a well," he said, putting his hat on.

The brim shaded his eyes, making them darker, more mysterious. It also made it harder to read his thoughts.

"I can't figure you out," she complained. "First,

you oppose the campsite and get it thrown out by the planning commission, then you offer a solution to the main problem. Why bother?''

''Danged if I know.'' He took her arm and walked down the steps with her. ''How about lunch?''

She realized she was hungry. Lately, she hadn't felt like eating. Breakfast almost nauseated her of late. ''Okay.''

''Wow,'' he said softly.

''Don't think it means anything.''

He chuckled. ''With another woman, I might. With you, I know better. You want to go to the Soup Kitchen?''

She nodded. Once they were seated at the local diner, he studied her with a narrowed gaze after they ordered. She began to feel self-conscious.

''You're thinner. Paler, too. Have you been sick?''

''Not really.''

He gave her an impatient frown. ''Don't talk in circles. Have you been sick or not?''

''No.'' She glared right back. ''I'm a big girl. I can take care of myself.''

''Okay, don't get your dander up. I was just asking.''

She realized she was being churlish. ''I haven't been eating regularly. With everyone gone, cooking a meal seems rather pointless.''

''Don't you have any guests?''

''Not now.''

He opened his mouth, then closed it. She eyed him warily, not sure what to expect.

''I was about to suggest you join us for dinner tonight," he said, "but Uncle Moses would probably have the preacher there, ready to marry us or lecture us."

Cybil's face had grown warm each time she'd run into the old codger in town the past month. While he'd always been friendly, now he greeted her as if she were his long-lost daughter. He so obviously wanted her and his nephew to get together. It was sort of sweet....

However, she didn't want to encourage his hopes. "I met the new first-grade teacher at church last Sunday," she mentioned to Mason.

"What the heck does that mean?"

She took exception to his snappish tone. "It means I met the new first-grade teacher at church last Sunday."

"No, it doesn't. It means you have something in mind for me and her. Forget it."

Their soup and sandwiches arrived. When the waitress was gone, Cybil snatched up her spoon and thought of rapping him across the knuckles. "She's in her early thirties, very pretty and extremely nice."

"Not interested. I moved here for tranquillity. Women are not conducive to that mood."

She smiled in spite of her annoyance with him. It occurred to her she was also relieved. She explored this idea worriedly. Mason was a wonderful lover, but they certainly were not involved...no thanks to him.

He was perfectly willing to carry on an affair, but she refused to get that entangled with him. It wouldn't be wise. She'd reminded herself of that fact every night for the past six weeks. Not that her body was listening.

A sharp twinge of need spiked through her.

Grimacing, she did her best to ignore it—and the man across from her—and began eating the soup. It was delicious. She practically inhaled the meal. He did, too. They finished at the same time.

"That was nearly as good as Maria's chicken gumbo," he declared. "Now for dessert..."

"None for me—" She shut up when she saw the flames leap into his eyes as he studied her.

"It's guaranteed nonfattening. In fact, it burns calories."

His low, sexy tone conjured up images she had fought to subdue for a month. "Not interested," she said firmly, almost convincing herself she meant it.

He grinned. With one finger, he touched her cheek and trailed a cool path down her hot skin. "Liar."

She pushed his hand away, then glanced around. Several pairs of eyes skittered away from hers.

"People are watching," she warned.

He met the eyes of the town librarian. He nodded and gave the woman a big smile, his mood obviously as sunny as the fall day. "How's it going?" he called out.

The librarian replied, gave them an approving smile and went on with her lunch. That opened the gate, and several other valley residents spoke or nodded to them, speculation in their eyes. The word of their lunch would be passed throughout the county by night.

Cybil sighed in resignation, her humor over the situation wearing thin. For some reason, she felt wretchedly tired. "I need to get home." And take a nap, was the rest of that thought.

"Me, too. We're moving stock into winter pastures now that we have the haying done. You finished yet?"

"Yes. I'll make it through the winter with no problem."

"Good."

She wondered if he meant that. He had been pretty quick to offer to buy her out when she'd mentioned cash-flow problems. Was that what he was after? Her ranch?

A slight feeling of nausea rolled through her stomach. Men had as many ulterior motives as anyone. Who knew that better than she did? She stood abruptly. He did, too.

"It's been lovely." She made her tone deliberately facetious, erasing the confused emotions he generated in her. She tossed money for her lunch on the table and hurried toward the door.

When she drove out of the parking lot, she saw him standing next to his truck, his eyes shadowed, watching her as she left. She kept her eyes straight ahead.

"YOU'VE LOST weight," Maria scolded. "Here, have another roll."

"I've had two already," Cybil protested.

"Are you eating regular meals?" Maria shook her head in answer to her own question. "Of course not. You're over there alone all the time."

"You sound like my mother used to." Cybil finished the last bite of homemade cinnamon bun and patted her mouth on the napkin. "Actually, I have lost five pounds. I'm not sick. I just don't feel like eating right now."

"You should go in for a checkup."

"I will." At her friend's sharp look, Cybil held up her hand in a Girl Scout pledge. "Scout's honor. In fact, I have an appointment at the end of the week."

"Good. Did I tell you I stopped by the school and had lunch with Enya over the weekend?"

"She called and told me. She also fussed because I didn't come up with you. I promised to attend a concert at the end of the month."

"Mason likes classical music," Maria mentioned with an impish grin.

"Please," Cybil requested, rolling her eyes. "Surely you haven't joined ranks with Moses on marrying me off to his favorite nephew, whose praises he is forever singing whenever I'm in sight. Although it is pretty funny." She pictured what Mason must be going through.

"Yes. The two of them have words about you nearly every day. The ranch hands have bets on who will give up first."

"Give up?"

"Moses wants Mason to court you. You know— candy and flowers, candlelight dinners. He gives out a lot of advice on how to proceed. It's driving Mason up the wall."

"Hmm, I like that last idea." With a laugh, Cybil pushed her lazy self out of the chair and said goodbye.

Outside, she headed for her truck at a brisk pace. Mason came out of the stable and reached the door of the pickup before she did. He opened it for her, then helped her up with hands on her waist.

Her skin tingled all along her torso. His hands were broad, his touch sure. She recalled a hundred other ways he had touched her. A tremor rushed over her.

"Thanks," she said.

He blocked the door when she would have closed it and crowded in close. "How's it going?"

"Fine."

"Did you and Maria have a nice chat?"

"Yes." She couldn't think of another thing to say. Instead, she was aware of the scent of horses and hay from the stables, of sweat earned in hard labor, of aftershave lotion and a certain masculine lustiness—

She pulled her eyes from his with an effort. It was much too dangerous to linger around him.

"Yeah. Me, too," he said softly. He touched the pulse that beat wildly in her temple, thus setting up another tremor that quaked through her. "I've missed you."

"You've missed the sex," she corrected flippantly.

She didn't like the yearning that assailed her whenever he was near. It made her vulnerable, and she had vowed six years ago never to allow anyone to become necessary in her life again. Besides, the whole man-woman attraction was downright ridiculous, especially at their age.

He shoved his hat off his forehead and rested one hand on the seat behind her, the other on the steering wheel. His chuckle was sardonic. "No, it's those constant barbs you throw at a man."

He leaned close. His breath touched her temple

where the telltale pulse pounded out of control. His lips caressed her there. Every muscle in her body jerked.

"Easy," he murmured. "This won't hurt a bit."

She blindly jabbed the key into the switch and started the engine. It roared to life like a dragon suddenly awakened. Mason pulled back and glared at her, the sexy softness leaving his eyes.

Laying his hands on each side of her face, he yanked her close and planted a hard kiss on her mouth. His tongue demanded entrance. She kept her lips firmly closed.

But then his lips softened and the kiss became an entreaty inviting her response. The magic wrapped its gold haze around her, and she was lost in a sensual cloud.

She placed a hand against his chest. His warmth seeped into her palm. He laid a hand over hers and pressed gently. She felt the strong, steady cadence of his heart.

Yearning filled her, reminding her of the wild delight she'd found in his arms. She tried to think of all the reasons she should avoid him, but not one rose to mind.

"Mason..." It was supposed to have been a protest, but her voice sounded stunned and lost.

"Yes to anything you want," he responded, threading his fingers into her hair and urging her forward so that the kiss was harder.

His tongue stroked hers in tender forays that whetted her hunger for more. The restlessness and unease that had haunted her for a month fell away. In its place was the stunning passion that bloomed each time she thought of him and his roaming kisses.

When they at last paused for air, she could only stare at him in dismay. Shaking her head, she put the truck into gear. He walked with her as the truck crept forward.

"When will I see you again?" he demanded, refusing to let her go.

"I don't know—"

"I'll be over tonight. We need to talk."

"Yeah, right."

He grinned, unabashed by her skeptical retort. "Uncle Moses thinks I should take you out to dinner and ply you with wine and soft words."

"That doesn't work with a modern woman."

"What does?"

"Why should you care?"

He stepped back. "Damned if I know." He slammed the door and walked away without looking back.

She drove off in a cloud of gravel dust, angry and not sure why. They seemed to have strange quarrels.

"WHAT DID YOU SAY?" Cybil stared at her doctor.

Janet pushed her glasses up on her nose and looked over her notes. "Nine weeks."

"Before that."

"You're pregnant."

Cybil shook her head. "That's impossible."

"I assure you, it isn't." Janet, who had been her doctor since the move to the ranch, looked rather puzzled.

"I can't have children. The doctor in Reno…"

The thought trailed away. There had been nothing specifically wrong with her. An unfriendly environment was the description she'd been given. Her secretions were too acidic. That could have contributed to the difficulty.

"Well, doctors have been wrong before." Dr. Platt laughed as if this were an old joke.

"But my husband and I…we never used birth control, not after the first two years of marriage…I never conceived."

"You have now." Janet stood and patted her shoulder.

Cybil had so many reactions she couldn't sort them out, except for one: happiness—pure, shining, I-can't-believe-this-miracle-is-happening-to-me happiness.

"A baby," she repeated, laying a hand over her abdomen, shaken by the wonder of it. "I had given up."

"Tell Mason I said congratulations." Janet chuckled as they left the office. She headed down the corridor to the next examining room.

Cybil went outside. The sun was still shining. The town still bustled with activity. The world had not stopped because Cybil Mathews was going to have a baby.

The enormity of it rocked her foundations. Janet's parting words echoed in her mind. Mason was going to be a father! What would he say? Then the next realization struck. He'd said he couldn't father children. And she had believed him! "I'll hang him from the hayloft winch," she murmured.

She drove home, her thoughts in a furious whirl. As she passed the Faraday place, she wheeled the truck into the driveway and came to a grinding halt at the barn.

"Where's Mason?" she asked a cowboy working in the paddock with a young horse.

"He went to the house."

"Thanks." She crossed the gravel and walked up the sidewalk, then the two steps onto the porch. She knocked instead of ringing the bell. The sound clamored through the house. It matched her feelings.

She heard footfalls inside. A man in boots. She balled her fists and tried to think what she should say.

The door opened. Mason's eyes widened slightly in surprise. "Well, come in."

She stepped forward and punched him in the stomach.

"Damn," he said. "What was *that* for?"

"Lying." She aimed for him again.

He grabbed her wrists. She tried to kick him. He sidestepped, wrestled her inside, shoved the door closed, then hauled her into his office. She struggled the whole way. He closed the door, then released her.

A hard smile appeared on his handsome face. "I'm delighted to see you, too, sweetheart, but try to restrain your passionate nature."

"If I never see you again, it'll be too soon, you...you..."

He settled on the corner of his desk. "Enough of the endearments. Tell me what's wrong. Don't bother mincing words. I can handle the cold, hard facts."

She propped her hands on her hips and glared for

all she was worth. He should have gone up in a wisp of smoke.

"I'm pregnant, that's what's wrong."

For a full five seconds, Cybil surmised, the words didn't register with Mason. When they did, his expression changed and he did the oddest thing.

He grinned. From ear to ear. He looked just like a kid who'd won grand champion at the rodeo. If he hadn't been standing still, she would have sworn he swaggered.

"If that isn't just like a man," she said. "Present him with a serious problem, and all he can do is act as if he's the world's greatest lover."

"Sit down," he ordered.

He took her hands and led her to a chair. She let herself be coaxed into sitting. The familiar fatigue overcame her. She could use a nap.

Meanwhile, her partner in crime, so to speak, shook his head, then he laughed.

"That's why you've been tired and out of sorts lately. And why you've been off your feed."

He actually managed to look concerned. But she had other things on her mind. "Why did you lie?" she demanded.

When she would have surged to her feet, he clasped her shoulders and gently restrained her.

"Be careful," he warned her. He propped a hip on the corner of the desk. "I didn't. The doctor said... Actually, it was Lorah who said..."

Cybil saw suspicion leap into his eyes.

"At that stage of our marriage, I believed her without question," he muttered. "However, she wasn't really interested in children. She must have lied." His eyes narrowed. "You said you couldn't have kids, either."

"My husband and I didn't use birth control. He and his wife had a child last year, so I thought that meant it had to be my fault." She sighed.

"Are you going to have it?"

She was stunned by the question. She wrapped her arms protectively across her waist. "Do you think I should get rid of it?" she asked, testing his reaction.

"No," he practically roared at her. "I'll take the kid if you don't want it."

"Why?" she asked, watching him closely as relief and happiness rose within her at his fervid declaration.

He ignored the question. "I'll pay you."

"How much?" she asked. Did he think he could barter for the child as if it were a calf to be purchased?

"A million," he said icily. "I'll give you a million dollars to have the baby and give it to me."

She rose and stood in front of him. She looked him straight in the eye and spoke very clearly. "I wouldn't give you a mongrel wolf to raise. This baby is *mine. I'll* raise it." She headed for the door.

He caught her before she escaped. "It's mine, too. I want joint custody."

Their faces were no more than four inches apart. "How do you know it's yours?" she challenged.

He didn't blink an eye. "If we go to court, DNA testing will prove my case. Won't it?"

She sighed. "Yes."

Releasing her arm, he touched a fingertip to her cheek. "Don't force my hand on this. We'll share the child..." He paused in thought. "I suppose we should marry."

The fact that some part of her was thrilled at this announcement horrified her. She couldn't possibly want to try marriage again. No, of course not. She stepped aside, away from his magic touch. "Absolutely not."

"I don't want my child to be illegitimate."

"I don't want to marry."

He eyed her as if she were a snake-haired hag. "You think I do?"

She shook her head. "At least we're in agreement on that. Marriage is impossible."

"No, it isn't. Look, there's no reason we can't marry, at least until the kid is born. Then we can divorce and share custody. We can be civilized about this."

She didn't feel civilized. She felt fierce and protective and maybe a little desperate. She didn't know how the law treated cases like theirs. "Why can't you be like a normal man?" she complained.

"How's that?"

"You should look for the nearest escape hatch at being informed of impending fatherhood."

"I'm forty years old, not a kid scared of taking responsibility for his actions. I've always wanted a family. You may as well sit. We've got to think this through."

The determined gleam in his eye made her uneasy. She had a vision of him hauling her off to one of those wedding parlors before she could stop him. "I need to go home."

"Uncle Moses," he muttered, then groaned. "He'll stage a shotgun wedding, for sure." Mason's grin was sardonic. "Hmm, this will be a new twist for the gossips—the gun will be pointed at the bride."

"You don't want to marry any more than I do," she reminded him. "Remember your ex-wife."

"I do. All too well. But you, thank God, are different. Give me credit for recognizing that from the first." He shrugged. "Well, almost from the first."

"From the dance, which is when you decided you wanted me," she corrected. When she'd let herself be engulfed by the magic of the music and the moment. How could she have been so foolish?

"I'd noticed you before."

"Really, this isn't getting us anywhere. I should go. I have to feed the stock."

He was suddenly close. "You can't do that heavy work. It might not be good for the baby."

"Of course I can. I'm not an invalid. Besides, help is impossible to find in the winter."

His eyes narrowed. "I'll send over one of the men. Who's your doctor? I need to talk to him—"

"Her."

Mason surprised her by grinning. "It must be Janet Platt. She's the only female doc out of the four in town. I want to talk to her. You're forty. That ups the odds."

"I'm in perfect health. You are not to interfere in my life, do you hear?"

He shook his head. "You should have thought of that two months ago, sweetheart."

She drew back when he bent toward her. She saw

the flames of passion in his eyes, the strangely lambent smile that lingered at the corners of his mouth. She realized he really didn't mind about the child, that he wanted it....

Her insides churned into a ball of confusion. She wanted...she wasn't sure what.

But she did know what he wanted. "No," she murmured, a protest against her own wildly blooming desire.

He touched her hair, then slipped his hand behind her head. "You're right. I want you. There hasn't been a day, or night, since the dance that I haven't thought of you."

So smoothly did he talk, distracting her with his words, that she hardly realized what else he was doing. Then she realized she was backed up against the door and his tall frame was touching her lightly all along their fronts.

"I especially want to make love when things go well. You can't believe how I want you," he murmured, then he kissed her, deeply, stirring her to her depths.

Cybil tried to resist. She hadn't stopped here to reenact the scenario that had gotten them into this predicament in the first place. But his lips were warm, gentle, enticing...sensuous...beguiling....

Pick one.

His hands caressed up and down her sides, then stopped beneath her breasts. He cupped their full weight. Against her abdomen, she felt the full length of his erection. Her body answered the call of his. It was as if life flowed into her from every point of contact.

He left her lips and moved down to her throat. His fingers plucked gently at her nipples. She thought she would explode with hunger.

"Mason, this is madness. We have to—"

Her breath fled as he kissed her breasts through her clothing. She wanted to tear their shirts off so they could touch skin to skin.

"The most enjoyable madness I've ever known." He lifted his head and held her gaze. "What can it hurt now if we take what we both want?"

He was right, but she was sure there was something wrong with this reasoning. She just couldn't think what it was at the moment.

Reaching behind her, he locked the door, then, wrapping his arms around her, he backed to the chair. Carefully, he drew her down with him until she straddled his lap. She released a troubled sigh and rested against him.

"I'm not going to make love with you," she declared on the off chance he might believe her.

He kissed her temple and smoothed her hair. "Let's get married tonight. We may as well get it over—"

She sat up, once more furious with him. "If you think seducing me will change my mind, you can think again." She pushed herself up and away from temptation, then started for the door once more. He strode in front of her and opened it.

"You're not to touch me again. I mean it," she stated firmly and tried, really tried, to believe it.

"What difference does it make when you're already expecting the child?" he demanded.

She sailed out without answering.

Uncle Moses stood at the living-room doorway. "Child?" he questioned. "You two are expecting a child?" His face creased into a thousand smile lines. "I guess we'll be having that wedding after all."

# 8

CYBIL WATCHED GLUMLY as Maria poured them each another cup of coffee and returned to the table. It was the second Sunday in November, two days after the debacle with Mason and his uncle. Mason had gone over to his uncle's side on the marriage thing. It was maddening.

"How can a person's life change so drastically in so short a time?" she demanded.

Maria smiled in sympathy, cut another square of brownie from the batch she'd brought over and laid it on Cybil's plate. "You need to eat."

"I'm not hungry."

"I always wanted food when I was carrying each of my three babies."

"I can't believe that old man."

"He wants the best for both of you," Maria soothed.

"He told everyone at church about the baby. The only thing he didn't do was pass out cigars. The preacher's wife urged me to do what's best for the child. I feel as if I'm caught in a *Twilight Zone* conspiracy."

"Maybe you should go ahead and do it."

Cybil gave her friend a worried glance. "Marry?

Without love and commitment?'' She wanted more for the baby.

Maria smiled as if relieved. "Maybe those would come later. Maybe after the baby is born, you and Mason will be so in love, you'll never want to part.''

Odd stabbing pains hit Cybil in the chest. "Oh, yeah, and that's fairy dust falling on the mountains less than a mile away.'' She glanced outside. "You had better head for the Faraday place before the snow gets here. It might turn to ice at this altitude.''

"I hate to leave you here alone.''

"I'll be fine. Actually, I like the solitude. This is a perfect afternoon for reading in front of the fire.''

After Maria left, Cybil paced the empty house like a lost soul. She wondered what Mason was doing and how he would act as a father. She blocked the thought, exasperated with herself for thinking of him so often. After building a fire, she lay on the sofa, read awhile, then napped.

MASON FLEXED HIS fingers and dashed for the house. The wind was bitterly cold. Random snowflakes hit his face as he ran. On the porch, he paused and considered knocking.

Cybil might not let him in.

He surveyed the cattle huddled in tight clusters against the storm. He walked along the fence, then went into the barn. He found the pickup inside already loaded with bales of hay.

Cursing her stubbornness, he drove into the pastures and tossed the bales to the cows who crowded around the truck. He checked the water in the trough, added some, then shut it off. He noted she'd already wrapped the pipes as protection from the freezing temperatures.

When he finished, he headed for the house. Once more at the door, he felt as unsure as a boy on his first date. He knocked and waited.

No answer.

Worry ate at him. It wasn't like her to let her stock go hungry. Maybe she'd had an accident.

After another rap got no response, he tried the knob. The door opened. He went inside. The warmth poured over him like a caress. He walked past her study and the dining room. In the kitchen, a pot of soup gave off an enticing aroma, but she wasn't there. He moved on.

A low fire glowed in the living room. Cybil lay on the sofa, sound asleep. She wore black slacks and a red sweater. Red fuzzy socks were on her feet. She looked...alluring.

He hung his hat and coat on the hall rack, then took off his boots and stood them in the corner. He laid his gloves beside them. Quietly, he entered the living room.

After building up the fire until it crackled, he sat on the brick hearth and warmed his hands. When he turned back to check on his companion, Cybil's eyes were open.

"Hi," he said. He cleared the huskiness from his throat. "Hope you don't mind my warming my hands. The windchill is around zero out there."

"No, that's fine."

She watched him warily, but there was still an air of vulnerability about her. Her hair was tousled. Her cheeks were sleep flushed. Hunger for her shot through him.

"I saw the hay in the barn and fed it to the stock. Was that what you intended?" He waited for her anger, but it didn't come.

"Oh. Yes. Thank you." She frowned slightly. "But you shouldn't have. I mean, I was going to do it."

"It was no trouble."

She sat up and smoothed her hair. "It's past six. I slept for a long time." She smiled as if embarrassed. "I seem to do that a lot nowadays."

He nodded. Looking at her curvy figure, he thought of the child taking shape within her. Joy etched a sharp ache of anticipation in him. He leaned over and laid a hand over her abdomen.

Cybil looked startled.

He smiled. "You're going to have to get used to this. I'm going to be around a lot from now on."

She pushed his hand away and pulled her knees against her chest. "Not at my house."

"Wherever you and the baby are," he corrected, his tone going hard with determination. "I won't be left out of my kid's life. I've waited too long for this."

That shut her up. She rested her chin on her knees and stared into the fire. He could see the flames reflected in her eyes, which appeared neither blue nor gray. They were dark and introspective at the moment.

Mystery lived in those depths. He found he wanted to explore there, to know this woman as he'd known no other.

"I won't be left out," he repeated.

"No, that wouldn't be fair."

He heard the uncertainty undercutting the statement. He knew she wondered at his motives. "I would never do anything to hurt a child. Or its mother," he added, an odd tenderness adding to the tumult he felt inside whenever he was around Cybil...or thought of her.

Moving over to the sofa, he sat beside her and slipped his hand over her tummy again. "When does he start kicking?"

"Four or five months, I think. I got some books, but I've just started reading them."

"Are we going to take classes?"

She looked at him blankly.

"You know, where we learn when to pant or to take deep breaths. I saw it on TV one time."

"You're planning on going, on being there when...?" She grinned in disbelief.

He gave her a level stare. "It's my kid. Of course I'm going to be there when he's born."

"It might be a girl."

"When will we know?"

"I'll have a sonogram at five months. Janet says she might be able to tell then."

He rubbed her stomach gently. "I can't feel it yet."

"Well, the whole thing is only about the size of an orange right now. It'll be another month or two before I really start showing."

A blush highlighted her cheeks. It made her seem young and endearing. He tried to shake off the tenderness that threatened to make him do something stupid, such as beg her to marry him, confess undying love or whatever to get her to agree. The thing was, he wasn't sure he didn't mean it.

No, he'd been down that road once before. He knew love was a polite name for an itch that didn't last.

Leaning his head against the comfortable sofa, he watched her stare into the fire. Their personal troubles dwindled into the background. The tension that had tightened his shoulders for weeks eased. He yawned.

Cybil's stomach rumbled.

He chuckled. "Have you eaten?"

"Not yet."

"Sit still," he ordered when she started to rise. "I'll bring it."

He found bowls and prepared them each a meal of soup and slices of buttered toast with milk for Cybil. He put on a pot of decaffeinated coffee.

They sat on the floor side by side and used the coffee table as their dining surface. When the food was gone, he took the dishes to the kitchen and brought in coffee and brownies he found in the cookie jar.

"You're a good cook," he complimented, wolfing a second brownie down.

"Maria made the brownies. I'm okay for ordinary things." She eyed him suspiciously. "You're being awfully nice tonight."

He laughed wryly. "I have some news."

"Uh-oh."

"Yeah, it's bad. Moses called my parents."

She licked a crumb off her lower lip. "And?"

"And told them about the baby." He leaned over and tongued a crumb off her chin, then lingered at the corner of her mouth. Unable to stand it any longer, he kissed her there, then on her lips when she looked at him. "I've been wanting to do that for days."

"You shouldn't.''

Her stern glance was meant to quell his libido, but it didn't. He wanted her. In his arms. Now.

He touched her abdomen, then slipped his hand upward and lingered under her breast. He wondered if they were heavier or if that was his imagination. He kissed her again.

This time, she responded the tiniest bit. Her mouth moved under his. He felt her sigh as her chest rose, then fell against his. Nuzzling her cheek, he closed his eyes and felt a peaceful sensation envelop him. It didn't erase the strum of passion in his blood, but instead seemed a part of it, the two intertwined in a way he couldn't explain.

"What did your parents say?'' She looked at him anxiously.

"They're delighted. They want to come visit.''

"And meet the hussy who's having your child?''

He smiled at her fatalistic tone. "They want to meet the woman Uncle Moses says is wonderful and perfect for me.''

She pressed her face against her knees. "This keeps getting worse. And I haven't even told my parents yet.''

"Wrong,'' he said huskily, sliding his arm under her and lifting her onto his lap. He pushed the low table over a bit to give them more room and cradled her against him. "*This* keeps getting better.''

He kissed her until she relented and kissed him back. The kiss went from warm to hot. He was breathing hard by the time they came up for air. He slipped his hand under her sweater and caressed her bare back. That's when he found out the interesting fact that she wore no bra.

"Cybil," he said. His fingers trembled when he raked them into her hair. The need was urgent now, a blinding drive toward completion and the wild sweetness of her lips and arms and body.

Half expecting her to demand he stop at any moment, he rose to his knees and laid her on the long sofa. He eased down beside her, careful to keep his weight off her body as he rolled toward her and claimed the lips that had turned rosy with desire. When she draped an arm over his shoulders, he relaxed and began to explore her curves.

"Perfect," he murmured, once more sliding his hands under the sweater and finding those smooth womanly treasures.

"It's the magic," she whispered. "I don't understand." Then she kissed him back as if there were no tomorrow.

And he didn't care if there wasn't. Because tonight…this moment…right now…was enough.

When he slid into the warmth of her body, he was glad they didn't have to use any barrier between them. He moved, flesh to flesh, against her and heard her cry of welcome.

He said a lot of things during the next hour, things he didn't exactly recall later, but the words, like the passion, seemed right. They exploded together, and it was just like the other times.

"Perfect," he murmured, settling her in his arms and pulling an afghan over them. "Perfect."

CYBIL KEPT HER eyes closed. She didn't want to face reality or Mason, either. He lay behind her, his body cupped to hers, one arm thrown casually over her waist.

Sometime during the night, they had gone to her bed. She hadn't murmured a word of protest. It had been nice to cuddle under the covers until their heat had warmed the sheets, then to fall asleep in his arms feeling contented, feeling loved....

Feeling delusional, she corrected. But being with Mason like this, everything seemed possible. He wouldn't be like her husband. Once he'd given his word, he would keep it. She sighed as confusion swept over her. Opening her eyes to the new day, she saw snow piled four inches thick against the window. She sat up, then settled down with a moan.

"Morning sickness?" Mason inquired, rising.

"Yes." She was surprised at his quick uptake on the situation. She was more surprised when he eased out of bed and, without a stitch, rushed to the kitchen. He returned after a couple of minutes, a triumphant grin in place as he held a cracker square aloft for her to see.

She couldn't help but smile at his foolishness. He sat on the bed and watched while she munched without lifting her head from the pillow. Shaking his head in amusement, he asked to use her shower. She nodded.

Mason exited the bathroom when she entered. His gaze swung over her nude figure in a way that was flattering.

Standing in the steamy spray, she considered her

feelings upon awakening with him. She suddenly wished she were eighteen again and in love for the first time. Back then, she'd been so sure life would go exactly as she'd planned. Then had come death. Later she'd found another love, but it had ended in betrayal and divorce. That had hurt terribly. And now...there was magic, stronger than ever before, but she had learned to be afraid of magic.

She still couldn't put a name to her reactions to Mason by the time she was dressed and heading for the kitchen. Pausing at the door, she watched him slide two omelets onto a plate. With quick movements, he buttered the toast and added the slices on each side of the omelets.

He looked up and grinned at her. "Breakfast is served, madam," he intoned. With a flourish, he set the plates on the table, then seated her.

When he brushed her hair aside and kissed the back of her neck, she trembled with a welter of mixed emotions, none of which she could read. It was maddening to be so uncertain and topsy-turvy. She wasn't like that....

Except she'd never been pregnant before, so how did she know what she was like?

"What's funny?" he demanded, taking the chair to the left of her.

"Nothing." At his slight frown, she expounded, "Morning sickness is a new experience. So is being confused all the time. It's like being a teenager again." She raised her shoulders at the weirdness of it all and let them drop before picking up her fork.

When he smiled, funny pangs echoed all the way

through her, like stones rolling into an abyss. She studied him intently, trying to figure out exactly what he wanted.

He looked rested, happy even. His gaze on her was lambent, filled with a tenderness she couldn't ignore. It was a fact—he really did want the child.

"What are you confused about?" he asked.

His voice dropped to a husky register that reminded her of last night. He'd said many things while they made love. He painted a rosy picture by telling her how beautiful she was until she almost believed him. He'd promised to be a good father to their child...and a good husband to her.

"We can live here, if you like," he'd murmured. "Or at the other ranch. We can have another child...."

Her breath stopped as that memory came to her. Another child. A delicious thrill winged its way to her heart. It had sounded so perfect then.

But this was the cold light of morning.

"Cybil," he called, returning her to the present.

"Well, I'm confused about us, for one thing. For another, I'm confused about what's best for the baby."

"Marriage," he said firmly.

She sighed. "We've both tried that."

"You were hurt more by your marriage than I was. By the end of the first six months, I was pretty sure I'd made a mistake. I was willing to give it a try, but I wasn't exactly surprised when she wanted out, or that she had another lover. You trusted completely, so the betrayal was more damaging. I'm willing to give you time, but I'd like for us to be married before the child comes."

Cybil ate the savory omelet slowly. "But we don't…I mean…passion isn't enough."

"We have more than that. We're both ranchers. Our land marches together. We have interests in common. It makes for a good merger."

What he said made sense, but she felt compelled to argue. "A business arrangement is fine for business, but not for people. The human heart is too complicated. Besides, you might meet someone—"

"No, I won't."

"You don't know that."

He gave her an impatient frown. "Yes, sweetheart, I do. Love is an overrated notion for sex. It's good between us."

She may as well save her breath. She could see he had made up his mind. Actually, she had to admit his concern for the child almost persuaded her. But… "Marriage," she murmured. "It's a big step."

"And you don't want to step off into the deep end again, right?"

She nodded.

"Think about it. In the meantime, I'm going to move over here."

She nearly dropped her coffee mug at this announcement. "You most certainly are not."

"Yep. It's too dangerous for a female, especially one in your condition, to be alone. Do you realize we're snowed in until either my boys can bring the plow through or the snow melts?"

She was stupefied. "How deep is the snow?"

"I'd say roughly a foot."

"We never get more than a few inches, three or

four at the most." So saying, she went to the back door and peered out the frosty panes. That was when she realized the snow was still coming down in lazy plumes and it covered the first strand of the stock fence. "We are snowed in," she said, the enormity of the situation hitting her.

"Yeah."

"Alone. Here at the end of the road."

"Uh-huh."

"You'll have to leave."

"I can't."

"You can borrow a horse."

He chuckled. "Do you have any checkers?"

The whole community would know he'd waited out the storm at her house. Somehow they would find out. Somehow? Huh. His uncle was probably on the phone to half the county by now. "Your uncle—"

"Will spread the word," he agreed with remarkable calm. "He's probably arranged the wedding with my folks by now."

Cybil began to get suspicious of Mason's sanguine attitude. "Did you plan this when you came over?"

"No, but it doesn't bother me." He grinned. "I plan to be over here a lot during the next few months."

She opened her mouth, then closed it. There was an air of finality about her tough neighbor. "You and your uncle are driving me right over the edge."

He nodded sympathetically. "That's what you do to me, honey…right over the edge." With a gleam in his eye, he rose and came toward her.

She jumped to her feet. "No, Mason. I mean it." She narrowed her eyes and tried to look stern. "We're not...I'm not... You just get that look out of your eyes.''

"What's the matter? You never seen a man go feed cattle in a storm?'' With that he donned his boots, jacket and gloves and disappeared into the great outdoors.

Cybil sat down weakly. There she was—all topsy-turvy again. It was the most maddening thing.

MASON HALTED INSIDE the barn. Cybil was there, rubbing down her mare with a burlap sack. He drove the pickup inside. She closed the door for him.

"I told you to stay inside,'' he scolded, unable to put any real heat into it. She looked good enough to eat with a line of snow on her cowboy hat and her long legs encased in tight jeans and boots. "It's a blizzard out there today. Did you hear the weather report?''

She shook her head, and snow flew off her hat. "I noticed the temperature had dropped and decided to bring the horses in since I have enough stalls for them. I wish I'd brought the cows to the barn pasture. It'll be safer and easier to feed them if the storm gets worse.''

"Right,'' he agreed. "I left the gate open and drove through it a few times. When they started ambling this way, I came on in. The weather news is bad—more snow expected for the next twelve hours. The passes are closed into Tahoe.''

She eyed him up and down, causing a stir in his blood. "It's a good thing I laid in supplies last week since it seems I'll have to feed you for the duration.''

Her exasperated tone did nothing to calm the storm that had invaded him. She was right. It was confusing to want another person this much. Or to think of her at odd moments at all hours of the day and night.

Seeing her bend over to spread the burlap on a sawhorse to dry, he moved instinctively, going to her and planting a kiss on the vulnerable line of her nape. He inhaled her sweet fragrance and thought of the night just past.

When she straightened and faced him, he stepped forward and gathered her close. He kissed her face while she watched him with a troubled mix of emotions in her eyes, which were dark gray in the twilight of the barn.

"If it weren't so damn cold, I'd show you what can be done in a stable with a little fresh hay and a horse blanket or two." He chuckled and let her go when she pushed.

"You have an exaggerated opinion of yourself if you think you'll get me into a pile of hay."

"Yeah?"

"Yeah."

He moved so that he was between her and the outside door. "Don't you know better than to challenge a red-blooded male that way?"

She gave the distance to the door and the far exit a calculating glance, then she sauntered forward until they stood chest to chest. Her breasts nudged him, tempting him to grab her up and rush into the nearest stall.

He refrained…heroically and with great patience.

"You're trying to push me into a rash act, but I'm

not going to let you crack my control. I'll give you just thirty minutes to stop that,'' he warned aggressively.

"In thirty more minutes, we'll be marooned in the barn. I prefer a warm house." She dashed around him.

He let her get far enough ahead to make it through the door. He followed and threw an arm around her when she slowed in the face of the wild wind that howled down from the mountain peaks above the valley. The snow was so thick it was almost a whiteout.

Fortunately, the house was close, and they made it to the porch without mishap. In the kitchen, they stomped their boots free of melting clumps on the throw rug.

"Sit," he ordered, then removed her boots and rubbed her cold toes.

"Ah, bliss," she murmured.

He hung up their outdoor gear, then scooped her into his arms. After plopping her on the sofa, he built up the fire and pulled out a checkerboard. "Two out of three?"

"I warn you—I used to play with my grandfather," she told him. "He was a mean player."

"I played with Uncle Moses."

She looked disgruntled. "He's the county champ."

"I'll try not to beat you too badly," he promised. An hour later, he had to eat those words as she jumped his lone crowned checker and swept it from the board. "Okay, that's your freebie. This time I'm not going to be easy on you."

"Ha."

He watched while she set the checkers in the starting position. Her fingers were supple as she moved quickly over the board. An air of quiet assurance surrounded her. He liked the capable way she did things, going about her work without asking for favors from anyone.

Not even him.

A lot of the women he'd known in the past thought nothing of making demands on the men they slept with. If Cybil had asked for help with the chores at her place, he'd have pitched in without thinking twice about it. It was the way things were done where he was from. Tit for tat. You scratch my back, I'll scratch yours.

The knowledge that she hadn't asked, had, in fact, made it clear that she expected to carry her own weight, made him feel...funny. As she said, it was confusing.

There were some feelings he could identify, though. He was fiercely protective of her and their child. Sometimes he felt the most overpowering tenderness, along with a need to touch her, that had nothing to do with making love, although that's usually where they ended up whenever it happened.

"What are you grinning about?" she demanded.

"I was thinking about how we end up making love whenever we're alone."

She gave him one of her scalding glances. "It wouldn't happen if you showed a bit more self-control."

"Me? You're the one who can't get enough of all the touching and hugging and kissy-face stuff."

"That was *not* a gentlemanly thing to say."

He edged around the coffee table and slid onto the sofa, catching her in his arms and blowing raspberries along her delectable neck. "But true. Isn't it?" he coaxed.

"No."

He scrunched his fingers into her sides. "Isn't it?"

She laughed helplessly and squirmed sinuously, driving him to the brink with her lush curves moving all over him.

"Isn't it?" He blew into her ear, then bit on the lobe.

"Maybe," she panted, "a little."

Easing his hands behind her, he stilled her wild movements with his body against hers, pinning her to the sofa. He looked into her eyes. The blue had gone dark as her eyes dilated with the passion that boiled just below the surface between them.

"It's never been this way before," he said.

"I know." Her gaze became troubled.

He smoothed the frown lines between her eyes. "It probably doesn't mean anything."

"Right." She didn't sound quite convinced.

"We're forty years old. We can handle this." *He* didn't sound quite convinced. The way the pulse was pounding at every pressure point in his body, he wasn't sure he could handle lying there with her without going further.

"The baby, too?"

"Yes."

He felt the tension seep from her body. When she yawned, he settled them a bit more comfortably, satisfied to hold her at this moment. When she drifted asleep, he eased away and covered her with the afghan.

Moving about the silent house, he contemplated life and its vagaries. He put on a confident front for Cybil, feeling she needed assurance from him—he'd read it wasn't good for the baby if the mother was upset all the time—but he was about as settled as a volcano during an eruption.

Having a family and children, things he'd once taken for granted, had seemed beyond his grasp. Now he thought about those very things most of the time. A man would be foolish to revive old dreams, especially with a woman who wanted as little to do with him on a permanent basis as possible.

But she wasn't the man-eater she wanted him to think she was. In view of her taking the teenager in and from other incidents Maria had mentioned, Cybil was downright softhearted. He smiled. So things could be worse.

When the phone rang, he grabbed it up before it disturbed Sleeping Beauty. "Yeah?" he said.

"There may be a break in the storm in the early afternoon," Moses informed him. "You want the boys to try to clear the road over that way, or do you want to stay there for another day or two?"

Mason stilled the clamor in his blood and tried to think rationally. Ah, hell... "Tell 'em to forget it. They can dig us out when the storm is over."

Moses cackled like a witch stirring a caldron.

# 9

CYBIL WOKE AND listened intently, trying to figure out what jarred her out of a sound sleep. The bellow rolled over the valley again. Mason struggled from the bed and looked out the window.

"I don't believe it," he said.

She joined him, standing on one foot to keep as much of her flesh off the cold floor as possible. In the driveway, snow up to his belly button, stood Fletch. He bellowed at the cows once more.

Mason sighed. "I'd better put him in the pasture. He might take a notion to go to town next."

Cybil dressed at the same time he did. She headed for the kitchen and started breakfast while Mason pulled on coat and gloves and boots for the trek outside. By the time she was ready to put the pancakes and bacon on the table, he returned. Rubbing his cold nose down her neck and sliding his hands under her sweater, he caused her to shiver.

"Where's the heifer he's attracted to?" he asked.

"In the far pasture."

"Poor ole Fletch. He'll be heartbroken when he doesn't find her straight off."

"Tough."

Mason washed up and took his seat at the table. "You're one mean woman."

"Remember that and we'll get along fine."

He tilted his head and studied her thoughtfully. "You're being defensive this morning. What brought on the armor plating?"

She was startled at his insight. The truth was she did feel vulnerable where he was concerned. "I don't know what you want of me."

"Yes, you do."

She shook her head. "I mean, *really* want."

His face became impassive. "We'll work it out."

It solved nothing to argue about what they were going to do. She knew that. But she felt trapped by fate. On one hand, she was elated at having the child she'd always wanted. On the other, she didn't want to involve her life with his. She felt too emotionally fragile around him.

"I don't want to need anyone," she murmured, thinking it out. "Here at the ranch, I've discovered things within myself that I don't want to let go."

"Such as?"

"Independence. Security." She smiled briefly. "In spite of the weather, the surprise appearances of stray bulls and the occasional mountain lion."

"Do you think you'll lose all that by marrying me?"

"By marrying, period."

He stared thoughtfully at her. "You know, with both of us feeling the same—being wary of entanglements—we would be natural together. We would both know what to expect."

"We should expect each other to be unfaithful to our marriage vows? No, thanks."

"I didn't break my vows. Neither did you. I meant that we would go into marriage with our eyes open, not expecting any of that hearts-and-flowers nonsense."

"We wouldn't confuse sex with love," she said.

He smiled in approval, as if she were a bright child who caught on fast. "Right."

"We'd have a sensible arrangement."

"Yes."

"No stars in *our* eyes."

"Exactly."

Cybil's fingers tingled. She wondered how he would react if she dumped a pail of snow over his head. Then she wondered why she wanted to. If she were contemplating tying the knot with him, what he said made sense.

Except it wasn't what she wanted. Before she could decide exactly what that was, a commotion outside caused her and Mason to peer out the window.

A tractor with a snowplow blade on the front came down the driveway, throwing snow in a graceful arc to the side. A pickup followed a short distance behind. The pickup stopped in front of the house while the tractor went to work clearing the space between the house and the barn.

"Your uncle is here," she said.

Mason touched lightly along her back as he watched the activity with her. "I suppose our respite is over."

She thought he sounded sad. The feeling echoed in her.

"YOU'RE LOOKING BETTER," Maria commented.

"I feel better." Cybil crossed her arms on the kitchen table and watched her friend remove pies from the oven. "I'm not sick anymore. That's a relief."

Maria smiled in sympathy.

Cybil wondered where Mason was, but she wouldn't ask. He hadn't appeared at her door at the crack of dawn as he usually did, insisting on helping her with the chores. He was the most maddening person. And the most endearing in some ways. She could get used to his bossy concern over her well-being. She wouldn't let herself do that, either.

Sometimes, when the hunger became too great, he stayed with her, sleeping in her bed, sharing his passion with her, mingling it with tenderness and a gruff sweetness that shook her soul. In those moments, the magic took them.

She sighed. Magic didn't last. *Three strikes...*

Her pulse picked up at hearing an engine in the distance. It was coming closer. From the window, she saw Mason stop, glance at her truck, then head for the house.

He brought the scent of winter with him when he stepped inside. "Well, hello," he said to her.

"Hi." She felt an unfamiliar shyness come over her. "Well, I'd better be going."

"Don't rush on my account," he said dryly but with a smile. He hung up his coat and hat. Maria brought him a cup of coffee. He joined Cybil at the table. "Are you joining us for Thanksgiving dinner tomorrow? Maria has promised us a spread fit for a king."

Maria carefully put two more pies in the oven and

set the timer. "She refused. Maybe you can convince her."

"Enya is invited, too," he said.

"She isn't here. Her mother asked her to visit." Cybil did feel somewhat bereft, but she and the girl had talked it over. She'd convinced Enya her mother should be forgiven if she wanted to make amends. The woman was now remarried and perhaps feeling more secure.

"If we married today, you would have to come," he murmured, quietly insistent and with an intensity in his gaze that was flattering.

They had discussed his insane idea regularly that month. She directed a repressive glance his way. "I wouldn't dream of intruding—"

A truck pulled up before the house, its horn beeping a staccato pattern.

"It's Uncle Moses," Mason said, going to the window.

"Along with some friends," she added, rising, too.

Mason closed a warm hand over her shoulder. "With my parents," he corrected, and heaved a deep sigh. "They told me they were supposed to go to friends for the holidays. We're in for it now."

Mason opened the door and let his relatives inside. They stomped snow off their boots and, in a flurry of chatter, hung up their coats and hugged Mason thoroughly.

Cybil stayed quietly out of the way. If she could have slipped out without notice, she would have, but since that was impossible, she waited by the window.

The attractive woman in a gray wool pantsuit and

Hermes scarf tied over a pink sweater turned to her. "You must be Cybil." She held out both hands. "I'm Anise, Mason's mother. This handsome rogue is his father. You must call us Anise and Sean. We don't stand on formalities."

Cybil laid her hands into the soft clasp of the older woman. Eyes the same color as Mason's looked her over, paused on her stomach, then swept to her face again.

"Sean, darling, come meet Cybil," she called. She sounded as if she came from the Northeast.

Mason's father was shorter and bulkier than the son, with iron gray hair and hazel green eyes. The lines on his face were mostly laugh lines. He was several years younger than Moses. She recalled Mason saying his dad had been born in the ranch house.

The older man smiled broadly at her. "So this is the woman Moses has been telling us about."

The most ridiculous thing happened. Cybil blushed, right up to her scalp. She could just imagine Moses's version of events.

"I wasn't sure whether to believe him," Mr. Faraday continued, "but you're as beautiful as he said."

Maybe Moses didn't mention anything else. "I'm very pleased to meet you," she said, forcing a weak smile. "How nice that you could join Mason for the holiday. He was just saying you had other plans."

She groaned internally. They'd obviously dashed from California to Nevada at the first chance to see how their son was faring. They probably thought the local hussy was trying to trap him into marriage or something equally bad.

"As soon as Moses told us about the baby, nothing could keep Anise from rushing up here at the earliest opportunity." Sean smiled benignly at his wife.

Anise released Cybil's hands only to step forward and lay one hand over her abdomen. "A child. After all this time." Misty-eyed, she gazed at her son. "I'm so proud."

"Can you feel anything?" Mr. Faraday asked.

"Not really. It's too soon," his wife said in the wise tone of one who knows. "I just had to give our grandchild a little pat of welcome, though." She patted Cybil's tummy, then stepped aside and patted Mason's cheek.

"Do you mind?" Sean asked.

Cybil shook her head in confusion, not sure what he was asking. He laid his hand over her abdomen and gave her a couple of gentle pats. The next thing she knew, Mason was also touching her. She moved back and gave him an indignant glance. He grinned.

"How about some coffee?" he said. "Have you had breakfast?"

"Only what they served on the plane. I'm ravenous," Anise confessed. "It must be all this fresh air."

Mason called Maria, who served some marvelous rolls with poached eggs in short order. Finished, she removed the last pies from the oven and returned to other tasks upstairs while they ate.

"I warn you, I'm going to take her to L.A. when we leave. She's a treasure," Anise confided, glancing after Maria.

"No way. I refuse to go back to Uncle Moses's burned pot roast." Mason poured more coffee for all of them, put on a fresh pot to brew, then snagged another roll.

"You could eat at Cybil's," Moses said.

Cybil saw Anise and her husband look at Moses, who nodded as if confirming some news. Glancing at Mason as he razed through the refrigerator for milk, then brought over the sugar and newly filled cream pitcher, she realized he was completely at home dealing with cows or with guests who carried the sheen of city life. A cosmopolitan but domesticated rogue. When his mother looked her way again, Cybil felt the blush start all over.

Mason resumed his seat, which was beside her. "We're discussing marriage," he said.

Cybil nearly fell out of her chair. "We are not!"

He turned a calm smile on her. "What were we discussing when the folks drove up?"

"It wasn't that kind of discussion," she reminded him heatedly.

"What kind was it?" Moses demanded. "Did you set the date? Or are you two still being contrary?"

"Cybil and Mason are clearly not ready to discuss the issue with us," Anise interceded for the couple. "I don't think we should push it."

Cybil felt wretched at the kind smile the other woman bestowed on her. The whole situation seemed to be worsening by the second. A warm pat on the leg from Mason was meant to calm and reassure her, she realized. When she glanced into his eyes, he sent her an intent scrutiny. He seemed to be asking something of her.

Sean leaned closer. "Don't let Moses get to you.

He thinks because he was the oldest kid in the family he can pry into everyone's affairs.''

"That's okay. I don't mind." She spoke directly to Mason's uncle. "We're still trying to sort things out. When we know what we're going to do, we'll tell you first."

"Good. How long before you think you'll know?" was his next question.

Mason burst into laughter. His parents joined in. Moses looked at them in surprise. Cybil smiled wryly.

"We'll tell you when we know, Uncle Moses," Mason promised. "So how are things in Tinsel Town?" he asked his dad.

Sean replied at length on the details of a contract for a production. "You won't be sorry you invested. This will be a blockbuster summer release."

"You invest in movies?" Cybil asked. "Isn't that riskier than betting on horses?"

"Not if you have an assured box-office success." He mentioned a big-name actor who had the starring role.

"Wow, I'm impressed. Are you going to invite him to the ranch?" She managed a starstruck expression.

Mason tapped her on the nose. "Get that gleam out of your eye. I'll lock you in the cellar before I let that womanizer on the place."

"Having a name star doesn't always mean success, though," his father admitted. He reminded them of a box-office failure of the previous year. "On the other hand, *Titanic* grossed a fortune with two unknowns."

"It cost a fortune, too," Cybil said, glancing uneasily at Mason. She spoke to his father. "How did you get into handling movie contracts?"

He told her of starting as an attorney for a talent agency, then a major studio before opening his own office.

Anise had been a costume consultant for period clothing. She had retired a few years ago. Cybil realized the woman must be in her late sixties, but she looked younger. Her husband was seventy, fourteen years younger than his big brother, Moses.

"I'm trying to get Sean to retire," Anise told them. "He's worked long enough. We have a small ranch in California that we visit as often as we can. Sean calls it a retread instead of a retreat. I'd like to sell the house and move there permanently."

Sean chuckled. "After dealing with producers and directors, I need more than a retreat. I need a whole new skin after fighting with them."

Cybil stayed another two hours, fascinated with the stories Mason's parents told from their experiences with the movie celebrities. Mason walked her to her truck.

"I would really like for you to join us tomorrow," he told her, his manner formal.

To refuse would be churlish. "All right. Your parents are very nice," she added sincerely.

He helped her into the truck as if she were fragile. As usual, her skin tingled at his touch. When she was safely strapped in, he stood there and watched her. She rubbed at the tension in her neck.

Strong fingers pushed hers aside and took over. "There was nothing to be nervous about. They liked you. Uncle Moses has been singing your praises for months.''

''That should have been enough to turn anyone off. Why didn't it—'' She stopped abruptly.

''Turn me off?'' he finished. He chuckled. ''You drove me nuts at times, you made me furious, but you are also the most interesting woman I have ever met.''

''Yeah, right.''

''You're thinking of movie stars. Hollywood has more than its share of phonies. You were real. I liked that.''

She craned her head around to give him a disbelieving glance. He tilted her head forward so he could rub her neck some more. After a bit, she felt his lips touch her nape.

Sensation ran riot through her—the tingles along her neck, the clutching somewhere deep inside, the leap of her heart. At forty, she shouldn't feel sixteen, she scolded.

It did no good. Her body had a will of its own. Why him? she wondered. ''Why now?''

''What?''

''Just wondering aloud,'' she explained. ''Why did my body respond now and not before? It's made for an awkward situation for all of us. I'm sorry.''

He took both her hands. ''I can't be sorry about the child. It's too much of a miracle.''

They smiled at each other, for once in complete agreement. When he laid a hand over her abdomen, she placed hers over his. They fell silent. It was as if, through touch, they were listening to their child.

''I told my family about the baby. They were as

thrilled as yours seem to be." She sighed, perplexed by it all.

He patted her hand. "That's good."

"Mason, I have a question."

"Yes?" he said encouragingly when she hesitated.

"Are you very rich?"

"No."

"Are you sort of rich?"

He grinned. "I have money, angel-face."

"That's what I was afraid of. Now everyone will think I'm a fortune hunter, as well as the hussy who tried to trap you into marriage."

He burst into laughter. "Some women think money is an added inducement to the relationship."

"Well, I don't," she said grumpily.

"I know. You're different, and I like that."

With that, he kissed her and closed the door, then watched until she drove out of sight. At her house, she retrieved her book and sat down to read after lunch. She identified with the heroine, who had as many doubts and uncertainties about the future as she had.

MASON AND HIS MOTHER ambled along the gravel road next to the pasture. They had no destination, other than a time of quiet together as they looked over the prime-beef herd lying in the grass.

The cows blew streamers of steam with each breath. Yearlings gathered and played butting games, already starting their push for status in the group.

To the east, the lower hills were covered with the remnants of the blizzard that had come through earlier in the month. To the west, the rocky peaks of the

Sierra Nevada Range sparkled with the thick layers of snow that would last until next summer.

"This place has been good for you," Anise remarked, tucking her hand into the bend of his arm. "There's a peacefulness in you I haven't seen before."

"I like it here."

"Do you think you and Cybil will marry?"

His mom rarely asked intrusive questions. It was a mark of her concern that she did now. He gave it the thought it deserved before answering. "I don't know. I'm committed to the idea, but she isn't."

"Because of her past marriage?"

"Probably." He watched the flight of an eagle across the valley. "I suppose it isn't easy for her to think of tying herself to a man again. She's independent and likes her life that way."

"Mmm, yes, I can see that."

"How did you and Dad make it through all the pitfalls of living together, especially in L.A.?"

Her laugh was rueful. "Children rarely remember the hard times, but do you think in a marriage that's lasted as long as ours the subject of divorce never came up?"

"I had wondered." He mused on the past. "You and Dad were always there. But I remember a time…" He hesitated about bringing the past up. His world, which he had thought was perfect until he was fifteen, had turned upside down when he had realized his parents were having problems. It had made him cautious about marriage long before he was old enough to think about it seriously.

"Once," she said softly. "There was one serious time."

He kept quiet, aware from the distant look in her eyes that she was remembering a time when life had not been good.

"A person makes many decisions in life," she finally said. "At that time I...your father and I...made a decision to continue the marriage. There are probably many such moments in a couple's life, most of them a ripple rather than a tidal wave."

"But the big ones can be devastating," he murmured, recalling the rage he'd felt upon learning his wife was unfaithful. And the grief, he admitted. Whether merely his pride or his heart, it had hurt.

"Yes. It usually involves a breach of trust. That's very hard to mend. Trust is a gift, freely bestowed when you fall in love, but once broken, it has to be earned."

Mason swallowed hard at the undertone of sorrow in his mother's voice. He knew when her trust had been broken. He remembered an actress who had been welcome in their home and who often visited, her manner wistful as she watched his family. That had been twenty-five years ago.

And never forgotten.

Anger with his father flared—a son's protective instinct toward his mother—then receded. His parents had worked through their time of sorrow. He realized that was the way he remembered the summer when he'd been fifteen—a time of sorrow. He'd heard bits and pieces of quarrels. He recalled his father's grim, guilty visage. Once he'd heard his mother crying when she'd thought she was alone. He squeezed her hand now in understanding and sympathy.

They walked in silence to the end of the ranch road, then turned back. The sun was warm on his back. The air was still. The valley wore a shine as if washed clean and ironed smooth. The peace of it filled him. A man and a woman could live out their years here in harmony....

"Have you told Cybil that you love her?"

He jerked around to stare at his mother. "Love?" he repeated in a shocked croak. His equilibrium returned. He laughed at the notion. "That's an overused term. I don't know what it means."

"It means you want to be with a person every minute of the day and night," his mom said with a lilt. "It means your pulse speeds up at the sight, or even the mere thought, of her and you think maybe you could spend the rest of your life with that person. It's a commitment of the heart. Have you told her?"

"You sound like Uncle Moses. He thinks I should wine and dine her—"

"Good idea. Why don't you try it?"

Mason sliced his mom a sideways glance. She returned it with a mock grimace, her mood playful now.

"Huh. First, she would laugh in my face. Second, she would tell me what a stupid idea it was."

"Third, she might like it. A woman needs reassurance at a time like this. Has she had morning sickness?"

"Yes."

"See?" she demanded as if this explained everything. "She feels unattractive and uncertain."

He thought that over. "Yeah, you may be right. She's complained a lot about being mixed-up."

His mom gave a soft exclamation as if she'd just discovered a profound truth. "Tell her you love her," she encouraged.

"Lie? She'd see through that in a minute."

"Would it be a lie?" Anise asked, pausing at the porch step and reaching up to touch his cheek. "You love her, and I think she feels the same about you."

Before he could think of words to convince her she was under a misconception, Uncle Moses and his father joined them from the direction of the barn. "The football game is on," his dad advised. "Let's see who's winning."

They trooped into the house. The fragrance of turkey and ham, of candied yams and pumpkin pie filled the house. Mason felt a hitch in the vicinity of his heart. His family had made a tradition of gathering on Thanksgiving Day to share the spirit of the occasion. Next year, he would make it a point to insist his sister come, too.

He heard an engine down the road. "It's Cybil," he said. "I'll help her in." He caught his mother's glance as he hurried back outdoors to wait and felt his ears grow warm. He was just being neighborly.

When Cybil parked, he strode forward and opened the door to the pickup. "Hi."

"Hello. Here, can you carry this?" She handed him a dish covered with foil.

Her cheeks were flushed an attractive pink, he noted, taking her hand when she slid out of the seat.

She bent back into the truck and fished out another covered container. "Okay, that's it."

When she turned to him and smiled, he noticed her eyes were the color of the sky, clear and blue and shining. For a second, he felt as if he were drowning.

"It's cold out here," she told him, and hurried toward the house. Her breath plumed in front of her mouth.

She wore makeup today. Her legs were encased in tights and dress shoes made like ankle boots. Her coat was unzipped, and he could see her dress was fitted under her full breasts and fell to the tops of her boots. She looked fashionably old-fashioned, like a pioneer in her Sunday best. Instead of homespun, her outfit was a velvety material of deep blue.

His palms tingled at the thought of running his hands over the sweep of her breasts and the curve of her hips.

In the house, Cybil was greeted warmly by his family and by Maria, who would be going to her daughter's house later that afternoon for their family dinner. Mason made himself useful and cheerfully followed the women's orders, adding a leaf to the table and gathering the extra chairs they would need. The two cowboys who worked the ranch all year would join them for the meal.

At one point, he stood back and watched as Cybil and his mother spread a green tablecloth and set the dining-room table with the good dishes.

"We need some pine boughs for the table," his mother decided. "To go around the centerpiece. What do you think?" she asked Cybil.

"I agree. I'll snip a few branches from the tree near the shed."

He went with her, making her put on her coat, plus a warm hat and knitted mittens he found for her. He grabbed the pruning shears from the shed and nipped off the branches she selected. When she had an armful and was protesting his cutting any others, he replaced the shears, then glanced around. They were out of sight of the house.

"Let's go. It's freezing out here," she complained.

"Yeah. Your nose is red." He chuckled when she made a face at him. Then, unable to resist, he bent over the greens and dropped a kiss on her rosy lips. "Mmm, that was good."

He kissed her again, this time taking her arms to pull her closer. She made muffled sounds, which he ignored.

"Real good," he murmured, and this time he opened his mouth and took the full taste of her.

She let him inside and stroked his tongue with hers, playing the lovers' game that came so naturally to them. When he raised his head, it was with a groan.

"I need more than that," he complained.

"We have to get back to the house."

He grinned because she sounded breathless and he realized one or two kisses weren't enough for her, either. Taking her arm, he guided her across the gravel compound between the buildings and into the house.

"Dinner is ready," his mother announced. Her eyes flicked from Cybil to him.

Mason glanced at Cybil to see if he'd somehow left evidence of his kiss on her. His mother's smile widened. He reached up and brushed his lips. His fingers came away a rosy pink. Giving his mom a warning frown, he wiped his mouth, then helped Cybil with her coat.

They ate and talked and laughed for the next two hours. Moses and Sean told stories of their early days on the ranch and compared the valley of then to now. They told about crews who came in to do the haying and the huge feasts the women fixed, which were eaten outside under the shade trees. They drank well water and glasses of cold buttermilk.

He watched Cybil surreptitiously. Her eyes sparkled as she encouraged the brothers to tell about their boyhoods. She listened avidly and laughed or crooned in sympathy, whichever the story in progress demanded. He found himself swallowing hard a couple of times to relieve a knot that grew in his throat for reasons he couldn't name.

At one point, his dad pointed to a basket of rosy apples on the sideboard. "My first gift to Anise was an apple. She was teaching a class on costume at UCLA. I was visiting the campus as part of a legal series on production contracts. I saw her and immediately tried to figure out how to arrange a meeting. I couldn't think of a way to approach her, but seeing a street vendor with apples, I hit upon the perfect line. I took her an apple. After that, I had her eating out of my hand."

Anise declared that wasn't true. "I felt sorry for him. That's why I agreed to a date. He blushed the whole time he talked to me and forgot to give me the apple until he was almost out the door."

Mason observed the shine of pleasure in Cybil's eyes as she listened to his parents' friendly banter. After lunch, he insisted Maria leave the dishes. Somehow he and Cybil were left alone to clean up the kitchen. He caught her in a yawn.

"You should rest," he said, feeling tender toward her because she had been kind to the people who meant the most to him. "Go to my room and take a nap."

She flashed him a humorous glance and shook her head. She covered bowls and stacked them in the refrigerator.

"When I was a kid, I used to visit my grandmother. I asked her how they kept food in the fridge before there was plastic to store them in," she murmured.

He cast her a questioning glance.

"They covered the bowls with plates. Later they used aluminum foil, then plastic wrap before Tupperware came out and everyone used that." She was silent a minute. "I thought of my grandmother's time as ancient because I couldn't remember a time before there was plastic." She gazed at him solemnly. "I wonder what our child will think of as something from the olden days."

Mason had an odd feeling inside, as if he were being compressed in a giant, invisible vise. It grew tighter and tighter. His heart began to pound...faster, harder.

"Mason?" she said, uncertainty in her voice.

He wanted to say something. Words filled his throat and stuck there. Light gathered within him, as radiant and warm as the summer sun, as he gazed at this woman who stared back at him in concern. "I think we should build good memories for our child,'' he finally said when the words, the feelings that overwhelmed him, wouldn't unknot and become clear. ''Think about that.''

She gave him a perplexed glance, then nodded, but it was in his mind that the words lingered and prodded and gnawed at him until he knew he had to take action.

# 10

_____

CYBIL WOKE AND listened intently. The wind had picked up. She could hear it piping around the eaves in high fairy notes. The elusive melody echoed the loneliness inside the silent ranch house.

Lazily, she swiveled her head and glanced at the clock on the mantel. Not quite midnight.

She stretched her arms toward the ceiling and yawned, then pulled her comfortable blue sweats back down over her waist. She supposed she should go to bed. But the sofa was comfortable, and she didn't feel up to moving.

If the six months ahead of her repeated the first three, she would sleep sixteen hours out of every twenty-four. That was probably nature's way of getting her ready for all the sleepless nights that would follow the birth.

She heard a thud. With a jerk of every muscle in her body, she realized someone was outside. On the porch!

Had she locked the doors?

A knock sounded just as she sprang to her feet. She froze for an instant, then relaxed when she heard Mason's voice outside. Shaking her head at her fright, she went to the back door. "Come in," she said, holding it open for him.

"Stay back," he advised.

He stepped over the threshold and, careful of her proximity, removed his hat and jacket. Snow drifted off him in light, airy flakes. He was dressed in jeans and a red flannel shirt over a white T-shirt.

She hung his outdoor gear on a peg by the door. "This looks like the year for blizzards. I can't believe we're having more snow."

"We haven't had this much since the last El Niño came through, what, three years ago?"

"Yes." She glanced at the kitchen clock, then at him. "I hate to mention it, but this is an unusual hour for calling on someone."

"I was going to wait until my folks left Sunday, but I couldn't stay away another minute." His quick smile upped her heartbeat. Then he gazed at her in a solemn fashion that stirred all the confusing feelings into a riot inside her.

"What?" she asked.

He shook his head, then took her hand. "Why aren't you in bed?"

"I fell asleep on the sofa."

"I figured as much."

Tenderness etched his voice and the gaze he turned on her while he tugged his boots off. He set them aside on the corner of the throw rug. She moved over to the counter. "Shall I make some coffee?"

"Yeah, it will probably be a long night."

She tried to make sense of this statement, then gave up. Mason would tell her what he wanted her to know in his own good time and not before. She noticed her fingers trembled while she put on a pot of decaffeinated coffee for the discussion she could sense was coming. "Oh? Why?"

"We have some talking to get through."

Her insides tightened up. He was smiling, but he looked dead serious. She sighed. No one confused her more than this man. "Your folks must think this is rather odd."

"They've gone to bed."

"Mmm," she said noncommittally.

"I couldn't sleep. I'll build us a fire," he volunteered, and padded into the living room.

"Great idea," she called after him, becoming a bit annoyed with his closemouthed tactics. What the heck did he want at this time of the night?

An answer came to her, causing heat to flush through her bloodstream. She had been almost painfully aware of him throughout the holiday meal at his place. When it had at last been over and she could graciously escape, she had taken off like a nervous goose.

But home had provided no refuge from her longings.

"Go sit down," Mason said, interrupting her musings as he turned back to study her. "I'll bring the coffee."

He pivoted her with a hand on her shoulder. She did as requested, more and more puzzled by his attitude...whatever that was. She couldn't figure him out.

When he entered the living room, he carried two mugs in one hand. In the other, he held a huge red apple. He placed the mugs on the coffee table. Sitting beside her, he gazed at the apple as if it were a crystal ball.

"This is for you," he said, holding it out.

She hesitated. The hair on the back of her neck rose as alarm spread through her. "How thoughtful," she said lightly, forcing herself to accept the fruit instead of staring at it as if it were the proverbial poison apple. "Are you trying to polish me up for a favor?"

"No."

His tone was deep, filled with portent that didn't escape her. "Then why?" she asked.

*Why are you here? What do you want? Do you mean to torture me this way?*

The questions hung unanswered in the air between them. He built up the fire until it snapped merrily. He added a pine bough from the basket beside the hearth. The scent of balsam filled the room. He sat beside her again.

"To tempt you, I suppose." He watched her for a long minute without smiling, then gazed into the fire.

She laid the apple down and restlessly stirred a small basket of potpourri on the side table, her eyes on his strong profile. Her mind was curiously blank, refusing to fill with words to break the tension that climbed steadily within her.

She had expected him to grab her up in a rush of passion when he appeared, but he hadn't. Instead, he was thoughtful and wore a slight frown of concentration.

"There is no easy way," he said.

"For what?"

"For us." He laughed briefly. "I may as well tell you point-blank and get it over with."

She shrank back from his announcement, unnamed fears stinging her heart the way the icy needles of snow stung the face when she went out in a driving storm. She steeled herself for an unpleasant declaration. "What?"

"My mother thinks we're in love."

She tried to make sense of the words.

His snort of laughter was sardonic. "Yeah, I knew you wouldn't believe it. But, wild as it seems, I guess it could be true."

"No, it isn't."

"How do you know?"

Cybil stood and paced in front of the hearth. "This whole situation is ridiculous." She maintained an outward calm, but inside, emotions erupted, burning holes through her equilibrium, making her delirious, dizzy. Unexpected tears pressed against her eyes, startling her. She tried to shield herself from the strange tumult.

He stepped in front of her and laid his hands on her shoulders. "One thing I do know—I want us to marry and live happily ever after the way they do in those sappy stories you women love." His gaze was troubled. "I think we owe it to the baby to at least try."

The light dawned. "Ah, that's what this is about. You've decided to use love words to get your way—"

"Honey, men use that trick to get into bed with a woman. I didn't have to do that with you." He tightened his grip. "This is too serious for games."

"You want the baby. You think you have a better chance at joint custody if we're married when it's born. I've already given you my word on that," she told him stiffly.

He sighed. "I told my mom it wouldn't work."

"You told your mom...you told your *mother* that you were coming over here to tell me a bunch of lies?"

"No, I told her you wouldn't believe me if I told you what she said."

The air pulsed between them. He moved his thumbs in tiny, intimate circles on her shoulders.

"What else did she say?" Cybil groaned at the breathless way she sounded. "Not that it matters," she quickly added. She wasn't going down this road again.

"She said I should tell you that I'm in love with you because it would make you feel better." He grinned, just a slight upturning at the corners of his sexy mouth.

"About what?" Cybil couldn't look away from his lips. Her own lips felt hot...needy....

"You tell me. You're the female. You're supposed to know these things."

She pushed his hands away and folded her arms across her chest. "I don't know anything," she said, suddenly close to tears. "I don't understand anything. Why can't men just tell the truth and be done with it?"

To her astonishment, he muttered an expletive and stomped out of the room. Her mouth dropped open.

"Where are you going?" she called, following.

"Home." He grabbed a boot. "I should have had my head examined for trying to talk to you."

She stuck her hands on her hips. "You didn't try

very hard,'' she said, compelled to point out the facts to him. She realized she didn't want him to leave. She wanted to hear more. She wanted him to convince her....

He dropped the boot and straightened. He stalked toward her. ''Talking is senseless. We communicate much better in other ways.''

She backed up a step. ''Don't you dare touch me.'' She realized that was the opposite of what she wanted.

''I've tried talking. It didn't work.'' He flashed her a wolfish grin. ''This way is much better.''

Before she could decide what to do, he swept her into his arms and carried her to the bedroom. With their noses no more than three inches apart, she glared at him the whole way.

He dumped her on the bed and ordered her to stay there. She pushed the covers down and arranged two pillows for a backrest. Ignoring her, he began to strip.

''I am not making love until we get this settled,'' she told him.

''It's settled. You just don't know it yet.''

''I will not be coerced. Or seduced,'' she added for good measure.

He smiled and tossed his jeans on top of his other clothing on the chair. He yanked his socks off and came toward her, his body flagrantly erect.

Her arguments faltered in the face of his blatant masculinity. She drew a shaky breath. ''This is ridiculous. I should have you arrested for trespassing.''

He plopped on the bed, took her face between his hands and kissed her breath away. He eased her down until he was half lying over her. ''Maybe we *are* in love," he suggested, pausing to gaze into her eyes, a questioning light in his. "It's a fact—we can't stay away from each other."

"Don't lie," she whispered, the oddly insistent tears coming dangerously close to the surface. "I can't bear it."

He slowly moved his hands from beneath her top. When she would have reached for him, he caught her hands and held her away. "I don't lie," he said in a quietly ferocious voice. "I've never lied to you. I never will. When you're ready to believe that, then we'll talk."

To her shock, he climbed out of bed and replaced his clothing. In another minute, he was gone. She heard the truck engine turn over, then the receding drone as he drove away. She sat there on the bed, stunned and empty and terribly alone. If she moved, she would burst into tears.

CYBIL PACED THE floor from the kitchen to the living room and back. She paused along the way to look out the windows. Mason hadn't returned. Instead, he'd sent one of his hands over to toss bales of hay to the stock and help her with the chores.

"Damn him," she said aloud.

Her voice echoed in the emptiness of the house. It had been a miserable weekend. She'd nearly called him a hundred times, but each time she'd hung up before it rang the first time, sure she was being foolish.

She closed her eyes and pressed a fist to her stomach. Maybe we *are* in love. Were they? Or was he saying that in order to get his way? She went to the door and gazed at the road, longing eating at her. Then she realized what she was doing...and why.

Across the pasture fence, the young heifer stood gazing dreamily off into the distance as if watching for her long-lost lover. Fletch hadn't visited since his last escape and subsequent return to the Faraday place.

Cybil rested her forehead against the cold window-pane of the back door and experienced the icy shock of truth hitting her. She, too, gazed across the meadows often, her thoughts centered on the ranch next door.

Oh. She felt helpless as she realized what had happened. Oh, Cybil, you fool.

She paced the house again, not knowing what to do with this newfound knowledge. To love, and not know it!

She paced some more. In the living room, she saw the apple he'd brought to her, to tempt her, he'd said, but what if it had meant more? What if it had been an offering...of his love? She picked the apple up. Maybe, like her, he didn't realize it. He'd skirted all around the idea, but love...it was terribly hard to admit to.

He wouldn't come to her again, not without a sign of encouragement on her part. She stared at the apple. An old verse she'd giggled over as a teenager came to her. An idea leaped into her mind along with it.

Lips pursed in uncertainty, she wrote a quick note, punched a hole in the paper and slid it down on the stem of the apple. Then she grabbed her truck keys and took off. If she was wrong, well, she'd just make a fool of herself. It wouldn't be the first time. But if she wasn't...

At the Faraday place, she found the house empty. Jack told her Mason and his relatives had gone to church. She took a deep breath and drove on. At the edge of town, she pulled into the parking lot of the small church. She drew another steadying breath, tucked the apple in her jacket pocket and went inside.

Mason, standing at the pew, talking to the rancher seated behind his parents, saw her at once. She tried to smile but couldn't.

His dark gaze raked over her black slacks and ankle boots, the blue sweater and the light makeup she'd put on. She walked to him, drawn by that compelling gaze, unable to look away.

"Cybil," his mother sang out cheerily. "Do come join us. There's room." And she made sure there was, right between her and Mason.

Cybil took the place without protest. She spoke to Sean and smiled at Moses, aware of the keen glance he gave her. She met his eyes. He smiled suddenly and nodded his head as if they'd come to some agreement. She smiled, too, but her heart beat very hard.

For the next hour, she sang or listened, but the words hardly registered. She heard Mason's pleasant baritone as if from a distance. His heat filled her senses.

At last the service was over. He took her elbow as they made their way down the aisle and out the door. Unable to bear the waiting another moment, she reached into her pocket and removed the apple.

"I have something for you," she said, and thrust it toward him.

With a suspicious frown, he took it and lifted the note from the stem. "'The Song of Solomon, 2:4-5.'" He raised a wary gaze to hers. "Is there a message in here for me?"

She nodded.

"I believe I can help," the minister said, peering over her shoulder. "I'm familiar with the verse. May I?" he asked her.

Cybil felt the heat seep into her neck. She squared her shoulders and looked Mason straight in the eye. "Yes."

"'...comfort me with apples, for I am sick of love.'" The minister smiled. "The poet would say 'with love' or perhaps 'from love,' rather than 'of love,' in today's vernacular."

Mason frowned. Cybil quivered under his gaze.

"Cybil, that's lovely," his mother said.

"I knew it," Moses added with a chortle.

"'...comfort me with apples,'" Mason repeated, "'for I am sick...with love'?" He looked at her.

She couldn't say the words, so she nodded and waited.

"Did you have to do this in front of the whole town?" he demanded.

"I wanted you to believe me." She felt the emotion start bubbling inside like a lava pot. If he didn't do something soon, she was going to explode. Or die from uncertainty.

"I see." He tossed the apple up, caught it, then took a big crunchy bite.

Around them, his family, the minister and his wife, the congregation of their neighbors, watched in rapt attention.

Mason handed the apple to her. She held it in confusion. He guided it to her mouth. She took a bite.

"Okay," he said. "I believe you."

"That I, uh…" She still couldn't say it.

"Yeah, that's what it had better mean. I'm not going to make a fool out of myself in front of a whole town for nothing." He turned and threw the apple as far as it would go, then he swept her into his arms and gave her a resounding kiss. "There, that's all the show you get," he told everyone when he lifted his head.

Taking her hand, he ran with her to her truck. Cybil handed over the keys and he made a quick getaway while their friends broke into laughter and shouts of encouragement.

He drove to her place. "Where we'll be left in peace," he told her. At the entrance, he stopped. "Where's the sign that says men aren't allowed?"

"I took it down," she confessed.

"I'll put it back up. Now that I have you, I don't want any other guys hanging around here. Got that?"

"I don't take orders," she informed him, sounding stubborn. Emotions churned relentlessly deep within, and the uncertainty returned. She gave him a curious glance. "Are you going to be a difficult husband?"

His gaze held a promise. "I'm going to be the best husband you can imagine."

She didn't know what to say to that and was silent while he followed the ranch road to her house. "I thought I'd put in the campsites up in those trees," she said when the silence became too intense.

He parked near the back steps. "You'd better put them in the meadow there so you can keep an eye on the campers."

His certainty that there would be trouble roused her stubborn streak again. "You have the vision of a dung beetle if you think the meadow will do. People don't want to camp on a treeless flat. They want shade."

"Are we going to fight about this?" he asked mildly.

"Yes." She began to feel maligned. She had declared her love in public. He hadn't said a word.

Uncertainty washed over her. Maybe his mother had been wrong. Maybe he really didn't want her....

He sighed and smoothed a hand over her hair. "Good. I love a stubborn-minded woman. I—"

A bellow stopped whatever he might have said next. He broke off and craned his neck to look out the back window of the pickup.

Cybil did, too. She couldn't help but laugh.

Fletch cut across the road, up through the yard and eased through a loose strand on the fence into the pasture, for all the world like a kid sneaking off on some adventure.

"It's a good thing most of the snow has melted on this side of the mountain," Mason said thoughtfully, "or else their honeymoon would be a cold one." He looked at her. "Where do you want to go on ours?"

"Are we going to have one?"

His frown was ominous. "Yes. Uncle Moses would sue us both for breach of promise if we don't marry.

Besides," he added, "I want to. I do love you, you know. I realized it for sure after I left the other night."

"I didn't until this morning. Then..."

"Then?" he prompted.

"I couldn't wait to get to you."

He released a breath as if he'd been holding it for a long time. "Where do you want that honeymoon?"

"Here," she said.

He nodded. "I'll take you to L.A., then Florida, for Christmas. I've often thought of us strolling along a white beach, you in a blue bikini, knowing other men can only look while I get to touch."

"I don't have a blue bikini," she admitted. She didn't have a bikini, period. "And my tummy will be sticking out by then."

After gathering her in his arms, he dropped kisses all over her face. "You'll be beautiful. I want everyone to see what we did together." He chuckled. "Forty years old, and I just now find out what it's all about."

"What?"

"Life. Love. The good things."

She smoothed the lock of hair off his forehead and caressed his mouth. "Oh, those." She spoke casually. So did he. But her heart was thumping.

"Yeah, those."

"So, your mother was right." She laughed because it all seemed so funny. The signs had been there— feeling young and confused again, wanting to see him, longing for his touch—but they'd had to find their way to each other slowly.

His gaze was tender. "Yeah, angel-face, she was right."

They stared at each other for a long moment, then they grinned. Taking her hand, he urged her out of the truck and into the house. Hand in hand, they went up the stairs, their need for each other stronger than any other at this moment. Later, there would be decisions to be made and vows to be said, but not now. This time was for them.

He kissed her, and the magic started. There was no need for a lot of words, only those that lovers whisper.

"Comfort me with apples," he murmured as they snuggled into the comfortable bed, bodies, hearts and souls touching. "No, make that kisses, lots of 'em..."

She heard the happiness in his voice. She saw the tenderness in his eyes. Her body, and maybe her heart, had known long before she had, but now she knew, too. The third time was definitely the charm.

# PATRICIA
# KNOLL

# Meant
# For
# You

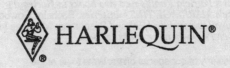

Dear Reader,

People frequently ask me where I get ideas for my books and I always say that good ideas come from everywhere, but the truth is I'm an unrepentant thief. I listen to stories other people tell me and adapt them for my books. I warn my friends and family not to tell me anything they don't want to turn up in a book someday. After a warning like that, it's amazing that anyone speaks to me.

I've picked up a number of good ideas from all the jobs I've held. Besides being a wife and the mother of four, I've taught school, worked as a librarian and as a secretary, and operated a care home for developmentally disabled children. My favorite occupation, though, is writing romantic comedies in which the characters get into challenging, humorous or outlandish situations and then work their way out. Each situation and set of characters is different, so sometimes the finished book is as much a surprise to me as it is to the reader.

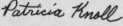

**Books by Patricia Knoll**

## HARLEQUIN LOVE & LAUGHTER
53—DELIGHTFUL JONES

## HARLEQUIN ROMANCE
3442—TWO-PARENT FAMILY
3462—A DOUBLE WEDDING
3502—ANOTHER CHANCE FOR DADDY
3530—WEDDING BELLS

*Don't miss Patricia Knoll's next two books in Harlequin Romance's MARRIAGE TIES miniseries.* Bachelor Cowboy *will be available in July 1999 and* Resolution: Marriage *in December 1999 wherever books are sold.*

# 1

"NOT AGAIN! PLEASE DON'T let this be happening again."
Caitlin Beck jiggled the key to her apartment door, easing
the knob the tiniest little bit to the left, then back to the
right as she twisted the key in the lock. When that didn't
work, she reversed the process. Still, the door remained
stubbornly locked.

"I asked Mr. Mellin to fix this," she muttered, frowning in concentration as she tried again. Frustrated, she
thumped her fist against the doorjamb. Of all days for this
to happen—yet again—this would be the one.

Murphy's Law in full force.

Caitlin set down her briefcase, balancing it against the
soggy bags of groceries she'd hauled up two flights of
steps to her door. On top, she stacked the envelopes she'd
taken from her mailbox in the downstairs foyer. She
crouched down to examine the lock. There was nothing
to do but call the building's handyman who was *supposed*
to help her out. The trick was to locate him.

Of course, she could step across the hall to her neighbor, but that would bring her more help, advice and information than she needed. She would much rather go into
downtown Crystal Cove and search the taverns until she
found Barney Mellin, the maintenance man she had hired
to help her out until she had full ownership of this building. It was a beautiful, Adam-style Georgian house that
had been converted into four apartments—which she in-

tended to convert back into a single-family dwelling. There were any number of young professionals looking for housing in Crystal Cove. This would make an excellent home for a family once the renovations were done. Of course, work couldn't resume until she was rid of the tenant across the hall.

The bottom two floors, scattered with stacks of tile and lumber, rolls of wallpaper and cans of paint, were a mess. She hated passing by it every day, regretted the time being lost, but no further work could be done until the legal problems were settled. And who knew when that would be?

Caitlin cast a dark glance at the closed door behind her, then went back to working with the lock, trying to coax it into opening.

She knew that her affection and attachment for this building were totally out of proportion to its beauty and worth, but she'd fallen in love with it the minute she had seen it standing on a cliff above Crystal Cove, its white-pillared front angled to catch the rays of the setting sun.

Sunset, she had discovered, was the best time to view it because the twilight masked its crumbling condition. She had taken the apartment before she'd had a good look at the place.

How could she have guessed that the stairs creaked as if they were going to collapse any second, the roof leaked and the hot water came from the shower in a pitiful trickle?

It probably wouldn't have mattered if she *had* known, she admitted with a sigh. She'd been besotted, and not only with the house and the small apartment tucked up under the wide-gabled roof directly across the hall from—

"Anything wrong, Caitlin?"

She remained in her crouched position for a minute as

she ran through a few choice words and tried to convince her heart to quit trying to choke her. She would have given almost anything not to have her body experiencing these wild physical reactions whenever she heard Jed Bishop's voice. There was absolutely no reason for it, but they wouldn't stop. Why did Jed always show up at the worst possible moment, anyway? He seemed to have a sixth sense where she was concerned.

"Caitlin? Is something wrong?" he asked again.

She straightened and turned around. Putting her hands behind her, she rocked up onto her toes and gave him a carefree smile. "No, Jed. Nothing at all."

"It *looks* like something's wrong."

Her breezy smile slipped a notch. "I can handle it."

His gaze traveled over her. "You're all wet."

Her eyes widened, her mouth dropped open in mock surprise and she stared down at her suit. "No kidding."

He ignored her smarty-pants theatrics and his thumb flicked out. "Doorknob stuck again, is it?"

"What makes you think that?" She pushed her damp hair out of her face with a nonchalant gesture as she shielded the door with her body. She hated this—being caught in an awkward situation, looking her worst. The rain had soaked her as she left her office. She'd stopped for groceries and received another drenching as she dashed into the market. Then, when her car wouldn't start, she'd stood in the downpour while a passerby had unsuccessfully tried to get it going.

The new hairdo she'd paid a small fortune for only the week before was no longer fluffed and perky. Instead, her chestnut hair was plastered to her head in some places and sticking up at wild angles in others. Her cream linen suit with its wide, sweeping skirt would have to go straight to the dry cleaners, as would her fuchsia silk blouse. She'd left for work looking professional and pulled together and returned home looking as if she'd been dragged backward through a knothole. An underwater knothole.

Her gaze skimmed over Jed. He, on the other hand, always looked good, even dressed in worn jeans and a long-sleeved T-shirt of charcoal gray. And, darn it, she wished she wouldn't notice. His black hair was carelessly tousled as if he'd pulled off one shirt and pulled on another and hadn't bothered to smooth his hair.

She knew exactly how he did it, too. Instead of grasping the T-shirt hem with crossed hands and pulling it over his head, he reached behind his neck and yanked it straight up and off, which meant the necks of most of his T-shirts were stretched out, and... Damn! Peeved, she looked away. She had to stop this.

He had been leaning against the door frame of his apartment. Now he sauntered forward, a knowing grin crooking one side of his mouth, his gray eyes full of wise-guy laughter. "I don't know, Caitlin. Maybe it's because you've dumped your stuff all over the hallway and I'm sure I distinctly heard some very colorful language coming from your ruby-red lips."

"Not until you showed up," she said sweetly, stretching those ruby-red lips into a patently fake smile. "And if you'd stay away, you wouldn't hear anything from me at all."

He shook his head. "Tut, tut, tut. I see we still have to work on our neighborliness—please note that I'm using the word 'our' in the loosest possible way. As far as I'm concerned, *my* neighborliness is just fine, while yours leaves something—"

"How about we don't get into that right now? If you

don't think I'm a good neighbor, you can always move out," she suggested. "My feelings won't be hurt."

"But you'll be lonely," he said, his voice dripping with sympathy. "And I would hate for that to happen."

"Loneliness isn't necessarily a bad thing, Jed, especially when the alternative is having you right across the hall from me."

Again that grin flickered devilishly and his voice dropped to a sexy rumble. "There's a third alternative. You could move in with me. I've got the larger apartment, big bedroom, big bed—"

"Big ideas," Caitlin broke in brightly. "But no thank you. You can continue to sleep in that big bed all by yourself."

He raised an eyebrow at her.

"At least without me," she added.

Why was it that *now* was the time she decided to get so smart? She should have wised up about three weeks ago, kept her goals in mind, discreetly sought information about Jed in Crystal Cove, paid attention to the battalion of women marching through his apartment day and night. She had never seen anything like it. Maria Rossi brought him fresh-baked goods from her family's bakery. Sandra Hudson showed up with curtains she'd sewn for his bedroom, as well as a bottle of champagne and two glasses. Raeann Forbes was writing a novel in which Jed appeared to have a starring role. Two elderly ladies, the Carlton twins, trotted up the stairs to bring him jars of jam and pairs of knitted slippers. There were so many others who sashayed in and out of his apartment that Caitlin had lost count.

Jed greeted them all with delight, inviting them inside. Caitlin tried not to notice how long the young, attractive ones like Maria, Sandra and Raeann stayed, but truthfully, she didn't think it was long enough for them to be indulging in anything illicit.

After all, she knew firsthand that Jed liked to take his time when making love. He said it was something that shouldn't be rushed, and... Damn! She gave herself a mental kick. Besides, it was none of her business if he had relationships going with three women at once, illicit or not.

She was *not* going to remember what it had been like to be in that big bedroom and big bed—at least not for the eleventh time today. She had made a bargain with herself that she would only think about it ten times a day and once she reached that limit, she wouldn't think about it again. Next week she was going to try for five times a day. Eventually the memory would fade away completely.

She was very organized and determined, which was why she was good at her job as an investment counselor and had achieved so much in the four years since college.

Her intelligence and determination had brought her this far. Unfortunately her intelligence had taken a leave of absence a few weeks ago, right around the time she had met Jed Bishop, but she had a grip on her determination that rivaled a first-time sky diver's grasp on his parachute's ripcord.

She pushed her damp hair out of her eyes and braced herself for further persuasions from him, but he gave her a knowing look and changed the subject.

"I've been home for an hour. Where have you been?"

"Working, Jed. It's an activity many people indulge in every day."

"And are they better off for it?" he asked smartly. "That's what I'd like to know."

"Most people think they're better off. It beats being hungry and homeless."

She'd tried to keep her tone light, but it must have betrayed something, because he gave her a swift look.

Caitlin kept her expression pleasantly neutral, hoping he would think it was a casual remark. She didn't really think she had fooled him, but he didn't pursue it. Instead, he said, "I work, Caitlin, only I don't work at the same job every day. I like variety."

There was no denying that. Some days he worked on his land-development deals or checked on the properties he owned around town; other days he drove a truck for his brother's trucking firm or coached basketball at a local youth club. Mostly he spent his time enjoying life.

That was another reason the women in town were so crazy about him. He had a devil-may-care attitude, a killer grin and an easy way of moving that suggested he could change direction at any second and would be happy to carry the nearest woman along in whatever direction he chose. It wasn't so much that he was the town bad-boy type, but more the why-don't-you-and-I-be-bad-together type. It was a combination compelling enough to attract most women. Including her.

He strolled across the hall, took the key from her hand and slipped it into the lock. Of course, it turned right away. Still bent at the waist, he pushed the door open with a touch of his finger, picked up her mail and her grocery bags and, with a deep bow, waved her inside.

Rolling her eyes, she grabbed her briefcase and marched into her living room, which was bright and enticing with its white walls, lushly upholstered sofa and chairs accented by fat primary print cushions, and healthy green plants. The decor was centered around a wall-hung Texas Star patterned quilt she'd bought at a craft fair last year.

She also had a number of found art objects on display.

She loved turning old things into lovely and functional items. She had taken a section of a garden gate, attached a mirror and surrounded it with silk flowers. Her tab-top curtains were hung from coils of electrician's tubing twisted into whimsical shapes above the windows. Her kitchen utensils rested in a can that had once held Italian plum tomatoes. These imaginative touches were at odds with the no-nonsense attitude she projected at work, but she didn't care. She could relax here because it was her home. At least for now.

Relieved to be in her apartment, she turned to Jed. "Thanks for your help," she said briskly. "I'll see you later."

Again that devil's grin flashed. "You know, that's a nice little dismissive tone you've got going for you there. I think I'll pretend I didn't hear it." He glanced around. "Don't I get some kind of reward for opening your door?"

"Obviously I loosened up the lock before you tried it," she said, dropping her briefcase and purse on the antique desk she'd refinished.

"Oh, obviously," Jed agreed, not even bothering to hide his grin.

Caitlin plucked the mail from his hand and took a moment to leaf through it.

Jed carried her grocery bags into the kitchen area and began unloading them.

"Make yourself right at home, Bishop," she said as she flipped through the mail, which she saw was mostly junk. She'd only lived in Crystal Cove a few months. How did all these sweepstakes and lottery entries track her down so quickly?

"Thanks, I will. Anything interesting in the mail?" he asked idly.

She gave him a look that would have had most people backing off. "Not that it's any of your business, but no."

"No love letters from some heartbroken boyfriend in San Francisco?"

She ignored him.

"Considering your line of work, I have to guess that any boyfriends you left there aren't the type to be heartbroken. Too busy watching the bottom line and counting their assets," Jed speculated.

"Jed, I'm not going to discuss anyone from San Francisco with you," Caitlin answered sharply.

To her irritation, he chuckled. "Fine. We'll leave everyone else out and talk about you."

"No."

"Caitlin, I've known you for nearly two months now—"

"Far too long, in my opinion."

"—and I've come to realize that you're not a woman who likes to take chances."

She couldn't argue with that, so she said nothing.

Jed stored some jars of pasta sauce in the cupboard and snapped it shut, then stood watching her with his hands on his hips. He lifted his chin, pointing it at the envelopes she still held. "You should fill out some of those sweepstakes entries and send them in. See what happens."

"I know what will happen. I'll get more. They follow me wherever I go." She tossed them down on the desk. "I'm convinced there are no real organizations anywhere that send these things out. I think these envelopes get together in some mailbox somewhere and breed like rabbits."

Jed's laughter rumbled across the room. "Why, Caitlin, that's the first vaguely bawdy remark I've ever heard you make."

"What can I say? You bring out the worst in me."

"You're damned cute when you say things like that."

Caitlin growled. It was impossible to insult him. Such comments rolled right off him and then he used them as ammunition to toss right back at her. And darn it, why did she have to fight the urge to smile at some of his comebacks?

"Seriously, Cait," he went on. "Why don't you take a chance on even one of those sweepstakes? You never know what luck might bring you."

"I believe in hard work, not luck." Caitlin cringed at her own prim tone. Good grief, when had she begun to sound so stuffy? That was an easy one to answer. When she had met Jed and he'd begun to railroad her into his way of thinking. Sounding stuffy seemed to be a way to establish a line of defense and maintain her independence.

"Then you're missing out on an awful lot in life."

"And you're just the person to tell me what to do to put some spice into my life, right?"

"Spice and sizzle," he confirmed.

The sizzle supplied by him, no doubt. She wished that didn't sound so appealing. "Did anyone ever mention that you've got a bad habit of arranging people's lives for them?"

Jed tilted his head back and pressed his lips together in a frown as he considered the ceiling. "Yeah. Bob Bailey mentioned that to me a year or so ago when I suggested he quit his job at his dad's auto body shop and move to the Cayman Islands."

In spite of herself, Caitlin was fascinated. "What happened?"

"After he told me to mind my own business, he did it. Bought a bar there, married one of the waitresses..." Jed paused and gave her an oblique glance.

"And?" she prompted, curious about why he was avoiding her eyes.

"And a hurricane blew in and wiped the bar off the face of the map."

Caitlin threw up her hands. "I rest my case."

"It was still the right thing for him to do," Jed insisted. "He hated working for his dad." He grabbed a bottle of beer which he had left in her refrigerator on his last uninvited visit and twisted off the cap. He examined the cans of diet cola in the door. "Anything I can get for you?"

"Out?" she asked wistfully.

He slapped the refrigerator door shut and gave her a friendly grin. "You know, if I wasn't such a secure guy, you might make me begin to think you don't want me around."

"I don't want you around."

She ignored the voice calling her a liar and told herself that she hadn't injured his feelings, that it was impossible to do so, but she saw some emotion flicker in his eyes and feared she had hurt him.

He didn't answer. Instead, he took a long, slow swallow of his beer and stared at her for several seconds, the color of his eyes going deep gray. She tried to imagine what he was thinking. It was easier for her if she thought of Jed as a mistake she'd made, then she didn't have to deal with the depth of her own distress because she'd slept with him without really knowing him. Something she had *never* done before. And worse, she was the latest of many women who had fallen for him.

But like it or not, she owed him. He had urged his elderly aunt Geneva to hire Caitlin as her financial adviser. Even though his aunt was on an extended vacation in Los Angeles, she had done so, calling Caitlin frequently for information and advice, for which she promptly paid a substantial fee. Those fees were helping to keep Caitlin's business afloat, and her talks with Geneva Bishop kept Caitlin's spirits up. Geneva was the kind of feisty, independent old lady that Caitlin intended to be. Best of all, Geneva had recommended Caitlin to several of her friends.

Looking at Jed now, Caitlin only seemed able to recall that his initial intervention had helped her start her business.

She knew her soft heart was going to get her into real trouble someday—if it hadn't already. She cleared her throat. "I didn't mean that quite like it sounded."

His eyes narrowed a bit. "Yes, you did. You want me to get out, but you never mention the alternative. You could sell me your half of the building and move out."

"Not if you offered me ten times its value," she answered in a testy voice. "Not now. Not ever."

With a shrug, Jed strolled into the living-room area. "Then we're stuck, aren't we?"

He sat down on her wicker couch, seeming to shrink it to the size of Barbie-doll furniture, and stretched his long legs before him. "I love the way you use words, Caitlin. It must come in handy in your work. Puts a man in his place."

"My words never put you in your place, which is across the hall, by the way."

"I guess I'm immune." He took another long drink of beer. "We're at an impasse over this house, Caitlin."

"Only because you're so stubborn."

"I'm not the stubborn one. Listen, we both want the same thing for this house, this whole project. There's no reason to dissolve our partnership."

"There's *every* reason."

Jed's jaw clenched. "When you get that blue-norther

tone in your voice, I know it's time to change the subject, but this isn't the end of the discussion." He paused as if mentally shifting gears, then said, "How was your day?"

Caitlin slowly released her breath through her teeth. "Fine, thank you."

"Liar. You're wet through and you look like a cat that someone tried to bathe."

Whereas *he,* with his feet stretched out halfway across her living room and his beer bottle resting on his flat stomach, looked like an advertisement for some pop psychologist's relaxation technique.

"If my appearance offends you, why don't you leave so I can change clothes?"

He wiggled his eyebrows at her lecherously. "Honey, you can change clothes while I'm here. It won't bother me at all."

"It will bother *me!*"

"You look plenty bothered already." Jed sat up and focused on her. "What's wrong, besides getting caught in the rain? If it's something to do with our partnership, I have the right to know. What happened?"

Why did she bother to fight it? Even as she asked herself the question, she struggled on. "Our soon-to-be-dissolved partnership," she stated firmly, but he only smiled. With a sigh, she said, "Nothing bad happened at work."

In fact, she'd had a good day, finally managing to convince Mrs. Harbel to put her money in some investments that would give her more financial independence and security over the next few years. She longed to share this little victory with someone. With Jed. But she already knew that telling him might tempt her into sharing further intimacies. She had learned that she needed to keep such information to herself. Unfortunately she had a hard time remembering that when she was around Jed.

She lifted her hand nonchalantly. "Everything's fine."

"Well, then, what is it?"

She growled her exasperation. "If you must know, my car wouldn't start after I stopped at MacAllen's Market. It's still there. One of the cashiers who was getting off work gave me a ride home."

Jed shot to his feet. He could move fast when he wanted to. "Why didn't you say so? Change into some dry clothes and we'll go get it."

"That isn't necessary, Jed. I'm sure it's nothing but a dead battery. The one that's in there is five years old. I'll call Charlie's garage and get it replaced tomorrow. I'll stop by there on my way to work, and—"

"Someone might steal it overnight."

Caitlin hooted with laughter. "My car? A thief would have to be pretty desperate to try making off with it."

"Why take that chance? You never know when a thief might come along and—"

"And what?" she asked. "Have a fetish for a twelve-year-old Nissan station wagon with mismatched fenders and a door that won't open?"

Jed's grin turned slyly reminiscent. "Maybe. Charlotte Ferris used to have a Nissan like that when we were in high school, and most of the guys in town—"

"Never mind," she interrupted.

She wished she didn't sound so prudish, but thinking of him with Charlotte Ferris, a tall, gorgeous blonde with approximately nine miles of beautifully toned legs made her feel a rush of something she refused to identify as jealousy.

"I've offered to lend you money to buy a new car, and

think how much more successful you would look tooling around town in a BMW or a Mercedes.''

This was an old argument. Caitlin held up her hand. "And have my clients thinking I'm so extravagant I can't handle my own money much less theirs? No thanks. I don't want your help, Jed. I know it's important to look successful and driving a nice car is part of that image, but I want to do this on my own. When I can afford it, I'll get a new car."

The corners of his mouth pulled down. "*Now* who's being stubborn? Go change your clothes. We'll get your car."

With an irate look, Caitlin turned away, entering her bedroom and closing the door carefully so she wouldn't be tempted to slam it. She might be stubborn, but if so, she'd been taking recent lessons from a master.

Her shoulders slumped as she stood by the door, not even cheered as she usually was by the sight of her high double bed with its brass frame and white eyelet comforter, and the fluffy white flokati rug on the smooth golden-maple floor. She loved this room, especially because of the ocean view, but today the sky, the water, everything outside was gray—reflecting her mood.

It had all seemed so simple, she thought morosely as she removed her damp clothes and hung them over the shower-curtain rod in the bathroom.

Since long before she had graduated from college, she had worked and saved every penny she possibly could from her job at the bank so that someday she could open her own office, be her own boss. She had made a careful study of the towns on the northern California coast. Her intention had been to find herself a hometown, one where she could settle and stay settled for the rest of her life, one where she could be part of the community.

Never again would she have to accompany someone who was skipping town one jump ahead of the law, nor would she awaken with a jolt, wondering where she was—what town or city, what room in which fleabag hotel.

Crystal Cove had seemed perfect. It was only an hour north of San Francisco, large enough to have many flourishing businesses and an influx of retirees and young professionals who could use financial advice from a hotshot young investment counselor named Caitlin Beck. At the same time, it had been small enough to possess the sort of friendly atmosphere she liked.

Who could have guessed Jed Bishop would come strolling into her office not long after she opened it, flashing that pirate's grin, appreciating her with his knowing eyes and melting her bones as soon as she reached out to shake his hand?

Who could have guessed that his request for information would lead to dinner, to numerous dinners, movies, dates, to a partnership in renovating this house, to moving in across the hall for the purpose of supervising the renovations, to a celebratory bottle of champagne?

To bed?

Who could have guessed that she, who weighed *every* decision carefully, would get herself into such a mess in such a short time?

Her distress wasn't only due to having slept with someone she didn't really know and love. It was because afterward she feared he saw her as one of his projects, like converting these apartments back into a single-family house, coaching basketball, helping people.

All those things were worthy, wonderful projects, but she didn't want to be one of them. She knew he saw her as a puzzle he needed to solve, but she didn't want to be solved. She wanted... She didn't know what she wanted.

All the women who visited him seemed to be wild about him, and he treated them with warm friendliness, greeted them with hugs and kisses. Why hadn't she *noticed* that he treated her the same way? That to him, she was just one of the crowd, only closer?

Because she had been besotted.

With a grimace, Caitlin jerked open her closet door and grabbed some clothes. It took her only a few minutes to change into a pair of slacks and a blue cable-knit sweater to ward off the September evening's chill. She combed her hair, and because it was a mess, hid it under a San Francisco Giants cap. Grabbing her raincoat, she left her apartment and met Jed in the hallway.

He gave her a quick glance as if approving her warm attire and the new color in her cheeks. Spying the cap, he frowned. "If you hadn't cut all your hair off, you wouldn't have to hide it under that cap."

"Thank you, Jed," she answered sassily. "You always know how to make a girl feel special. If you're going to get my car started, hadn't we better leave now?"

He gave her a disgruntled look, but took her arm and accompanied her down to the sweeping, pockmarked driveway where he'd parked his golden-yellow Mustang. The garage out back was falling down, so neither of them used it.

Caitlin was grateful to see that the rain had stopped, though she didn't expect to see the sun. The clouds sulked on the horizon.

Once they were seated in Jed's car, he reminded her to fasten her seat belt and they took off with a roar.

Caitlin had ridden with Jed before so she knew what to expect. She braced herself against the dashboard, but the turn from the driveway onto the pavement was made on two wheels at warp speed. The force plastered her against the door, and as she struggled upward and gasped for air, she said, "That giant sucking sound you hear is me peeling my face off the window. Can't you slow down?"

He grinned as he flashed her a glance. "What's the point of driving a sports car if you're not going to use all this speed and power?"

"A long life?" she suggested, grabbing the armrest to avoid catapulting into his lap as he took another curve. "Jed, you're a terrible driver."

He gave her a dry look. "Oh, please stop, Caitlin. These showers of praise are embarrassing."

Caitlin turned her face to the window as she bit her lip. Darn him. He was making her laugh again, charming her, exactly as he charmed every female.

The tires shrieked as they reached the town limits. He slowed to a crawl as they passed through a school zone and eased into MacAllen's parking lot. He cruised to a stop and Caitlin worked her fingernails out of the padded dashboard. They left little half-moon shapes behind. "Thanks for the flight," she gasped.

"Anytime."

"Yeah, anytime I want to know what my maximum heart rate is."

"Think of it as aerobics without all that annoying sweat," he advised as he unfolded himself from the Mustang and held out his hand for her car key. "Come on, let's take a look at your car."

"It's a dead battery, Jed. All we have to do is open the hood and—"

"I'll check and make sure."

Of course he would. Exasperated, Caitlin handed over the keys.

Jed tried the engine and was met with nothing but a grinding sound. He cranked it a couple of times, listening carefully. "Must be the battery," he observed, tilting his head in thought. Caitlin wanted to hit him.

"I'll get my jumper cables," he said. "Then we'll see if we can start it."

Caitlin would have offered to help, but he seemed to want to do it himself. She moved away and stood watching the early-evening shoppers stopping for last-minute necessities as she had done. She held the door for a petite elderly woman who emerged from the market pulling a two-wheeled wire cart on which her groceries were loaded.

She glanced up at Caitlin, who was struck by the woman's direct gaze and clear blue eyes. "Thank you, my dear," she said, stopping for a few seconds to look searchingly into Caitlin's face.

Caitlin was about to speak, but something in the woman's expression stopped her. She had an odd little triangular face, hardly lined although she was stooped with age. Her hair was snow white and thick, curling around her face. Her startling bright eyes studied Caitlin for a few more seconds taking on a vague, faraway expression, then she seemed to focus again and she said, "Hello. I was beginning to wonder when I would see you."

The warmth in her soft, quavery voice made the statement sound as if they had met before, were, in fact, close acquaintances.

Caitlin stared, trying to place the woman, but failed. In her work, she had met a number of older women in town, but she didn't remember this one. Deciding the woman was a bit addled, Caitlin smiled kindly and said, "It's nice to see you again, too."

Immediately the woman straightened and blinked at her. "What do you mean, again? We've never met before." With a shake of her head, she moved through the door.

Taken aback, Caitlin released the door to let it slide quietly shut while she gazed after her. Her first response was to laugh, but instead, she shivered. Strange. She felt as if the old woman had seen right into her soul.

Caitlin watched her as she made her way across the sidewalk, carefully avoiding cracks, even lifting her little cart over them. Smiling, Caitlin recalled the old saying "Step on a crack, break your mother's back." This woman seemed to be a strict believer in that, though Caitlin couldn't imagine that the elderly woman's mother was still alive. After several minutes of avoiding the tiny fissures in the sidewalk, the woman reached the curb, stepping off first, then turning to pull the cart onto the crosswalk. One of the bags shifted, and she stopped to set it right. Then she seemed to spy something in the gutter and bent to retrieve it.

Caitlin straightened in alarm when she heard a car approaching. The swish of tires on wet pavement told her it was going much too fast for these conditions. Quickly she glanced around and saw it speeding down the street, its blinker indicating the driver was going to turn at the corner where the old woman was wrestling with her cart.

"Wait!" Caitlin shouted, starting forward. Jed dropped the jumper cables onto the engine and spun around to see what was happening.

Automatically he reached out a hand to her, but Caitlin dashed past him. Grabbing the cart, she shoved it aside and wrapped her arms around the woman, pulling her onto the curb. An instant later she felt Jed's arms close around them both and he dragged them back as the car swept past. It sent up an arc of water, drenching all three of them.

Caitlin Knoll

the curb. A servant took the hat for 1 It was close enough, though, and he caught them between the car . . .
you know what came in the car directions all over a book

# 2

---

"WHAT THE....? DAMN," Jed sputtered. With one hand, he swiped water from his face. "Fool driver."

Caitlin gasped in outrage over the drenching they had taken. "Of all the rude...!" Looking down, she realized she was clutching the woman they'd rescued and Jed was still holding them both. Automatically she loosened her hold on the woman, but stayed close, lightly touching her arm in case she needed steadying. She shifted away from Jed and spoke to the woman. "Are you all right, ma'am?"

The woman brushed water from her face and flipped drops of it from her curly hair. As she shook out the front of her long black raincoat and stomped water from her old-fashioned high-top rain boots, she treated her rescuers to a rueful look. "Well, I'm as wet as a codfish, but I'll survive." Her words were hearty, but her voice wavered. She cleared her throat. "I wonder if my groceries did. I'll be very put out if my fresh bread is ruined."

She started for the curb, but Jed strode ahead of her. "I'll get it, ma'am." He grasped the handle of her little cart and pulled it to safety, then peeked into the bags and said, "Everything looks okay. I guess it's a good thing you answered 'plastic' when they asked."

"Oh, yes, plastic," the woman said. "It's astonishing what they can do with that now. So much more versatile than cellophane."

Caitlin and Jed exchanged puzzled glances. "Yes, ma'am," he said.

Suddenly she gave Jed a sparkling look from her bright blue eyes. "Such polite language. What is your name, young man?"

"Jed Bishop."

She nodded slowly and a smile of recognition spread across her face. "Bishop, of course. Your parents have raised a true gentleman. I knew they would."

Jed gave her a quick scrutiny. "I don't think we've met. Do you know my parents?"

"My name's Reenie. Reenie Starr, and don't be ridiculous. Of course I don't know your parents. I just arrived here."

His eyes darkened in confusion. "Well, then, I don't understand what you mean."

"That's all right," she said, patting his arm. "You don't need to."

Jed glanced at Caitlin again, who smothered a laugh. She recalled the comment Reenie had made while Caitlin had held the door for her, saying she'd been wondering when she would "see" Caitlin. The woman's mind seemed to be wandering.

"I don't?" Jed began, but Reenie veered off to another topic.

"Well, that was lucky," she said. "You were here at exactly the right moment." She glanced up. "It's working already," she said in a tone of pleased wonder.

"What's working?" Caitlin asked, still wiping dirty water from her face. If she'd known she was going to get wet all over again, she never would have changed out of her suit and put on clean clothes.

"The luck, of course." She opened her palm and showed them a shiny object. "'See a penny, pick it up, all the day you'll have good luck,'" she quoted in a sing-song voice.

Jed and Caitlin looked at what the woman held in her hand, then glanced at each other. Jed cleared his throat. "Excuse me, ma'am..."

"Reenie," she supplied pertly.

"Reenie," he said. "That's not a penny. It's a copper-colored beer-bottle cap."

She squinted at the item, then dug in her pocket. She pulled out a pair of glasses, popped them on and frowned through the thick lenses. "Well, I'll be darned. You're right." Perplexed, she shook her head. "My eyesight's not what it used to be, but squashed flat like this it looks exactly like a penny."

"And picking it up nearly got you flattened in the street," Jed said.

"Uh, Jed," Caitlin warned, fearing his pointed language would offend the lady. "Ma'am...Reenie. You really shouldn't have lingered in the street like that."

"Well, how was I to know the speed limit had been raised to such an outrageous number? Thirty-five miles an hour. Why, that's appalling." She blinked suddenly, gazing at the stop sign. "No wonder the driver didn't stop. Some trickster has painted that stop sign red, instead of yellow. Someone should speak to the city council about that."

"Yellow stop sign?" Caitlin asked.

"Ma'am, stop signs haven't been yellow since the nineteen fifties," Jed told her.

Reenie glared at him. "I knew that," she said with a firm nod. She shook her finger at him and frowned. "I know what you're thinking."

His eyebrows rose. "You do?"

"You're thinking that I'm off my rocker, that my cheese has slipped off its cracker, but it's not true."

Jed's lips twitched. "No, ma'am. I understand. Your cheese is still firmly attached to its cracker."

She beamed at him. "That's right." Turning, she reached out to pat Caitlin's arm as she had done with Jed. Her hand was cool. "No. You're wrong. I did the right thing by picking up that penny even though it isn't a penny. It brought me luck. You were there to save me."

Caitlin looked at Jed. This time it was his turn to shrug. "I don't think that was luck," Caitlin said gently.

Reenie's eyes brightened as she turned to Caitlin. "Of course you don't, dear. I'm well aware that you don't really believe in luck, do you? Only in hard work and self-sufficiency."

"Well, I…" Good grief, how had this little lady known that? Caitlin's amazement must have shown on her face, because Jed's grin flickered.

Reenie had her back to him. He lifted his hand and tapped a finger against his temple to indicate what he thought of her mental acuity.

Without turning around, Reenie said, "I thought we'd agreed I'm not crazy, young man. Merely ancient. Be careful, I may think the only gentleman your parents raised was your brother, Steve."

Jed's mouth flopped open and color climbed his cheeks. "I'm sorry, I… How do you know I have a brother named Steve?"

Reenie didn't answer. Instead, she took Caitlin's hand and folded the bottle cap into it. "There, I think you need this. It'll teach you a good lesson." She took the handle of the cart and said, "I must be on my way now. I'll be seeing you again."

Jed recovered his much-vaunted manners and stepped

forward. "Why don't you let us drive you home, Ms. Starr?"

"Now, really," she said in a long-suffering tone. "I'll be very offended if you don't call me by my first name. Otherwise how will I know you're my friend?" She moved away without giving him time to think up an answer. "No thank you, young man. It's not far. Only up Old Barton Road."

Jed frowned. "Only one person lives up Old Barton Road," he said. "And she's gone."

"I know," Reenie answered, and once again started off. "I'm not there yet because I'm still here." Jed and Caitlin exchanged blank stares as Reenie stepped to the curb.

This time, she paused to look both ways before stepping from the curb, but she glanced back to give Caitlin a warm smile. "Your hair looked much better long. I'll bet your young man here thought so, too," she said, nodding at Jed. "It was very soft and feminine. I think he liked to touch it. Men do, you know. My Harvey always said my long curls were my best feature." She touched her hair and regret lined her face for a moment. "But it's easier for me to keep this way, and he's no longer here to care."

Caitlin was startled. Her own short hair was covered by a baseball cap. Questions sprang to her lips, but Reenie was already turning away with a wave. Caitlin watched, dumbfounded, as the tiny figure made her way across the street and down the sidewalk, disappearing around the corner that led to the old gravel road.

"Well, I'll be damned," Jed said, running his hand through his damp hair. "Do you think we just met a witch?"

A shiver ran across Caitlin's shoulders and she glanced uneasily at the bottle cap in her hand, but she said dismissively, "Don't be silly. She's only a sweet old lady. Maybe a little addled."

Jed nodded as he contemplated the direction Reenie had gone. "There really isn't anything down Old Barton Road except my aunt Geneva's house at this end, and we both know she's out of town. There's no one renting her little apartment out back, and my whole family has orders to stay away from there. Says she doesn't want us prowling around. On the cliff at the other end, there's a wrecked farmhouse someone slapped together back in the thirties. Steve and I used to play there as kids. I'm amazed now that the place didn't collapse around our ears. It's got an incredible view. Developers have been coveting it for years. *I've* been coveting it for years, but the owner won't sell, so I know Mrs. Starr can't be living there."

"Well," Caitlin said, still worried, "maybe she's a little confused and will find her way all right." She turned an uncertain gaze on him. "You think so, don't you, Jed?"

His eyes met the worry in hers. "Tell you what," he said briskly. "Let's get in my car and drive up that way, make sure she gets home okay, then we can come back and get your car."

Caitlin sent him a grateful smile. "You're a pal, Jed Bishop."

Jed snorted. "Nicest thing you've said to me in three weeks. If I'd known that was all it took to get you to be reasonable, I would have been trotting little old ladies across every street in Crystal Cove."

"To quote our new friend, 'Don't make me take back what I said'," Caitlin responded, giving him a retiring look. With a quick step, she headed back to his car.

While she was fastening her seat belt, Jed picked up his jumper cables, slammed the hood of her car, then hopped into the seat beside her. They pulled out of MacAllen's parking lot and were soon tooling up the street.

When they turned onto the dirt road, Caitlin sat up straight, looking for Reenie. As they passed Geneva Bishop's closed-up house, they saw that the road ahead of them was empty.

There was no sign of the little old woman even though they drove all the way up to the dead end by the farmhouse with its caved-in roof.

Jed waved his hand toward the open car window. "See, she's not here. She probably got her bearings straight and headed on home."

"I hope you're right." Caitlin looked again at the bottle cap Reenie had given her. She had the unsettling feeling that something important had occurred, but she didn't know why she thought that. That was just a fanciful notion, she told herself as she shoved the bottle cap into her jeans pocket. When she looked up, Jed was studying her.

"Something on your mind?" he asked.

"No, no, not at all," she answered, but his skeptical look told her he didn't believe her. She turned away, wishing she wasn't so easy to read. Or at the very least, she wished things were better balanced and he was as easy to read as she seemed to be.

He should have been, she thought, staring down at her hands resting in her lap. His quick grin and easygoing manner should have been those of a man whose thoughts went no further than tomorrow, or at the most, no further than his Saturday-night date.

It wasn't that way, though, which was why she'd been so off balance since meeting him. Maybe it was also why it had been so easy for him to tumble her into bed—or rather, there had been no tumbling to it. It had been pure finesse.

She might as well face it. She liked things in her life to be well ordered and settled, and he'd been unsettling her from the start.

Jed was still watching her. Caitlin glanced at him, then away from those gray eyes that saw too much. To her relief, he said nothing.

He turned the car around and they went back to the market. He jump-started her car and promised to install a new battery the next day, but Caitlin had to put her foot down when he offered to buy one for her.

"I *always* pay my own way, Jed," she told him bluntly once her car was idling with its usual rumble-and-cough rhythm.

"Yeah, I'm learning that about you." Jed slammed the car hood closed. "I don't know why you won't accept a loan for a car. I know from our partnership papers that you've got a good credit history. The bank would give you a loan in a minute. I've offered several times. I'd do it for any of my friends. I've given dozens of them."

She knew that, and it was another reason she didn't want one. She didn't want to be bailed out like so many other people who depended on him. She realized now that was part of the reason she'd entered into the partnership with him, so that he would see her as a serious business-woman and not simply another person he needed to rescue. "And I've turned you down several times. I wish I had a new car, but it will have to wait until I can afford it. I won't accept a loan."

"It's only money, Caitlin. It can be paid back."

She didn't know how to answer that. She couldn't argue with his easygoing attitude and she was unwilling to explain her fear of debt. Money wasn't as easy to replace as he seemed to think. Besides, it wasn't the money itself, but the security it offered that appealed to her.

Finally she said, "I'll take care of the battery myself, Jed. Tomorrow."

Surrendering, he held up his hands, but his lips tightened and he shook his head at her stubbornness. "All right, then. Let's go home. I'll be right behind you in case you have any more trouble."

Caitlin nodded her thanks and drove home, aware of him behind her, wishing she wasn't so conflicted about what was right for her—independence—and what she wanted—Jed.

When she reached the old Victorian house, she parked her car, waved her thanks to Jed and hurried inside. She was anxious to take a nice, relaxing bath, put on warm pajamas and fix herself some dinner—not a sandwich tonight, but something hot and nourishing.

However, her phone was ringing when she mounted the stairs and she hurried in to answer it. Her phone rarely rang. Since she was new in Crystal Cove, she knew few people other than her clients, and they never called her at home.

She answered briskly on its fifth ring and a male voice on the other end said, "Ms. Beck? This is Gordon Carrow of Carrow Classic Cars and Auto Restorations."

Caitlin smiled. Maybe he was calling to give her an estimate on restoring her car. Too bad hers wasn't a classic. It was merely a clunker.

Caitlin sat on the sofa with a whoosh of breath. After this afternoon's experience, she sincerely wished she could take this man up on whatever great deal he was no doubt going to offer her. Sighing, she asked, "Yes, Mr. Carrow, what can I do for you?"

"Ms. Beck, it's what I can do for you—or maybe I should say it's what you've done for yourself."

Caitlin rolled her eyes. She really didn't have time for this. She wanted a bath and dinner, but she found it impossible to be rude to people on the phone. She had helped pay her way through college by making unsolicited calls, known as cold calls, for a telemarketing firm. She knew what it was like to have the phone hung up in her ear, so she couldn't do that to this man. She scraped at the bits of mud on her shirt while she waited patiently for the pitch. It wasn't long in coming.

In an excited voice he said, "You, Ms. Caitlin Beck, are the winner in the Crystal Cove Merchants' Harvest Bonanza! Congratulations!"

Caitlin didn't answer, waiting for him to go on.

"Ms. Beck, did you hear me?" he asked hesitantly, some of the excitement draining from his voice.

"Yes, I did, Mr. Carrow. It was very nice of you to call and let me know that. Now, what exactly is it I have to buy in order to win whatever it is I've won?" she asked politely.

There was a lengthy pause. "Uh, miss, I think maybe you're not hearing me. You don't have to buy anything. You signed up for the Harvest Bonanza Grand Giveaway."

Vaguely Caitlin recalled the posters and banners she'd seen around town the past few weeks. They advertised special deals and giveaways at many of the retailers. She couldn't recall signing up for anything, though. Uncertainly she said, "I'll take your word for it, Mr. Carrow."

Although her tentative response probably wasn't what he had expected, Mr. Carrow went on, "Well, anyway, we had the drawing today and you're the proud owner of a fully restored, beautifully reconditioned 1957 Chevrolet Bel-Air.''

Caitlin straightened abruptly. "Excuse me?"

"We'd like to bring it over tonight if possible," Mr. Carrow continued. "I've got a video crew all ready to go, so we can tape you receiving the keys. We sponsor the *Midnight Movie* on Channel Six and we'd like to show the tape on our commercials tonight."

Her heart beating fast, Caitlin wheezed, "Is...is this a joke?"

He laughed. "No, I assure you it's no joke. To prove it, we'll be there in an hour with your car." He paused, then added, "If you've got family and friends close by, maybe you'd like to invite them over. They can be in the video, too. Let me confirm your address." He rattled it off and, in a daze, Caitlin confirmed it. With a cheery goodbye, he hung up.

Caitlin sat staring at the receiver. This was incredible. Slowly she replaced the phone and sat trying to recall exactly when she had entered the Bonanza giveaway at Carrow Classic Cars and Auto Restorations. Never. She had never even been there. Of course, she could have signed up at some other merchant in town, but she didn't think so. She never did that sort of thing.

This had to be a hoax. She grabbed the phone book and leafed through it rapidly to find Carrow's phone number. When she called back, the phone was answered by a receptionist who confirmed the information, congratulating Caitlin on her snappy red Bel-Air. "You'll be the envy of your friends," the woman said.

"No kidding," Caitlin breathed. "But I...I don't remember even entering the contest. I only moved here a few months ago."

"Oh, well, that explains it," the woman said breezily.

"Every new resident was entered automatically as a sort of 'welcome to Crystal Cove' gift. There was an announcement in the *Crystal Cove Clarion*."

"I...I guess I didn't see it," Caitlin said faintly. Her mind was spinning. "Well, thank you. Thank you very much."

When she hung up the second time, Caitlin sat stunned for a moment, then jumped straight up off the couch with a crow of joy, threw her hands into the air and did a little jig of delight around the room. She couldn't believe this. She'd never won anything before in her life.

Who could she tell? Her best friends, Tony and Anna Danova, were in San Francisco. She knew hardly anyone here, except for.... Her dance slowed to a stop, her hands fell to her sides, and she looked at her apartment door, imagining the man who was across the hall.

She could tell Jed that she'd won a car, not a new one like he'd been encouraging her to buy, but a classic, a red one, and she had to tell someone or burst with the news.

Before she could give it further thought and talk herself out of being impulsive, she whipped open her door and dashed across the hall. She knocked, then did a fancy little two-step while she waited for him to answer.

When the door opened, she whirled around excitedly to see him standing in the entrance, briskly drying his hair with a small white towel. When he saw her, he looped it around his neck and looked at her with interest.

"Yes, Caitlin?"

She focused on his face. "Jed, you'll never guess..." Her eyes traveled rapidly downward, spied his hands loosely clasping the ends of the towel, framing his chest, sharply defining the muscles there. Then her gaze dropped lower—to his stomach. There were muscles there that she knew from firsthand experience were as hard as a slab of marble.

Completely against her will, her tongue darted out to wet her lips, and her gaze shot back to his face, which was taking on a puzzled look. She hitched in a breath and tried again. "You'll never guess—"

"You said that already," he interrupted in a voice one breath away from a chuckle.

"What…you'll never…" Her words stumbled over themselves, withered up in her desert-dry mouth, then blew away.

While she had been on the phone and then dancing around her apartment, Jed had been in the shower.

He was barefoot, had on jeans, zipped but unbuttoned, and no shirt. The hair that curled across that washboard stomach of his, already dark, was nearly black with dampness. The scent of soap and aftershave eddied out to tantalize her.

An unwanted memory of touching him, being held and loved by him, burst through her. She had tried so hard to suppress that memory, but it had been there all the time, waiting to pop out like a genie from a magic lamp, ready to tempt and torment her. The sight, the scent of him, had desire sifting through her, gathering strength until it kicked her right in the belly, nearly sending her sprawling on her bottom.

Eyes wide, mouth falling softly open, Caitlin looked up at him. Her bottom lip trembled before she bit down on it, bringing it under control.

Jed's politely interested smile underwent a slow, blatant change until it held the usual teasing she knew so well. Being Jed, he knew exactly what her problem was!

"Something wrong, Caitlin?"

She cleared her throat, but still her answer came out as

if someone had stepped on her toe. "No!" She softened her tone. "Uh, I mean, no."

"Do you see something you like?"

Did she ever! Her face turned a bright pink. She was being ridiculous. It certainly wasn't as if she'd never seen him half-dressed—much less than half-dressed—before. She wasn't going to give him the satisfaction of knowing how he was affecting her. She would never hear the end of it.

That thought stiffened her resolve. She had fought this for three weeks now. She knew she could conquer it. Besides, it had been at least an hour since she had passed her limit of thinking about him only ten times a day.

She took a deep breath, but still she stammered when she answered. "I...I just received a call. I...I've won a car."

Jed's face went blank. "You're kidding."

"It's true. Fully restored," she quoted. "Beautifully reconditioned. I'll be the envy of all my friends."

Happiness bubbled through her and she laughed. The expression on Jed's face changed from the teasing look to something more serious, more alert. His eyes sharpened subtly.

Caitlin gave only fleeting notice to it as her explanation tumbled from her. Breathlessly she ran through everything Mr. Carrow had said, concluding with, "...and the receptionist said I was entered automatically as a new resident, and...and I won."

"The Harvest Bonanza Grand Giveaway. I wondered if they had a winner yet."

"They do. Me."

"That's great, Caitlin, " he said, grinning. "Congratulations. I'm certainly envious. Gordie does excellent work."

"Fully restored," she parroted again, still in something close to shock. She blinked. "Beautifully reconditioned."

Jed laughed, causing her to realize that she was babbling. Blushing, she rolled her eyes comically. He chuckled again, then his brow creased.

"It must be the luck that old lady was talking about," he speculated in a thoughtful tone as he crossed his arms over his chest and leaned against the doorjamb.

"Old lady?" Caitlin's eyes glazed at the sight of those spectacular muscles that bunched and stretched when he crossed his arms. She almost wished he wouldn't stand like that, but if he didn't how could she enjoy this show?

"The old lady at MacAllen's," Jed responded. "She said it would teach you a good lesson."

"MacAllen's?" she asked, finally lifting dazed eyes away from his magnificent pecs to focus on his face. He was watching her with that knowing smile of his.

"Oh!" Caitlin slapped her hand against her jeans pocket. The bottle cap was still there. She drew it out and flipped it in the air. It's shiny surface caught the reflection from the hall light, winking tantalizingly at her. She caught it and examined it for a moment. It was only a flattened bottle cap, after all. Some of her excitement began to cool. "I don't think so, Bishop," she said briskly. "It's a coincidence."

"Oh, that's right. You're the one who doesn't believe in luck."

That was before she had won a car, she thought. "I only said I believe more in hard work than in luck."

Jed's grin kicked up one corner of his mouth. "But this time, it's luck, not hard work that brought you what you needed. Maybe Reenie Starr *is* a witch," he concluded. "After all, you did wish for a new car."

"Oh, come on, Jed. It's not like a fairy godmother suddenly appeared to grant my wish. Saying I wished I had a car was...the kind of thing...anyone would say under the circumstances.'' She flapped her hand at him. ''Oh, never mind. Bishop, I'm not going to get into this discussion. I've got to go get ready. They're bringing the car tonight and they're going to videotape it for a television advertisement.''

''But first, you came to tell me. Caitlin, I'm touched.''

''Don't be,'' she said repressively. She realized with relief that she was getting her equilibrium back. A little teasing from Jed put her right back where she should be— businesslike, responsible, totally unaffected by the sight of his tousled hair, sexy grin and bare chest. Totally unaffected, she assured herself, taking another quick inventory. And that odd warmth she was feeling was hunger. After all, she'd had no dinner. The fact that the warmth wasn't in her stomach, but in a place a little bit lower that was strictly feminine didn't mean a thing. Congratulating herself on that bit of logic, she lifted her gaze to meet his again. ''Mr. Carrow told me he would be here in an hour and I should invite my friends to be in the video and...''

Darn! Why had she let herself in for this? Thinking of Jed as a friend was only going to get her into something she certainly didn't want.

Jed straightened, his gray eyes gleaming. ''When Gordie and the video crew are gone, we should celebrate.''

''No,'' she snapped, remembering how their last celebration had gotten so out of hand. ''After they're gone, I'm taking my new car for a drive, and—''

''You want me to be your first passenger.'' Laughing softly, Jed stepped toward her. ''That's the best offer I've had all day.''

"It wasn't an offer, I... Oh, forget it!" Whirling around, she rushed to her apartment, had a short tussle with the balky knob, then whirled inside and slammed the door.

# 3

JED SHRUGGED and stepped back into his own apartment, shoving the door shut with his elbow.

Hell's bells, he never knew where he was with her. He shook his head as he headed into his bedroom to finish dressing. That wasn't true, he thought. With her, he was out of her life, across the hall, out in the cold, *way* out in the cold.

He reached for his shirt, put it on, and began buttoning it with quick little twists of his wrist. He had no one to blame but himself. Two months ago he had taken one look at her and pure lust had raised its insidious head. Damn. He could have sworn he'd conquered that devil when he was about twenty-two.

Then, when she'd opened her mouth and started talking and he'd realized there was an actual brain inside that beautiful head, he'd completely lost it.

Jed tucked in his shirt, then smoothed his hair. He was the first to admit that he liked women. Okay. To tell the truth, he loved women, and he'd never had much trouble attracting them because they seemed to like him, too.

Caitlin had been a challenge, though. Right from the beginning, when he'd seen her in her office dressed in one of her San Francisco financial-district power suits, he'd been intrigued. His younger sister, Diana, said there was an indefinable quality that showed whether or not a woman had class. He'd never known what that meant until he'd met Caitlin, with her sleek chestnut hair curving around her chin, her big golden-brown eyes staring at him through the lenses of those reading glasses she affected, in hopes, he was sure, of making herself look less feminine and desirable. It hadn't worked. He would have found her desirable if she'd been dressed in a gunnysack.

He had only gone into her office that day to introduce himself and talk to her a bit. His imperious aunt Geneva had called from Los Angeles, where she was visiting friends, to say she had a little nest egg to invest and had heard there was a new investment counselor in Crystal Cove. A woman. Geneva had assigned him the task of finding out if Caitlin seemed trustworthy.

He could have given Aunt Geneva the advice she needed, but despite the fact that she had three brothers and numerous nephews, she didn't much like men. She had never married or had any inclination to do so, and whenever possible had sought out women in any profession she dealt with. Until recently she had taken the advice of a male stockbroker. However, now that there was a woman available, she insisted that she wanted a woman's advice. As ordered, he'd gone to obtain one of the brochures that detailed Caitlin's experience in financial matters and her philosophy about investing.

As it turned out, he'd picked up the brochure to send to his aunt and he'd convinced Caitlin to have lunch with him. They had talked about common stocks, mutual funds and investment portfolios while his ungovernable imagination had been picturing her talking about other things, her full lips welcoming him to her, her eyes dark with promise, with passion. In his mind, he saw her reaching for him.

Quite a leap, considering that sitting at one of the small

tables at Margie's Café, all he'd been able to see of her were her hands, face and satiny throat.

It was the voice that had come out of that throat that had captured him, along with her serious expression, accented by occasional flashes of humor and a vulnerability in her eyes that she masked with a businesslike manner.

On the spot he'd come up with his crazy plan to get her to invest in the house he was renovating—though he certainly hadn't needed an investor. He'd guessed right away that she wouldn't let him get close to her for the normal man/woman reasons, so he'd scrambled around for another one. Using the house had seemed logical. It was an excellent investment.

Jed grimaced. It was true that his plans occasionally didn't work out as he'd thought they would. Diana said it was because he didn't consider the consequences, but she was wrong. It was only that the consequences sometimes caught up with him before he was ready for them.

A prime example was the partnership with Caitlin.

He saw now that she really hadn't the money to spare, but once she'd seen the old house, she had fallen in love with it. Even then, she'd tried to be practical, reasoning that she shouldn't invest on a whim, that such a move would make her look untrustworthy to her clients. He'd finally convinced her, though, that the money would be an investment in her future. He'd had to promise that she could get out of the deal whenever she wanted. She didn't want out of the deal now, though. She wanted to buy *him* out, making payments that would fit into her budget. She'd even been determined to forgo a new car to do it.

He had thought he was making real progress, especially when they'd consummated their partnership, so to speak, but she had awakened the next morning with a panicked look in her eyes. That was when good old Mr. Consequences had kicked him in the butt. With breathless excuses and apologies, she had dashed from his apartment into hers while he'd hopped along behind her demanding explanations while trying to get into his skivvies.

Since that morning, she had kept him at a distance. In his opinion she had reacted in a way that was completely out of proportion to what had gone on between them.

Not that it hadn't been good, Jed thought as he reached for his keys and pocket change. In fact, it had been damned good. He wouldn't mind repeating the experience every night for a while. After that, they would be good friends. That was how it had worked out with all the previous women in his life. He liked it that way. However, this particular woman wasn't so inclined.

That was when he'd finally understood that Caitlin Beck might be a successful career woman with brains and ambition, but she had secrets he hadn't expected. As far as he was concerned, that wasn't fair. He'd always been involved with uncomplicated women before. Mostly they had been interested in one of two things: a good time or a good husband. He was still friends with most of the women in the first group and he'd managed to deflect those in the second group to a male acquaintance interested in the husband part.

It hadn't taken him long to realize that he'd made a bad mistake by rushing Caitlin; he should have wooed and coaxed her. He knew women needed time, finesse, romance. He knew that, but he'd rushed her, anyway.

When she had begun insisting she would buy out his half of their renovation project, he had actually been given a little hope. After all, she wouldn't be so insistent if she was apathetic toward him.

Still, he had been confused, so he had switched modes and begun treating her with the same teasing attitude he used with his sisters and his old girlfriends, but hell, that wasn't working, either. She had a breezy answer for every one of his teasing remarks. When she got home, she ducked into her apartment across the hall and he didn't see her unless he bullied his way in—which he had begun doing every night.

Maybe it was only his ego doing his thinking for him, but he couldn't help the feeling that the way she had pulled back and begun avoiding him didn't really involve him entirely. There was something else going on that he couldn't quite get a handle on. Lately he'd been thinking that there must be a man back in San Francisco she was still involved with.

Ego talking again, he thought ruefully—she had to be involved with someone else or she wouldn't be so reluctant to become involved with him. He was old enough to know that if a woman wasn't interested, she simply wasn't interested, but he didn't think that was it. After all, he'd seen the look in her eyes when he'd opened the door. She wasn't as immune to him as she pretended.

Still, he ought to be ashamed of the way he kept pushing himself into her life. His only excuse was that she was a puzzle that intrigued him.

He'd always been a sucker for puzzles.

Jed rolled his shoulders, trying to ease the tension there as he told himself to forget her for a little while. He was expected at his folks' house, along with the rest of the family, for their regular monthly dinner. If he didn't show up, his mother would arrive on his doorstep with concern and a quart of chicken soup.

A smile glimmered in his eyes as he thought about asking Caitlin to go with him, but she had resisted all his attempts to get her to meet his family. Besides, she was going to be busy in about forty-five minutes taking deliv-

ery on one of Gordie's cars, one of those for which good
old Gordie usually received as much as fifty thousand
dollars. He would love to know how the Chamber of
Commerce had talked Gordie into donating it.

If she was a normal red-blooded American girl—and
despite recent indications to the contrary, he knew she
was—Caitlin was going to love that car.

Jed paused as he was reaching for his car keys. He
recalled the look of uncomplicated delight in Caitlin's
eyes. She'd won a car and he'd been the first one she'd
told.

Running his hand over his chin, Jed considered how he
could use this situation to his advantage. She had no family here, or anywhere, as far as he could determine. Since
she was new in town, she had few friends yet. It would
look good if there was a cheering crowd around when she
took possession of her new set of wheels.

With a calculating grin, Jed reached for the phone.

WHAT DID ONE WEAR to accept delivery of a gift of a
classic car worth thousands of dollars? Caitlin wondered
as she stood surveying the contents of her closet. Slacks
were out. Her last clean pair was now spotted with muddy
water. A suit wouldn't work. Those were only for work,
and Jed had told her they made her look unapproachable
and as humorless as a tax collector with an ax to grind.

She would show him. Caitlin reached far back into her
closet and pulled out a dress of electric blue she'd bought
when Anna Danova had bet her that she didn't have the
nerve to wear it. Her friend had been right. It had hung
in her closet for nearly a year.

Holding it up and viewing it with a critical eye, Caitlin
realized that the dress wasn't anything fancy, but its fitted
waist and slim skirt weren't her usual style. Neither was

the V-neck that cried out for a glittering necklace. In fact, it was very nearly a party dress, and she almost always stuck to business attire.

She reached up, intending to put it back, but then muttered, "Oh, why not?" It wasn't every day that she won a new car, or anything else for that matter. She wasn't a risk taker. Caitlin thought about her night with Jed. Well, maybe she was an occasional risk taker.

Exasperated with her waffling, she pulled the dress on, figuring it would probably be a very long time before she had a better opportunity to wear it.

A few minutes later she was standing before the mirror checking her hair and makeup when she heard cars coming up the circular drive. She flew to the window, straining to see her new car through the gathering dusk. But her apartment was at the corner of the house and the window afforded only a glimpse of the driveway, so she couldn't see much except for a line of cars. How many people was Mr. Carrow bringing with him, anyway?

Too excited to wait for them to ring the doorbell and fearful they might trip over the piles of building materials in the entryway, Caitlin rushed from her apartment. She flew down the stairs so fast they barely had time to creak. She heard Jed's door open as she hurried, and knew that he was following. He was always around, giving her his advice and opinions, so why should she think tonight would be any different? This time, though, she was glad he would be there. She wanted to share this moment with someone.

When she reached the bottom of the stairs, she scrambled across the entryway, then stood for a second with her hand pressed to her stomach while she regained her breath. Finally she walked sedately to the door and opened it, aiming a warm but professional smile at the person who stood there.

Caitlin's smile sagged and she had to drop her gaze ten inches to make eye contact with her visitor. This wasn't Mr. Carrow. It was a girl of about eleven who had a mouthful of braces and an armload of accordion. As soon as she spied Caitlin, she grinned hugely, hitched up her instrument and swung into a loud, off-key rendition of "Roll out the Barrel."

The noise was teeth-gratingly awful.

Stunned, Caitlin stared down at the little girl who was running her fingers over the keyboard, only hitting about every third note correctly and compressing the squeeze box with cheerful enthusiasm. She was working so hard at her music that the tip of her tongue could be seen caught between her silver-lined front teeth.

Whoever this girl was, she looked so endearing that Caitlin didn't have the heart to follow her first inclination and clap her hands over her ears. The child broke her concentration for a second and looked up at Caitlin with another grin.

Caitlin's eyes narrowed. Where had she seen that grin before?

Its twin appeared over her right shoulder as Jed came up behind her and put his arm around her waist. "Hi, Jessie," he said to the little girl. "Sounds great. Those lessons are really paying off." He looked past her. "Where are your mom and dad?"

The girl broke off her playing in midsquawk. "Hi, Uncle Jed. Dad said I should bring this to provide the music for the party. He said everyone should get the pleasure of listening, not just him and mom."

Jed cleared his throat and Caitlin knew he was swallowing a laugh. "Your dad is all heart."

"He told me you'd say that." She nodded back over her shoulder. "Here they come. Mom needs help getting out of the car now." She gave Caitlin a frankly curious look. "Is this the lady who won the car?"

"Yes." Stepping from behind Caitlin, Jed urged her forward. "Caitlin Beck, this is my niece, Jessica Bishop. You'll meet the rest of my family in about two minutes."

Caitlin, always scrupulously polite, except perhaps with Jed, could only nod at the girl before her gaze dropped once again to her instrument. Taking that as her cue, Jessica whipped into another spirited number—"When the Saints Go Marching In." It didn't sound much better than the last song. Grinning, Jessie marched into the house.

This time Caitlin couldn't help wincing.

Jed looked down at her. "She's barely started lessons," he said by way of explanation.

"I thought so," she answered in a mild tone. "Uh, Jed? Why the accordion? It doesn't seem like something that would interest most girls her age."

"Jessie's not like most girls. She thinks it'll help build up her chest."

*"What?"*

"Seriously. She's afraid of being flat-chested, so she took up the accordion."

"You're making that up."

"It's the truth. She considered the tuba for a while, but I told her about a girl I used to date who played the trombone. It didn't work out, though. All that lung power she had built up made her hard to kiss. The suction was incredible."

"Jed! You didn't say that to your niece."

His eyes twinkled. "Hey, what kind of uncle would I be if I let her play an instrument that might ruin her future love life?"

Caitlin tried to sputter out an answer, but he distracted her by pointing to the front yard. "Here comes the rest of the crew."

Caitlin's eyes lifted and darted around the yard where cars were being parked every which way. People began pouring out of the vehicles and streaming toward her. Everyone seemed to be carrying plastic containers, trays or paper bags.

She finally found her voice. "Jed, why is your family...?" Finally her brain caught up with her ears and she recalled what Jessica had said. "Party?" she asked, turning to him. "Jessica mentioned a party. *What* party?"

"For you," he said. "It's not every day a friend of mine wins something like this, Cait, so I called all of them to come take a look. I knew you wouldn't mind."

"You take a great deal for granted, Bishop."

Unrepentant, he nodded. "It's one of my more endearing qualities. Besides," he added, "you're dressed for it. I've never seen you wear anything like this before." He reached up and ran the tip of his finger beneath the hem of her sleeve. "Nice."

Before his touch could build up any serious shivers in her, Jed moved past her to help a very pregnant woman who had paused at the bottom of the stairs. She seemed to be gathering her strength to make the climb. Jed hurried down and put his hand under her elbow. "Hi, Mary. How's it going?"

"I wish it would go," she sighed, leaning on his arm and resting a hand on her tummy. "If this pregnancy lasts much longer, these babies will be born big enough to play soccer."

He put his arm around her and gave her a sympathetic squeeze, then looked up at Caitlin. "This is my sister-in-law, Mary, and my brother, Steve."

Mary gasped out a hello and congratulations as she gave Caitlin a warm handshake and went inside in search of a place to sit down. Steve, who looked like a slightly older, but more serious version of Jed, followed with a couple of bottles of wine tucked under his arm and a cake balanced on one hand.

"Head on into the parlor," Jed called after them. "There's a chair for Mary and boxes for everyone else to sit on. We can set up sawhorses and planks for tables."

"The parlor?" Caitlin asked, aghast. "That place is a mess."

"Well, where do you suggest? Your apartment is too small and you've avoided coming into mine like you think I'm going to grab you and ravish you right there on the floor. Besides, Mary couldn't make it up those stairs. The doctor says it's twins."

More questions popped into Caitlin's mind, but she didn't have time to ask them because she was busy meeting Jed's mother, Laura, and his father, Dave, his sister, Hailey, her fiancé, Aaron, and his two uncles, Frank and Burton.

"I've got another sister, Diana, but she lives in Sacramento."

Caitlin, who was having her hand squeezed and her arm pumped by his uncle Burton, answered with a dazed nod. "Oh, well, that's too bad."

He laughed.

Everyone was carrying some type of food or drink. Jed's mother even had a tablecloth, a stack of paper plates and napkins, and bags of plastic dinnerware.

Caitlin couldn't remember the last time someone had done something so nice for her, and she didn't know what to say, but it looked as though she wouldn't need to say anything. Jed was pointing toward the driveway.

"Here comes Gordie with your car and his video crew. Hop on out there and I'll get my family to be your cheering section."

Moving at a trot, Jed ducked into the house while Caitlin whirled around to catch sight of her new vehicle. Her eyes strained in the fading light, but her breath stuck in her throat when she saw the beautiful two-tone car, white on top and candy-apple-red on the lower half. Majestically it made the sweeping turn to the front of the house. She was grateful to note that the driver was careful to avoid the potholes in the asphalt. She would hate to see the Bel-Air lose one of its wire wheel covers.

Eagerly she descended the steps as the car reached the front of the house, followed by a minivan that had a man with a video camera hanging out the window. He swung the camera around and pointed it directly at her, filming as she watched the classic Chevrolet come to a stop.

Caitlin fell hopelessly in love with this marvel of Detroit car-making ingenuity. Besides its perfect, shiny paint job and glistening wire wheel covers, she could see that the inside was elegantly upholstered in purest white.

Excitement bubbled through her as she rushed toward Gordon Carrow, who was stepping out, smiling at her. He was a short, wiry man in his fifties who wore a dark suit, a white shirt and a natty bow tie. He was holding the keys in his hand. As soon as she approached, he tossed them into the air jauntily and caught them with a snap.

"You must be Caitlin Beck," he said. "The Crystal Cove merchants are happy to present you with the prize in this year's Bonanza Giveaway." With a flourish of his wrist, he indicated the car.

"I'm happy to receive it," she gulped, and he smiled. As the video crew poured out of their van, he turned and gave them some instructions. At the same time, Jed's family came out of the house, congratulating her and exclaiming over her good fortune. The cameraman nearly tripped over himself as he filmed the Bishops' reactions.

Waving his arms and shouting instructions at the Bishops, Gordon Carrow organized them so that, the tape rolling all the while, they were clapping enthusiastically as he turned the keys over to Caitlin. She accepted with stammered thanks, and the Bishop family surged forward to get a better view of the car.

After asking permission of the dazed new owner, Jed's father, brother and uncles opened the hood to inspect the engine. The women gave it a cursory look, then leaned in the windows to examine the inside.

In the melee, Caitlin found herself pushed up against Jed, who put his arm around her protectively.

Gordon Carrow shouted, "We need something for a grand finale."

Jed growled, "It's a thirty-second commercial, Gordie, not a production of *Grease*."

Gordon wasn't listening. He wrinkled his brow and scratched his head, obviously deep in serious thought. "Something dramatic," he muttered. "Something that will make viewers of the *Midnight Movie* sit up and take notice—remember Carrow Classic Cars and Auto Restorers."

"Gordie, those viewers are mostly insomniacs. They're a captive audience. They won't care."

Gordon gave him an injured look.

"Oh, for Pete's sake," Jed said. He put his hands on Caitlin's shoulders and whirled her around. "How about this, Gordie?"

He bent Caitlin back over his arm theatrically and pressed his lips to hers.

"Perfect," Gordon squealed excitedly. "Roll the tape. Roll the tape!"

The tape rolled, Gordon Carrow shouted enthusiastically, the video crew whistled in appreciation, the entire Bishop family turned to watch, and Caitlin's world spun out of control.

All she could do was clutch at Jed's shoulders and hang on for the ride. And a wild one it was. It could have been a chaste kiss played up only for the camera. With Jed in charge, it became a slick, sensual meeting of breath, then mouths, then, when his tongue traced the seam made by her closed lips and they shuddered open, of tongues as well.

She should stop this, Caitlin thought hazily, even as she felt Jed's hands skim over her back, pulling her in closer. Her own hands shot up to circle his back where she could feel the muscles bunch and strain against her palms.

Oh, she didn't want this, she thought as she met him touch for touch. She didn't want to remember what it had been like, to remember how badly she had needed him and how wonderful it had felt to be taken by him.

Finally he raised his head, and even though it was almost full dark now, the light from the video camera still shone on him and she could see the glittering triumph reflected in his eyes.

Caitlin pushed at his shoulders and he swept her back to her feet as the light from the camera cut off.

Head spinning, she turned blindly to Gordon. "Please don't...don't use that," she said breathlessly, stumbling away from Jed.

"Nonsense," the spry little man said. "It'll make a great ending."

Caitlin gave him a furious look, then turned her ire on

Jed. "I have a professional image to maintain, Jed. What will my clients think when they see that?"

Jed shrugged. "Lucky, lucky girl?" he asked innocently.

"Oh, you're impossible."

"So I've been told. Listen, why don't we worry about this later? I'll bet Gordie's got some papers for you to sign, and you probably want to take your new car for a ride."

Since she was already the center of interest for the entire crowd, Caitlin decided to let the matter drop until they were alone. Besides, she *was* eager to take her new car for a drive.

Pointedly she turned away from him to finish her business with the car dealer. As soon as that was done, Gordon and the camera crew packed up and prepared to leave. Caitlin dashed upstairs for a jacket, then invited the Bishop women to accompany her on her maiden voyage.

As they drove away, Jed's mother leaned out the window and insisted that the men get the food ready while they were gone.

It took Caitlin a few minutes to get the feel of the car. It was so much bigger and more powerful than her little compact. After driving a few miles, she turned the car around carefully and drove back to the house. She dropped off the women and picked up the men, except for Jed who said he would wait. The Bishop men all looked as if they would love nothing more than to be behind the wheel of the car themselves, but they didn't ask, which Caitlin took as a sign that their manners were better than Jed's.

By the time she returned from the second trip, Caitlin felt more confident about handling the car, but she was still cautious.

She parked in front of the house and they all streamed inside to eat. Caitlin was impressed by the flexibility of the family. They didn't seem to mind serving themselves from a makeshift table consisting of boards perched on two sawhorses, sitting on top of boxes of floor tiles and eating from plates balanced on their laps.

They were genuinely nice people who were as pleased with her good fortune as she was. Caitlin found herself envying Jed his family.

It was quite late before everyone left, and Caitlin closed the door behind them with a happy smile. She turned from the entryway to find Jed right behind her.

"Got the keys to your new car?" he asked.

"Of course." She pulled them from the pocket of the jacket she'd left by the front door.

"Then it's my turn for a ride."

"Forget it, Bishop," she said automatically, slipping them back into the pocket and folding the jacket over her arm.

He walked toward her, hands outstretched innocently. "Hey, I'm not asking to drive."

"Yet," she added sardonically.

He stopped before her, tucked his hands into the back pockets of his jeans and bounced on his toes. "I'm not going to point out that you owe me."

"What for?"

"Inviting my family over so you'd have some friends around."

"Well, then, thanks Jed." There was no denying that she had genuinely enjoyed meeting them. "But I didn't realize you had invited them so you could blackmail me into getting a ride in my car."

His forehead creased in irritation. "Why do you insist

on putting the worst possible spin on everything I say and do?''

Shamed, she knew it was a defense mechanism. Maybe an unfair one. Glancing away, she cleared her throat. ''Sorry.''

''You're forgiven. Let's go.''

She could have put her foot down and told him no, but she knew that would be petty. She did manage to give him a pointed look and say, ''All right, but I'm driving.''

''Whatever you say, ma'am,'' Jed answered, hustling her out the door.

Caitlin tried to give Jed the same kind of cautious ride she had given his family members, but once they pulled onto the highway, he said, ''Honey, quit driving like a little old lady.''

''I'm not going to drive like you do!''

''You've got a V-8 engine in this thing powerful enough to blast you to the moon. Why don't you open her up and see what she can do?''

Caitlin gripped the wheel and gave him a sideways glance.

''Chicken?'' he taunted.

''Of course not,'' she answered. ''I simply don't see the need. That would be dangerous.''

''There's no one on this road,'' he said, cutting her off and spreading his hands wide to indicate the empty highway that stretched before them. It was one of the few straight sections on the coast. ''Do it for fun. Quit analyzing things for once and do it.''

Stung, she turned with a flounce and faced the road. She punched down on the accelerator, the classic car bucked, then took off with a deep-throated roar.

''That's more like it,'' Jed crowed in triumph. He settled back, propped his right arm in the window, stretched his left one along the back of the bench seat and relaxed.

Caitlin spared him a glance again and decided that with his black hair flying in the wind blasting in the open window and his triumphant grin stretched from ear to ear, he looked for all the world like the king of the road.

As they sped along, her initial caution gave way to a pure sense of thrill at the car's power. It was fun, for once, to put aside her usual prudence and be a bit reckless.

She laughed out loud, causing Jed to lean over and grip her shoulder in shared excitement.

"Come on, I bet she can do even better than this."

Recklessly encouraged, she pressed her foot down on the accelerator a bit more.

Heady with excitement, she laughed and glanced in the rearview mirror.

That was when she saw the flashing blue and yellow lights.

# 4

CAITLIN'S JOY DIED an instant death and her heart jumped into her throat, where it stuck like a giant gumball. Immediately her foot slammed onto the brake, and the car began coasting to a stop. It took longer for her to slow the massive vehicle than it ever had with her Nissan. She had a moment's panicked thought that the officer might think she was deliberately stalling. As she steered the car onto the shoulder of the road, she cast a fiery look at Jed.

"'An engine in this thing that could blast me to the moon? Open her up and see what she can do'?" she quoted furiously as she shut off the engine and fumbled for the emergency brake. "Well, now we know, don't we? She can get a ticket."

Jed looked behind them. "Hey, it doesn't have to be a ticket. You can probably get by with only a warning if you know how to talk your way out of this."

"Talk my way out of it?" she asked incredulously.

"Sure. You have to know how to do it right."

"And I'll bet you're going to tell me, too, aren't you? Save your breath. I don't need any more advice from you." She began searching through the jacket pocket where she'd put her wallet.

"Hey, it's probably Don Brentanski. He loves pretty women. All you have to do is smile at him the right way and he's putty in your hands."

Caitlin's eyes narrowed. "Are you suggesting I use *sex* to keep from getting a ticket?"

"Hell, no. I'm not saying you need to sleep with the guy. Just be nice to him."

"That's disgusting!" She stuck her nose in the air. "I will treat him with professional courtesy and I'm sure he'll treat me the same way."

Jed flicked his hands as if washing them of this situation. "All the same, it wouldn't hurt to take my advice. First of all, get out of the car slowly and carefully and walk back to meet him with your license and registration in your hand. Admit you made a mistake. Smile, apologize, tell him it's all my fault if you want to, and he'll go easy on you."

"The only mistake I made was listening to you in the first place!" she shot back as the patrol car came to a stop behind her. She glanced in her rearview mirror and saw that the officer was writing something. Her license-plate number, no doubt. She turned back to Jed as she jerked her thumb to indicate the patrolman. "I'm not going to jump out and go sashaying back there like I'm trying to flirt my way out of this."

Jed looked as if she'd injured him. "A little flirting never hurt."

"I'm going to forget you said that." She tossed her hair, then recalled it was now too short to toss. She ignored Jed as she planned how she was going to deal with this. She drummed her fingers on the steering wheel. "I've never been stopped for speeding before or for any other traffic violation. If I tell the patrolman that, I'm sure he'll understand."

"He might, but I know Brentanski. He'd like it a lot better if that information was delivered with a warm...smile."

Caitlin fumed as she waited for the officer to get out of his car and approach her. Why had she listened to Jed? Why did her common sense always seem to take a vacation when she was around him?

"Come on, what can it hurt?" Jed urged. "I admit I got you into this, so I'm simply trying to give you some advice to talk yourself out of it. Get out of the car, smile, be friendly, turn on the charm. Assuming you've got any," he added dryly.

Caitlin's eyes snapped at him, but she found herself actually considering it. After all, she'd never been in this situation before. He might know what he was talking about. If she didn't try this and ended up with a ticket for speeding, he would say she should have tried his method. Either way, she couldn't win.

Grabbing her wallet out of her jacket pocket, she reached for the door handle. "All right," she said. "But this better work."

"I guarantee it."

"Ha!"

Forgetting what Jed had said about moving slowly and carefully, Caitlin whirled out of the car, erupting onto the shoulder of the road as if she'd been catapulted from a slingshot. Her foot landed in a pothole, snapping the heel off her pump. She staggered a few steps, jerked her foot out of the shoe and looked down, astounded, at her stockinged toes. When she bent to pick up the shoe, she overbalanced and had to do a hopping dance to keep from falling face first.

"O-o-o-o-h!" she raged, grabbing the shoe and jamming it back on her foot. Disgusted, she kicked the broken heel aside.

"Miss, have you been drinking?" the officer asked as he approached.

Startled, Caitlin looked up to meet his stern gaze. She snapped to attention and tried to manufacture the serious demeanor of a Supreme Court justice. "No! Certainly not."

"How much alcohol have you consumed tonight?" he asked as he lifted his powerful flashlight and shone it in her face.

"None." Stunned, Caitlin blinked at him. Realizing he was serious, she beat down a spark of panic and said, "I swear, Officer. I haven't been drinking anything stronger than iced tea."

He swept his light over her blue dress. "Looks like you've been to a party."

Caitlin straightened her spine, wishing the low neckline could magically roll up to cover her throat. Hastily she began buttoning her jacket over her chest. Then, afraid she'd made herself appear guilty, she put her chin up in hopes of appearing assertive. "Well, I have, in a way, but—"

"But there was no drinking?" he scoffed.

"Well, there was, but I didn't drink."

He gave her a suspicious look. "I guess we'll find out when I give you the Breathalyzer test. Could I see your driver's license and car registration, please?"

"Of course. I'm perfectly willing to cooperate." Caitlin fumbled in her jacket. She dropped her wallet, swiped it up from the ground, only to drop it again. Muttering under her breath, she took a firm grip on it, removed her license and handed it over.

He took it, studied it, examined her face, studied the photo again. She repressed a hysterical laugh. She could see that his name was indeed Brentanski, and he had all the necessities for dealing with the criminal element—gun, mace, nightstick. He looked like a giant, a long, lean, tough arm of the law—and totally devoid of a sense of humor, not that she was tempted to start cracking jokes. And she certainly wasn't going to try Jed's suggestion and begin flirting!

Caitlin stood at attention and tried her best to look like a responsible citizen. Behind her, she heard the other car door open. She glanced up to see Jed. He gave her a sharp nod and a frown as he mouthed, "Smile," at her.

At least that was what she thought he said since she couldn't see him well in the strobelike brightness from the patrol car's bubble lights. She wrinkled her nose and stuck her tongue out at him exactly when Brentanski lifted his head. The officer gave her a startled look. She closed her mouth and looked up as if studying the stars.

"Hello, Brent," Jed said, clearing his throat. Caitlin knew he was trying to swallow a laugh. "Nice night, isn't it?"

Caitlin instantly decided that if he was laughing at her, she was going to strangle him when they got back in the car—if she wasn't on her way to jail by then.

The officer looked up. "That depends, Jed. It's not a good night for drinking and driving, if that's what you've been doing."

Jed leaned on the car and rested his forearms on the roof. He gave the other man an easy grin. "No, no, Brent. We'd never do that. Why, Miss Beck here hardly ever drinks alcohol. She's very careful about what she drinks."

Caitlin frowned at Jed and said through her teeth, "I'm sure Officer Brentanski isn't interested in that, Jed." If she didn't shut him up, he would probably blurt out that half a bottle of champagne, however, was enough to talk her into bed.

"Sure he is, Cait. The more responsible citizens we have in Crystal Cove, the easier his job will be." He turned back to the officer. "Miss Beck is new to Crystal Cove. She's opened her own business as an investment counselor. In fact, she helped your aunt, Emma Harbel, today. She's going to put her money in some mutual funds and annuities."

Caitlin stared. How had Jed known that? He circled the nose of the car to stand beside her. Again he mouthed, "smile," at her, then lifted his shoulder and winked at her, giving her the cue to flirt with Brent. She raised her hand and formed a fist, but he grasped it in his and held it between them.

"Oh, yeah?" Brent asked, pausing in his examination of Caitlin's license. "What kind of mutual funds and annuities?"

"Low risk, I assure you," Caitlin said hastily as she tried to work her fist out of Jed's grasp. Failing that, she elbowed him in the ribs. He bent over with a whoosh of breath. Satisfied that she'd hurt him, she managed to smile weakly as she spoke to the patrolman. "Your aunt's money will be completely safe."

Brentanski's palm rested on the handle of his gun. He had thick, dark eyebrows that formed a straight line over his eyes. When they drew together, Caitlin was reminded of an approaching thunderstorm. "That money better not be from Uncle Tip's life-insurance policy. She was supposed to let my wife have that to start up a mushroom-growing business. We were going to build sheds out back of our house."

Caitlin's smile collapsed. The money *had* been from Tip Harbel's insurance, but Caitlin wouldn't tell Brent that because of client confidentiality. All she could say was, "Oh?" but her crestfallen expression gave her away.

"Well, hell," the officer groused. "Thanks a lot. Now I'm going to have to go to the bank and get the money."

He fixed Caitlin with a malevolent glare. "Can I see your registration, please?"

Before she could answer, the other door of the patrol car opened and a man climbed out. "Okay if I join you, Brent?" he asked, sauntering forward.

*Heck yes,* Caitlin thought. *Let's make it a foursome. The more the merrier.* Maybe her good friend Jed would say something to make this newcomer think she was an ax murderer.

When Brentanski stepped back to speak to the man, she looked over at Jed. "Will you please shut up?" she hissed. "And let go of my hand."

"I was only trying to help," he answered in an insulted tone. "And I'm holding your hand so you won't deck me. Policemen don't like rude motorists."

"So far, you've *helped* him think I'm a drunk and a thief trying to do his wife out of her business, and I'm not being rude to *him,* you're—"

"Hello, Al," Jed said. His gaze flashed to Caitlin's angry face. "Caitlin Beck, this is Al Gresham, editor and publisher of the *Crystal Cove Clarion.*"

"Also chief reporter and photographer," the man said cheerfully.

Caitlin looked down and to her horror saw that the man carried a camera. She prayed he wouldn't decide to take her photograph and plaster it all over the weekly paper beneath a headline reading, Financial Adviser Picks up Hints on Local Traffic Laws.

"How do you do?" she asked in a sinking voice. Could this night get any worse? She'd gone from the peak of happiness to the gutter of indignity in only seconds, thanks to her own foolishness in listening to Jed. She gave her hand a sudden twist and managed to get it away from him.

"Your registration, Ms. Beck?" the officer prompted.

Holding her head high, she turned away and limped to the car, where she opened the glove compartment. It was empty, as clean as the windswept prairie. Her luck—if she believed in luck—seemed to be continuing its downward spiral. There was no registration form. Hadn't there been one in all those papers she'd signed for Gordon Carrow? She couldn't remember.

Swearing under her breath, she stood, manufactured a cheery smile and said brightly, "I could run it by your office in the morning, Officer Brentanski, because it doesn't appear to be here."

He seemed to swell indignantly, rocking up on his toes and tucking his tongue into his cheek as he considered her. "Where would it appear to be?" he asked. "You're aware, aren't you, that you're supposed to carry your registration in your vehicle at all times?"

"And I do. Oh, I do," she assured him as embarrassment broke over her in a tidal wave. "At least, I always carry it in my car, my old car. I mean, my other car," she babbled. "But you see, I only got this car a little while ago, and—"

"She got it off Gordie's lot," Jed supplied.

"Gordie's?" Brentanski's eyes narrowed as they swept over the classic car. "You two didn't take one of Gordie's cars, did you, for a little joyriding? Maybe a little necking in the woods?"

"Necking?" Jed hooted. "Brent, are you stuck in the sixties? We're not a couple of teenagers."

"You know what I mean," the officer said.

Caitlin rolled her eyes. "No, Officer Brentanski, we aren't doing anything illegal."

"Except riding around without the registration," Jed volunteered.

She gave him a look that shot daggers. "Stop *helping* me," she growled, then looked back at the patrolman with a falsely happy smile. "I won the Crystal Cove Merchants' Harvest Bonanza Grand Giveaway. The prize was this car. We were trying it out, but I'm afraid Mr. Carrow forgot to tell me where the registration is. Uh, maybe it's not in my name yet, but—"

"You won the car?" Al Gresham asked excitedly. He lifted his camera. "I've got to get a few shots of this. It'll make great copy for next Wednesday's paper. 'The winner of the car celebrates by getting a ticket.'"

Caitlin's heart stopped. She held up both hands. "No, please," she whimpered.

Jed looked at her and finally began to clue in to her distress. "Hey, Al, you don't want to do that."

Too late. Caitlin threw her hands out to stop what was about to happen, but the newspaperman began snapping pictures. She heard the shutter click at least six times.

"No," she said. "Don't. Please don't print that."

Jed started after Al, but the man skipped back to the patrol car, jumped inside and locked the doors. "Al, you always were a damned jerk," Jed said, rattling the door handle and pounding the flat of his hand against the window. Al held up the camera and grinned, which infuriated Jed even more.

While Jed was yelling at Al, the patrolman seemed to take pity on Caitlin. No doubt he was more concerned about the possibility of a homicide, so he gave her a speech about safe driving and always carrying her registration, then let her off with a warning, which she signed and accepted with shaking fingers. Fervently she promised to get the registration form right away and always keep it in the car.

Jed stalked back to her as Brentanski returned to the

patrol car and Al unlocked the door for him. Caitlin was grateful that the policeman seemed to have forgotten about the Breathalyzer test. No doubt Al would have wanted to photograph that, too. She was grateful when another car zoomed by, catching Brent's attention. The officer started the patrol car, switched off his blinking lights and followed the other vehicle.

"Are you all right?" Jed asked when they were alone.

Caitlin threw up her hands. "My whole professional life in Crystal Cove flashed before my eyes, but oh, yes, I'm just dandy. No thanks to you," she tacked on. Furiously she whipped around, forgetting about the pothole by her car door. She stumbled and snapped the heel off her other pump.

"Aaargh!" Bending down, she grabbed the heel and threw it across the highway, then took off both her shoes and sent them sailing, too.

"Aw, Caitlin, it's not that bad," Jed said, standing by her door.

She pushed him out of the way, jerked open the door and fell inside. The finger she pointed at him shook with rage. "You kissed me for an advertisement on the *Midnight Movie*. You twisted my arm to take you for a ride where you encouraged me to speed—"

"Oh, come on," he said, growing angry, too. "That was your decision."

"Yes, it was, fool that I am. I don't know why I ever listened to you. You almost got me a ticket, nearly got me having to take a Breathalyzer—"

"Hey, that wasn't my fault. You were the one who fell out of the car like a sailor after a three-day shore leave."

She was too furious to be deterred. Waving away his objections, she said, "You almost let them think I'd stolen this car, and then you couldn't keep your mouth shut so that Mr. Happy Snappy took my picture for the paper.''

''I tried to get it away from him,'' he pointed out.

''If you hadn't said anything, it wouldn't have been necessary.''

''Oh, for crying out loud, Cait, he was looking for something to photograph. That's why he was out with Brent tonight. That's why he had his camera in his hands. He would have taken your picture, anyway. Besides, everyone knows they never get anything right in that paper, and—''

''That's not the point!''

''Caitlin, you're not being logical.''

''Logic has no place here or I wouldn't be out on this highway with you!'' she yelled.

Jed must have realized he'd said the wrong thing because he held up his hands placatingly. ''All right, forget that. I don't understand why you're so mad about me kissing you in a TV advertisement and about your picture being taken for the paper.''

''Because I'm *trying* to build a professional reputation in this town.'' Her hands were still trembling, but she reached down and started the engine.

''A couple of incidents like this won't affect that.'' Jed stalked around the car and reached for the door handle. ''People know you're trustworthy. You're overreacting.''

That was too much. Caitlin hit the accelerator and the tires spat gravel as the car lurched ahead.

''Hey, Caitlin. Stop!'' Jed shouted. His hand was on the door handle. He held on to it as he sprinted to keep up.

''No!'' she hollered back, but she had to pause as she pulled off the shoulder and onto the roadway. When she did so, Jed slapped both hands down on the door frame and dove inside headfirst as she accelerated.

Jed landed with his head almost in her lap and his feet dangling out the window. He'd banged his elbow on the door frame, but at least he was inside the car. He looked up at Caitlin's face and decided instantly that he had never seen an angrier woman. Logic hadn't worked in trying to calm her down. Maybe he should try charm.

She glanced down at him and swiped an elbow at his head. He ducked away from her. "Sit up straight," she ordered. "With your feet hanging out like that, people will think I've got a dead body in here."

As they entered the Crystal Cove city limits, the streetlights illuminated her face. Jed examined the murderous look in her eyes as he sat up, rubbing his elbow. "They wouldn't be far wrong," he muttered.

She ignored him.

"Caitlin, you worry too much about what people will think," Jed goaded her.

"I have to, Jed, if I'm going to be successful."

"Your success doesn't depend on a couple of incidents like this. It's built day by day, like you've been doing since you moved here."

"A couple of incidents like this won't help."

Jed rubbed his hand across his face to see if the coldness in her tone had frost forming on his eyebrows. He opened his mouth to tell her to calm down, but then he snapped it shut. She *was* calm. Icily so, and it alarmed him. Icy indifference was the last thing he wanted from her. He tried again. "Caitlin, your clients or potential clients who see the TV advertisement or the picture in the paper will think you're a good sport."

She threw him another angry glance, but she didn't answer. He gave up trying to convince her.

They reached the house a few minutes later and Caitlin pulled to a stop. As they climbed out of the car, Jed decided it would be in his best interests to apologize. Though he'd only been trying to help, things had gone badly wrong—at least in her eyes.

He strolled around the front of the car as she carefully locked the doors and said, "Thanks for taking me for a ride, Caitlin. I'm sorry you got stopped."

She flicked a glance at him. "I'm sorry I listened to you. I think I'm the one who got taken for a ride."

"Oh, come on, Caitlin!" Jed exclaimed, losing his patience with her single-minded stubbornness. "You're overreacting. Sure some people will see the TV ad and—"

"And *everybody* will see the newspaper."

"But who's going to care?"

"Me!" Caitlin jabbed a thumb at her chest.

Jed balled his hands into fists and punched them down to his sides. "Why won't you listen to me? This isn't going to harm you professionally. The people who know you will be glad for your good fortune. Those who don't will be envious, but so what? Either way, it will mean free publicity."

"Not the kind I want!" Caitlin took a deep breath and clutched her hands together so hard her knuckles were white.

Jed shook his head, breathed a gusty sigh and muttered, "I should have wrestled that camera away from Al, the little twerp. Maybe I'll raise his rent."

Caitlin frowned at him. "Raise his rent?"

"I own the *Clarion* building."

Caitlin stared at him as an admittedly crazy thought formed in her head. "Jed," she said slowly, "if you own the building, that means you have a key."

"Sure," he shrugged. "Why?"

"Because if you've got a key you can get into the *Clarion* office."

"Why would I want to...?" He gaped at her. "You want me to break in and get those pictures?"

Caitlin nodded vigorously. "Don't you see that's the best solution?"

"It's breaking and entering!"

"Not if you've got the key."

"I've got the key, but I've also got a rental agreement in which I promise not to come into their offices unless it's an emergency."

"Well, what do you think this is?" she demanded.

"This is hardly a threat to life and limb."

Caitlin glared at him. "That shows how much you know," she said grimly. She looked down at his legs as if trying to decide which one to break first.

He gave her a wild look. "Aren't you the one who was worrying about risking your professional reputation? How would it look if we broke in and got caught?"

*"We?"*

"You don't think I'm going to do this *alone,* do you?"

"Does that mean you'll do it, then?" she asked eagerly, jumping on the part she wanted to hear.

Jed opened his mouth and she was sure he was going to refuse, but then his head tilted back and he assessed her with a calculating gleam in his eyes. "On a couple of conditions."

Warily she asked, "What conditions?"

"I'll let you know after we finish at the *Clarion* office."

"There you go with that 'we' again."

"That's one of the conditions. If I do this, you're coming with me."

She held up her hands. "Wait, wait, wait. I'm not going to agree unless I know what the other conditions are."

"You don't have any choice," he said smugly. "You need me to do this for you, so you have to do something for me. It's a one-time offer. Take it or leave it."

She really didn't like the way this was headed. She rubbed her knuckles across her forehead. "Oh, Jed—"

"Take it or leave it," he repeated. "And we'll shake on it." He stuck out his hand.

Reluctantly Caitlin looked at him, then down at his hand. This was a risk. She didn't like risks. Every one she'd taken with him had shaken her up. Still, the thought of her picture in the paper getting a speeding ticket was a risk, too. Maybe, as Jed had said, she was overreacting, but this was a small town, and she had to think of her image.

"Oh, quit looking like I'm trying to hand you a live grenade," Jed groused. "This is a straightforward business deal. I do something for you. You do something for me."

Her bottom lip thrust out as she thought it over. "Why do I have the feeling this isn't as cut and dried as you're making it sound?"

"Because for some reason I have yet to figure out, you've talked yourself into thinking I'm the bad guy."

"I never said you were."

"Oh, forget it," he said, dropping the hand he'd been holding out. "Trust me. I'm not going to do anything to hurt you."

Where had she heard that before? Caitlin wondered. Oh, yes. How could she have forgotten? He'd whispered those words to her when he'd taken her to bed. She had believed him then, been enthralled and touched by his tenderness. He hadn't hurt her. He'd treated her with all the care his words had promised.

Caitlin put a stop to those thoughts and could almost hear the brakes screeching in her brain. She was getting way off track. He was right. He hadn't done anything to hurt her then and he wouldn't now. He'd never pretended to be anything except what he was, an outgoing, friendly guy who made no promises. *She* was the one who'd made that night into something it wasn't.

Drawing a steadying breath, she reached out, grabbed his hand and gave it a quick, sharp shake. "It's a deal. Let's go." She whirled back toward her new car.

If he was surprised by her sudden capitulation, he didn't show it. Instead, he called out, "Wait, Caitlin. You need to change your clothes."

Ruefully she glanced down at the bare toes sticking through her shredded stockings. "Oh, yes, I may need shoes."

"Not only shoes. You need to change all your clothes. Do you have anything dark?"

"Dark?"

"We're breaking and entering, remember? We've got to be dressed right."

"Well, I have some black leggings and a sweatshirt," she said.

"Perfect. How about a black cap?"

"Maybe." She frowned at him. "Shall I see if I can find a stick of night camouflage makeup?"

"Have you got one?" he asked hopefully.

"No."

"Well, maybe we can smear some mud on our faces," he suggested.

"Are you kidding?"

"Wait and see. Let's go get changed." He shooed her

into the house, up the stairs and into her apartment. "Make it quick," he said, leaving her at her door.

As instructed, Caitlin scrambled into her leggings, sweatshirt and black sneakers. Because the outfit had no pockets, she hooked a fanny pack around her waist, then placed a small flashlight and her keys inside.

She wasn't sure why she had to go through all this simply to stroll into a building that Jed actually owned, but she had told herself she was going to trust him and she was anxious to keep those awful pictures of her from being published. As she dressed, excitement ran through her. She had never done anything like this before. When she met Jed in the hallway, she saw that he was dressed in a similar outfit, though his sweater was navy blue.

She gave it a close look. The hem sagged, the neck was too wide, there were several dropped stitches right in the center of his chest, and loose ends of yarn stuck out here and there. Besides these charming features, it was big enough for two people to crawl inside and have a picnic. "Nice sweater," she said, trying to keep the humor out of her voice. "Did it come with its own tent pole?"

"It is a little big," Jed admitted. "Suzy Briscoe knitted it for me." He stretched his arms out in front of him and put his wrists together. "If I keep the sleeves pushed up, you can't even tell that one sleeve is two inches longer than the other."

Caitlin dipped her chin so he couldn't see the laughter in her eyes. "Is this her first attempt at knitting?"

"Nah. I've got three more of these, but this is the only dark one." He gave her an innocent smile. "Suzy feels bad because she dumped me last year for Dan Welby."

"Are you sure you didn't dump her and this is her revenge?" Caitlin asked. Somehow she couldn't resist some gentle jabs at him and at Suzy's sweater, but she didn't understand the nip of jealousy she felt.

"You don't like it?"

"It's fine," she said. "Precisely what you need for a little breaking and entering." She grasped his arm and started for the stairs. "Let's go. What are you going to do, by the way?"

"I figure Brent's shift probably ended at ten. He would have dropped Al by the *Clarion* office and Al would have left the camera there and gone home."

"What makes you think Al didn't go home and take the camera with him?"

"Because he's an obsessive-compulsive little creep who likes everything in its place, including his camera."

"Sounds like you know him."

"We went to school together. He used to keep his pens and pencils in neat little rows in his desk," Jed said in disgust. "He charged daily rental to anyone who borrowed one from him, with an extra ten cents added if you chewed it, sharpened it too much or wore it down and *forgot* to sharpen it."

Caitlin squinted at him skeptically. "That can't be true."

"Why would I lie?" Jed asked. "I used to save his butt when the other guys beat up on him. I'm beginning to regret that."

Caitlin grinned. "So what's your plan for getting the film back?"

"We'll wait around outside the *Clarion* building to see if Al is coming back. If he doesn't, we'll know he's already been there. Then we'll go inside, get the camera and retrieve the film."

Her eyes widened. "That's it? Walk in the front door and get the film. That's your plan?"

He flashed his riverboat-gambler's grin. "Well, the back door actually, but yeah, that's pretty much the plan."

"I thought you said you didn't want to do this because we would be breaking and entering."

"We'll be in an office we have no right to be in. That's bad enough."

Caitlin skidded to a stop. "And for that, we needed dark clothing?"

"Not really," he answered, his grin growing wicked. "I wanted to see you in a pair of leggings." He glanced down at her slim legs. "Nice," he said appreciatively. "I've got a thing for leggings. Tights, too. Someone should have thought of shrink-wrapping women's legs years ago."

Caitlin gave him a sharp look. "I'd love to know what goes on inside your head."

He wiggled his eyebrows comically and leered at her. "Honey, I think you already know. Besides, you would have frozen in that dress, and..."

When his voice trailed off, Caitlin stopped on the stairs and turned around. "What?"

His glance darted around the stairway as he avoided her gaze. "I didn't like the way Brent and Al were looking at you."

Was that jealousy she heard? In spite of herself, she was delighted. "How were they looking at me?"

"Like you were a safe-deposit box and they had the only key."

With a laugh, Caitlin preceded him through the front door, then waited while he locked it. When she headed for her new car, he pulled her back. "We'll go in mine. If Al is around he might see yours and remember it because it's so noticeable."

Caitlin glanced at Jed's golden-yellow Mustang. "And yours isn't?"

"At least he hasn't seen it in the glare of rotating bubble lights." He slanted her a sheepish look. "Well, at least not recently. Maybe he won't remember who it belongs to."

Resisting the urge to remind him that it was probably the only car in town that had broken all known land-speed records, she climbed inside, fastened the seat belt and tightened it.

Amused, Jed watched her. "Don't cut off the circulation to your legs," he warned. "You might not be able to run if we need to make a quick getaway from the cops."

Caitlin braced herself as they took off like a cannon shot. "Then you'll have to carry me."

# 5

WITHIN MOMENTS, THEY WERE cruising through Crystal Cove. Jed turned into the parking lot behind the building that housed the *Clarion* and wedged the Mustang into the farthest corner, behind the Dumpster. "In case someone sees it from the street," he whispered, glancing around furtively. There were no lights on in the building. They waited for several minutes, but saw no one. Jed checked the glowing dial of his watch. "It's after ten. Al's probably already been here. Let's go get that film."

They exited the car quickly, but nearly dove back inside when they heard a rustling noise in the Dumpster, then relaxed with a sigh of relief as a cat appeared briefly on top, spied them and ducked back inside. Jed and Caitlin took a couple of deep breaths to steady their nerves.

"Probably one of Mrs. Zachary's cats," Jed whispered. "She's got about a hundred of them living with her in that house across the alley and they're all as mean as she is."

Caitlin nodded and pummeled her heart back down into place.

They scurried across the parking lot, gazes sweeping the area and the alley behind to make sure they were unobserved and no more cats were going to leap out at them. They had a few nervous moments when they reached the well-lit back door and Jed's key didn't seem to fit, but then it turned and they were inside. Jed quickly punched in the code for the alarm system, and they both gulped for oxygen.

"Now I know why I didn't want to do this," Caitlin said. "I don't have the nerve for it."

"Relax. All we have to do is see if Al brought the camera back, find out if the film is in it, take it and get out of here." He took a flashlight from his pocket, covered the beam with his fingers so that only a small amount of light came through, then carefully played the light around the back hallway.

"Piece of cake," Caitlin agreed, though she wasn't too sure. "Won't Al notice there's no film in the camera? And how do we know we'll get the right roll of film?"

"I doubt he'd have used more than one roll. There's not that much happening in Crystal Cove on a Friday night—which is why he was so hot to get your picture."

"How fortunate that I get to be the featured attraction on a slow news day."

Jed chuckled, then he pulled her close and spoke in her ear. "Get behind me," he urged, "and stay close."

"Is that really necessary?" she asked, fully aware that the brush of his breath against her ear was causing wildly erotic thoughts to blossom.

"Nah, I've just always wanted to say that."

She rolled her eyes, but did as he said, moving close behind him. Trust Jed Bishop to turn breaking and entering into a game. They moved down the hallway to a large room where a row of desks stood. Caitlin had been in here before when she'd placed an ad announcing the opening of her office, but she hadn't paid much attention to the layout. "Where's Al's office?"

Keeping her close behind him by reaching around and placing his hand at her waist, Jed used his other hand to shine a tiny beam of light around the room. "It used to be the one on the right, but it looks like they've rearranged things. We'll have to look around.''

Caitlin unzipped her fanny pack and pulled out her own small flashlight, then zipped it shut again. ''We'd better split up to search or we'll be here all night.''

''Okay. You go to the left. I'll go to the right. We're sure to find it.''

''Got it.'' Cautiously they moved away from each other. She knew it was silly, but without Jed's presence, her stomach felt jittery. Turning away to the left, she felt a tug on her fanny pack and reached down to adjust it. She headed for the first open door on the left, which loomed like a dark cavern. She'd only taken a few steps when she heard something topple over.

''Jed, what was that?''

''I didn't hear anything.''

Sure her overactive imagination was playing tricks on her, she frowned. They'd better find that film fast and get out of here before her imagination really went into overdrive. She took a few more steps and heard several more things fall.

''Jed, you can't tell me you didn't hear that.'' She swung her flashlight toward him. ''You knocked something over.''

''I did not,'' he insisted. ''I'm standing in the center of the room.''

''Well, be careful, anyway.''

They had each taken a few more steps when they heard more things hitting the floor. Caitlin spun around. Even more crashes and thumps. ''Jed! What are you *doing?*''

''Not a damned thing. What are *you* doing?'' He swung his flashlight around to her face.

Caitlin blinked when the narrow beam hit her in the

eyes. "I'm *trying* to find Al's office, but you keep knocking things over."

"*Me?* I haven't touched a thing."

"Well, stop it," she said, exasperated. He made a rude noise at her. They both turned away, heading in opposite directions. This time she heard the distinctive sound of a pencil holder hitting the floor, spraying its contents across the tile, then there was another muffled thump, and she was brought up short by something tugging on her fanny pack again. "What in the world...?" She reached for the fanny pack and pointed the flashlight at it. A long string of yarn extended from the zipper and off into the darkness. She followed it with the beam of her flashlight across the room, over three desks whose tops were a shambles, to the back of Jed's head.

"Hey," she said. "Look."

He whipped around, pulling the thread taut and sweeping the surface of another desk. A framed photograph clattered to the floor, followed by a lightweight tape dispenser. A top-heavy halogen lamp wobbled on the edge of the desk, and Jed made a lunge for it, scooting it back barely in time. Dumbfounded, he stared at her.

"It's your sweater," she said frantically. "A loose end on the back caught in the zipper of my fanny pack. It's unraveled and knocked over everything between us."

"Well, then, come here," Jed growled. He reached behind his back, snagged the thread and began reeling her in.

"Wait," she called out. "Let me unzip..." Too late. Jed's hard tug on the yarn pulled her across the floor, she hit the corner of a desk and sprawled across it, clearing the top with her outspread arms. Her elbow hit the corner of a computer monitor, and she had to scramble to grab it and keep it from toppling over the edge.

Jed was beside her in a second, helping her stand, pulling the loose yarn from the zipper. With a tangle of crumpled-up yarn and his flashlight in one hand and his other hand wrapped around her arm, he turned her so they could survey the damage. The area around them was a shambles. "Oh, great," he murmured. "We've got to clean this up."

"How will we know what goes where?" Caitlin asked, bending to grab a handful of items from the floor.

"We don't. We'll have to—" He spun around. "What was that?"

She shot to her feet when she heard the slam of a car door. "Someone's coming!"

They whirled toward the front windows. A patrol car could be seen pulling away from the curb. "It's Al," Jed said. "Brent's dropped him off."

"I thought you said—"

"How was I supposed to know the two of them would be late? They probably stopped off for coffee and doughnuts."

"Let's get out of here." Leaving behind the mess they'd made, they sprinted for the back of the building. "Do you think he'll know we've been here?" she asked.

"He'll know *somebody's* been here. And even Al's smart enough to think it was us." Jed shot back. "I've got a key, remember? And he knows we don't want those pictures published. He might figure out we were trying to get our hands on the film."

They whipped the back door open and tumbled out. A loud shriek had them jumping out of their skins. They both looked down at a squirming black-and-white ball of fur.

"Mrs. Zachary's cat," Caitlin said, nearly hyperventilating in her fright. His tail was caught under Jed's foot. He lashed around wildly. "Is he okay?"

Thinking fast, Jed bent down and scooped the animal up, grunting in pain when claws made contact with his unprotected hands. He examined the feline quickly. "Yeah. Spitting mad, but okay." He bent to put the cat down. "Let's get— Hey, I know what to do." Turning, he tossed the cat inside the back door, then closed it and locked it.

Caitlin gaped at him. "What did you do that for?"

"Al will think the cat got inside somehow and did all that damage and that one of his staff left the alarm off. We'll be in the clear." He grabbed Caitlin's arm and sprinted for the car. "But we'd be smart to get the hell out of here."

Caitlin didn't bother to respond. He was right, but they had failed in their mission. Her unflattering picture was going to appear in the paper. Still, that was better than lining up for a mug shot at the police station. She gripped Jed's hand and ran.

Jed and Caitlin didn't stop running until they reached the car. They crept out of the parking lot, with their lights off, coasted by the front windows, where they could see Al darting wildly around the brightly lit room. He was waving his arms, yelling and attempting an Irish jig.

"I guess he found the cat," Jed said in a mild tone.

Caitlin, high on adrenaline, answered with a wild giggle.

"I'm no expert at lipreading, but I never would have guessed Al knew so many four-letter words or that he knew how to dance like that," Jed said.

Once they were beyond the building, Jed flipped on the headlights, stepped on the gas and raced for home. He noticed that, for once, Caitlin didn't complain about the speed of his driving. She was as glad to get away from there as he was. When they reached home, they rushed in their front door and slammed it shut.

Still shivering from fright, Caitlin waited on the stairs while he locked the door behind them and then joined her.

"What do you think happened when Al got hold of that cat?" she asked, her golden-brown eyes sparkling wickedly.

With a grin, Jed placed his hand on the railing and nodded toward it. "Probably the same thing that happened to me."

Caitlin looked down and gasped at the raw, red scratches on his hands. One was deep enough to have drawn dots of blood along its length "Oh, Jed," she said, horrified. "Why didn't you say something?"

"What would have been the point? I don't have a first-aid kit in the car, and besides, I was busy making our getaway."

"Come into my apartment," she said, taking his arm and tugging upward with a gentle touch as if he'd suddenly become an invalid. "I've got some antiseptic cream we can put on the scratches. You don't think those will leave scars, do you?"

Jed almost said he could take care of the scratches himself, but then told himself not to be a fool. This was the first time Caitlin had shown such solicitous concern for him. He should milk it for all it was worth. He would need all the sympathy he could garner when he sprung the second half of their agreement on her.

"I guess we'll have to wait and see," he said in a long-suffering tone.

His lips pinched together as if he was stifling the pain. He'd seen Steve Martin do that in a movie, and it had worked up sympathy from the female lead pretty effectively.

Caitlin ushered him into her apartment, had him sit on the couch, then bustled around finding cotton balls, hydrogen peroxide and antiseptic cream. He sat back, enjoying himself, and decided he didn't mind this at all. When she bent over to lay the items out on the coffee table, he had a nice view of her sweetly rounded bottom. He would have given it a little pat if he hadn't known she'd turn around and belt him. It was pleasant to have a woman fussing over him, though he admitted he'd had more than his share of it in his life. Even though he was one of four, he'd been pampered. When he'd moved out on his own, he'd discovered there were plenty of women who liked doing things for him. That was okay, because he'd done things for them, too. He'd fixed their cars or their roofs, dragged their cats out of trees. Caitlin was the first woman he'd been with—short-lived though it had been—who didn't want him to do anything for her.

Funny, it hadn't occurred to him sooner to have *her* do something for *him*. She was a nurturing, caring person with all the little old ladies whose finances she handled. It was only him she kept at a distance, but he thought the experiences they'd shared tonight might go a ways toward changing that.

He held out his hands when she ordered him to and watched as her slim, efficient fingers dabbed hydrogen peroxide on the scratches.

His breath hissed in. "Ouch!"

She winced in sympathy and gave him a melting look. "I'm sorry. I didn't think it would sting so much."

He lifted his chin. "I'm strong. I can take it."

She giggled again as she dabbed on the antiseptic cream. It was a sound he'd never heard her make before tonight and he liked it. He never would have suspected she was a giggling kind of woman. "There," she said, capping the tube and laying it aside. "That should take care of it."

"Thanks," Jed said. He looked around. "I don't suppose you'd let me have a beer, would you?"

"Why not? You paid for them." She brought him one, then sat in the chair opposite him. That wasn't good. He wanted her nearby.

He was considering telling her that and working the sympathy angle when she looked up and said, "I really appreciate what you tried to do tonight, Jed. Getting the film back, I mean."

"Too bad we didn't succeed. I'll talk to Al again tomorrow and see what I can do, but this is Friday, and the paper goes to the printer tomorrow, so it may already be too late."

She grimaced. "I know."

"Listen, Cait—"

She held up her hand to stop him. "Don't tell me again that it won't affect my reputation in this town. I'm not ready to hear that." She frowned at the floor for a moment, then glanced up. "We had an agreement and I'm willing to honor it. What is it I'm supposed to do for you?"

Dread settled in Jed's stomach. He took a sip of his beer. "Well," he began slowly, "it's part of the Harvest Bonanza celebration...."

He let his voice trail off. It sounded so silly and he didn't know why he'd let himself get talked into it again this year. Caitlin nodded, her earnest face encouraging him to go on.

Jed gulped in a deep breath, expelled it, then took a sip of his beer as he mumbled something.

Caitlin leaned closer. "What did you say? A bachelor, what?"

"Auction," he mumbled again, swallowing more beer. He felt color climbing his cheeks in a blush. Gad, when was the last time he'd done that?

"You're kidding." She sat back and stared at him.

"Nope. They've done it every other year for ten years. I think it's way outlived its time, but the women in town seem to like it, and there's usually a few new bachelors in town who get roped into it."

"And this year, you're one of them?"

"Yeah. I've managed to duck it most years by being out of town, driving for Steve, but my mother threatened to disinherit me if I skipped it this year. The women's club puts it on and she's the current women's club president. They use the money to buy books for the school libraries."

"Oh, well, it's for a good cause, then," Caitlin said, sitting back and looking at him with teasing enjoyment in her eyes.

Jed frowned. "I'm not one of those who believes the old 'anything for a good cause' routine,' especially after what happened two years ago."

Caitlin sat forward eagerly. "Why? What happened?"

Steeling himself to face the memory, Jed said, "The Carlton twins bought me and my promised date of an evening on the town in San Francisco."

"That sounds like fun, but..." Caitlin paused, her gaze going inward for a second, then her eyes widened. "The Carlton twins. The two ladies who bring you jam."

"And crocheted booties."

"I think they're supposed to be slippers."

"With pom-poms on the toes?" Jed asked, horrified. "Baby-blue ones?"

"I've never seen you wear them," Caitlin pointed out, her sympathy lost in a wave of amusement.

"I don't. I use them to polish my car."

"And this all started with the bachelor auction two years ago?"

"Well, no. I'd been in the bachelor auction before and they'd bought me each time. It was sort of a tradition."

Caitlin thought about the other females who visited his apartment. "Didn't any *younger* women get to bet on you?"

"They tried, but Edith and Evelyn intimidated them into giving up by glaring at them. There may have been voodoo dolls involved, too, but I'm not sure." He winced. "Probably crocheted ones."

She tried to picture it and failed. "So you've been on more than one date with them?"

"Three. The first two weren't too bad, but the third was...bleak."

"That's too bad," she said sympathetically. "I understand that the bachelor auction must be a community-wide affair and all, but isn't it a little strange for them to want a date with you? I mean, they're a little old for you, aren't they?"

He nodded sorrowfully. "They don't look their age, what with the red hair color, blue eye shadow, gold spandex pants and sequins, but yeah, they're in their seventies."

In spite of her sympathy for him, Caitlin erupted into laughter. He gave her a disgruntled look. "You wouldn't have thought it was so funny if you'd been there. Edith, who is definitely the dominant twin, forgot her hearing aids, so I had to bellow at her all evening. When she doesn't have her hearing aids, she tends to shout, as well,

so everyone in the restaurant heard her yelling that she
had to have stewed prunes every day or she couldn't—''

"I get the picture," Caitlin said, holding up her hand
and laughing even harder.

"Well, good, because I didn't want to have to spell it
out. All that was bad enough, but then Evelyn's dentures
broke, the top plate split right down the middle, so she
couldn't eat anything. She took the thing out and waved
it around for all to see while Edith screamed at her to put
the damned thing back in her mouth."

"Oh, no!" Weak with laughter, Caitlin was sitting back
on the chair, holding her sides. "What ha...happened?"

"Well, the date ended early, real early, and we started
home. Evelyn sat up front with me on the way to the city,
and Edith was supposed to sit up front on the way home,
but Evelyn said she'd be carsick if she had to sit in the
back since she hadn't had any dinner."

"Because of the broken dentures."

"Right." Jed nodded and sipped his beer, trying not to
shudder at the memory. "So Edith refused and the two of
them got into an argument right there in the parking lot,
Edith saying Evelyn always got her own way because she
was older by ten minutes and Evelyn saying—" He broke
off. "Well, actually, I don't know what Evelyn was saying because I couldn't understand her."

"Because of the broken denture," Caitlin said again,
choking with laughter.

"Yeah. Anyway, we finally got home with both of
them sitting in the front bucket seat, jabbing each other
in the ribs, and I swore not to be part of that auction
again."

He watched as Caitlin sat up and fumbled for a tissue
in the box by her chair. She swiped tears from her eyes.
He had never seen her laugh so hard. Seeing her like this

caused a fist of desire to curl itself up and punch him right in the stomach. He set his beer down and licked his lips. He could imagine kissing that soft, giving mouth of hers. The one taste he'd had this evening, hours ago now, hadn't been nearly enough. He wondered if there was some way to maneuver her into another one.

"Jed, how do you get yourself into these things?"

"Luck of the draw." He shrugged.

"There's got to be more to it than that."

He should have known she wouldn't accept an easy answer. He took another swallow of beer, then rubbed his hand over his jaw. "You know I like to help people," he said finally.

"Oh, yes," she answered, lifting an eyebrow at him. Obviously she was recalling the incident with Brent and Al.

"It's kind of a lifelong thing. My sister Diana is diabetic, and since I'm a year older, I always kind of looked out for her. After she grew up and left home, I guess I expanded my helpfulness to other people."

"Whether they want it or not," she added dryly.

"Hey," he protested, "you'd be surprised how many people can't make plans and decisions on their own and want a little help and advice. Besides, it usually works out for the best—with a few minor adjustments."

Caitlin chuckled. "So, how did you let yourself get talked into this bachelor auction again if you swore not to?" she asked.

"My mom signed me up and then told me about it. I kept thinking I could get out of it, but so far, no deal. That's where you come in."

She gave him a cautious look. "Me?"

"Yeah, I want you to buy me."

"You do? Why?"

"Because then I'll know I'm being bought by someone who's at least relatively normal."

"Thanks a lot!"

"You know what I mean. Edith and Evelyn don't have any real romantic interest in me. It's only that they're so competitive with each other. They get tired of each other's company and they get lonely. Somehow they've convinced themselves that I'm bored and need their help. They don't want me to be lonely."

Caitlin's mouth dropped open. "*You?* Women march through your place like General Sherman's troops through the South."

Jed's eyes widened and he sat up straight, staring at her. What was this? he thought. His smile morphed into a knowing grin. "Oh, yeah?" he said. "You've been keeping track of my visitors?"

She lifted her chin. "Certainly not. I happened to notice. In a purely casual way, of course."

He chuckled. "Of course."

"Now go on with what you were saying," she instructed. "The Carltons think you're lonely..."

"And bored. They have a thing against being bored. They think it's a deadly disease, so they try to liven up my life."

"Sounds like they've succeeded."

"No kidding." Jed sat forward and gave her a pleading look. "Come on, Cait, you don't want to see me on another date from hell with the glitter twins, do you?" When she grinned, he said, "Don't answer that!"

Caitlin tilted her head and pursed her lips as she thought it over. He *really* wished she wouldn't do that. "Well, I do owe you for trying to get that film back."

"Good. I'll give you the money to buy me. Remember

you've got to outbid everybody and don't let any audience mutterings about respect for old age get to you."

"I understand. But Jed, you've got so many girlfriends, couldn't one of them...?"

"I've got lots of *friends* who are women, but most of them are involved with someone. Besides, you're the one who owes me a favor."

"I see," she said, then gave a long-suffering sigh. "All right. I'll do it, and I'll be stalwart no matter how many little old ladies threaten me with canes and false teeth."

"Hold that thought." Jed let his eyes drift partly shut and gave Caitlin a sly look from beneath his lashes. "You do understand, though, that you'll then be committed to an actual date with me?"

She blinked. Obviously that hadn't occurred to her. Slowly she put her hands on her hips. "I don't think so, Bishop."

He leaned forward and met her gaze. "I know so, Ms. Beck. After all, you're very concerned about your reputation. How would it look if you backed out of an agreement?"

Caitlin's mouth opened and closed a couple of times. He had her and they both knew it. Before he lost his advantage, Jed stood up and moved toward the door. "See you," he said.

Caitlin bounced out of her chair and dashed after him. "Wait a minute, Jed."

"Can't," he said, swinging open the door. "Gotta go."

She whirled in front of him and slammed it shut. "It's one thing to help you out, but—"

Since he didn't like the direction that statement was heading, Jed shut her up in the best way he knew how. He kissed her.

He meant for it to be casual, light, a teasing way to

head off her arguments. Instead, the instant their lips touched, it became sweet and tender. He wanted her, but if she knew how much, it would scare her off yet again, and he didn't want that to happen, so he tasted and tempted her, wooing her with the touch of his lips and tongue.

Caitlin's lips trembled open, accepting what he offered. Her hands clasped his upper arms as if she wanted to push him away, then they moved up and over his shoulders, blazing a heat trail in their wake. Jed made a low, growling sound in his throat and reached out to wrap his arms around her and hold her close as he tilted her head back to deepen the kiss.

Damn, he thought dizzily, damn, he'd missed this. One night with her hadn't been enough. A thousand might not be enough. This wasn't the way it was supposed to be, he thought hazily. He loved women, but liked things free and easy, loose, mutually satisfying and temporary. This didn't feel temporary. He pulled back and stared down into her eyes which had gone deep gold with desire. He'd done that to her, he thought with a wild moment of triumph. He'd made her feel that level of passion. The look in her eyes almost caused him to drag her back to finish what he'd started, but somehow better sense prevailed. He carefully set her away from him, then moved her from where she blocked the door.

"Good night, Cait," he said. "Remember our agreement."

She nodded as if her head was attached to a spring, then her face clouded. "Agreement?"

Before she could remember, and before that dazed, sexy look on her face got to him, he scooted out the door and across the hall.

JED ARRIVED AT Caitlin's office the next morning carrying coffee and doughnuts. He set them on her desk as she turned away from her computer and greeted him with a surprised look. He twirled a straight-backed chair around and pulled it up to the edge of the desk, then sat, straddling it backward.

"It's Saturday, Caitlin," he said. "Why are you working?"

Caitlin removed her reading glasses, laid them on the desk, then took a deep breath. The morning was cool and, along with the coffee aroma, he'd brought the scent of fresh ocean air in with him.

*Easy, girl,* Caitlin thought as her heart fluttered. She had relived his kisses a hundred times last night, had dreamed about him all night and here he was in the flesh.

She'd thought she could escape by coming to work, but he'd followed her. She felt her heart soften. How lucky could a girl get? "I have a few things to do," she said.

"You work too hard."

"That's what Eunice tells me." Eunice Grandy came in several hours a week to help Caitlin out with secretarial duties. She was a whiz at keeping the office organized, and Caitlin planned to hire her full-time as soon as she could afford it.

"I've been to the *Clarion* office," he announced.

"Have you?" Caitlin picked up a doughnut and took a delicate bite.

"Lots of talk over there about a mysterious cat that somehow got inside and wrecked the place."

"No!"

He pulled his face into a long, serious frown. "It's true. Al found the cat still inside the office last night. It was quite a battle to get it outside again."

Caitlin sipped her coffee, though she thought she might

choke on rising laughter, and viewed him over the rim of the paper cup. "Who won the battle?"

"From the scratches on Al's face, I'd say the cat won."

"Oh?"

"Yeah. Al said the cat stood about two feet high and weighed fifty pounds."

"Hefty cat."

"Or an average-size bobcat."

"Are they native to this area?"

"This is the first I've heard of one," Jed said, grinning, delighting in their shared secret. "Poor Al had to use a whip and a chair to get the monster out the door."

"Brave man."

The two of them looked at each other and burst out laughing. It took them several minutes to calm down. Finally Caitlin drew in a shaky breath and said, "What about the photos?"

"He won't budge, says the public has a right to see them, that the car you won is part of a community-wide project, blah, blah, blah."

Grimacing, Caitlin tried to stem her disappointment. "That's pretty much what he told me when I phoned him myself." No doubt the pictures would be as bad as she feared.

Jed studied her face for several seconds as he sipped his coffee. "I'm sorry," he said, startling her into looking up and meeting his eyes. The laughter they had shared was fading. "I didn't realize how much this would upset you," he went on. "Or at least, when you told me, I didn't understand."

She was so astonished she didn't know quite what to say. She stumbled around for a reply. "Oh, I see..."

"And I thought this might be a good time to talk about our partnership."

Her eyes grew wary. "What about it?"

"If you'll agree to stop trying to dissolve our partnership over the house, we can get the renovators back to work on the place. All this wrangling between us is taking up time we can't afford. Besides, now that winter is coming, we'll be having a lot of bad weather, which will delay the work even more, especially on the roof."

That sounded reasonable, though she wasn't ready to admit it. Her demand that they dissolve their partnership had been a knee-jerk reaction on her part. A reaction against the commitment she felt she'd made when she'd slept with him. She had wanted to distance herself from him, to keep from being one of the former lovers he'd turned into a friend who baked cookies for him or knitted him sweaters. It had been an immature reaction. She could see that now, and while she still wanted to be cautious, she also owed him for what he'd tried to do for her last night.

"Then what will happen when the work is done?" she asked.

He sat back and spread his hands as if he was the most easygoing and reasonable of men. "Then we'll sell the house at a tidy profit, dissolve the partnership and walk away with a nice chunk of change in our pockets."

She considered it for several seconds. "That sounds easy," she said.

"It will be easy," he said. "Then you agree to it?"

In spite of what she'd been telling herself, she was still reluctant. It meant living right across the hall from him for several more months yet. She had to be realistic and ask herself if she could resist the temptation he offered. She looked at his tousled black hair, the sexy slant of his gray eyes, the fullness of his lower lip that could kiss so devastatingly. She admired the casual way he sat with his wide shoulders at ease, his arms folded along the back of his chair, his legs splayed. Heat hopscotched up her spine. She could handle the temptation he offered.

And pigs could fly.

Jed sat forward, leaning over her desk to look into her face. "Cait, do you agree?"

"Sure." Her voice had shot up as if she'd been pinched. She cleared her throat, took another sip of coffee and repeated, "Sure."

He gave her a puzzled look and rubbed his chin. She recalled how it had felt to have that smooth jaw moving over her skin. *Focus, girl,* she told herself. *Focus.*

"All right then," Jed responded. "I'll call Appletree Construction and tell Terry Appletree to get back to work on the house. Also, I'll get Barney Mellin to tear down the old garage. There should be enough usable lumber left over for him to build a carport for your car. Maybe one for mine, too."

Pleasure flushed through her. Her hand lifted to her heart. "Why, Jed, thank you. That's so thoughtful. I don't know what to say."

"Don't say anything. From now on we'll be true partners and things will run as slick as greased glass," he said with a grin.

"That's...that's wonderful," she stammered. At last things were going to be resolved. This was what she had been wanting for weeks. Wasn't it?

He stood up quickly as if afraid she would change her mind, then grabbed his coffee and another doughnut. "I'll see you later, Caitlin. Like I said, I'll make those calls right away, then I'm going to be out of town for a couple of days. I promised Steve I'd drive a truck down to San Diego for him. Be back Monday night. Don't forget Friday is the bachelor auction."

She'd almost forgotten about that. Before she could say anything, he pointed a finger at her. "Don't try to get out of it. A promise is a promise. A deal is a deal."

"A sucker is a sucker," she responded.

With a wink and a wave, he was out the door. Caitlin turned back to work and tried to concentrate on the rows of numbers that came up on her screen. She was going to focus on work, not on how very much she was going to miss him.

# 6

"OF COURSE I'M NOT SAYIN' Mabel's wrong to be mad at me about this. I mean we were still teenagers when we got married. How was she supposed to know I'd turn out to be so devastatingly attractive to women?" Terry Appletree finished laying out the squares of counter tiles, then gave Caitlin an aggrieved look as he picked up his tile cutter.

"She couldn't have known, Terry. It's a burden that both of you will have to bear and share together," Caitlin answered sympathetically, pinching her lips to keep from smiling.

As promised, Jed had called both Terry and Barney Mellin to resume renovations on Monday. She had stopped by after work to see how Terry was coming with the kitchen. She was pleased to see that he had already installed the new stainless-steel sink and had begun laying the ceramic tile. She'd barely said hello before he'd begun telling her about the troubles he was having with his wife's jealousy. "The important thing is to never give her any reason to doubt you," she counseled.

He sighed and nodded his head. "You're right, but I can't help it if women look at me and find me attractive."

Caitlin made a sympathetic noise but didn't say what she was thinking—that attractiveness was in the eye of the beholder. Terry was a big man who wore slouching jeans that rode low on his hips directly under his Santa

Claus belly. He hitched them up frequently, but they always headed south again within a few seconds. He had shaggy blond hair that curled around his face, and a beatific smile that gave him a cherubic appearance. It wasn't a deceptive appearance. He wasn't very bright, but he was good-natured. He also seemed to have an unshakable belief that women lusted after him, though she'd honestly never seen any indication that he encouraged it or that this problem actually existed.

Caitlin sympathized with him because he seemed so genuinely aggrieved by this, and because he didn't use this belief to flirt with her or hit on her. Why should he? In his mind, he had enough women hungering for him already.

While Terry was working in the house, Barney Mellin, thankfully sober, was busy tearing down the old garage and sorting the wood to build a carport. Caitlin was anxious to use it for her new car. She had already found a buyer for her old one, the teenage grandson of a client. The boy wanted to fix it up. Caitlin figured the poor kid should finish that chore by the time he was a grandfather himself.

She'd been thrilled to drive her new car into town that morning, with a quick stop by Carrow Classic Cars to pick up the registration form so she could get the title changed into her name. Many people had congratulated her on her good fortune that day. She only hoped their smiles didn't turn to mocking laughter when the *Clarion* hit the stands on Wednesday.

She knew Jed was probably right—she was worrying about it too much. Of course, he didn't know she had good reason for wanting to avoid negative publicity. He knew much less about her than she knew about him. A fact he'd pointed out many times when she'd ducked his questions.

"I'll leave you alone and let you work, Terry. Call out if you need anything," Caitlin said.

"Sure thing, Ms. Beck. Hey, Jed told me you've been having trouble with your doorknob, so I took it apart and oiled it. Barney said he'd fixed it already, but he lied. Should be okay now."

"Why, thank you, Terry," she said, pleased that the problem was solved and that Jed had been so thoughtful.

He nodded his acknowledgment and switched on the radio he kept with him. As she left the room, the sounds of some new alternative rock group filled the lower floor. She was starting up the staircase when she felt a rush of cool air and turned to see two women at the open doorway.

"Hold the door," one of them said.

"*You* hold the door," the other responded. "I've got my hands full."

"And I don't?" The second one tried to elbow her way past with the result that they both got wedged in the doorway. The Carlton twins, dressed exactly alike from the hot-pink caps on their heads of flaming orange hair to their yellow spandex slacks and slick black leather boots.

Each of them held a casserole dish in her hands and had her elbows stuck out. After several jabs at each other's ribs and much jostling, wriggling and grunting, they stumbled inside.

Even if she hadn't seen them before, Caitlin would have known these were the Carlton twins by the proficiency they showed with their elbows. They stopped inside the door to exchange furious looks.

Deciding she'd better intervene before they started

throwing the casserole dishes at each other, she asked, "May I help you?"

They stopped glaring at each other and glanced up, noticing her for the first time.

"Who are you?" one of them asked.

She walked forward, smiling, to meet them in the center of the entryway. "I'm Caitlin Beck."

The two ladies exchanged a look that seemed to say, "Oh yeah?" Caitlin had seen them come to visit Jed before, but they obviously hadn't seen her. The first one drew herself up to her full five feet and gave Caitlin a stern look. "I'm Edith Carlton and this is my sister, Evelyn. We've come to see Jed Bishop."

"I'm afraid he isn't here."

"Oh? And exactly where would he be?" Evelyn asked suspiciously, shoving Edith aside so she could command Caitlin's attention.

"He's driving a truck for his brother, Steve, to San Diego. He'll probably be home tomorrow night."

"Uh-*huh*," Evelyn said, giving Caitlin a speculative look.

"I *see*," Edith chimed in. Her gaze roamed over Caitlin's russet-colored suit and matching pumps. She began to move around Caitlin in a clockwise motion, examining everything from her shiny cap of hair to her subtle gold-stud earrings. Evelyn began moving in the opposite direction, making the same survey, her casserole dish held high and away from what she obviously feared were Caitlin's prying eyes. The two women stopped before her and stood side by side, the shoulders of their identical electric blue baseball jackets brushing against each other. From beneath the brims of their pink caps, their orange bangs erupted right over their suspicious blue eyes.

"And how come you know so much about his where-abouts?" Edith asked.

"I live here, and—"

"What?" The two women straightened as if someone had jabbed them with a hot poker. They exchanged censoring looks. "You live here. With Jed?"

"Well, not—"

"What kind of young woman are you, anyway?"

Caitlin's mouth dropped open. "Excuse me?"

"Does his family know about you?" Evelyn asked.

Caitlin looked from one to the other of them. They were examining her as if she was a particularly unpleasant variety of pond scum. "Know what about me?"

Edith pinched her lips together and leaned forward. In a fierce whisper she said, "That you live with him?"

"I don't live *with* him," Caitlin said in exasperation. "I live across the hall from him in the other upstairs apartment."

"Uh-*huh*," said Evelyn again.

"I *see*," repeated Edith.

The two of them shared a look that all but screamed, *A likely story.*

"Good grief," said Caitlin in a faint voice. There was no way that she was going to convince them. Edith looked at Evelyn, who nodded knowingly.

"Well, sister," Evelyn said. "I guess we'll have to see about this."

"Yes, indeed, we will. Jed deserves better." As one, they turned and headed for the door.

Better?

"Wait," Caitlin called out, scrambling after them.

They stopped and turned. "Yes?" Their faces were grim.

"What exactly do you think is wrong with me?" Caitlin asked, lifting her hands, palms out. Did they see her as a tramp, a loose woman—what? Older people had different values. Could they be horrified because she and Jed lived so close to each other? That hardly seemed creditable, but who knew?

Edith gave her a look straight out of the deep freezer. "You *look* ordinary," she announced in ringing tones that equated the word with an infestation of head lice. Turning, she swept through the door. Or would have, if her sister hadn't been in the way. Again there was a short tussle as they once again tried to get through the opening at the same time, but then, they popped through, and the door closed behind them.

A full two minutes later, Caitlin managed to crank her jaw up where it belonged and shut her mouth. "Ordinary?" she said. "Ordinary?"

That was bad?

She thought about the outfits they wore and glanced down at her own unadorned suit. Well, maybe it was to them. What business was it of theirs, anyway? It wasn't as if she and Jed were involved. Engaged. Married.

Insulted, Caitlin turned to the stairs and stomped up to her apartment. This was war, she decided. Poor Jed, putting up with those two busybodies all these years. He deserved a break from them.

And as for herself, Caitlin thought, she might be a lot of things, but she wasn't *ordinary!*

"I DON'T REALLY THINK they see my nephew in romantic terms," Geneva Bishop said. "At least I hope not."

Caitlin wasn't so sure. Geneva had called her as she usually did as soon as Caitlin opened her door on Tuesday morning. As she sipped her coffee and looked at the *Wall*

*Street Journal,* she'd told Geneva about the upcoming bachelor auction and the visit from the Carlton twins.

"Then what is it?" she asked.

"I think they feel proprietary toward him. Since I'm not there, they think they need to watch out for him."

"He's thirty years old and he's got oodles of family around here who could watch out for him," Caitlin said.

"Yes, but you see, they're incurably nosy and they think Jed should live an exciting life. They think everyone should, but for some reason, they've fixated on him. They think he's going to settle into being boring."

Or settle for someone ordinary, Caitlin thought, still miffed. "Jed could never be boring," she said.

"They're crazy," Geneva said flatly. "This could get tricky at the bachelor auction."

"No kidding."

"I'll have to give this some thought. Maybe I can come up with a suggestion to help you out. In the meantime, we have financial matters to discuss." She launched into a series of questions and comments that had Caitlin scrambling for answers.

Fifteen minutes later, Caitlin hung up, forgot about the Carlton twins and spent the rest of the day happily engaged in writing up various investment plans to propose to another of Geneva's friends. When Eunice arrived, they prepared a mailing for potential clients from a list Caitlin had acquired from the Chamber of Commerce. By the time five o'clock arrived, Caitlin was pleasantly tired and satisfied with the day's work. She had received a call from Jed's mother, who wanted her to speak to the women's club about investments. Caitlin had accepted eagerly and anticipated an increase in her clientele afterward.

Before leaving for the day, Caitlin gathered up her purse, briefcase and jacket and laid them on her desk, then went into the small washroom at the back of her office. When she came out, she was startled to see Reenie Starr sitting in the chair opposite her desk.

"Mrs. Starr!" Caitlin exclaimed, hurrying forward. "Hello."

Reenie looked up with a vague smile. "Hello, my dear. Isn't it a lovely day?"

Caitlin looked outside. Clouds were filling up the horizon. Rain had been forecast. "Um, yes," she said.

Seeing Caitlin's puzzled look, Reenie turned and glanced out the window. "Well, when did that happen?" she asked, shaking her head. She rapped her knuckles against her forehead. "You must think I've got a few cracked eggs."

Caitlin smiled. "Oh, no, Mrs. Starr."

Reenie's face pinched. "Oh, yes, you do, but you're wrong. I simply forget things sometimes. Just like you're forgetting to call me Reenie."

Caitlin settled herself on the corner of her desk. "We all do. In fact, I was so surprised to see you I forgot to tell you about my good fortune."

"Your car," Reenie said. "I heard about that. So the penny brought you luck?"

Caitlin opened her mouth to remind Reenie that the "penny" had actually been a flattened bottle cap and she wasn't so sure that was what had brought her the car, but she'd already hurt Reenie's feelings, so she said, "Yes, ma'am, and thank you."

Reenie's eyes narrowed shrewdly. "You don't sound like you mean that."

Caitlin answered with a weak shrug.

"I thought not," Reenie said with a sniff. She reached into the pocket of her black raincoat and pulled out something that dangled from a key chain. She handed this to Caitlin.

Caitlin stared at the basinlike object with the wooden water tank for several seconds before it made sense to her. "An old-fashioned toilet?" she asked.

Reenie's face turned pink with pleasure. "Actually we used to call them water closets. My late husband was a plumber, you know."

"No, I didn't know that," Caitlin said in a faint voice. "How...nice."

"I tried to find a rabbit's foot key chain for you, because it's a time-honored symbol of good luck—though probably not to the poor rabbit who used to own it," she added sadly. "But I couldn't find one, so I got you that, instead. It will bring you good luck and teach you another good lesson. As the penny did."

Caitlin wasn't quite sure why she was being the recipient of all these lessons in good fortune. She really couldn't think of what lesson she'd learned last Friday night, unless it was one on how to win a car, nearly get arrested for drunk driving, participate in breaking and entering, agree to buy Jed in a bachelor auction and almost end up making love to him all in one evening.

In other words, the Jed-Bishop-could-talk-her-into-anything lesson.

She eyed the key chain warily. She wasn't sure she was ready for another evening like that one.

Reenie stood suddenly. "It's time for me to go," she announced.

Caitlin scooted off her desk. "I was about to leave myself. Please let me drive you."

"No thank you, dear," Reenie said breezily. "I can manage."

"But it's going to rain."

Reenie turned and gave her a stern look. "I can manage," she repeated firmly. "Rain won't hurt me."

Caitlin subsided reluctantly. Managing on her own seemed to be very important to her new friend. "Well, okay."

With a satisfied nod, Reenie left the office. Caitlin took another look at her newest good-luck charm, laughed softly and quickly stuffed it into her purse. She turned off the lights and locked the door. Outside, she made a quick scan of the sidewalk. Reenie had disappeared.

"For a little old lady, she sure can hustle," Caitlin murmured. "Maybe she is some kind of spirit."

Thunder rumbled and rain began to spatter the ground. Caitlin cast another concerned look along the street, then climbed into her car and headed home.

THE STORM PICKED UP WATER and wind as it met the flow of air moving in from the Pacific, buffeting the old house. Caitlin was awakened from a fitful sleep by banging noises. Thinking it was another loose shutter, she turned over and put the pillow over her head when she heard her name called.

"Caitlin! Wake up. I'm drowning," Jed shouted from the hallway.

Startled into wakefulness, she bounded out of bed and stumbled from her room, fleeing toward his voice without thinking to turn on the light. She had heard him arrive home a little while before she'd gone to bed, but he hadn't been over to see her. Even though she wanted to tell him about the visit from Edith and Evelyn, she knew he was tired. She had told herself she wasn't disappointed she hadn't seen him.

"I'm coming," she yelled. "Hold on." She banged her knee into the edge of a table. "Oomph," she grunted as she careened against the corner of the sofa and tripped over the rug, finally half-falling against the door with a thud. "Ouch," she yelped as pain shot from her shoulder and knee.

"Cait, what's wrong? Are you okay?" he called through the door.

Fully awake now, she hit the switch for the overhead light. Wincing at its brightness, she tried to rub her knee and shoulder as she worked the locks on the door.

"Caitlin, answer me!"

"No, I'm not okay." She flung open the door and blinked at him. "What do you want?"

He stood barefoot in the drafty hallway wearing a white T-shirt with a stretched-out neck and baggy gray sweat-pants. His black hair fell over his forehead in a tumble. A blanket and pillow were clutched to his chest. "I need a place to sleep," he said, giving her a forlorn look.

Caitlin frowned at him. "Try your bed," she suggested, and started to close the door on him.

Jed's hand shot out to keep it open. "I can't. It's wet."

"You wet the bed?"

He muffled a laugh. "*I* didn't, smart mouth. I forgot and left the window open while I was gone. The rain came in and soaked it. I'd sleep on the couch, but it's too short for me."

"Bend your knees," she suggested, and again tried to close the door. Jed was too quick for her. He simply pushed the door wide open, gathered her close and frog-stepped her backward into the apartment.

"Come on, Caitlin, have a heart. I've driven all the way from San Diego today. I gotta get some sleep." In the middle of this tale of woe, his gaze focused and roamed over her. "By the way, I like the spiked-hair look. It's sexy. Cute pj's, too. Did they come with bunny feet in them?"

Immediately shivers swept over her. To her alarm, her nipples peaked and pushed against the soft waffle-knit cotton of her pajamas. They *were* cute pajamas, and her favorites, long-sleeved and covered with tiny yellow rosebuds. To cover her reaction, she hunched her shoulders and crossed her arms at her waist. She gave him a disgruntled look. "My sofa is even shorter than yours," she said.

"Yeah, but it folds out into a bed."

"A very short one."

"And you've got that big ottoman I can put at the end for my feet." He was already hotfooting it toward the sofa and gathering up the pillows and cushions. "It'll be perfect."

"Well, 'perfect' is probably overstating it," she said grumpily, but she didn't insist that he leave. "I should throw you out."

He glanced up with a grin, looking rumpled and sexy himself with his sweatpants riding low on his hips and his clean white T-shirt a contrast to his tanned skin. His smile was pleased and more than a little smug. "The fact that you aren't proves that your good judgment is—"

"On vacation." Her toes curled against the cold floor and she shivered again. "Someplace warm, no doubt."

"Still working strong, even when you're awakened at midnight," he finished, ignoring her interruption.

"Humph," she said, but in the bright light of the apartment she could see that his face was lined with exhaustion. He did need sleep and she was being petty to deny him a place on her couch. Really, the only reason she was reluctant was that the sight of him had her thinking lustful thoughts, which were making her weak in the knees.

Mentally she gave herself a thump on the back of the head. *Be strong, girl,* she thought. *You can take it.*

Turning, she strode briskly to the linen closet in her bedroom and returned with some sheets and another blanket. As he made his bed and scooted the ottoman to the end, she stood back and watched. He was really very efficient. She recalled how impressed she'd been with the cleanliness of his apartment the night they'd slept— *Never mind.*

"What's been going on around here while I've been gone?" he asked as he tucked in the sheet.

Caitlin told him about the work Terry and Barney had been doing and about the strange encounter with the Carlton twins—though she left out their statement that she was ordinary. That still stung.

He winced. "Maybe I shouldn't have asked you to help me out. This bachelor auction could get ugly."

"I grew up in a tough neighborhood," she said absently. "I can handle it."

He tossed the pillow onto the bed and turned to her. "A tough neighborhood?"

Before he could ask her any more about that, she said, "Besides, I've got a new good-luck charm. Mrs. Starr came by today and gave me a toilet."

*"What?"*

Caitlin told him about the encounter with Reenie. She took the water-closet key chain from her purse and showed it to him.

He took it from her and examined it, then handed it back. "She thinks this will bring you luck? Hey, what's wrong?"

Caitlin was rubbing her knee and shoulder, which were still smarting.

"I banged into the table and the door while trying to

rescue you from drowning," she said in a disgruntled tone.

"You deserve a medal. You were wounded while trying to save a comrade." Dropping the blanket, he moved closer to examine her injuries.

Caitlin tried to bat him away, but he simply picked her up and deposited her on his newly made bed, then tugged up the leg of her pajamas to inspect the red spot on her knee. "Well, see, here's your problem right here."

"What?" She tried to struggle upright, but he held her down with a hand on her uninjured shoulder.

"Your knee's too bony. See, it sticks out right here, begging for things to bang into it."

"It is *not* bony." She tried again to sit up, but he held her back, gently but firmly.

"Quit wiggling. I've got to see if it's okay."

"Bishop, it's not a major trauma. I only bumped it."

"You never know," he responded in a somber tone. He picked up a brass candlestick that sat on the end table, wrapped it in the corner of the blanket and tapped the reflex area below her kneecap. Her foot flew into the air.

"Seems okay," he approved.

"I wish it had kicked you," she said, sitting up stiffly. She eyed the candlestick as he set it back on the table. "Where'd you learn to do that, anyway?"

"I used to date an orthopedic surgeon," he said. "An expert on anatomy. She taught me everything I know."

"I'll bet."

"Now let me look at your shoulder." He tugged at the neck of her pajama top, his clever fingers making quick work of unbuttoning the buttons.

"Stop!" she yelped, grabbing for the front of her top. "My shoulder is fine."

His eyebrows drew together. "Can't be too sure. It might be dislocated."

"I'd be in agony if it was. Didn't your orthopedic girl-friend teach you that?"

"Honey," he growled, "you'd be amazed what I learned from that woman."

"No, I wouldn't," she responded sweetly.

He answered her with a leering grin as he eased her pajama top off her shoulder and gave her creamy skin an appreciative once-over. "Looks okay to me," he said. His head lowered and his lips brushed her skin. "In fact, it looks great." He kissed her shoulder blade. "Couldn't be better."

Heat sizzled through her. Her voice was thin and reedy as she said, "Uh, Jed?"

"Yeah?" His breath whispered against her skin.

"It's, uh…the other shoulder."

He paused and looked up. "I knew that. I *did,*" he said defensively as her eyes widened in disbelief. "I thought this one might be hurting in sympathy. And don't look at me like my cheese is slipping off its cracker."

The desire building in her eased a bit and she giggled. He responded with a comical wiggle of his eyebrows.

Against her better judgment, Caitlin relaxed. Enthralled as usual by his method of getting what he wanted, she stopped fighting him. How could Edith and Evelyn ever think he might settle for a boring life?

Turning her head, she looked into his face, inches from her own. His eyes were teasing and testing her, his hands warm and vital on her skin as he pulled up one side of her pajama top and smoothed the other off her throbbing shoulder.

With his gaze holding hers, Jed massaged her skin, his fingers rubbing over the flesh and then working deep to ease the tension that had tightened her muscles at the moment of his touch. He placed a kiss at the base of her neck. "Why are you so tense, honey?"

"Because you're kissing me."

He laughed. "You know, some people think that's a good thing." He opened his mouth against her skin and the heat of his breath seared her.

"Oooh, it's a good thing all right," she answered. Heat, awareness, fright and wonder all bounded through her, chasing away the need to resist him. Words came to her mind, but couldn't make the journey to her lips.

Delight and dread warred in her as Jed lowered his head once again and caressed her skin softly with his lips. When she moved restively, he murmured, "It's all right, Caitlin."

She didn't know if he meant her shoulder or her needs, which he seemed to understand.

"I'm sorry you hurt yourself on account of me," he said. "I won't let it happen again."

Caitlin couldn't look away from the solemn promise in his gray eyes. What was he promising? Was he giving her some kind of talisman against physical pain? Mental? Emotional? A vow that, whatever happened, he would keep her from being hurt? That couldn't be it, her practical nature insisted. No one could make that kind of promise to another person.

But maybe. Her needs and desires yearned to believe such a promise. If so, she should grab on to it, hold that promise, because she would certainly need it later. "Jed, I—"

"Don't say anything," he instructed, lifting his lips from her shoulder. Drawing her along with him, he lay back on the bed so that she lay sprawled across his chest. She had forgotten that her top was unbuttoned, but the brush of his soft T-shirt against her breasts reminded her. In a moment of panicked confusion, she put her hands on his shoulders and arched upward. Her breasts lifted from his chest, her nipples peaked and hardened. Stunned, she watched as his gaze went from her face to her breasts, then back to meet her eyes, which were staring at him.

"Well, now," he said in a low, rumbling voice. "That's about the prettiest sight I ever saw."

Caitlin whimpered.

"What's the matter, Cait?"

She swallowed. "I…I think that if sanity's going to put in an appearance, now might be a good time."

He lifted his head and she could see that his eyes were deep and mysterious. "Haven't you heard, Cait? Sanity's way overrated."

Her lips trembled. "I…I don't know about that…."

"Shut up and kiss me, Cait."

She started to answer, to say, "Okay," but she only got as far as forming the *O*, which seemed to suit Jed fine, because he fit his lips onto hers and kissed her with deep thoroughness as if he wanted her to remember this kiss, to compare it to every other one. There was no comparison, though. The touch of his lips, teeth and tongue had wildly erotic thoughts blossoming in her mind.

Her hands came up and around his shoulders. She kissed him back, delighting in the taste and texture of him, his tenderness and warmth. At that moment she couldn't remember why she'd run from him that time, weeks ago, when he'd given her such pleasure, made her feel so treasured and wanted. Hazy thoughts of not wanting to be temporary in his life or to be one of the many women who dangled after him, of him saying he wasn't the marrying kind, drifted through her, but didn't stay. She didn't want to think about those things. She wanted to feel him, his solid weight on her, his strength filling her. She wanted…so many things she couldn't put into words, but she would try.

"This is really, really nice," she murmured, her lips against his jaw. It was a truly wonderful jaw—strong, definite, smooth. *Smooth?* She drew away and gave him a dubious look. "Did you shave before you came over here?"

He'd been giving the base of her throat his undivided attention, but now he lifted his head. "Yeah. Why?"

"Were you hoping that we would…?" She gestured to the sofa bed beneath them.

"And if I was?"

"Don't answer a question with a question," she instructed, but then his hand moved from her waist to her breast. "Doh…ho…nn't distract me."

"Then answer my question first."

"I…think you…must be…a real optimist," she moaned.

He chuckled softly and moved his hand in a slow rotation. It sent her heart into a pounding rhythm that would have made any flamenco dancer proud. "Oh, yeah?" he mocked. "But so you know, I shaved because I forgot my razor when I left for San Diego and I was pretty grubby after two days in Steve's rig."

"Ohhh," she breathed, drawing out the word on a thread of desire. She was almost sure she'd had some clever thing ready to say, but it had vaporized along with her common sense. "I'm glad," she confessed, instead. "It feels so good. You smell so good."

"Oh, honey." Jed buried his nose against her throat. "If this is a feel-good-smell-good contest, you win."

"Thank you." Leaning away, she blinked at him, her

tawny eyes gone smoky with desire. "Why don't you kiss me again and let's see how that feels?"

The slumberous desire in her eyes combined with the moist fullness of her lips and her flushed face, telling Jed that he could make love to her now to their mutual delight. She would be with him every step of the way.

Jed did as she'd asked, kissing her with the passion that was rising inside him like an irresistible tide. But a tiny voice of conscience insisted on being heard. What would happen in the morning? Would she run from him again? This might turn out to be another of his plans that went awry.

And it had all started because he'd missed her. Damn, how he'd missed her the past two days. He'd thought a dozen times about calling her, but what would he have said? That he couldn't go another mile without hearing her voice?

How could he do that and maintain his image as an easygoing, laid-back guy who never let serious thoughts about a woman interfere with his life? He couldn't, that was all. He liked helping people, doing things for them, but he didn't like to get too deeply involved in their lives. And even if he *had* been thinking in terms of commitment, he knew *she* wasn't.

The very act of *thinking* the word "wife" made his mouth go dry. Neither of them were ready for that, in spite of the attraction that simmered and occasionally boiled between them.

Slowly, carefully, he rebuttoned her top. "You'll be fine. Nothing's hurt beyond repair."

She blinked, still fighting her way out of the sensual haze he'd created. "Hurt?"

"Your shoulder."

"What about it?"

His lips twitched. "You bumped it. I was checking it. Remember?"

"Oh." She pulled air into her lungs, but the increase in oxygen didn't seem to help the function of her brain. "Sure. Sure I do," she lied.

Jed shook his head, seemed to be trying to swallow a laugh and sat up, pulling her with him. He managed to get them both to their feet.

"Thanks for the bed," he said, standing suddenly and lifting her to her feet. "We both need to get some sleep."

Dazed, she turned toward her room. "Yes, I, um… That's a good idea." She wanted to say something more, to leave him with a quick retort or rebuttal, but none came to her mind. She looked at him, her eyes full of questions and uncertainties, then turned and went into her bedroom. She closed the door carefully behind her and leaned against it.

Why had he stopped? Because neither of them was ready. That much was obvious, even to her mushy brain. She felt buffeted by unfulfilled desire, but she should be grateful to him for stopping. One of them had to show some sense. They had made love once before and it had complicated things. Neither of them needed that to happen again.

It was good that he had stopped, she thought. Good. She nodded decisively and headed for her bed, then took a right turn and marched to the bathroom for a cold shower.

# 7

"NOW REMEMBER, CAIT, I'm depending on you." Jed knotted his tie, straightened the ends, made a sound of disgust and ripped out the knot. Why couldn't he get the damned thing right?

"I know." Caitlin was standing by his bed, leaning up against the tall corner post of the footboard. She was watching him with undisguised amusement.

"No matter how much money Miss Edith and Miss Evelyn bid, you've got to bid more."

"I understand, Jed."

He turned from the mirror and gave her a suspicious look. "Have you ever been to an auction before? Any kind of auction?"

He didn't like the innocent shrug she gave him. "No."

"Things could get nasty," he muttered. "Real nasty."

She lifted an eyebrow at him. "Jed, it's not like we're going into combat."

"That's what you think. You've met the Carlton twins. Do they look like the type to give up easily?"

"Well, no."

"They've been calling my family members all week, including my sister-in-law, Mary, who doesn't need the extra stress since she's about to go into labor any minute, and my aunt Geneva in L.A., who told them to mind their own business."

"What have they been calling about?"

Jed turned back to the mirror. Hell, he should have kept his mouth shut. After their near lovemaking episode, they had gone back to their usual prickly, bantering relationship. It was best that way, he was sure of it, and she seemed to agree, because she hadn't mentioned it, either.

He whipped the end of the tie around and made a new knot. "I wish I didn't have to wear this damned thing," he groused.

"You've retied it four times," Caitlin said. Walking up behind him, she put her hand on his shoulder and urged him around. Batting his hands away, she adjusted the knot herself. Jed liked the feel of her hands brushing the underside of his jaw. He liked the scent of her perfume as it subtly teased his sense of smell. He heartily approved of the new dress she was wearing. It wasn't one of her usual business suits, which he detested. And it wasn't as sexy as the blue dress she'd worn the night she'd won the car. This one was pale lavender, almost the color of smoke with a short, snug skirt that did great things for her already perfect legs. The top was a little too modest and high-necked, but hey, he wasn't complaining. At least it didn't have the battalion of buttons that usually graced her clothing. This one had an easily accessible zipper that—

"What were the Carlton twins calling your family about?" she asked again.

He gave a start when she cut into his fantasy, and he realized how far he'd let his mind wander. A quick look at her intently interested face told him he'd be wise to stick to his original topic of conversation.

"I've always hated ties ever since my days at Sunday school when I had to wear one to please my mother. Now, here I am at thirty, and still doing things to please her."

"Jed?"

"Did you have to wear uncomfortable clothes to Sunday school to please your mother?" he asked.

"My mother wasn't the churchgoing type, Jed. Answer my question. What have the Carlton twins been calling your family about?"

"Uh, nothing, I— Aargh!" he squawked as she tightened the knot on his tie and cut off the circulation to his brain. "Ca-ait," he wheezed, reaching for her wrists. "Stop."

She loosened the knot, but he didn't like the determined look in her eyes.

"All right, all right. They've been trying to get information about you. About whether or not your intentions toward me are honorable."

"Are you kidding?"

"Now, Cait, that shouldn't surprise you, considering their visit here on Monday," he soothed. "They're protective of me."

"They're nuts," she muttered.

"True, and that's why you need to watch yourself during the bidding. You've got the money?"

"Every penny you wiped out of your bank account." She paused and chewed her lip, an unconscious action he found wildly erotic. He wondered if she'd let him have a go at it. Probably not, he decided with a sigh. After the kiss they'd shared a few nights ago, she'd gone back to treating him with her usual breeziness, but she might as well have a big sign attached to her chest saying, "Touch me and die." If he tried to take a taste of her lips, she'd probably bite his tongue. But damn, it might be worth a try in spite of his determination not to get serious about her.

Before he could do anything idiotic, she stepped back,

gave him a worried look and said, "If I pay a lot of money for you, people won't get the wrong idea, will they?"

"That depends."

"On what?"

"On how much money you think is a *lot* of money."

She tilted her head and considered him. "For you, anything more than fifty-seven cents."

"If that's as high as you're willing to go, you're dooming me to another evening of broken dentures and elbows in the ribs." He wiggled his eyebrows at her. "But the higher you're willing to go, the more attractive I'll seem."

"Well, that's a terrible burden to have to bear, but that's not what I was thinking. I was wondering if people will think that I, a financial adviser, was being foolish with my money."

His expression collapsed into a frown. "Here we go again. Why do you worry so much about what people think? The *Clarion* came out day before yesterday and you haven't had huge numbers of clients calling up to cancel their dealings with you, now have you?"

"Jed, I don't *have* huge numbers of clients in the first place."

"But how many calls have you received since Wednesday congratulating you on your car and asking about your financial services?"

Caitlin looked down at her hands. "A few."

"A few?"

She tossed her head back and stuck her chin out at him. "Oh, all right, many. I've had many calls. You were right and I was wrong and I shouldn't have been so worried about the photo, even though I looked like a deer caught in headlights."

"So why are you *still* worried about what people will

think? I've never known anybody who worries about that as much as you do.''

"Says the man who wants me to pay a lot of money for him so people will think he's attractive." She rolled her eyes. "Jed, people *know* you're attractive. All they have to do is look at you, and besides, all those women you've got parading through this place are testimony to that." She turned away. "Hadn't we better go?"

He wasn't going to let her get away with that, either. He reached out and snagged her hand. "I want you to pay a lot for me so Edith and Evelyn won't, but, honey, I didn't realize it bothered you that so many of my friends are women."

"Good heavens, why should it bother me?" she asked evasively.

"That's what I'm wondering. I also didn't realize you think I'm attractive."

She lifted her free hand and examined her fingernails. "Oh?"

He kept a firm grip on her hand. He wanted answers. "Are we talking people-don't-run-screaming-when-they-see-me attractive or baby-I'm-hot-for-your-body attractive?"

Her eyes grew wary. "Not-ashamed-to-be-seen-with-you-in-public attractive." She wrenched her hand from his and glanced at her watch. "My goodness, look at the time. We'd better go."

She whirled away, snatched up the handbag she'd laid on his bed when he'd called her into his apartment to help him with his tie, then seemed to realize exactly where she was and skittered away from the bed. He lifted his hand to hide a grin as she hotfooted it out of the bedroom and marched across his living room. He was making her nervous, or being in his apartment was making her nervous. For some crazy reason he didn't mind that at all.

He grabbed his wallet and keys, snagged his navy blue blazer off its hanger and followed her out the door. He'd been dreading this night for weeks, but now he was beginning to think it might get pretty interesting.

"Sold to the lady in the red dress for eight hundred dollars, a date with one bachelor by the name of Ted Wilkinson and the romantic day he's planned on his sailboat." The auctioneer, who happened to be Jed's uncle Frank, looked up and grinned as Ted left the small stage that had been set up at the front of the room. "I've sailed with Ted, young lady," he said. "I suggest you pack some motion-sickness pills."

The crowd laughed and settled down to wait for the next bachelor to appear. Caitlin looked around the large main room of the women's club, which was packed with club members, bidders and people from the community who had dropped in to enjoy the fun. And it was fun. Her idea of a women's club had been blue-haired ladies sitting around drinking tea and gossiping. This one seemed to have its share of older women, but there were lots of younger ones, too, and they all appeared to have embraced the single goal of making this auction a success. Mrs. Bishop had greeted her with warm enthusiasm and reminded her of her promise to be a speaker at one of their upcoming meetings. Seeing the diversity of the group, Caitlin was already planning a talk that would cover everything from college finances to individual retirement accounts. She should join the group herself. After all, she was a member of the community now.

Warily she eyed the Carlton twins, who sat two rows in front of her and had turned around several times already to throw dark looks in her direction. Did they know she was going to bid on Jed? Or were they still perturbed that such an ordinary woman as she was had the nerve to attend the auction? Whatever. The next few minutes were going to be dicey.

The two ladies were dressed to kill in sequined spandex dresses—lime green tonight. They also wore feathered boas of the same color and purple hats decorated with ostrich plumes. The people behind them had to duck and dart around in order to see.

Frank interrupted her thoughts. "Our next eligible bachelor is my nephew Jed Bishop." When his name was called, Jed stepped from a curtained area beside the stage and mounted the steps.

He was almost knocked over by the sigh of pleasure that went around the room. Caitlin couldn't have agreed more. He looked fabulous. His midnight hair was perfectly combed, his jaw was freshly shaven and the navy blue blazer he wore complemented his eyes and hugged the substantial width of his shoulders. He glanced up and grinned, then aimed a wink in her direction. At least she thought it was in her direction, but most of the other women must have thought so, too, because there was a collective intake of breath as if he'd stopped half the hearts in the room.

Caitlin put her hand over her own pounding heart. If this kept up, the women's club would be handing out pacemakers before the evening was over.

"The date Jed is offering will be an evening of dinner and theater in San Francisco," Frank went on. "Finishing up with a romantic midnight cruise around the bay. Let's start the bidding at one hundred dollars."

Before Caitlin could even open her mouth, six women were on their feet, shouting. She had only a moment to recognize Maria Rossi and Raeann Forbes before Edith and Evelyn Carlton joined the melee, shooting upward and hollering out their bids in voices that could have summoned hogs from a faraway bog.

Frank stumbled back, and Jed, looking stunned himself, had to grab him and hold him upright. It took Frank a few seconds to collect himself, but he finally got the bidders under control, though he couldn't seem to keep the amounts from leaping upward a hundred dollars at a time. Caitlin joined in the bidding, but fearing she couldn't be heard, stood up like the other bidders and called out her offer.

One by one, the other women dropped out, giving disappointed shrugs or laughing with their friends. Pretty soon, it was down to only Caitlin bidding against the Carlton twins, who turned and gave her drop-dead looks whenever she called out a bid. They seemed to think they were the only ones who should bid on Jed because that was the way it had always been. Caitlin would have felt sorry for them if they hadn't been so nasty about ordinariness. She smoothed the short skirt of the dress she'd bought for the occasion. Ordinary, indeed!

"The bid stands at two thousand dollars," Frank called. He glanced over at his sister-in-law. Jed's mother shook her head as if she couldn't believe it, either. "Do I hear two thousand one hundred?"

"You bet you do," shrieked Edith.

"Two thousand three hundred," Caitlin called.

The Carltons turned and gave her looks that promised dire revenge. Caitlin answered with a confident smile. She was actually beginning to enjoy this, but there was still a part of her that didn't want them to be angry at her.

The Carlton twins faced the front, squared their shoulders, and Evelyn called out, "Three thousand."

A collective gasp traveled around the room. This was far more than any of the other bachelors had brought in. Caitlin gulped. Jed had given her three thousand to bid on him, saying it would never go that high. The last time he'd been involved in this, Edith and Evelyn had paid only half that amount for a date with him.

Caitlin's eyes shot to Jed's face, which was turning pale. He sent her a panicked look. She started to shrug, indicating she didn't know what to do, but out of the corner of her eye, she saw Edith turn and give her a smug, superior smile, indicating she was sure they'd won.

*Oh, yeah?* Mentally Caitlin pushed up her sleeves, spit on her hands and got ready to fight. The heck with caring if they got angry at her. They were the ones who had turned this into a personal campaign by calling her ordinary, then asking Jed's family about her. Stretching onto her toes, she called out, "Three thousand five hundred."

Jed jerked as if someone had zapped him with a cattle prod. His gaze swung to her face. She gave him a firm nod and he grinned. He knew she was into her own money now.

The people around them were beginning to realize that there was something personal going on here. All eyes fixed on Edith and Evelyn to see what they'd do next. They held a hurried consultation and Edith called out, "Four thousand."

Like fans at a tennis match, everyone in the room turned to Caitlin, who blanched momentarily, but then decided to fight on. Jed was depending on her! He'd been telling her that for a week. She couldn't let him down. Looking up, she saw that he was watching her with admiration for the determination she was showing. That was all very fine, she thought, nearly hyperventilating when Edith and Evelyn glared at her again, but he wasn't the one the Carlton twins were plotting to sell into white slavery! She broke out in a sweat and someone nearby handed her a tissue. With a hurried thanks, she blotted her forehead, wadded the tissue and called out, "Five thousand."

Attention whipped back to the Carltons. Evelyn was the spokesperson this time. She gave Caitlin a "top this" look and called out, "Six thousand."

Tossing her head, excited and high on adrenaline, Caitlin kicked off her shoes, climbed onto her chair, threw her hands into the air and yelled. "Seven thousand dollars!" Looking directly at the two ladies, she tacked on, "Ha!"

The Carltons threw her a look that should have killed her on the spot and sat down abruptly. Clutching their purses in their laps, they stared straight ahead.

"Sold to the lady on the chair," Frank called. The room erupted into cheers, Caitlin looked down, dazed to realize that she was, indeed, standing on her chair. Embarrassment swept through her, but before she could clamber down, Jed bolted off the stage, rushed to her and whipped his arms around her waist. Laughing, he swept her down into his arms and kissed her. The room went wild with whistles and catcalls.

Caitlin threw her arms around his neck and kissed him back, then drew away and said in shock, "I bid seven thousand dollars for a date," she gasped. "With you!"

He laughed and kissed her again. "Don't sound so horrified. Maybe you'll get your money's worth."

"I'd better," she answered as he set her back on her feet and steadied her while she tried to find her shoes and the audience laughed and clapped. She glanced around, accepting congratulations and thinking that the crazy things that had happened to her and that she'd done in the past week had made her feel like more a part of the community than she ever had before. When Jed's arm clamped around her waist and he drew her to him, she realized that home wasn't simply a place, it was a feeling and she felt it in this room, with this man.

Shaken by the knowledge, she pushed away from him, gave him a trembling smile and sat down. The people seated nearby rearranged themselves so that Jed could have the seat next to her. He parked himself there and accepted the congratulations of the crowd. Looking quite pleased with himself, he stretched his arm across the back of Caitlin's chair and sat back, ready to enjoy the rest of the auction.

Caitlin gave him a sidelong look. "Don't let this go to your head," she advised.

"Too late, honey," he said, flashing his devilish grin at her. "There's something about having women fighting over me that really gives my ego a boost."

She smiled sweetly. "If your ego had any more of a boost, it could fling the space shuttle into orbit."

He grinned and turned away as his uncle began the bidding on the next bachelor. The frenzy of bidding on Jed had started the ball rolling, and the next several men carried high price tags. By the time it was over, the book fund had nearly fifteen thousand dollars in it and Jed's mother appeared to be on the verge of fainting.

Jed glanced over his shoulder as they walked to her car and said, "Uh-oh."

"What is it?" she asked, busily digging in her purse for her keys. She felt an incredible light-headedness that she knew was a result of the adrenaline rush she'd just been through. She hoped it wouldn't affect her driving. She glanced around to see that Edith and Evelyn were bearing down on them. "Uh-oh is right," she said.

"Jed, it looks as though this is the end of our friendship," Miss Edith announced.

Jed cast a quick glance at Caitlin. "It is, Miss Edith? Well, I'm sorry to hear that, but why can't we still be friends?"

"Because you and this girl have embarrassed us," Evelyn answered primly. "This was a setup between the two of you, wasn't it?"

"Yes, it was."

Caitlin gave him a swift glance. She hadn't expected him to lie, but she hadn't thought he'd be so quick to admit the truth, either, to these two nosy ladies.

"Humph," Evelyn said. "All these years we've been looking out for you, trying to keep you from having a dull life and now we see it meant nothing to you. We thought we were your friends, but you've embarrassed us in front of the whole town."

Jed nodded his head. "I understand how you feel, but the truth is, I finally realized I'm not good enough for the two of you."

Caitlin's eyes widened and she choked back a laugh.

Edith glared at Jed. "What do you mean?"

He dropped his head as if he was ashamed of himself, then lifted it to stare earnestly at them. "The date we had for the last bachelor auction wasn't very good. It was my fault. I know that, but you two were so kind and bravely carried on trying to make it seem like you were having a good time with me." His frown deepened. "But I know the truth. I bored you, didn't I?"

The Carltons looked taken aback. "Why, we didn't—"

"Oh, don't try to deny it," Jed said, lifting his hand and assuming the air of a martyr. "Sure, I'm young, but I'm boring. I know it and I accept it. The two of you are too kind to say it, but it's true. I know you felt obligated to continue trying to change me, but I think we all know it's hopeless. I'm in a rut and the worst part is, I like being in a rut.''

Caitlin stared, amazed at the web of fabrications he was weaving. She wondered if he would catch himself in it. She glanced at the Carlton twins. They exchanged looks.

"I didn't mean to embarrass you tonight and neither did Caitlin," Jed went on, "but I felt like it was better to make a clean break and not saddle you with someone as boring as me." The look he gave them was as soulful as an injured puppy's.

Edith lifted her hand. "But this girl—"

"She's boring, too," Jed said morosely. "That's good in an investment counselor, though, in case you ever need her help or advice."

Talk about damned with faint praise. Under her breath, Caitlin muttered, "Don't do me any favors, Bishop."

He was still talking. "In fact, we're going to go home now. She'll go into her apartment and read the *Wall Street Journal* and then go to bed and drink a glass of warm milk. I'll go to my apartment and watch television. My favorite science program is on—'All About Fungus.'"

Evelyn looked stunned and then sympathy began to show in her eyes. "But your date in San Francisco? That'll be exciting." She glanced at her sister. "At least we thought so."

"Yeah, maybe, but I like things to be calm, you know. The play we're going to see is very avant-garde. The actors sit on stage and don't move for two hours."

"They don't move?"

"Not a muscle, and the cruise around the bay is actually a medical test for a new motion-sickness pill. If I don't barf, they'll pay me fifty dollars."

Caitlin erupted into violent coughs as she choked back a whoop of laughter and fought the tears of mirth in her eyes. Frantically she scrambled in her purse for a tissue, found one wrapped around something hard and angular. It took her a moment to realize it was the old-fashioned water-closet key chain Reenie had given her.

Jed lifted his hand. "See what I mean? Caitlin is a good friend. She did this so you wouldn't feel obligated to buy me at the auction, but she's in tears at the thought of having to go out with me. Aren't you, Cait?"

"Yes. Really, ladies, I wish you'd find someone else to help. He's hopeless."

Jed held out his hands to Edith and Evelyn, who grasped them and gave him looks of intense pity. "You've got to forget about me," he said. "You've got to let me live my boring life. I truly wish you'd find someone else. Someone more worthy of your interest. In fact, something's been worrying me." He manufactured a concerned look. "You don't think dullness is contagious, do you, Caitlin?"

Now what? She cleared her throat. "It's hard to say."

"Oh." As one, Edith and Evelyn dropped his hands and backed away.

"I...I see what you mean," Edith said. "You're...you're absolutely right. We need to use our energy, our enthusiasm for...for life, to help someone else." She grabbed her sister's arm and dragged her away. "Good night, Jed, and, uh, Caitlin. We'll see you."

The two women hurried across to their car and left with a squeal of tires.

"You're not good enough for them? You're boring? *I'm* boring? Where did you come up with that?"

He gave her a self-satisfied grin. "Pretty good, huh? I mean, considering it was spur-of-the-moment. I should have realized they'd be embarrassed and angry. I had to placate them somehow."

"Oh, I think they were placated. They also think you're crazy."

He opened the car door for her and then closed it after she'd slid behind the wheel. Climbing into the passenger side, he made himself comfortable and said, "Maybe they'll find a new interest in life, though, and stop crocheting booties for me."

"Have you considered introducing them to Terry Appletree and Barney Mellin? Now *there's* a couple of interesting men."

Jed grinned in agreement. As she started the car, she glanced down, surprised to see she still held the key chain. In fact, she'd been holding it when she'd said she wished the Carlton twins would find someone else to help. Maybe that wish would come true, she thought, dropping it into her purse, and there would be two fewer women making the pilgrimage to Jed's apartment. She would have less competition, and... Whoa!

"What's the matter?" Jed asked.

"Nothing." Her voice shot up, then dropped. "Nothing."

"You sound like you've got the hiccups."

"I'm fine." She pulled out of the parking lot and started home.

He didn't look like he believed her, but he changed the subject. "About the date we're going on..."

"To watch stationary actors in an avant-garde play, then take part in a motion-sickness study?"

"I really know how to show a woman a good time, don't I?"

"I can't wait."

"Good. When shall we go?"

She shot him a teasing glance. He was too full of himself right now, she decided. "How about a year from next Friday?"

"Next Friday? Sounds good," he answered breezily. "You gonna let me drive your car?"

"In your dreams."

They launched into an argument that carried them all the way home and up the stairs to their apartments. It broke off only when Jed heard his phone ringing and hurried inside to answer it. Caitlin went into her own apartment and closed the door, then wandered restlessly from the living room to the bedroom and back. After the excitement of the auction, their crazy conversation with Edith and Evelyn, then their argument on the way home, her *apartment* seemed boring. Being with Jed was fun. Far too much fun for her peace of mind, she decided ruefully. The thought of going out on an actual date with him set her stomach fluttering with excitement.

When she heard a knock on the door, she hurried over to find Jed standing there. His eyes were shining. "Mary's in labor," he announced. "Two weeks early."

"Oh. Do you think everything will be all right?"

"Yeah, Steve says so." Jed paced into her apartment and then turned. "That was him on the phone. He was on his way to drive a rig to Boise, but was called back because of Mary. I'm going to go in his place. I'll be gone a couple of days."

"Okay," Caitlin answered, hearing the way her voice dipped into the toes of her shoes.

"You'll have to keep tabs on Terry and Barney while I'm gone. They know you're my partner, so what you say goes."

"Yes, of course." Knowing they were on the same side gave Caitlin an inexplicable glow of happiness. "Maybe

I'll set them up with Edith and Evelyn while you're gone.''

"Do that, and don't forget we have a date next Friday night," he said, pointing a finger at her. "And don't even *think* of trying to get out of it."

Eyes wide, she said, "I wouldn't dare."

He bent from the waist and gave her a peck on the cheek. "Good girl. You're learning."

"The truth is, I don't want to miss out on the opportunity to go out with someone as boring as you. Besides, what if Edith and Evelyn ask about our date? I'll need to tell them how many times I drifted off to sleep during the play."

"I don't think that will happen," he said, his eyes twinkling. "I forgot to mention that in the play the actors sitting perfectly still for two hours are also buck naked." With a laugh and a wink, he gave her another kiss and whisked out the door. "I'll call you," he said.

Smiling, Caitlin closed her door. This place was going to be awfully quiet for the next couple of days. In a few minutes she heard his footsteps going down the hall, and then the house was as silent as she'd predicted. Thinking of him on the road and of Mary in labor, Caitlin was too keyed up to sleep.

She couldn't believe she'd added thousands of dollars of her own money to buy a date with him at the auction. Even more surprising, she was glad she'd done it, which showed exactly how much she had changed in the past few weeks. She felt ashamed of the way she had snapped and skirmished with him over the house and so many other things, and even though she said teasingly that she didn't want to go out with him, she was looking forward to their date.

Caitlin moved around the room straightening a few

things, then paused when she heard the downstairs door. Had Jed forgotten something? Or had he forgotten to lock the door and it had been caught by the wind that was beginning to kick up?

She walked out into the hallway. "Jed?" When there was no answer, she descended the stairs. The door was standing open. With a shake of her head, she closed and locked it, then started back to her apartment. She happened to turn her head as she passed the parlor, then whirled around with a gasp of surprise when she saw who was there.

Reenie Starr sat on an old chair in front of the empty fireplace.

# 8

WITH A YELP, Caitlin fell back, her hand to her throat.

The old woman turned to look at her. "Hello, Caitlin dear. I'm sorry I startled you."

"Mrs. Starr, Reenie," Caitlin gasped, swallowing to force her heart down to its proper place. "Where did you come from?"

Reenie blinked at her. "Well, from home, of course, and then right through your front door. You were very thoughtful to leave it open for me."

"But what are you doing here?" Caitlin asked as she approached. "It's going to storm soon." As if in emphasis, thunder rumbled, moving ever closer.

"That's all right, dear. I'm dressed for it." She indicated the rain boots, yellow rain slicker and white rain hat she wore.

"You didn't walk here, did you?" Caitlin asked in alarm. "It's very dangerous to be out on the road at—"

"I'm fine," Reenie said, waving Caitlin's concern away. She held out the hem of the coat. "See? This has been decorated with some kind of reflective paint, exactly like a highway sign. Remarkable."

Caitlin smiled at the wonder in the old woman's voice. "Where did you get it?"

"Oh, I happened to walk by the fire station and there were several of these hanging right inside the door. Wasn't that considerate of the firefighters? The people in this town are so nice. I traded my black raincoat for it. It's very dangerous to be walking around at night in such dark clothes.'' She looked down at her new attire with pleasure. ''I'll have to return it, of course, as soon as I'm finished with it.'' Her voice was edged with regret. ''Too bad, but I suppose it *is* rather heavy for everyday wear.''

Caitlin bit her lip to keep from laughing. She could imagine the surprise of a member of the Crystal Cove volunteer fire department if he ran in to grab his equipment and ended up with a little old lady's sensible raincoat, instead. ''I think returning it would be a good idea,'' she said. ''It might be needed.''

''I suppose so,'' Reenie said sadly.

''Mrs. Starr, why are you out on a night like this? Didn't you know it's going to rain?''

''Oh, yes, but I had to come and talk to you. It's very important. Won't you sit down?'' She wriggled in her chair and sat back, then folded her hands in her lap and gave Caitlin an expectant look as if she was ready to tell a story.

''Of course,'' Caitlin said. ''But why don't we go up to my apartment? I've got the heat on and it's much more comfortable than this drafty room.''

Reenie pulled her coat around her. ''I'm perfectly comfortable here,'' she said. ''And besides, I can only stay a minute.'' Her voice took on an urgency that had Caitlin removing a stack of fireplace tiles and a tube of caulking from a rickety folding chair and pulling it up opposite the old woman.

''What is it, Mrs. Starr?''

''I don't think I'll ever get you to call me Reenie,'' the woman said. ''Well, never mind. I guess it's understandable, considering your line of work. Most of your clients are my age. Lots of people nowadays don't respect age, you know," she said in a regretful tone. "That's not why I'm here, though. I came to ask if the key chain helped you at the bachelor auction tonight."

"I'm not sure if it brought me luck or not." Caitlin explained what had happened at the auction and in the parking lot afterward.

"Well, then, I would say it did," Reenie answered, her eyes twinkling. "You have a date with Jed and he might be free of the attentions of Edith and Evelyn." She sniffed. "They were always silly girls."

"Oh, you know them?"

Reenie started to answer, but then a look of confusion drew her thin, white eyebrows together. "I... shouldn't..." Her voice trailed off vaguely and she shook her head.

Caitlin reached out and touched her hand. "Are you all right, Mrs. Starr?"

Reenie blinked, her eyes cleared, and she gave Caitlin a sunny smile. She covered Caitlin's hand with her own in a surprisingly strong grip. Then she pulled away and reached into her pocket. "I have another good-luck item for you." She tried to pull something out, but it seemed to be too large and bulky. She had to work at it for a moment before it came free. Finally, she held it up.

Caitlin stared. "A bone?"

Reenie beamed and nodded. "I found it on my way over here. I think some dog buried it, then dug it up and forgot about it. Quite fortuitous, I must say, since I knew you'd need it."

Caitlin reached for it and was surprised to find the heavy thing was warm in her hand. She lifted puzzled eyes to Reenie, who smiled.

"A dog's bone," Caitlin said in a flat voice.

"I'm sure you've heard the old saying that even a bad dog can find a good bone sometimes."

"Uh, er, yes, of course," Caitlin responded, though she'd never heard that saying before in her life. Was Reenie saying she was the "bad dog" or that Caitlin was?

"I looked for a horseshoe, but didn't see one, so the bone will have to do. It will teach you another lesson, as the penny and the key chain did. " She examined Caitlin keenly. "You did learn something from the penny, didn't you?"

Caitlin blinked and tried to control her amazement at her strange gift. "Learn something?" she asked faintly. She'd certainly learned not to try to convince Reenie that the penny was actually a flattened bottle lid. "Why, yes, I suppose I did," she answered, instead.

Reenie nodded, her floppy-brimmed rain hat bobbing over her eyes. She reached up to push it back. "You learned that wonderful things can happen when you least expect them, and that you have many more friends than you thought you had."

Caitlin thought of her new car, of meeting Jed's family and of her upcoming date with him. "Yes, I did."

"The bone may teach you that what you want isn't always what you should have."

Caitlin thought that was probably asking a great deal of a leftover part from a long-dead cow.

Reenie stood suddenly. The huge fireman's coat engulfed her tiny frame. Her serene face smiled from between the floppy rain hat and the sagging collar of the coat. "Well, it's been nice chatting with you, but I have to go now," she said.

As she started for the door, Caitlin scrambled to her feet. "Let me drive you," she said hurriedly. "The storm is coming and you shouldn't be out on the street—"

"Oh, no, dear," Reenie said. "I'll be perfectly all right."

Caitlin turned and sprinted for the stairs. "Nevertheless, I'll drive you. Please wait right here while I get my keys."

She hurried upstairs to her apartment. She set the bone down on her desk, thought better of it and set it on the floor. She grabbed her keys and purse and dashed out once again. She stopped in the parlor doorway and saw that her guest was gone. Whirling around, she ran to the front door, then down the driveway all the way to the street, calling Reenie's name. But the old woman was gone, as thoroughly as if she'd never been there at all.

Frustrated, Caitlin threw up her hands. "How does she *do* that?"

She turned back toward the house. How could a little old lady disappear so quickly and completely? And so consistently? Worried, Caitlin jumped into her car and made a hurried trip up the highway that led to Crystal Cove, but no sign of Reenie.

Back in her apartment, Caitlin picked up the bone. Reenie said she'd found it on the way over. That meant she'd probably walked by the home of someone who had a dog. All Caitlin had to do to find her was see who had a dog and... But then three-fourths of the people in Crystal Cove had a dog. Maybe she'd have better luck trying to find Reenie through the more usual ways. Caitlin had asked a few people if they knew Reenie, but no one seemed to have seen her, except the people at MacAllen's Market, who said she was an infrequent customer.

The phone rang, startling Caitlin. With the bone still in her hand, she reached for the receiver. When Jed's voice came over the line, she was disconcerted by the thrill of pleasure that shot through her. Her voice was breathless when she said, "Hello, Jed."

"Hi," he responded, then paused. "I called to tell you I think I left the front door unlocked."

"Yes, I know. I took care of it."

"Is something wrong? You sound funny."

There was no way Caitlin was going to tell him that the sound of his voice made her heart hop into her throat. Instead, she looked at her newest good-luck charm again and said, "I'm fine, but I've had another encounter with Reenie Starr."

"Reenie? The old woman from the market? The one who gave you the bottle lid?"

"And the key chain. And now I've got a bone to add to my growing collection."

"Excuse me, did you say 'bone'?"

Caitlin explained Reenie's reasoning, though she couldn't really justify the lady's shaky logic.

"Okay, I think it's official now. You've got the nuttiest guardian angel in heaven, but hey, you can't complain. She's looking out for you. The bottle cap brought you a car," he reminded her. She could hear the smug grin in his voice. "The key chain got you a date with me. What more could a girl want?"

"Humph," she snorted.

"Now, Cait, that's the most unladylike sound I've ever heard you make, unless you count those little sounds you make in the back of your throat when I—"

"Jed!" Heat washed through her, staining her cheeks, and she protested in shock, even though she knew she sounded like someone's maiden aunt.

"Those are more of a purring-cat kind of noise, so I don't think they really count as human sounds, ladylike or otherwise, but they're damned sexy."

In frustration Caitlin banged the bone down on the desktop, nicking the finish. She stared at the mark furiously. "Oh, I wish you would be quiet. I wish you wouldn't talk at all and just listen to me!"

"Sure, Cait," he answered in a tone of pure innocence. "What did you want to say?"

What *did* she want to say? *Don't remind me of what it's like to make love to you?* Who needed a reminder? She thought about it all the time. "Nothing," she finally answered. "Have a safe trip."

"You miss me already," he gloated. "I really am touched. I've got to get Steve's rig on the road. In the meantime, think about our date."

"You wish," she muttered as she hung up, but it was true that she was looking forward to Friday night.

Caitlin ran her knuckles across her forehead. Why was it that when she was with him, she couldn't seem to recall her reluctance to get involved with him? Somehow things like her background, his laid-back attitude, the way his former girlfriends stayed around to look after his welfare didn't seem that important right now.

Obviously she was suffering from some kind of emotional overload. Yeah, that was it. She'd had too much excitement tonight what with the bachelor auction, the visit from Reenie and all. There was only one cure for this problem.

She headed for the kitchen and the pint of cherry-chocolate-cheesecake ice cream that sat waiting in the freezer for exactly this kind of emergency.

CAITLIN DROVE HOME from work the next afternoon feeling pleased with herself, though a little groggy since she hadn't crashed from her self-induced sugar high until after midnight. Still, she felt elated over the day's events. She'd had a stimulating conversation with Geneva Bishop, who had shared the news that there were two new members to her family. Mary had given birth to a boy and a girl. Geneva was thrilled, even if one of the twins was a boy. Caitlin would love to know what had happened to make Ms. Bishop so distrustful of men. Caitlin had reported on the bachelor auction and told Geneva about the odd little woman, Reenie Starr, who seemed to pop up at strange times and places, full of advice. Geneva had surprised Caitlin by suggesting that she listen to the woman. Geneva's statement had been, "You can learn a lot from an old broad."

Caitlin had been amused by this "Genevaism." She'd been on her own so long, she wasn't sure she knew how to take personal advice from others, even from someone as sweet and sincere as Reenie Starr.

However, the whole conversation with Geneva had made Caitlin hopeful. Later in the day, she'd discovered that a mutual fund she'd encouraged some of her clients to invest in was doing better than expected, and it had given her a feeling of satisfaction to know she was responsible for her clients' financial security. Maybe that bone *had* brought her luck.

When she turned into her driveway, Caitlin saw Mr. Mellin's truck beside Terry's in the driveway. With both men working, the house would be finished and on the market by spring, then she would be able to move on with her life. She couldn't imagine why her heart sank at that thought. As she stepped out of the Bel-Air, she heard the high-pitched whine of a power saw.

When she stopped in the hallway to pick up her mail, she saw that Terry was using the saw to cut new decorative moldings for the windows to replace the rain-damaged ones. He turned off the saw when he saw her and flipped the protective goggles to the top of his head. He nodded toward a cellular telephone he'd left on a sawhorse and said, "Jed called. He said he'd be home late tomorrow. He ran into some heavy rain."

"Oh," Caitlin responded. "That's too bad. I..." She paused, not sure what she'd been about to say. The mental image of Jed driving an eighteen-wheeler on slick roads sent shudders of fear rippling up her spine. Surely he wouldn't try it at his usual breakneck speed. "Thanks for telling me, Terry."

Terry pulled his goggles down. "No problem," he said, then gave her an interested look as he added, "He didn't sound too good."

"He didn't?"

"Nah, but it might have been a bad connection. He said for you not to wait up for him."

"I wouldn't have any reason to," she said, though she knew she'd worry about him until he arrived.

Terry grinned. "Yeah, right." He switched on the saw once again, drowning anything further she might have said.

Caitlin rolled her eyes. She didn't know why she bothered to deny it. After her chair-hopping performance on Friday night, everyone in town probably knew there was more than a business partnership between them. She fervently wished she knew what that something was.

The next night, when she finally heard the sound of a car crunching gravel in the driveway, recognized the roar of the powerful engine of Jed's Mustang, relief washed over her.

She waited at the top of the stairs, ready to speak to him as soon as he came up, but the slow, deliberate scrape of his feet on the steps alarmed her. He sounded as if each foot weighed fifty pounds and he had to struggle to lift them.

When she caught sight of him leaning on the banister

as he ascended, Caitlin forgot about her irritation with him and flew down to meet him. One of his arms was laid along the railing, and his head was bent as if he had to summon strength for each step. The brush of her slippers on the stairs caused him to look up.

"Jed! Are you all right?"

"Hi, Cait," he said in a voice that sounded raw and raspy. "How's it going?"

"That's what I'd like to know," she said, hurriedly placing her arm around his waist and propping her shoulder beneath his arm. Heat from his body seared through his shirt and jacket, telling her he was burning up with fever.

"Hey," he responded with a lopsided grin, "this is all right. You're acting like you're actually glad to see me. You've never greeted me like this before. In fact, you're usually ready to throw something at me."

In the muted light of the hallway, she noted his bleary eyes with alarm. "Not tonight," she said, trying to keep the fright out of her voice. "Maybe tomorrow." She reached up to brush his hair out of his face. His feverish skin almost scorched her fingers. "How on earth did you drive an eighteen-wheeler in this condition?" she asked.

"I'm tough," he answered, but he leaned on her gratefully.

"Oh, I can see that," she answered, wrapping both arms around him to keep him steady on his feet.

He gave her another smile, but when he tried to speak, nothing came out. He looked at her in surprise as he mouthed the words, "My voice."

"Maybe this won't be all bad," she muttered, making him frown. "At least you can't boss me around."

"Wanna bet?" he whispered.

Together, they got him upstairs and into his apartment.

Caitlin steered him straight to his bed. He waited, leaning on the bedpost while she turned back the covers, and then he collapsed across the bed as if all his strength had been used in climbing the stairs. He sighed as his eyes closed.

Alarmed anew, Caitlin looked at the way he sprawled bonelessly across the navy blue sheets. She had never seen him like this before. Carefully she sat on the bed, lifted one of his feet and began untying the laces of his sneakers.

He roused enough to mutter, "'S'all right. I'll do that in a minute."

She ignored him, removing his shoes, then tucking him under the covers. He seemed to have fallen asleep, which was probably the best thing for him, but she knew he'd sleep better if she got some aspirin down him.

Caitlin knew there was no aspirin in her apartment, so she searched his bathroom for a bottle, but found none. Finally, feeling like a snoop, she looked in his kitchen, then returned to the bedroom where she located a small bottle in his nightstand, beside a box of condoms.

As soon as she saw it, her gaze flew to his face. Her breath caught, then she exhaled in a sigh of relief when she saw that his eyes were closed and he seemed to be completely unaware of what she was doing. Quietly she removed the bottle of aspirin and closed the drawer. Turning, she hurried to the kitchen for a glass of water.

That box of condoms made her remember the night she'd slept with him, his compelling touch, his gentle humor, the care he'd taken to protect her by using one of those condoms.

Caitlin paused as she filled the glass with water from the tap. Had he used any condoms since that night? Had there been any reason for him to? Since she lived across the hall from him, she was aware of his comings and goings. As far as she knew, none of his frequent female visitors had spent the night with him.

Water filled and overflowed the glass. Hurriedly she turned off the tap, then stood with the dripping glass in her hand. He'd been gone for several nights in the past couple of weeks, though. Could he have met someone?

It was absolutely none of her business. She whipped a towel off the counter, wiped the glass and carried it into the bedroom. With difficulty, she roused Jed long enough to get him to swallow a couple of aspirin and gulp down some water. When he fell back against the pillows, she tugged the covers over him and turned to leave the room.

Her feet slowed to a stop as she approached the doorway. She eased around silently to see that Jed seemed to have fallen instantly asleep, if she could judge by his closed eyes and regular breathing.

How many condoms were in one of those boxes, anyway? It wouldn't hurt to look, she thought. As a consumer, she needed to know information like that. It might be useful someday.

Nonchalantly she wandered back to the bedside, gave Jed another quick peek, then leaned over to open the drawer as silently as possible. With as much stealth as a burglar, she removed the box, checked to see that it was supposed to contain six condoms, then gingerly lifted the lid. There were five foil packages inside. Which meant that if the box had been new when she and Jed had made love all those weeks ago, he hadn't used any since. Elation soared through her and she made a quiet sound of satisfaction. Horrified that she might have awakened Jed, she whipped her head around to see that he was awake and staring at her.

"Strolling down memory lane?" he asked in a raspy

drawl. His dark eyes brightened, but not because of his fever.

Embarrassment flooded Caitlin. She closed the box and dumped it back in the drawer, then slapped it shut. "Certainly not," she said.

Jed grinned. "Nah, not you. You're honest enough to tell me when you want me to make love to you." He nodded toward the nightstand. "Tell you what, why don't you write your name on the ones you want me to use, and as soon as I feel better—"

"Oh, shut up," she said, whipping around and fleeing from the room. She crossed his apartment in quick strides, dashed through the hall and into her own place, closing the door behind her and then bolting it. Her hands flew to her burning cheeks.

What had she been thinking? She had no real interest in how many condoms he used, did she? The number of women he slept with was his business, not hers. Still, she couldn't ignore the satisfaction and elation that she felt knowing the box was still almost full.

JED WAS SICK for three days. Caitlin insisted that he needed to see a doctor. She took it as a sign of how truly terrible he felt when he agreed to let her take him to the clinic. He came home with prescriptions to treat the symptoms of his flu and instructions to stay in bed, rest and drink plenty of fluids.

"Like I didn't already know that," he groused.

"It's better to have a professional opinion," she said in a pedantic tone that hid her relief at knowing he would be well in a day or two.

Once he was back in bed, Caitlin took him bottles of juice, checked his temperature and fed him aspirin for the fever. The next day, his mother came with quarts of chicken soup and news of the newest members of the family. After Laura Bishop assured herself that her younger son was getting better and would be cured with her soup, she left him to sleep and went to Caitlin's apartment. The two of them sat at the small kitchen table, shared a pot of coffee and studied pictures of the newborn twins, who were to be named Susanna and Bradley.

When Jed's mother left, Caitlin again thought of what a warm and generous family he had and wondered if he knew how lucky he was.

By Sunday afternoon she had little to do. She wandered around her apartment for a while, then straightened the items on her desk. She stubbed her toe on something and looked down to see the lucky bone Reenie had given her. Smiling, she turned it in her hands, examining the dirty surface.

Caitlin started to put it down, then decided to show it to Jed. Besides, she should probably heat up some more of the soup his mother had brought him. Carrying the bone, she crossed the hall to find Jed lounging dejectedly on his sofa, morosely leafing through a magazine. When he saw her, his eyes lit up and he leaned back, resting one arm along the back of the sofa and grinning expectantly at her.

Caitlin hid a smile when she saw the eager challenge in his eyes. She didn't think he had his voice back yet, but he had other ways of making his wishes known. Who'd have guessed he could communicate as well without that glib tongue of his? That those dark eyes of his could be so expressive? And so sexy? On second thought, she had to admit she'd already known about the sexy part.

"Hello, Jed. You seem to be feeling better."

He shrugged in response, then gestured for her to sit down.

She handed him the dog bone as she perched in the chair opposite him. "Remember when I told you about Reenie's visit? This is what she gave me. Maybe it'll help you."

He took it from her and gave her a curious look. "Did it do anything for you?" he whispered.

"Not really. I—" She stopped and stared at him, recalling the night of Reenie's visit.

"What?"

Caitlin's eyes widened as she gazed at him, then at the grimy item in his hand. "Nah," she said after a minute, then turned her head and gave him a guilty glance out of the corner of her eye. "Nah," she murmured, shaking her head. "No way."

"What?" he asked again.

"Oh, nothing." She stood suddenly and crossed swiftly to the door. "I'm glad you're feeling better, Jed, I'll—"

"You'll stop right there," he ordered.

Even though the command was whispered, it rocked her to a stop. In an instant he was behind her, his hands were on her shoulders, and he was spinning her around, forcing her to look at him. "'Nah' what?" he demanded. His voice faded out on the last syllable, but it was still insistent.

"Jed, there's nothing to it. Only…my imagination."

"Tell me."

Caitlin breathed a theatrical sigh. "Reenie came by and gave me that thing."

"We've already established that."

Her hands fluttered. "Okay, okay. I took it upstairs and I was holding it when I talked to you on the phone."

He frowned at her, then his brow cleared and his eyes snapped wide open. "And you told me you wished I'd shut up."

"Well, I don't think I said it quite like that," Caitlin answered defensively.

He gaped at her. "You put a curse on me."

"Oh, don't be silly. I did not."

"You *did*. You put a curse on me."

"Don't be ridiculous. I'm not some kind of a witch." Before he could answer, she added, "And neither is Reenie. She's just...different."

He ignored that. "You put a curse on me. Did you do it on purpose?"

She twisted her shoulders, trying to dislodge his hands. "It was a coincidence! The wildest kind of...of chance."

"Like the smashed bottle lid and the call from Gordie and the car?"

Caitlin's mouth opened and closed a couple of times. "Well—"

"And that goofy key chain and the Carlton twins finally losing interest in keeping me from a boring life?"

Caitlin rolled her eyes. "No. That was only some quirk of fate."

"Luck, you mean?" he whispered in a silky tone.

"Yes, all right. Luck." Her eyes flew up to meet his triumphant ones.

"But, Caitlin, you don't believe in luck."

She lifted her chin. "Maybe I've changed my mind."

"And you're willing to admit it, too." His smile grew into a grin. "Cait, my girl, I think you're making progress." His voice seemed to be growing stronger, or maybe it was because she was so close that she could hear him better. He ignored her attempts to escape him, wrapped his arms around her and leaned close. His gray eyes had lightened to silver and his lips were tilted in a devilish smile. "But you owe me a forfeit for putting this curse on me."

"I didn't!" She avoided his lips when they came close to her and fixed him with a severe look. "And stop trying to give me your flu."

"I'm not contagious anymore," he said. "In fact, I'm completely well."

"Who told you that?"

"My mom," he said, blinking innocently. "And I'm sure you realize moms know everything."

"She said that to make you feel better."

"Uh-uh. My mom used to be a Cub Scout den mother. She always tells the truth. Moms are supposed to. Didn't yours?"

Caitlin avoided his eyes and tried to wriggle from his grasp. "Not that I can recall. Jed, why don't you let me go?"

"No." He had gone very still, and for a moment, he looked down into her face with searching intensity before her gaze skittered away. He then pulled her so close a molecule of air couldn't have passed between them. Her belly was pressed up against his, her breasts flattened against his chest. The position was intimate yet playful, and to her shame, arousing. "I like this," he said. "And you do have to pay me a forfeit."

She felt a sizzle of heat stirring, but she managed to tilt her head back and roll her eyes at him dismissively. "I suppose you mean a kiss?"

"Oh, no." His voice broke, then dipped into low tones. "A kiss wouldn't begin to satisfy me." He lowered his head and ran his cheek along the side of her face. "I want something that lasts much longer than that. Something—" he nuzzled behind her ear "—hot and sweet and fulfilling." She shivered. "Something we can both participate in, have fun with." She felt his teeth scrape ever so lightly along her neck. "Something we can draw out until we're both wild with excitement, satisfaction, even joy."

The longer he talked, the more her heart pounded.

"Jed, I... I suppose you mean—" her voice dropped as low as his "—sex."

His smile changed from a wickedly teasing grin to one of such sweetness that her breath was stolen away. "Oh, sweet Caitlin," he whispered. "You are so strong and bold and yet so fearful, and not at all ready for that."

"I'm not?" Her voice trembled with disappointment.

"No, you're not. I rushed you the last time, but I'm not doing it again. When we make love again, you're going to be ready."

She wanted to insist that she was ready now. Instead, she said, "But what about something hot and sweet and...and satisfying?" she asked.

He kissed her lightly on the forehead. "Actually I was thinking of hot chocolate, but keep the other in mind, and I'll get back to you on it."

"Oh, you!" She whirled from his arms and gave him a furious look.

"Don't blame me," he said. "You're the one with sex on the brain."

Her eyes dropped to a noticeable bulge directly below his belt. "Not the only one," she answered.

He turned away from her with a small laugh. "Well, maybe not," he amended. "Now, how about that hot chocolate?"

"I'll make it for you," she said ungraciously, forgetting she had come over in the first place to heat some of Laura's chicken soup for him. She headed for the kitchen, where she found the ingredients she needed and began making the hot beverage. She knew how much he liked to eat, so she wasn't surprised to find a well-stocked pantry, including cocoa and sugar. She could have made hot chocolate in the microwave, but she needed something to keep her busy, so she took a pan from the cupboard to heat the milk on the stove burner.

She was grateful to have something to occupy her because her mind was seething with self-recriminations. Just because Jed talked to her in a slow, sweet, sexy way was no reason for her to let her imagination run away with her. Just because he held her close and she could feel her own arousal, and *his*, didn't mean she should automatically begin having visions of the two of them together, in bed, entwined.

Caitlin's hand shook as she stirred the milk in the pan. It was time for her to face facts. She was far more attracted to Jed than was good for her. All the time she had spent thinking about him these past weeks had only fixed him more firmly in her mind and in her heart. Her plan about thinking of him only ten times a day had long since been blown to the four winds.

When he had come home sick, when he'd needed her, she had been glad to help him. She had felt useful, as if what she was doing for him couldn't be done by anyone else. She had felt important to him.

Even now, when she had virtually volunteered to sleep with him—her face burned at the memory—he had made it clear he wanted something as mundane as hot chocolate. She hadn't felt rejected. Somehow she knew he was easing her toward what he wanted from her. It wasn't simply sex. He wanted the part of her that she had refused to let him see, refused to share with him.

So what was stopping her?

# 9

"WHAT'S THIS?" CAITLIN asked, glancing at the television as she handed Jed his hot chocolate. She settled on the other end of the sofa with her own. He'd been flipping through the television channels and had decided on something with the grainy appearance of an early seventies made-for-TV movie.

"Science-fiction movie," he said, immediately engrossed. He sipped his drink and made an approving noise. "Thanks."

On the screen a sweet young thing with a body like a young Pamela Lee was parading around in scanty underwear. "I can tell it's science fiction," Caitlin agreed. "No one has a body like that."

"Please notice how I'm keeping my eyes firmly glued to the screen and not letting them stray longingly toward your body while saying, 'Oh yeah?'"

"Duly noted." She squinted at the action on the screen. "Now what's happening?"

"There's a giant spider hiding in her underwear drawer. That's how he gets his jollies. When she opens the drawer, he's going to jump out at her, mad because she's spoiling his fun."

Caitlin set her cup down on the coffee table, propped her feet up beside it and said, "How do you know that?"

"I've seen it before."

The girl was now running bath water. "On purpose?

Or was someone holding you hostage and torturing you by making you watch this?''

"Something like that. It was one afternoon a few years ago while I was baby-sitting Jessica. It's called *Spider World*. I thought it would be educational."

"You mean like 'All about Fungus'?"

Jed chuckled. "Yeah." He set his empty mug beside hers and made himself comfortable by scooting down onto his spine and propping his hands behind his head. "I'll get you up to date on the plot."

"This thing has a plot?" Five minutes later the girl was pouring bath oil into the water. Inside her underwear drawer, a fuzzy black spider with red eyes was peeking coyly through the leg of a pair of her bikini panties.

"Pay attention," Jed instructed. He launched into a story about softball-size rocks from outer space that turned out to actually be radioactive spider eggs. While the unsuspecting citizens of a quiet Arizona town went about their dusty desert days, the spiders plotted to take over the world.

"See?" he said. "They're launching their dastardly plan now. When they hatch, they grow fast." Jed pointed to the screen where another spider, approximately the size of an eighteen-wheeler, was moving at the speed of a slug through town. "That guy only hatched about ten minutes ago."

Citizens were running and screaming, jumping into pickup trucks and speeding away so fast their vehicles overturned in thick tangles of cactus. In one shot a man crawled out of his wrecked truck and began plucking cactus spines from his tongue. Caitlin winced in sympathy.

The spider watched all the action with his malevolent red eyes, then closed them and fell asleep. The panicked townspeople didn't seem to notice.

"Fascinating, isn't it?" Jed asked.

"I think I'd use the word 'stupefying.'" She flapped a hand at the TV. "Look—even the spider is bored to death. Uh, Jed?"

"Yeah?"

"I think I'm having a déjà vu here."

His attention still on the screen, he gestured toward the other room. "Oh? Well, you know where the bathroom is."

She slapped his arm. "I mean I have the feeling I've seen this before."

He turned an admiring look on her. "You mean you like stupid old movies, too?"

"No. I mean this spider reminds me of something. I think it was an art-and-science project we did in first grade. We had to make spiders out of foam balls spray-painted black, with red sequins for eyes and black pipe cleaners for legs."

"Hey, maybe your teacher worked as the special-effects director on this movie," he said, sitting up. "What was her name? We'll look for it when the credits roll."

On the screen, townspeople had returned and were poking the spider with sticks. "Why are they doing that?" she asked.

"They want it to wake up so they can run from it again. I guess they don't get much exercise out there in the desert. Caitlin? What was your teacher's name?"

Mesmerized by the idiocy of this movie, she barely heard him. "I don't remember," she answered. "I went to three different schools that year, so I don't remember which teacher had us do the spiders."

Jed reached for the remote. "Why did you go to three different schools?" he asked, switching the set off. "Was your dad in the military?"

Caitlin blinked and looked up. It took her several seconds to realize what she'd said. Good grief, she hadn't meant to say that. She stood suddenly. "No. No, he wasn't. It was just me and my mom. We moved a lot. Listen, I've got to go. Thanks for the…" She glanced around, unable to remember why she was there. "Whatever," she said. Shaken, she turned toward the door, but stopped and glanced back when the phone rang.

Jed ignored the phone and was beside her in a flash. When she reached for the doorknob, he pressed his hand against the door so she couldn't open it. "Caitlin, what's the matter with you?"

She looked up at his puzzled face. "Nothing. I just remembered something I need to do. At my place."

"What? Hide in the closet?"

She had no answer. They both knew she couldn't come up with an excuse for this behavior. In fact, she wasn't exactly sure why she had reacted to his question with panic. Old habits died hard. Confused, she shook her head at him, not sure what to say.

Jed had no such problem. He took her by the hand and led her back to the sofa, but before he reached it, the phone rang again. He gave it a distracted look. "I'd let the answering machine pick it up, but it might be Steve or Mary needing something. Then you and I are going to talk. And don't argue. I'm not a well man. If you argue, I might have a relapse." As if he was afraid she'd take off if he let go of her, he pulled her with him to the desk where he picked up the receiver.

"Hello?"

Faintly Caitlin could hear a woman's voice on the other end. It wasn't his sister-in-law. This woman's voice was deep and sultry. Deciding instantly that she really didn't want to be where she was, Caitlin attempted to pull away, but he reeled her back.

Jed shot a swift, uncomfortable glance at Caitlin as he answered. "Hi, Maria. How's it going? Oh? Where did you hear that? No, I've got a touch of the flu." He faked a cough and Caitlin rolled her eyes at him. This was the first she'd heard of a cough.

Jed smirked at her, then paused to listen. As he did so, Caitlin tried to twist her wrist from his grasp, but he stopped her by pulling her arm behind her back and bringing her close. He held her firmly as he spoke into the receiver. "That's sweet of you, honey, but not necessary. My mom's been here with her chicken soup."

Caitlin was close enough now to hear Maria say, "I could come over and heat some for you."

His eyes glinted wickedly as he met Caitlin's eyes. "Thanks, but my neighbor's here. She's keeping things plenty hot."

Caitlin's eyes widened and she aimed the heel of her sneaker at his bare toes, but he bent at the waist, dragging her feet off the floor. Outraged, she dangled in midair. "Let go of me, Jed," she demanded, but he ignored her.

"Is that your neighbor?" Maria asked, then her voice cooled. "Oh, the one who bid for you at the bachelor auction? She made quite a spectacle of herself."

"She's nuts about me," he said.

"In your dreams," Caitlin said, trying to wriggle from his grasp.

Realizing he was about to lose his grip on her, Jed spoke hastily. "Thanks for calling, Maria. I've got to go. My hands are full." While Maria was still speaking, he hung up, wrapped both arms around Caitlin and frog-marched her back to the couch. He tossed her down on it and gave her a ferocious look that seemed to nail her in place.

Jed pointed a finger at her nose. "We're not going to do this anymore," he said.

"Do what?" she asked warily.

"This business of your secret life."

"My secret life?"

"We've known each other for almost three months. We've lived across the hall from each other, become business partners, lovers, and I *thought* we were friends. I have lots of friends, but not one like you. For some reason you seem to think I can't be trusted. You hoard information about yourself like it was gold. Are you a participant in the federal witness-protection program? Hiding out from a Chinese tong? From your family? What gives?"

Caitlin had never seen him so angry. In fact, she'd never seen him angry at all. It slowly dawned on her that he was furious because she had hurt him. She didn't know what to say. She couldn't defend her actions, because she knew he was right. Now somehow it didn't seem that important to keep her secrets anymore. Hadn't she been thinking that while she was in the kitchen?

"Jed," she began, "I wouldn't be hiding out from my family. I don't have one. I don't have anyone."

His hands lifted to rest at his waist. He frowned as he looked into her eyes. "Cait, everyone has someone."

"No, they don't. I don't."

"Tell me about it," he said, sitting down beside her on the sofa.

Her hands clenched together in her lap, but he reached down and pried her fingers apart, holding her hands in his. He lifted his chin at her as if urging her to go on.

She took a deep breath. "I know you think I'm too

focused on work, on providing for my future. I don't believe in luck because, until I started providing for myself, took control of my own life, I didn't seem to have anything but *bad* luck.''

His anger had faded away, replaced by compassion. ''How long have you been providing for yourself?''

''Since I was sixteen. That was when my mother abandoned me.'' Caitlin looked away and stared at a painting over his desk. It was of a ship on a storm-tossed sea being beckoned to port by the beam from a lighthouse.

''Abandoned you? You mean, she walked off and left you?''

''That's right.''

''But…but mothers don't do that.'' Horror rose in his voice.

Caitlin raised an eyebrow.

''Well, I guess they do,'' he said, shaking his head.

''Yes, and in a way, I was grateful to her for it.''

''Why would you be grateful?''

''I was grateful she didn't do it sooner. My younger life wasn't anything great, believe me, but at least she kept me with her. My mother had me when she was fifteen. She was a runaway, probably didn't know who my father was. At least, it's not listed on my birth certificate. We lived all over California. Usually left one city or another one jump ahead of the law.'' For a moment Caitlin felt the confusion and fear she'd known as a child wash over her. She must have shivered because Jed pulled her closer and tucked her head under his chin. His arms enfolded her in a cocoon of safety she couldn't remember ever feeling before.

''Go on,'' he urged. ''You've come this far.''

''Jed, she was an alcoholic, a sometime drug user, a petty thief—and a prostitute, and not necessarily in that order. I didn't know what a prostitute was until I was about nine and one of my friends, I think we were in San Diego then, couldn't come home to play with me because her mom said mine was a hooker. I didn't know what that was. When I found out, I realized why there were always so many men around our place. Anyway, one day, when I was sixteen, I came home from school to find that almost everything was gone from the cheap little apartment we'd been renting. Weeks later she wrote from Las Vegas, said she was sorry. Anyway, the rent was paid for the month, so I got a job working as a waitress and I stayed. It was a scramble."

She stopped for a moment and pulled back to look at his face. Above all, she didn't want him to feel sorry for her or to think she'd done it all on her own. "People were kind," she said. "Tony Danova, the owner of the restaurant where I worked, let me take food home. When I was a senior, he and his wife, Anna, paid for my senior pictures. They bought my prom dress, too, and took pictures of me wearing it." She smiled at the memory.

"It's good you had someone, but..." Jed's voice faltered. "Your mother dumped you when you were *sixteen?*" Now his voice had a tone she'd never heard him use before. Puzzled, Caitlin looked up and saw rage simmering in his eyes. "Why would she have done something like that?"

"She had a new boyfriend who didn't want a kid around, though I wasn't much of a kid at sixteen, but she chose him, instead of me." Caitlin freed one hand from the confining afghan and touched Jed's face. "I don't begrudge her that. In fact, I was glad. It meant I didn't have to worry about her anymore, make excuses for her, cover for her—clean up after her, dodge her drunken boyfriends. Maybe it was selfish of me, but I could finally concentrate on myself, on getting what I wanted." She gave him a lopsided smile. "And what I wanted was stability—emotional, mental and financial."

"Didn't the court step in?"

"They didn't know. No one knew for a long time." She winced. "I'm not proud of this, but whenever I needed my mother's signature on something for school, I forged it. I had goals, you see. I couldn't get mixed up with the child-welfare system. They would have gotten in my way, tried to put me in foster care, do what was 'best' for me, but I *knew* what was best for me—being an honor student, getting a scholarship, an education, a career that would give me security."

Jed stared at her, feeling humbled and ashamed. He'd known she was smart and her beauty was obvious. He hadn't realized she was a self-made woman. In fact, he'd never known the truth of that phrase until now.

"My mother died a few years ago. Cirrhosis of the liver. She was thirty-six years old. Her life hadn't amounted to anything." Caitlin lifted her head and Jed saw the sadness in her eyes change to determination. "I'm not going to be like that," she said firmly. "I'm *not*."

"No, you won't." He caught her hand and pressed his lips to it. "Caitlin, I think you're my hero." He shook his head. "I wish I'd known some of this before."

She pulled away and gave him a look that of weary resignation. "Jed, do you really think that someone who's been on her own for as long as I have finds it easy to confide in others?"

His eyes narrowed as he looked down at her. "I think you confide in my aunt Geneva."

"Not this stuff," Caitlin said. "Only things about you. Besides, that's different."

"Because she's a woman?"

"A wise, elderly woman," Caitlin said. "And they're long-distance confidences, if you know what I mean. It's harder to say things, personal things, face-to-face."

Which told him exactly how much it meant that she'd confided in him. "I guess it is."

When he touched her face, he was amazed to see that his hand was shaking. For an easygoing guy with a laid-back attitude toward relationships, responsibilities, to life in general, he was suddenly feeling a ton of obligations, all of them to this slim chestnut-haired woman who seemed to know so much about strength.

He understood now. He understood why security was so important to her, why she hated the time that had been wasted the past few weeks on the renovations of this house, why she'd been so embarrassed by the television ad where he'd kissed her publicly and by the photograph and article in the paper. Even though those things had turned out well, it must have been difficult for her because they had brought her the kind of attention she didn't want. He wished now that he'd understood, but how could he when she hadn't told him?

It was time for him to make up for past mistakes. He cupped her cheek with his hand and tilted her face up to his.

Caitlin looked into Jed's eyes and saw something there she hadn't seen before. Along with the compassion she'd already noted was tenderness.

"I want to make love to you, Caitlin."

Her heart began a slow, steady beat that seemed to pulse from her toes to her hairline. "You...you do?"

"It'll be different this time," he said.

She reached for him, signaling that she was ready for him at last to make love to her. As naturally and effort-lessly as if she'd done this a hundred times, Caitlin wound her arms around his neck and brought her lips to his. "I know," she said.

His mouth came down on hers, fierce with need. He stood, pulled her into his arms and carried her to his bed.

Caitlin heard the mattress sigh, felt it give beneath her as Jed set her down on it, then swiftly removed his clothes to lie beside her.

Caitlin looked into his face, at his eyes sheltered by his thick brows, the set of his jaw, his gently smiling lips. The last time, they'd made love in a rush of heat, influenced by champagne, by elemental needs. Those needs were still there, but this time they were making love with a consciousness that had been missing the first time.

Caitlin's eyes drifted almost shut and through the screen of her lashes she could see the intensity in his face. Her heart overflowed with warmth and tenderness when she realized he was trying to make this as memorable and wonderful as he could.

He was succeeding beyond his sincerest expectations.

When Jed's hands touched her, they were as soft as the her sweater, which he eased over her head. He lifted one strap over her shoulder and down, then the other. He swept her bra aside, then paused to look at her. His eyes glittered.

"You are so beautiful, Caitlin."

His earnest voice made her believe she was beautiful in a way she never had before. Caitlin relaxed and felt the heat and tension build as his hands skimmed over her skin. His hands were followed by his lips, which took their time in exploring the soft texture of her throat. Caitlin arched her neck with a husky moan.

"There you go again," Jed murmured. "Making those noises that drive me wild."

She gave a breathy laugh. "Do you want me to stop?"

"Hell, no," he murmured, moving to her shoulder. "I don't ever want you to stop. In fact—" his mouth moved to the swell of her breast "—I want to hear it often, nightly, in fact, for years."

Fear shivered through her. "Jed, I don't think that's such a good—" His mouth found the peak of her nipple and her objection exploded in a blast of heat. Her fingers dug into his shoulders. "Jed!"

He trailed kisses to her other breast. "Tell me that you belong to me, Cait," he whispered.

Her hands skimmed down his arms, then up again to cup his face. "What?" she asked against his lips.

He looked into her eyes. "I said, I want you to say you belong to me, as I belong to you."

"Jed, I don't know." Her voice caught. "I've never belonged anywhere, and—"

"Forget about that. You belong to me. We belong together."

The word "belong" seared into her brain. Was it true? She couldn't think clearly with his mouth on hers, his hands on her, readying her for his possession.

It seemed so right, as if she did belong to him, as if all the wanderings and upsets of her life had somehow brought her here, to this moment, to this man. But saying what he wanted her to say was such a big step she didn't know if she could do it.

"Never mind, Caitlin," he said after a moment. He lifted himself away from her and looked into her eyes. Even in the shadows, she could see compassion and tenderness there. "It'll come."

Her throat clogged with gratitude as he said it. Her arms came up and around him, holding him tight. She kissed him, caressed him, showing him with her body what her mouth couldn't seem to speak.

When she did so, the heat between them built even further. Her body begged for fulfillment. He responded, giving her what she asked with whispered murmurs, arousing touches and finally by sinking himself deep inside her.

Caitlin arched upward, her hips lifting to take him in. She gasped as he began to move in a slick, sensual, satisfying dance that brought them both to the peak. When it hit, her eyes flew open to see him above her, his face set, his eyes full of joyous tenderness. Sensation crashed through her, colors exploded in her head, and his prophetic statement came true. She did belong to him.

DID SHE REALIZE what she'd done? Jed wondered. He couldn't move away from her yet. He couldn't break that bond, but he didn't think she realized how strongly they'd forged one between them. Once she started to think about it, she would worry. In fact, she might panic. She was too quick to figure things out once she started thinking.

Jed thought it might be a damned good idea if neither of them did much thinking right now. He lowered his mouth to hers and began the arousing dance once again.

Caitlin moaned when his mouth settled on her breast. "Jed?"

"Relax, honey," he said. "We've been waiting a long time for this night. Let's make the most of it."

He could feel her wanting to protest, could almost see the words forming on her lips, so he sealed them inside her by placing his lips on hers. "There's a time for talk," he murmured. "But this isn't it. At least not yet."

This time, there was no more hesitation, no more resistance. To his joy, he saw she was smiling. "Yes, Jed," she said.

He returned to the pleasure of driving them both wild.

Caitlin wrapped herself around him and joined him in the journey.

CAITLIN AWOKE TO FIND Jed's arm around her, his leg entwined with hers. A glance at his bedside clock told her it was still two hours before she had to begin preparing for work.

She lay with her arm hugging Jed's and tried to analyze her tangle of feelings. There was fear, but she couldn't quite determine its source because it didn't feel like what she'd experienced when she'd awakened with Jed all those weeks ago. She was touched by tenderness and warmth for him, and she wasn't as worried. That *had* to be progress.

She didn't think she had moved, but Jed's arm tightened around her and he spoke into her hair. "You think too much."

She smiled. "How can a person think too much?"

"I don't know many people who can do *any* thinking at this hour of the morning, but if anyone can manage it, you can." He shifted and turned them both so that they lay thigh to thigh, belly to belly. "Don't think," he said, and she could almost hear the smile in his voice as he said, "Just feel."

And feel she did. Caitlin felt his hands smoothing over her body, his mouth on hers, his body pressing down on her, into her. He was gentle, he was rough, he made her want to laugh and to weep. When he brought her to the peak of fulfillment, she gasped and cried out, then lay limp in his arms.

After several long minutes Caitlin opened languorous eyes and focused on him. The sun was coming up, its first rays stealing across the room so that she could see his face. His hair was tousled from her hands, his lips as swollen from kisses as hers were, his dark eyes so serious and steady that wariness had her pulling away to look at him. "Looks like *you're* doing some thinking now."

"I am."

She didn't like the heaviness of his tone. "What, Jed? What is it?"

"We didn't get our Friday-night date," he said slowly. "In fact, none of this has worked out the way I'd planned."

"Exactly what had you planned?" His expression made her nervous because she couldn't read it. Was it regret?

"I didn't expect to get sick."

"No one ever does."

"No, but I thought when we made love again it would be the usual," he admitted with a shrug. "Dinner, theater." His smile flickered. "Seduction."

His tone, the solemn look in his eyes so unlike him that a chill swept through her. She edged further away from him. She didn't like what he was saying, either. "The usual?"

"Yes." His voice was low, his words hesitant as if he was sorting them before speaking. "I thought it would be so easy, that the one night we spent together weeks ago wasn't anything unusual, that if we did this—" his hand swept down her body "—it would be great for a while, then I could turn you into a friend like…"

"Like all the other women in your life," Caitlin finished for him. Clearly it was regret she was seeing and hearing. Hurt blossomed and she spoke before she thought, but hating the cynicism in her tone. "I'm not surprised. That's what I expected to happen, too. You're good at it."

"Good at it?" he asked, staring at her. "Good at what?"

Caitlin pulled away completely and he let her go. "Good at keeping your former girlfriends as friends, at continuing to take care of them. You said yourself it's because you were responsible for your sister. It's a habit you've developed." Caitlin reached for the sheet, but he was lying on top of it. When she tugged at it, he scooted away from her so she could cover herself. She gave him a smile as brittle as old parchment. "But you don't have to worry about me. I don't need you to take care of me. I've always taken care of myself, remember?" Sickness rolled in her throat and she felt as if she was suffocating, but she struggled on. "You don't have to worry about me hanging around, knitting sweaters for you, bringing you brownies from the bakery, or…or making you the featured sexy hunk in a book I'm writing."

Jed's eyes grew stormy as he listened to this little speech. "You know, if you'd let me finish what I'm trying to say—"

"There's no need," she said. "I'm not going to be an albatross around your neck. We're neighbors, business partners. This—" her hand swept out to indicate the bed and the two of them "—was fun, but don't feel like you have to repeat it."

"Repeat it?" He stared at her. "Have you listened to a single word I've said either last night or today?"

She didn't want to burst into tears, but she didn't know how much longer she could keep from it. How had all this gone so wrong? She glanced around, looking for her clothes. Escape was uppermost in her mind. Escape before she indulged in pure humiliation. "Well," she answered in a vague tone, "people say things they don't mean, and—"

"I don't!" Jed rolled off the bed and stood glaring at her. After a few seconds, he turned and sifted through the covers they'd tossed from the bed to find her jeans and sweater. He handed them to her.

Her hands trembled as she took the items from him. They dropped from her hands, fluttering down like her damaged dreams. "Jed, I—"

"I don't know what kind of man you think I am, Caitlin, but you've lived across the hall from me for months now. I thought we knew each other. I thought we were friends. I thought you'd know this wasn't just sex."

Caitlin stared at him, waiting for him to say that it was love, but the words didn't come. And she couldn't seem to form the words herself.

Jed turned away and picked up his own clothes. "I'm going into the kitchen to make coffee while you get dressed. Then we're going to talk about this." He turned and strode from the room.

# 10

CAITLIN LIFTED HER HAND as if to stop him, but then she grabbed her clothes and hurried into them. While he was in the kitchen, she scurried past him and dashed for the front door. She heard him call her name, but she kept running, whirling inside her own apartment and closing the door. Then she leaned against it and fought for breath.

She loved him. That was why this was so terrible. She loved him and he wanted to turn her into one of his drop-by-and-check-on-Jed friends. Caitlin's hands clasped together at her waist. She couldn't do that because she realized now she'd been in love with him for weeks, probably since the day he'd walked into her office with his killer grin.

Her eyes full of distressed tears, Caitlin stared blindly at the clock and saw it was time for her to get ready for work. Sure, she could do that, she thought as she pushed away from the door, stumbling slightly as she did so. She would concentrate on work until she could decide exactly what she was going to do.

She hurried through her preparations for work, barely noticing what she was doing because her mind was consumed with Jed, with her feelings and reactions. She needed help or direction of some kind, but didn't know who to ask. Her best friends, Tony and Anna, were in San Francisco. She could ask them, but it seemed unfair after weeks of not contacting them to suddenly spring this problem on them. Besides, she'd always kept her own counsel. Her friends would be flabbergasted if she called and asked for advice on her love life.

She couldn't ask anyone. She had to work this out for herself. That decided, Caitlin grabbed up her briefcase and purse and headed for the door. As she reached for the knob, she heard heavy footsteps in the hall. At first she felt a moment of panic, but then she realized it couldn't be Jed. It sounded like this person was wearing boots. Maybe Terry had come to work early.

She jumped when the visitor rapped on her door. Cautiously, she opened it to see a tall figure clad entirely in black. He was facing away from her, but when he turned around, her jaw dropped.

"Jed?"

Her bewildered gaze traveled over him. He hadn't shaved, so his jaw was shadowed with the beginnings of his beard. His hair was slicked back, and he wore a black T-shirt, black leather jacket and pants and heavy biker's boots.

"Come on," he said, reaching out and grabbing her wrist. He plucked her purse and briefcase from her hands and dropped them inside the door, then closed it.

"Jed!" she protested, trying to pull away as he dragged her out into the hall. "What are you doing?"

"Something I should have done months ago," he growled, his face so grim.

"Whatever this is better not include violence," she said.

"It should, but it won't." He pulled her into his apartment, closed the door and locked it. There was another lock near the top she had never noticed before. He locked this one with a key and slipped it into the pocket of his skin-tight leather pants. At any other time she would have taken a moment to admire how beautifully those pants hugged his powerful thighs and terrific tush, but right now she was too stunned to do anything except gape at him.

"Why are you doing this? And why are you wearing those clothes?"

"To show you that the days of Mr. Nice Guy are over."

"They are?"

"Yup," he said, advancing on her. "No more Mr. Nice Guy."

She backed away, her golden-brown eyes wide and wary. "O…kay," she said, trying to humor him. "Why no more Mr. Nice Guy?"

"Because I'm going to prove to you that I don't intend to treat you like all the other women in my life—not that there are that many," he added in a tone of righteous indignation. He lifted his hand and counted them off on his fingers. "My mother, my sisters, my aunt, a few friends." He wiggled his thumb at her. "That leaves room for you. Take off your jacket."

"Room for…? What?"

He put his hands on his hips and stuck out his jaw. "I said take off your jacket. It's ugly, anyway."

Caitlin had never seen him like this. Where was the laid-back fun guy she knew? Oh, yes—no more Mr. Nice Guy. She looked down at her sensible brown-and-black pin-striped suit jacket. Well, okay, maybe it wasn't her most attractive, but it wasn't ugly. She lifted her head. "Jed, why would I want to take off my… Oh!" He'd stepped forward and stripped it from her arms.

He strode to the bathroom with it dangling from his hand, and a few moments later she heard the shower running. She scurried after him and arrived at the very moment he tossed it into the tub.

"Jed!" she shrieked. "Have you gone crazy?"

"Yeah. Now your skirt."

"I'm not taking off my skirt so you can ruin it by throwing it into the shower!" she shouted. Her amazement was finally giving way to anger. Who did he think he was, anyway?

He shrugged. "Okay. *I'll* do it."

When he reached for her, she tried again to pull away, but he was a man with a purpose. He had her out of her skirt in less than ten seconds despite her struggles. He tossed it into the shower along with the jacket. "Now your blouse."

Caitlin was learning. She skimmed out of it in record time and threw it at him. "That's as far as I go," she said, standing before him in her underwear. "Until I find out what's going on here."

"Panty hose," he said in disgust. "Those, too."

"No!"

"Yes." He started toward her.

"Okay, okay." She took them off and he snagged them, one-handed, from the air as she threw them at his head. They went into the trash. He cranked the shower off, grabbed her hand and hauled her into his bedroom.

"Jed," she said, sawing back on her arm. "If you think we're going to solve this with sex..."

"No. I tried that already. In fact, I tried it twice and it didn't work because you wake up the next morning thinking you know everything and won't even listen to me. We're not doing that again," he said, stabbing a finger at her. Turning, he grabbed something from the bed and handed it to her.

Caitlin blinked. It was a set of biker clothes like his. Leather pants, jacket, black T-shirt.

"These were my sister Diana's," he told her. "Put them on."

"Are you kidding?" She knew she'd wasted her breath as soon as she said it. The determination in his face told her he wasn't. She grabbed the T-shirt and slipped it over her head and then began struggling into the pants, which were too small. Diana must be a tiny woman, she decided as she worked them up her hips and struggled with the zipper. "Now, will you tell me what this is all about?"

Seemingly satisfied that she was doing what he wanted, he picked up a pair of boots and some socks and gave them to her. When she was completely dressed, he said, "I've got a secret life and no one has ever shared it with me before."

"A secret life?"

"Yup." Some of his irritation with her seemed to be fading and a silvery glow of anticipation began shining in his eyes. "I've got a Harley Fatboy parked in a shed behind my dad's garage. We're going for a ride down the coast highway. No one's been on that bike with me since Diana moved to Sacramento. You're the first."

She met his eyes and a smile started to form. "Why me?"

"That's what I was trying to tell you a while ago when you ran off." He paused, took a breath and went on, "This didn't turn out like I'd planned because I've fallen in love with you."

"You have?" Caitlin asked softly.

"I can't treat you like all my other old girlfriends because I don't want you to *be* an old girlfriend. I want you to be my wife."

"You do?" A blend of amazement and joy clogged any more words she might have said.

Jed waited a second, an edge of uncertainty slipping into his face. "Well, how about it?"

Maybe she couldn't speak, but she could move. Caitlin rushed into his arms. "Yes," she managed. "Yes."

He swept her up and kissed her, long and slow. Breathless, she pulled away, her eyes shining with tears. "I didn't know that I loved you until this morning."

"Better late than never," he growled, and kissed her again. "So, when will you marry me?"

"Anytime you say."

He grinned. "An easy woman. I like that. What about a honeymoon?"

Her eyes glinted with mischief. "Anywhere you say."

He rewarded her with another kiss. "Can I drive your car?"

Caitlin came up on the toes of her biker boots, wrapped her arms around his neck, planted a long, hard kiss on him and said, "Not on your life."

THEY WERE MARRIED in November in the little church Jed's family had attended for forty years. It seemed that half of Crystal Cove was there, and even more came to the reception at the community center.

Caitlin's dress was the kind young girls dream of, with yards of white satin and lace trailing behind her. Her practical soul had balked at the expense, but the romantic nature growing in her said that she would only be marrying once, so she'd better do it up in style. Her friends had come from San Francisco, Tony Danova to give her away and wife Anna to be her matron of honor. Jessica Bishop was her only bridesmaid.

For the reception Jed had hired a three-piece band, who were set up at the end of the basketball court. The group only seemed to play fast numbers, which the guests liked. Even Steve and Mary were dancing, though not in time to the zippy music. They were each holding a twin as they glided around the edge of the big room.

Caitlin smiled at them as they moved past, then grinned at her own husband, who was holding her close while trying to execute a complicated series of steps. He took her hand and spun her in a twirl. "Is this an actual dance," she asked through her laughter, "or are you making this up as you go along?"

"Well, you know I'm an impromptu kind of guy," he said. "And besides, if I keep you moving fast enough, no one else will try to cut in and dance with you. I have no intention of sharing you with anyone."

They whizzed past his parents, who were sitting this one out. Caitlin waved as they passed in a blur. "You married me under false pretenses. I thought you were laid-back, easygoing."

"Not if there's a chance someone might try to make a move on my wife."

"I think you're overreacting. Besides, I'm getting dizzy." By digging in her heels, she managed to slow him down. "Why don't we get some punch?"

With a good-natured shrug, he grabbed her hand and parted a way through the crowd. It took a while because they were stopped so often by well-wishers.

Jed had his hand at her waist, guiding her along, when he spoke in her ear. "Hey, look, there's my aunt Geneva."

Caitlin craned her neck to see. "You're kidding. Where?"

"Right where we're headed—over by the punch bowl. Mom says she was at the ceremony, but she refused to come through the reception line. She says those things take too long. I'm supposed to bring you over to meet her."

"Well, let's go," she said, eagerly pulling him along. She couldn't wait to meet her mentor, the woman who'd sent so much business her way and given her such valuable advice.

Geneva Bishop turned out to be tall and rangy, like the rest of the Bishops. She had short white hair and steady gray eyes. She shook Caitlin's hand and smiled her approval. "You've done well, Jed."

Jed lifted an eyebrow at her and smiled. "High praise from you, Aunt Geneva. I'm flattered."

"Don't be," she said repressively. "It was meant as a compliment for Caitlin."

"I should have known." He hugged Caitlin closer. "Compliment her all you want, Auntie. It won't turn her head. She's too smart to be affected by your effusive flattery."

"She *is* smart," a voice said from behind Geneva. "Smart enough to keep you in line."

Caitlin and Jed looked and their mouths dropped open as Reenie Starr stepped up with a cup of punch. "Hello, dear," she said. "I'm so happy for both of you." She glanced around. "This is a lovely reception."

"Mrs. Starr!" Jed said.

"Reenie!" Caitlin exclaimed.

"The very same," she said, her eyes twinkling. "You knew I'd come to your wedding, didn't you?"

Jed lifted his hand and rubbed his jaw. "To tell you the truth, we thought you were a ghost or a witch or something from that way you have of disappearing so fast."

She shook her head. "I only disappeared fast when you offered help. I didn't need it. I like being independent."

"That's the way you'll be when you're old, Caitlin," Geneva said, and smiled at Reenie.

"Do you two know each other?" Caitlin asked.

"Since we were children, though I moved away from here when I was a young girl," Reenie answered. "Geneva and I met by chance in Los Angeles a few months ago and got reacquainted."

Caitlin stared at the two of them, then spoke to Geneva. "How come you didn't tell me you knew her when I told you about her on the phone?"

Geneva's gray eyes sparkled as she took a sip of her punch. "Because she's hiding out from her children, of course."

"They want to put me in a *home*," Reenie said, outraged. "They think I can't take care of myself because sometimes I get a little addled. When I met Geneva again and told her about it, she offered to let me come stay in the little apartment behind her house for a while."

"Well, I'll be dam...darned," Jed said. "When you said you lived down Old Barton Road, you really *did*." He looked at his aunt. "And that's why you told the family to stay away from your place."

"None of you needed to be nosing around there, anyway," Geneva answered with a sniff. "And Reenie needed some time alone to prove she'd be all right."

"Yes," Reenie confirmed. "I kept to myself and took care of myself so my children would see I can still be on my own. I call and check in with them every once in a while."

Caitlin and Jed exchanged laughing glances. "Well," Caitlin said, "I'm glad to know you weren't a figment of my imagination."

"I'm solid, all right." Reenie reached out to grip Caitlin's hand firmly. "See? And I recognized you the first time we met because I'd seen your picture in the brochure Jed sent Geneva. She'd told me all about you, and when I moved up here, we kept each other up-to-date." She and

Geneva exchanged smiles like a couple of conspirators. "And I knew you didn't believe in luck because your brochure said so. 'Hard work and knowledge are what build a successful portfolio,'" she quoted.

"Oh." Caitlin blinked. She gave Jed an apologetic smile. "I see now. When I told Geneva things about Jed, she told you, and you came to talk to me about him."

"That's right. Geneva and I felt you needed some wise counsel. After all, she's been dealing with the men in the Bishop family for a long time. She knows how difficult they can be."

Jed shook his head as he took this in. "So you were looking out for Caitlin all along."

"Yes, but I don't think there was really any need. She's managed well for herself," Geneva answered.

"There's one more thing," Reenie said. "I'm the owner of that old farm on Barton Road you've been trying to buy for so long. My maiden name is Barton. The farm belonged to my father, but it failed during the depression and no one ever tried to farm that land again. I didn't want to see the property spoiled by a big development of condominiums and golf courses, but if you still want to buy it, I'll sell it to you."

Caitlin felt Jed give a start. "Why, I—"

"There's one condition, though," she broke in. "You and Caitlin must build yourselves a home there, one to share with your children when they come along."

Caitlin looked up at Jed, who opened his mouth, then closed it again. He seemed stunned. She'd never seen him ⬛⬛⬛ for words, so she spoke for both of them. "Thank ⬛⬛⬛ That's exactly what we'll do."

⬛⬛⬛ "Perfect."

⬛⬛⬛ the arm. "Why don't you ⬛⬛⬛ of our family?

Since you're going to be staying with me for a while, you'll want to get to know them." The two women melted into the crowd.

Jed gaped after them. "You know what this means?"

Caitlin placed her arm around his waist. "It means we'll have a house on some lovely property."

"Yeah," he said in a strangled voice. "Right up the road from my aunt. She'll want to baby-sit, you know."

"That's okay."

"That's what you think," he said, giving her a horrified look. "Whenever she baby-sat for us when we were little, she made Steve and me join our sisters for tea parties!"

Caitlin burst out laughing. "She was only trying to erase your gender bias."

"You sound exactly like her." He grabbed two cups of punch from the table and handed one to her, then clinked his cup against hers and encouraged her to drink up. "There's only one thing to do," he announced when he'd drained his cup.

"What's that?"

"Figure out some way to make sure we only have girls! I'm strong enough to hold my own against all you women, but I'm not going to wish it on a son."

With that said, he whisked the cup from her hand and whirled her onto the dance floor again. Caitlin went gladly, eager to take on the challenge of their life together. She'd chosen well, she thought: a hometown, a home, Jed Bishop to love, someday children of her own. Who needed wishes or luck?

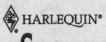

at a loss
you, Reenie.

She beamed at the
Geneva touched her friend on the
come along and meet the other member

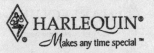

# COMING NEXT MONTH

## #5

### DOWNHOME DARLIN' by Victoria Pade

When Abby Stanton's fiancé calls off the wedding because he claims she's too boring, Abby sets out to prove him wrong. Abby becomes a "wild woman" for one night and corrals herself a cowboy. Now boot-wearin' Cal Ketchum has to convince darlin' Abby that he has something more permanent in mind....

### THE BEST MAN SWITCH by Liz Ireland

The last thing in the world best man Grant Whiting wants is to be set up with the maid of honor at his friend's wedding. So he blackmails his identical twin brother into performing the *best man switch*. Only after the bridesmaid decks Grant's brother is he forced to take his brother's—that is, *his own*—place and realizes he's found the woman of his dreams...who considers him the man of her nightmares!

## #6

### FOR THIS WEEK I THEE WED by Cheryl St.John

Francie Karr-Taylor needs a husband—but only for a week. So she convinces Parrish McKinley to help. He and his kids come to her reunion—as her happy family. Parrish isn't eager to get involved in such a crazy plan, but one look at Francie told him she was desperate. And after all, it wasn't like she was talking about forever—was it?

### 50 CLUES HE'S MR. RIGHT by Alyssa Dean
*Real Men*

Reporter Tara Butler is thrilled with her assignment from *Real Men* magazine: updating "49 Things You Need to Know about a Real Man." Maybe this is her chance to meet a real man— not the romantic duds she's dated. But when she's paired with sexy Chase Montgomery, who doesn't have a real man quality to him, she begins to wonder if her list is wrong...

HARLEQUIN · FIVE DECADES OF ROMANCE · CELEBRATES

In July 1999 Harlequin Superromance®
brings you *The Lyon Legacy*—a
brand-new 3-in-1 book from popular
authors Peg Sutherland, Roz Denny Fox
& Ruth Jean Dale

# 3 stories for the price of 1!

## Join us as we celebrate
Harlequin's 50th Anniversary!

Look for these other
Harlequin Superromance®
titles wherever books are sold July 1999:

**A COP'S GOOD NAME (#846)**
by Linda Markowiak

**THE MAN FROM HIGH MOUNTAIN (#848)**
by Kay David

**HER OWN RANGER (#849)**
by Anne Marie Duquette

**SAFE HAVEN (#850)**
by Evelyn A. Crowe

**JESSIE'S FATHER (#851)**
by C. J. Carmichael